When a hero surrenders...

"You have plans for tomorrow?"

She moistened her lips with her tongue. "Just the usual. Cleaning, laundry, groceries. I'll be done by noon."

"I'll call you."

"I'll answer." Inwardly wincing at the sappy response, she seized an impulse, one she hadn't felt in a long time, leaned forward, and brushed his mouth with hers.

Again his fingers tightened around hers, and his gaze turned dark with emotion—surprise, uncertainty, temptation, desire. Finally he smiled, just a little, and let her go as he opened the door.

Almost immediately, though, he stepped back, slid his hand into her hair, dislodging her ragged ponytail, and he kissed her back. It was innocent and sweet and hinted that he wanted so much more...

A Hero to Come Home To

MARILYN PAPPANO

FOREVER

NEW YORK   BOSTON

Forever
Hachette Book Group
237 Park Avenue
New York, NY 10017

www.HachetteBookGroup.com

Printed in the United States of America

First Edition: June 2013
10 9 8 7 6 5 4 3 2 1

OPM

Forever is an imprint of Grand Central Publishing.
The Forever name and logo are trademarks of Hachette Book Group, Inc.

The Hachette Speakers Bureau provides a wide range of authors for speaking events. To find out more, go to www.hachettespeakersbureau.com or call (866) 376-6591.

The publisher is not responsible for websites (or their content) that are not owned by the publisher.

*To the members of the Oklahoma Army National Guard, thank you
for your service, your honor, your duty, and your bravery.
And for the families of those who did not return, I promise your
loved ones' sacrifices will never, ever be forgotten.*

Specialist Kyle A. Brinlee
Killed May 11, 2004

Sergeant Buddy J. Hughie
Killed February 19, 2007

Sergeant Daniel M. Eshbaugh
Killed September 17, 2008

Corporal Michael E. Thompson
Killed September 17, 2008

Chief Warrant Officer 3 Brady J. Rudolph
Killed September 17, 2008

Second Lieutenant Jered W. Ewy
Killed July 29, 2011

Specialist Augustus J. Vicari
Killed July 29, 2011

Staff Sergeant Kirk A. Owen
Killed August 2, 2011

Sergeant Anthony Del Mar Peterson
Killed August 4, 2011

Second Lieutenant Joe L. Cunningham
Killed August 13, 2011

First Lieutenant Damon T. Leehan
Killed August 14, 2011

Specialist Joshua M. Seals
Killed August 16, 2011

Private First Class Tony J. Potter Jr.
Killed September 9, 2011

Specialist Christopher D. Horton
Killed September 9, 2011

Sergeant Bret D. Isenhower
Killed September 9, 2011

Sergeant Mycal L. Prince
Killed September 15, 2011

Specialist Francisco J. Briseno-Alvarez Jr.
Killed September 25, 2011

Specialist Sarina N. Butcher
Killed November 1, 2011

Sergeant Christopher D. Gailey
Killed November 1, 2011

Acknowledgments

To the Smart Women Who. You know who you are, and you know why.

To my son, Brandon Pappano. Staff Sergeant, Airborne, Korea, 173rd, Vicenza, Iraq, and Afghanistan: Thanks for letting me borrow your Army career. Thank you more for being a son, a soldier, a husband, and a father I can be so very proud of.

And, as always, to my husband, Robert Pappano, United States Navy (Retired). You not only gave me the support I need for this job, but your Navy career provided the plots, the settings and the characters for so many of my books. You're the best asset any author could have and the best husband a woman could ever ask for.

The greatest casualty is being forgotten.

—Wounded Warrior Project

Wife. The toughest job in the Army.

—Unknown

A Hero to
Come Home To

Prologue

Thirteen months, two weeks, and three days.

That was the first conscious thought in Carly Lowry's head when she opened her eyes Tuesday morning. It was like an automatic tote board, adding each day to the total whether she wanted it to or not.

Thirteen months, two weeks, and three days. The way she marked her life now. There weren't events or occasions, no workdays or weekends, holidays or seasons. This was the only important passage of her time.

Thirteen months, two weeks, and three days since the helicopter transporting Jeff had been shot down in Afghanistan. Since her own life had ended. Her stubborn body just didn't recognize it.

Closing her eyes again, she groped for the remote on the nightstand and hit the power button. The morning news was on, though she paid it little mind. She didn't care about the latest bank robbery in Tulsa, or the sleazy lawyer's newest excuse to keep his high-profile client out of court on homicide charges, or which part of the city had construction woes adding to their morning commute.

Here in Tallgrass, Oklahoma, none of those things had happened in a long time. It was a great place to raise kids, Jeff had told her when they'd transferred here. Low crime rate, affordable cost of living if they discounted the air-conditioning bill in the dog months of summer, and all the amenities of Fort Murphy right next door. He'd loved downtown, with its stately buildings of sandstone and brick, none taller than three stories, as solid as if they'd grown right up out of the soil. He'd liked the old-fashioned awnings over the shop windows and the murals of cowboys, buffalo, and oil rigs painted on the sides of some of those buildings, along with restored eighty-year-old ads, back when phone numbers had only three digits. He'd loved the junk stores, where detritus of past lives showed up, their value and sometimes even their purpose forgotten. Rusty faded pieces of the town's history.

He'd loved *her*. Promised their time in Tallgrass would be good. Promised that when he retired from the Army, they would settle in just such a little town to finish raising their kids and turn gray and creaky together.

He'd broken his promise.

A sob escaped her, though she pretended it was a yawn and threw back the covers as if sleep might entice her if she remained in bed one minute longer. Truth was, crying every night wasn't conducive to a good night's sleep.

She avoided looking in the mirror as she got into the shower. She knew she had bed head, her pajamas made no attempt whatsoever at style, and her eyes were red and puffy. When she got out ten minutes later, she concentrated on the tasks of getting dried, dressed, and made up instead of the signs of tears, the fourteen pounds she'd gained, and the simple platinum band on her left hand.

She was ready for work early. She always was. While a cup of coffee brewed in the sleek machine she had bought as a surprise after Jeff had coveted it at the PX, she opened the refrigerator, then the pantry, looking for something to eat. She settled, as she did every morning, on oatmeal labeled as a "weight-control formula." She ate it for the protein, she told herself, because she needed the energy at work, and not because those fourteen pounds were huddled stubbornly on her hips and plotting to become twenty. To help them along, she added creamer and real sugar to her coffee, then topped off the meal with two pieces of rich, chocolate-covered caramel.

It was still too early for work, but too late to stay in the house any longer. After making sure the papers she'd graded the night before were inside her soft-sided messenger bag—of course they were—she stuffed her purse in, too, before grabbing her keys and heading outside to the car.

It was a chilly morning, but she didn't dash back in for a jacket. A utilitarian navy-blue one was tossed across the passenger seat. Since college, she'd kept one in the car for cold restaurants, not that she ate out much anymore. Eating alone was bad enough; doing it in public exceeded her capabilities.

Two miles stretched out between her neighborhood and the Fort Murphy gate, then less than another to the post's school complex where she taught. Most soldiers reported for duty an hour or more before school started, so she could wait that much longer at home and make the

trip in less time, but moping was as well done in the car
as at home.

She moved into the long double-lane line turning off
Main Street and into the post. The only traffic jams Tallgrass ever saw were outside the fort's two main gates in
the morning and afternoon. Jeff had liked to go to work
early and stay late because life was too damn fun to sit
idle in traffic.

He'd never sat idle.

Finally it was her turn to show her license and proof of
insurance to the guard at the gate, who waved her through
with a courteous, "Have a good day, ma'am."

Oh, yeah. Her days were so good, she wasn't sure how
many more of them she could handle.

"You need to talk to someone," her sister-in-law had
advised her in last week's phone call.

*"To who? I've talked to the grief counselors and the
chaplain, I've talked to you, I've even tried to talk to
Mom."* Carly's voice had broken on that.

Lisa's voice had turned sympathetic. *"You know your
mom doesn't 'get' emotional."*

A thin smile curled her lips as she turned into the
parking lot for the schools. None of her family "got"
emotional. Mom, Dad, and three brothers: scientists,
every last one of them. Logical, detached, driven by
curiosity and rationale and great mysteries to solve. Unfortunately, she, with her overload of emotion, wasn't the
right sort of mystery for them. They were sympathetic—
to a point. Understanding—to a point. Beyond that,
though, she was more alien to them than the slide samples under their microscopes.

Easing into a parking space, she cut off the engine.

Large oaks, with last fall's brown leaves waiting to be pushed aside by this spring's new ones, shaded the U-shaped complex. She worked in the one ahead of her, the elementary school; the middle school was, appropriately, in the middle; and the high school stood across the vast lot behind her.

Only two other employees had beaten her: one of the janitors and the elementary principal. He was a nice guy who always came early—problems of his own to escape at home, or so the gossips said—and brought pastries and started the coffee in the teachers' lounge. He was about her father's age, but much more human. He understood emotion.

Still, she didn't open her car door, even when the chill crept over her as the heater's warmth dissipated. The comment about her mother hadn't been the end of her conversation with Lisa. Her sister-in-law had returned to the subject without missing a beat. *"You need to talk to someone who's been there, Carly. Someone who really, truly* knows *what it's like. Another wife."*

Lisa couldn't bring herself to use the word *widow*, not in reference to Carly. Carly couldn't, either.

"I don't know…" She could have finished it several ways. *I don't know if I want to talk to anyone. I'm all talked out.* Or *I don't know if talking could possibly help. It hasn't yet.* Or *I don't know any other wives whose husbands have died.*

But that wasn't true. Wives—widows—didn't tend to stay in the town where their husbands had last been assigned. They usually had homes or families to return to. But she knew one who hadn't left: Therese Matheson. Well, she didn't actually *know* her, other than to say hello. Therese's kindergartners were on recess and at lunch at different times than Carly's third-graders, and their free periods didn't coincide, either.

But Therese had been there, done that and had the flag and posthumous medals to show for it. Therese really, truly knew. Would it hurt to ask if they could meet for dinner one evening? One dinner wasn't much of a commitment. If it didn't pan out, so what? At least she would have eaten something besides a frozen entrée or pizza.

Therese would be at school before the eight-fifteen bell. Carly would find out then.

"Tuh-*reese*, where's my pink shirt?"

Thirteen-year-old Abby's voice had always had a shrill edge, from the first time Therese Matheson had met her, but it had grown even worse over the past months. It was designed to get on her nerves quicker than a classful of kindergartners who'd had too much sugar, too much whine, and not enough rest.

"Tuh-*race*," she murmured for the thousandth time before raising her voice enough to be heard upstairs. "If it's not in your closet, Abby, then it's in the laundry."

Footsteps reminiscent of a *Jurassic Park* T. Rex resounded overhead, then Abby appeared at the top of the stairs. She was barely a hundred and ten pounds. How could she make such noise? "You mean you didn't wash it?"

Therese bit back the response that wanted to pop out: *How many times have I told you?* Instead, keeping her tone as normal as possible, she said, "You know the policy. If it's not in the hamper, it's not going to make it to the washer."

The girl's entire body vibrated with her frustration. "Oh God, the one day a week we don't have to wear our uniforms and we *all* decided to wear pink today, and now I can't because *you* can't be bothered to do your job! My mom *always*..." The words faded as she whirled, her pale blond and scarlet hair flouncing, and stomped back to her room.

Your job. Therese leaned against the door frame. Being a mother was work, sure, tumultuous and chaotic, absolutely, but it wasn't supposed to be a *job.* It was supposed to be balanced by love and affection, common courtesy and respect. While their little family had an overabundance of tumult and chaos and resentment and hostility, there was precious little of the good things that made the rest worthwhile.

"Oh, Paul," she whispered, her gaze shifting to the framed photo above the fireplace. "You were the glue that held us together. Now that you're gone, we're falling apart. I'm trying, I really am, but..." Her voice broke, and tears filled her eyes. "I don't think I can do this without you."

For as long as she could remember, she'd wanted a husband and children, and for the last six years, she'd wanted Paul's children—sweet babies with his ready smile, his good nature and sense of humor, his endless capacity to love.

She'd gotten his children, all right. Just not in the way she'd expected.

A distant rumble penetrated her sorrow, and her gaze flickered to the wall clock. She blinked away the moisture, cleared the lump from her throat and called, "Jacob! The bus is coming."

Again heavy steps pounded overhead, then her tall, broad-shouldered stepson took the stairs three at a time. Only eleven, he was built like his father and shared the same coloring—dark blond hair, fair skin, eyes like dark chocolate—but that was where the similarities ended. Where Paul had been warm and funny and considerate, Jacob was moody and distant. Paul had been easy to get along with; Jacob was prickly.

Not that he wasn't entitled—rejected by his mother and abandoned, however unwillingly, by his father. Therese tried to be there for him, to talk to him, to comfort him, and God knew how often she prayed for him. But the last time he'd let her hug him had been right after Paul's funeral fifteen months ago. It seemed the harder she tried, the harder he pushed her away.

He paused only long enough to grab the backpack in the living room, then the door slammed behind him. He didn't say good-bye, didn't even glance her way.

Therese tried to take a calming breath, but her chest was tight, her lungs so compressed that only a fraction of the air she needed could squeeze through. In the beginning, right after she'd gotten the news of Paul's death, the difficulty breathing, the clamminess, the fluttering just beneath her breastbone, had been an occasional thing, but over the months it had come more often.

People asked her how she was doing, and she gave them phony smiles and phony answers, and everyone believed her, even her parents. She was afraid to tell the truth: that every day was getting worse, that she was losing ground with the kids, that her stomach hurt and her chest hurt and her head was about to explode. She did her best to maintain control, but she was only pretending. Whatever control she had was fragile and, worse, sometimes she *wanted* to lose it. To shatter into nothingness. After all, *nothing* couldn't be hurt, couldn't suffer, couldn't grieve. *Nothing* existed in a state of oblivion, and some days—most days lately—she needed the sweet comfort of oblivion.

Another rumble cut through the rushing in her ears, and she forced her mouth open, forced Abby's name to form. Unlike Jacob, Abby didn't ignore her but glared at her all the way down the stairs. Contrary to her earlier shriek, she was wearing pink: a silk blouse from Therese's closet. It was too big for her, so she'd layered it over a torso-hugging tank top and tied the delicate fabric into knots at her waist.

Abby's defiant stare dared Therese to comment. Just as defiant, she ground her teeth and didn't say a word. She had splurged on the blouse for a date night with Paul, but no way she would wear it again now. If it was even salvageable after a day with the princess of I-hate-you.

The door slammed, the sudden quiet vibrating around Therese, so sharp for a moment that it hurt. The house was empty. *She* was empty.

Dear God, she needed help.

She just didn't know where to get it.

As the warning bell rang, Carly left her class in the capable hands of her aide and made her way to the kindergarten wing that stood at a right angle to her own wing. Therese Matheson's classroom was at the end of the hallway, next to a door that led to the playground. It was large and heavy, especially compared to the five-year-olds that populated the hall, but since five-year-olds were proven escape artists, it was wired with an alarm to foil any attempts.

Therese stood in the hallway, greeting her students, ushering the stragglers into the room. Pretty, dark haired, she looked serene. Competent. So much more in control of herself than Carly. For a moment, Carly hesitated, unsure about her plan. What could she possibly have to offer Therese?

Then she squared her shoulders, fixed a smile on her face and approached her. "Hi, Therese, I'm Carly Lowry. Third grade?" One hand raised, thumb pointing back the way she'd come. "I, uh...My husband was..."

Sympathy softened Therese's features even more. "I know. Mine, too."

A pigtailed girl darted between them, pausing long enough to beam up, revealing a missing tooth. "Hi, Miss Trace."

"Good morning, Courtney." Therese touched her lightly on the shoulder before the girl rushed inside.

Kindergartners were unbearably cute, but Carly couldn't have taught them. That young and sweet and cuddly, they would have been a constant reminder of the kids she and Jeff had planned to have. Would never have.

"I was, uh, wondering...well, if you would mind getting together for dinner one night to—to talk. About...our husbands and, uh, things. If...well, if you're interested."

Therese considered it, raising one hand to brush her hair back. Like Carly, she still wore her wedding ring. "I'd like that. Does tonight work you?"

Carly hadn't expected such a quick response, but it wasn't as if she had any other demands on her time. And if she had too much time to think about this idea, she very well might back out. "Sure. Is Mexican all right?"

Therese smiled. "I haven't had a margarita in months. The Three Amigos?"

It was Tallgrass's best Mexican restaurant, one of Jeff's favorites. Because of that, the only Mexican food Carly had since he died had been takeout from Bueno. "That would be great. Does six work for you?"

Therese's smile widened. "I'll be there."

The bell rang, the last few kids in the hall scurrying toward their classes. Carly summoned her own smile. "Good. Great. Uh, I'll see you tonight."

An unfamiliar emotion settled over her as she walked back to her own classroom. Hope, she realized. For the first time in thirteen months, two weeks, and three days, she felt hopeful. Maybe she could learn how to live without Jeff, after all.

Chapter One

One year later

It had taken only three months of living in Oklahoma for Carly to learn that March could be the most wonderful place on earth or the worst. This particular weekend was definitely in the wonderful category. The temperature was in the midseventies, warm enough for short sleeves and shorts, though occasionally a breeze off the water brought just enough coolness to chill her skin. The sun was bright, shining hard on the stone and concrete surfaces that surrounded them, sharply delineating the new green buds on the trees and the shoots peeking out from the rocky ground.

It was a beautiful clear day, the kind that Jeff had loved, the kind they would have spent on a long walk or maybe just lounging in the backyard with ribs smoking on the grill. There was definitely a game on TV—wasn't it about time for March Madness?—but he'd preferred to spend his time off with her. He could always read about the games in the paper.

Voices competed with the splash of the waterfall as she touched her hand to her hip pocket, feeling the crackle of paper there. The photograph went everywhere with her, especially on each new adventure she took with her friends. And this trip to Turner Falls, just outside Davis, Oklahoma, while tame enough, was an adventure for her. Every time she left their house in Tallgrass, two hours away, was an adventure of sorts. Every night she went to sleep without crying, every morning she found the strength to get up.

"There's the cave." Jessy, petite and red haired, gestured to the opening above and to the right of the waterfall. "Who wants to be first?"

The women looked around at each other, but before anyone else could speak up, Carly did. "I'll go." These adventures were about a lot of things: companionship, support, grieving, crying, laughing, and facing fears.

There was only one fear Carly needed to face today: her fear of heights. She estimated the cave at about eighty feet above the ground, based on the fact that it was above the falls, which were seventy-two feet high, according to the T-shirts they'd all picked up at the gift shop. Not a huge height, so not a huge fear, right? And it wasn't as if they'd be actually climbing. The trail was steep in places, but anyone could do it. She could do it.

"I'll wait here," Ilena said. Being twenty-eight weeks pregnant with a child who would never know his father limited her participation in cave climbing. "Anything you don't want to carry, leave with me. And be sure you secure your cameras. I don't want anything crashing down on me from above."

"Yeah, everyone try not to crash down on Ilena," Jessy

said drily as the women began unloading jackets and water bottles on their friend.

"Though if you do fall, aim for me," Ilena added. "I'm pretty cushiony these days." Smiling, she patted the roundness of her belly with jacket-draped arms. With pale skin and white-blond hair, she resembled a rather anemic snowman whose builders had emptied an entire coat closet on it.

Carly faced the beginning of the trail, her gaze rising to the shadow of the cave mouth. Every journey started with one step—the mantra Jeff had used during his try-jogging-you'll-love-it phase. She hadn't loved it at all, but she'd loved him so she'd given it a shot and spent a week recovering from shocks such as her joints had never known.

One step, then another. The voices faded into the rush of the falls again as she pulled herself up a steep incline. She focused on not noticing that the land around her was more vertical than not. She paid close attention to spindly trees and an occasional bit of fresh green working its way up through piles of last fall's leaves. She listened to the water and thought a fountain would be a nice addition to her backyard this summer, one in the corner where she could hear it from her bedroom with the window open.

And before she realized it, she was squeezing past a boulder and the cave entrance was only a few feet away. A triumphant shout rose inside her and she turned to give it voice, only to catch sight of the water thundering over the cliff, the pool below that collected it and Ilena, divested of her burden now and calling encouragement.

"Oh, holy crap," she whispered, instinctively backing

against the rough rock that formed the floor of the cave entrance.

Heart pounding, she turned away from the view below, grabbed a handful of rock and hauled herself into the cave. She collapsed on the floor, unmindful of the dirt or any crawly things she might find inside, scooted on her butt until the nearest wall was at her back, then let out the breath squeezing her chest.

Her relieved sigh ended in a squeak as her gaze connected with another no more than six feet away. "Oh, my God!" Jeff's encouragement the first time she'd come eye to eye with a mouse echoed in her head: *"He's probably as scared of you as you are of him."*

The thought almost loosed a giggle, but she was afraid it would have turned hysterical. The man sitting across the cave didn't look as if he were scared of anything, though that might well change when her friends arrived. His eyes were dark, his gaze narrowed, as if he didn't like his solitude interrupted. It was impossible to see what color his hair was, thanks to a very short cut and the baseball cap he wore with the insignia of the 173rd Airborne Brigade Combat Team. He hadn't shaved in a day or two, and he was lean, long, solid, dressed in a T-shirt and faded jeans with brand-new running shoes.

He shifted awkwardly, sliding a few feet farther into the cave, onto the next level of rock, then ran his hands down his legs, smoothing his jeans.

Carly forced a smile. "I apologize for my graceless entrance. Logically, I knew how high I was, but as long as I didn't look, I didn't have to *really* know. I have this thing about heights, but nobody knows"—she tilted her head toward the entrance where the others' voices were coming closer—"so I'd appreciate it if you didn't say anything."

Stopping for breath, she grimaced. Apparently, she'd learned to babble again, as if she hadn't spoken to a stranger—a male stranger, at least—in far too long. She'd babbled with every man she'd met until Jeff. Though he'd been exactly the type to intimidate her into idiocy, he never had. Talking to him had been easy from the first moment.

"I'm Carly, and I hope you don't mind company because I think the trail is pretty crowded with my friends right now." She gestured toward the ball cap. "Are you with the Hundred Seventy-Third?"

There was a flicker of surprise in his eyes that she recognized the embroidered insignia. "I was. It's been a while." His voice was exactly what she expected: dark, raspy, as if he hadn't talked much in a long time.

"Are you at Fort Sill now?" The artillery post at Lawton was about an hour and a half from the falls. It was Oklahoma's only other Army post besides Fort Murphy, two hours northeast at Tallgrass.

"No." His gaze shifted to the entrance when Jessy appeared, and he moved up another level of the ragged stone that led to the back of the shallow cave.

"Whoo!" Jessy's shout echoed off the walls, then her attention locked on the man. The tilt of her green eyes gave her smile a decided feline look. "Hey, guys, we turn our back on her for one minute, and Carly's off making new friends." She heaved herself into the cave and, though there was plenty of room, nudged Carly toward the man before dropping to the stone beside her. She leaned past, offering her hand. "Hi, I'm Jessy. Who are you?"

Carly hadn't thought of offering her hand or even asking his name, but direct was Jessy's style, and it usually brought results. This time was no different, though he hesitated before extending his hand. "I'm Dane."

"Dane," Therese echoed as she climbed up. "Nice name. I'm Therese. And what are you doing up here in Wagon Wheel Cave?"

"Wishing he'd escaped before we got here," Carly murmured, and she wasn't sure but thought she heard an agreeing grunt from him.

The others crowded in, offering their names—Fia, Lucy, and Marti—and he acknowledged each of them with a nod. Somewhere along the way, he'd slipped off the ball cap and pushed it out of sight, as though he didn't want to advertise the fact that he'd been Airborne. As if they wouldn't recognize a high-and-tight haircut, but then, he didn't know he'd been cornered by a squad of Army wives.

Widows, Carly corrected herself. They might consider the loose-knit group of fifteen to twenty women back in Tallgrass just friends. They might jokingly refer to themselves as the Tuesday Night Margarita Club, but everyone around Tallgrass knew who they really were, even if people rarely said the words to them.

The Fort Murphy Widows' Club.

Marti, closest to the entrance, leaned over the edge far enough to make Carly's heart catch in her chest. "Hey, Ilena, say hi to Dane!"

"Hello, Dane!" came a distant shout.

"We left her down below. She's preggers." At Dane's somewhat puzzled gesture, Marti yelled out again, "Dane says hi!"

"Bet you've never been alone in a small cave with six women," someone commented.

"Hope you're not claustrophobic," someone else added.

He did look a bit green, Carly thought, but not from claustrophobia. He'd found the isolation he was seeking, only to have a horde of chatty females descend on him. But who went looking for isolation in a public park on a beautiful warm Saturday?

Probably lots of people, she admitted, given how many millions of acres of public wilderness there were. But Turner Falls wasn't isolated wilderness. Anyone could drive in. And the cave certainly wasn't isolated. Even she could reach it.

Deep inside, elation surged, a quiet celebration. Who knew? Maybe this fall she would strap into the bungee ride at the Tulsa State Fair and let it launch her into the stratosphere. But first she had to get down from here.

Her stomach shuddered at the thought.

After a few minutes' conversation and picture taking, her friends began leaving again in the order in which they'd come. With each departure, Carly put a few inches' space between her and Dane until finally it was her turn. She took a deep breath...and stayed exactly where she was. She could see the ground from here if she leaned forward except no way was she leaning forward with her eyes open. With her luck, she'd get dizzy and pitch out headfirst.

"It's not so bad if you back out." Despite his brief conversation with the others, Dane's voice still sounded rusty. "Keep your attention on your hands and feet, and don't forget to breathe."

"Easy for you to say." Her own voice sounded reedy, unsteady. "You used to jump out of airplanes for a living."

"Yeah, well, it's not the jumping that's hard. It's the landing that can get you in a world of trouble."

On hands and knees, she flashed him a smile as she scooted in reverse until there was nothing but air beneath her feet. Ready to lunge back inside any instant, she felt for the ledge with her toes and found it, solid and wide and really not very different from a sidewalk, if she discounted the fact that it was eighty feet above the ground. "You never did say where you're stationed," she commented.

"Fort Murphy. It's a couple hours away—"

"At Tallgrass." Her smile broadened. "That's where we're all from. Maybe we'll see you around." She eased away from the entrance, silently chanting to keep her gaze from straying. *Hands, feet, breathe. Hands, feet, breathe.*

Dane Clark stiffly moved to the front of the cave. A nicer guy would've offered to make the descent with Carly, but these days he found that being civil was sometimes the best he could offer. Besides, he wasn't always steady on his feet himself. If she'd slipped and he'd tried to catch her, she likely would have had to catch him instead. Not an experience his ego wanted.

His therapists wouldn't like it if they knew he was sitting in this cave. He'd only been in Tallgrass a few days. The first day, he'd bought a truck. The second, he'd come here. The drive had been too long, the climb too much. But he'd wanted this to be the first thing he'd done here because it was the last thing he'd done with his dad before he died. It was a tribute to him.

The women's voices were still audible, though all he could really make out was laughter. What were the odds he would drive two hours for a little privacy and wind up sharing the cave with six women—seven if he counted the pregnant one, now handing out jackets—from the town where he was stationed?

It really was a small world. He'd traveled a hell of a lot of it. He should know.

Sliding forward a few inches, he let his feet dangle over the edge. God, how many times had doctors and nurses and therapists told him to do that? Too many to think about, so instead he watched Carly's progress, her orange shirt easy to pick out against the drab shades of rock and dirt. Why had she volunteered to lead the climb if she was afraid of heights? To prove she could?

Finally, she jumped the last few feet to the ground and spun in a little circle that he doubted any of her friends noticed. She joined them, and what appeared to be a spontaneous group hug broke out, congratulating each other on their success.

He'd had buddies like that—well, maybe not so touchy-feely. Still did, even if they were scattered all over the world. But after years filled with one tour after another in Iraq or Afghanistan, a lot of them were gone. Sometimes he thought he couldn't possibly remember all their faces and names. Other times, he knew he would never forget.

After posing for more pictures, the women headed away from the falls. With the trail empty as far as he could see, he stood up, both hands touching the rock just in case. Time to see if his right leg and the miracle of modern medicine that served as his left could get him to the bottom without falling on his ass.

He succeeded. Uneven ground made for uncomfortable walking, the prosthetic rubbing the stump of his leg despite its protective sleeve. It was odd, standing, moving, climbing, without more than half of his leg. He could feel it, and yet he couldn't, sensed it was there but knew it wasn't. It was the damnedest thing—sometimes the hardest of all to accept.

He stood for a moment watching the water churn where the falls hit, giving the ache in his leg a chance to subside. Another month or two, and the pool would be filled with swimmers on weekends. He'd always liked to swim, and his various medical people had insisted he would again. He wasn't so sure about that. He'd never considered himself vain, but putting on trunks and removing his prosthesis in public...He wasn't ready for that. He was beginning to think he never would be.

Determinedly he turned away from the water and started for the parking lot. It wasn't far, maybe a quarter mile, sidewalk all the way, but by the time he reached his pickup, his leg and hip were throbbing, and the pain was spreading to his lower back. The two-hour drive home, plus a stop for lunch, would leave him in need of both a hot bath and a pain pill, but he didn't regret the trip.

Dane drove slowly through the park and onto the highway. Once he reached the interstate, he turned north, then took the first exit into Davis. A quick pass through town showed the fast-food options, and he settled on a burger and fries from Sonic. He was headed back to the interstate when traffic stopped him in front of a Mexican restaurant. Inside were the seven women from the cave, toasting each other, margarita glasses held high.

He'd noticed without realizing that most of them wore

wedding rings. Were they just friends from Tallgrass, Army wives whose husbands were stationed there or maybe soldiers themselves? Carly, at least, had some military experience, with the way she'd pulled the name of his old unit out of thin air. And neither she nor Jessy nor any of the others had sounded as if they were native to Oklahoma, though he knew how easily accents could be picked up and lost. Best bet, they'd been brought to Tallgrass by the Army, and when their husbands deployed, so did they.

But he knew from firsthand experience there were worse ways for a wife to entertain herself when her husband was gone than hiking with her girlfriends.

He reached Fort Murphy in good time, turning at the end of Main Street into the post's main entrance. A sandstone arch on either side of the four-lane held engraved concrete: WELCOME TO FORT MURPHY on the left, a list of the tenant commands on the right, including the Warrior Transition Unit. That was the unit that currently laid claim to him. In the future...

Once he'd had his life all laid out: Twenty years or more in the Army, retirement, a family, a second career that left him time to travel. He'd thought he might teach history and coach, open a dive shop or get into some type of wilderness-adventure trek business. Now he didn't have the vaguest idea what the future held. For a man who'd always known where he was going, it was kind of scary, not knowing where he was going or how—or even if—he could get there.

After clearing the guard shack, he drove onto the post, past a bronze statue of the base's namesake, cowboy, actor, and war hero Audie Murphy. The four-lane passed

24   *Marilyn Pappano*

a manicured golf course, a community center with an Olympic-size pool and the first of many housing areas before he turned onto a secondary street. His quarters were in a barracks, opened only months ago, small apartments to help their occupants adjust to life outside the hospitals where most of them had spent too many months. Dane's own stay had lasted eleven months. Long enough to bring a new life into the world. *Not* long enough to adjust to a totally new life.

He was limping painfully by the time he let himself into his apartment. Tossing the keys on a table near the door, he grabbed a beer from the refrigerator and washed down a couple pills, fumbled his way out of his jeans, then dropped onto the couch before removing the prosthesis. He had two—one that looked pretty real from a distance and this one that seemed more of a superhero bionic thing. He was grateful to have them—he'd seen nonmilitary people forced by the cost to get by on much less efficient models—but neither was close to the real thing.

Absently rubbing his leg, he used the remote to turn on the television, then surfed the channels. There were lots of sports on today that he didn't want to watch. They reminded him too much of his own years playing football and baseball and running for the pure pleasure of it. No chick flicks, no talking animals, no gung-ho kick-ass action movies. He settled on a documentary on narrow-gauge railroads that let his mind wander.

How had he filled his Saturday afternoons before the amputation? Running for his life sometimes. Taking other people's lives sometimes. Jumping out of helicopters, patrolling barren desert, interfacing with locals. Before Iraq and Afghanistan, it had been riding his motorcycle through the Italian Alps, taking the train to Venice with his buddies, sightseeing and drinking too much. Hanging out, using too many women badly trying to get over his failed marriage.

He replayed weekends all the way back to his teens. Chores, running errands, homework, extra practices if the coach deemed them necessary, dates on Saturday night with Sheryl. Before she'd married him. Before she'd fallen out of love with him. Before she'd run around on him—adding insult to injury, with guys from his own unit.

He was over her. By the time she'd actually filed for divorce, he'd been so disillusioned by her affairs that he hadn't cared. But there was still this knot of resentment. They'd been together since they were fourteen, for God's sake, and she hadn't even had the grace to say "It's over." She'd lied to him. Betrayed him. She'd let him down, then blamed him for it.

And her life was great. She'd gone back home to Texas, married a rich guy who only got richer and lived in a beautiful mansion with three beautiful kids.

Dane's mother gave him regular updates, despite the fact that he'd never once asked. *"You let her get away,"* Anna Mae always ended with a regretful sigh.

Yeah, sure. *He'd* screwed up. It was all his fault. To Sheryl and Anna Mae, everything that had gone wrong was his fault, even the IED that had cost him his leg. *If you'd listened to Sheryl and me and gotten out of the Army…*

A dim image of the women he'd met that day—Carly, Jessy, and the others—formed in his mind. Did they lie to their husbands, betray them, let them down? It would be easy to think yes. The unfaithful-always-ready-to-party military wife was a stereotype, but stereotypes became that for a reason.

But today, after driving to the park, hiking to the falls, and climbing up to the cave, he'd rather give them the benefit of the doubt. That was something normal people did, and today, he was feeling pretty normal.

"Do you ever feel guilty for looking at a guy and thinking, 'Wow, he's hot; I'd like to get to know him'?"

The quiet question came from Therese, sitting on the far side of the third-row seat of Marti's Suburban. Carly looked at her over Jessy's head, slumped on her shoulder. The redhead's snores were soft, barely noticeable, and due more to the third margarita she'd had with lunch than anything else, Carly suspected. Jessy was full of life until she got a few drinks in her, then she crashed hard.

"You mean, do I feel like I'm being unfaithful to Jeff, his memory, our marriage, his family, myself? Yeah. We had such plans." Regret robbed her voice of its strength. "Life wasn't supposed to turn out this way."

"But are we meant to spend the rest of our lives honoring our husbands' memories and...alone?"

Alone. That was a scary word even for women as independent as the Army had forced them to become. Even before their husbands had deployed to Iraq and Afghanistan, they'd been gone a lot, training at various bases around the country. They'd worked long hours to get themselves and their troops combat-ready, and most home-life responsibilities had fallen on their wives.

But then, *alone* had been okay. There had been an

end to every training mission, to every deployment. The men had come home, and they'd made up for all the time missed.

For the seven of them, though, and the rest of the margarita club, the last return home had been final. There would be no more kisses, no more hugs, no more great sex, no more making up for missed time. There were only flags, medals, grave sites, and memories.

Yes, and some guilt.

"Paul wouldn't want you to spend the rest of your life alone."

The words sounded lame even to Carly. Lord knows, she'd heard them often enough—from friends, from her in-laws, from therapists. The first time, from a grief counselor, she'd wanted to shriek, *How could you possibly know that? You never met him!*

But it was true. Jeff had loved her. He'd always encouraged her to live life. He would be appalled if she grieved it away over him instead. Her head knew that.

Her heart was just having trouble with it.

Therese's laugh broke halfway. "I don't know. Paul was the jealous type. He didn't want me even looking at another guy."

"But that was because *he* was there. Now…" It took a little extra breath to finish the sentence. "He's not."

A few miles passed in silence before Therese spoke again. "What about you guys? What if one of us…"

After her voice trailed off, Fia finished the question from her middle-row seat. "Falls in love and gets another chance at happily ever after?"

Therese swallowed, then nodded. "Would it affect *us*? We became friends because we'd all lost our husbands.

Would a new man in one of our lives change that? Would we want to share you with him?"

"Would he want to share you with us?" Ilena asked. "What guy would want his new girlfriend spending time with a group that's tied at its very heart to her husband's death?"

Shifting uncomfortably, Carly stared out the window. She had other friends—a few from college, teachers she worked with, a neighbor or two—but the margarita club, especially these six, were her best friends.

She wanted to say a relationship could never negatively affect their friendship, but truth was, she wasn't sure. She'd had other best friends before Jeff died—they all had—other Army wives, and they'd grown apart after. They'd shown her love and sorrow and sympathy, but they'd also felt a tiny bit of relief that it was *her* door the dress-uniformed officers had knocked at to make the casualty notification, that it was *her* husband who'd died and not theirs. And they'd felt guilty for feeling relieved.

She knew, because she'd been through it herself.

She forced a smile as her gaze slid from woman to woman. "I'll love you guys no matter what. If one of you falls in love, gets married and lives the perfect life with Prince Charming, I'll envy you. I'll probably hate you at least once a week. But I'll always be there for you."

The others smiled, too, sadly, then silence fell again. The conversation hadn't really answered any questions. It was easy to say it was okay to fall in love, even easier to promise their friendship would never end. But in the end, it was actions that counted.

The closer they got to Tallgrass, the more regret built in Carly. Though their times together were frequent—

dinner every Tuesday, excursions every couple months, impromptu gatherings for shopping or a movie or no reason at all—she couldn't ignore the fact that she was going home to an empty house. All of them were except Therese, who would pick up her resentful stepchildren from the neighbor who was watching them. They would eat their dinners alone, watch TV or read or clean house alone, and they would go to bed alone.

Were they meant to spend the rest of their lives that way? Dear God, she hoped not.

By the time the Suburban pulled into her driveway, Carly was pretty much in a funk. She squeezed out from the third seat, exchanged good-byes with the others, promising to share any good pictures she'd gotten, and headed toward the house as if she didn't dread going inside.

It was a great starter house, the real estate agent had told them when they'd come to Tallgrass. *"That means 'fixer-upper,'"* Carly had whispered to Jeff, and he'd grinned. *"You know me. I love my tools."*

"But you never actually use them."

But the house was close to the fort, and the mortgage payments allowed plenty of money left over for all those repairs. Jeff had actually done some of them himself. Not many, but enough to crow over.

She climbed the steps he'd leveled and inserted the key in the dead bolt he'd installed. A lamp burned in the living room, a habit she'd gained their first night apart, shining on comfortable furniture, good tables, a collection of souvenirs and knickknacks and, of course, photographs. The outrageously sized television had been his choice, to balance the burnished wicker chair she'd chosen for her reading corner. Likewise, he'd picked the leather recliner to hide at least part of the froufrou rug she'd put down.

Their life had been full of little trade-offs like that. He would load the dishwasher if she would unload it. He would take his uniforms to the dry cleaner for knife-sharp creases, and she wouldn't complain if he wore sweats at home. She mowed the lawn, and he cleaned the gutters.

She'd stayed home, and he'd gone to war and died.

And she missed him, God, more than she'd thought possible.

To stave off the melancholy, she went to the kitchen for a bottle of water and a hundred-calorie pack of cookies. Before she reached the living room again, her cell phone rang.

It was Lucy. "I sent you some pictures. Check 'em out." She sounded way too cheerful before her voice cracked. "Norton, don't you dare! Aw, man! I swear to you, that mutt holds his pee all day just so he can see my face when he soaks the kitchen floor. Gotta go."

"Hello and good-bye to you, too." Carly slid the phone back into her pocket and made a turn into the dining room, where her computer occupied a very messy table. She opened her email, and pictures began popping onto the screen—group shots, individuals, posed, candid, all of them happy and smiling.

No, not all. She hovered the cursor over one photo, clicking to enlarge it. Their cave-mate Dane. He was looking directly at the camera, a hint of surprise in his eyes as he realized he was being photographed, as if he wanted to jerk his gaze or his head away and didn't quite manage.

It was a stark photo of a good face: not overly handsome, with a strong jaw and straight nose, intense eyes and a mouth that was almost too sensitive for the rest of his features. He looked capable, a command-and-control kind of guy, except for his eyes. They were tough to read, even when she magnified the photo until the upper half of his face filled the screen, but there was definitely something haunted—or haunting?—about them.

He had a story to tell, and probably a sad one. It wasn't likely she would see him again to hear it. Tallgrass wasn't a large town, but it was easy enough for people to live their lives without ever running into a specific individual. Unless Dane had a child at the elementary school or happened to crave Mexican food on a Tuesday night, they would probably never see each other again.

Whatever his story, she wished him well with it.

Chapter Two

Last one out of the truck before Marti headed toward her own home, Therese stared at the house from the driveway. It was two stories, white siding with red brick, a narrow porch lined by flower beds and a patch of neatly manicured lawn waiting for spring to turn it green and lush.

They had been married six years before Paul got orders to Fort Murphy, and ordinarily they would have rented an apartment in the beginning, but he'd just found out that his ex-wife was sending the kids to live with them. Up to that point, Therese's exposure to Abby and Jacob had been limited to a few rushed days twice a year. She'd been excited about the move, actually buying a house and forming a real family with his children.

Lord, had she really thought it would be that easy?

It hadn't been, not from the start. Her presence in Paul's life had put a serious roadblock in the kids' hopes that their parents would get back together, one they hadn't recovered from when Catherine packed them off to live with their dad. Finding herself? Needing *me* time?

Therese had wanted to smack the woman. The time to find herself was before she had children or after she'd raised them to be responsible, self-sufficient adults. At eight and ten, Jacob and Abby had been neither self-sufficient nor adults. Just deeply wounded children longing for the stability they'd lost.

Things had never been smooth, then Paul had died and Catherine had declined to let the kids return home to California, claiming she just couldn't handle the burden in her grief.

They were her *children*, not a burden, Therese had pointed out when Catherine delivered the message in a phone call. And just how much grief could the woman have? *She* was the one who'd had an affair, who'd left the marriage, who'd filed for divorce. *She* was the one who'd broken Paul's and the kids' hearts. But Catherine hadn't budged.

Paul's children. Not a burden. Even if Abby still resented her, still expected maid, chauffeur, and restaurant service, still thought the world revolved around her and Therese was the drudge whose sole reason for existence was greasing the axle. Even if Jacob was still sullen, rarely looking at or speaking to his stepmother—though, for the record, he paid Abby no notice, either. In his opinion, they were both just nuisances put there to test him.

Paul's children.

Giving herself a mental shake, she walked past the car and took the steps to the porch. Hitting the autodial button for their neighbors, she braced her cell between her shoulder and ear while she unlocked the door, then stepped inside. Even empty, the house wasn't peaceful. The air was filled with tension, as if it couldn't escape the four walls or the doors that were constantly being slammed. *Lord, how much longer?* Would things ever get better for them?

"Hi, Marsha," she said when her friend answered. "I'm home so you can send the kids over any time. Did they behave?"

Marsha laughed. "Don't you know kids always behave better for other people than they do for their parents? They were fine. Abby and Nicole went to a movie, and Jacob and Liam played video games all day. I'm sure their eyes are still crossed. Did you have a good time?"

"I did. The park was beautiful, and the exercise did me good. I appreciate you keeping them. Let me know next time you and Will want a date night. I'd be happy to return the favor." She wasn't lying. Having company didn't change Jacob's behavior—Liam was sullen just like him—but Nicole's presence always made Abby straighten up at least a bit.

"I'll take you up on that. I'll pry the boys loose from their games and point them your way."

"Thanks." Therese headed straight to the kitchen, leaving her purse and phone on the counter, hanging her keys on a cat sculpture nearby. As she placed a frozen pizza in the oven, she mused about Marsha's choice of words. Pointing the kids her way ... sounded like aiming a weapon.

"Oh, Paul, the things I do for love," she whispered.

It was less than fifteen minutes before the front door slammed. The pizza was cooling on the counter, and Therese was tossing together a salad—literally: bagged lettuce, cherry tomatoes, and a container of diced cucumbers. Wearing a scowl, Jacob gave his hands a poor excuse for a wash, grabbed a bottle of pop from the refrigerator, and headed for his usual seat at the table.

"Jacob, get the plates and silverware." Therese's voice sounded fairly neutral, considering it was about the thousandth time she'd made the same request. For about the thousandth time, he grunted—why did males think that was an appropriate response to *anything*?—and obeyed.

Abby, on her cell with Nicole, was taking her turn at the sink. First she'd demanded, then wheedled her way into getting the phone by pointing out she could use it to stay in touch with Therese. Not once in the six months since had she ever called Therese, and Therese was pretty sure that, if *she* called Abby, the girl wouldn't answer. But it had made her happy . . . for a while.

"Three glasses of ice," she reminded Abby when she dried her hands.

"I don't want ice."

"I do." It was one of her few requirements for living in her house. They ate like civilized people, with dishes, drinks in glasses and everything. "And tell Nicole goodbye." No phone calls during dinner, either.

"I gotta go. It's dinnertime. Talk to you later."

Therese could actually hear the eye-roll in Abby's tone.

Once they were seated at the table, she held out her hands. Nearly three years, and the kids were still reluctant to take her hands, bow their heads or even say *Amen* to the blessing. Their *mother* never made them wait when they were starving just to say a prayer. *She* never made them sit at the dinner table and answer questions about their stupid day, or ordered them to set the table or expected them to clean up afterward or forced them to eat food they didn't like.

"This isn't your mother's house," Paul had firmly reminded them. *"When you live in our house, you follow our rules."* Even though saying the blessing wasn't something he'd done, either, before meeting Therese.

"Amen," she finished, but kept her eyes closed just a moment longer, silently adding a *PS* to the prayer. *Lord, we're drowning here. Please throw us a lifeline, at least for the kids. I'm a pretty strong swimmer, but help them, please.*

A little bit of hope wouldn't go unappreciated, either. Because sometimes it seems mine is running out, and I can't let that happen. No matter how much they hate it, I'm all they have.

The somber thought stiffened her resolve as she said another soundless *Amen*.

But it also sent a tiny shiver down her spine.

The Bible might have intended Sunday as a day of rest, but that was rarely the case on the Double D Ranch outside Tallgrass. It wasn't even noon yet, and so far Dalton Smith had barely slowed down since sunrise. After feeding the cows in the east pasture and the mares with foals in the back field, making sure the new babies were nursing and checking that none of the pregnant cows had wandered off to give birth away from the others, as they tended to do, he'd gone in for breakfast with his brother Noah.

Right after the meal, the kid had left for Stillwater, where he was a sophomore at Oklahoma State, trying to decide whether a plain old ag degree was good enough for him or if he'd rather be a vet. Raising palominos and Belted Galloway cattle, Dalton figured a vet in the family would be a good thing, but that would mean another four years for vet med school after Noah got his bachelor's. Seeing that he was paying the tuition, Dalton also figured the sooner he got out and started working, the better. He could use some help on the Double D.

Thoughts of his other brother, Dillon, stirred in the back of his mind—a place he definitely didn't want to go. Swallowing the last of the water, he crushed the plastic bottle and tossed it into the recycling bin next to the door and started for the house. He was halfway there when he saw the pickup parked at the side of the road next to the horse pasture. A few feet away, a man rested his arms on the top rail of the wooden fence.

Though Dalton wasn't much for socializing, he knew all his neighbors. Hell, he'd lived on the ranch his entire life. This man was a stranger. Probably just admiring the animals. Most people did.

He had a headache and was ready for lunch, and after that, there was still a dozen things he needed to do before bedtime, including the book work he put off every week until Sunday. He didn't want to visit with anyone.

But he also didn't trust strangers. The man could be just admiring the horses, or he could be up to no good. A rancher in the next county had just lost six head of cattle in a pasture that ran alongside the road to some nut job with a bow and a dozen arrows.

Dalton changed directions, heading down the yellow grass butting up to the gravel driveway. As he got closer, he saw the truck was so new he could practically smell it.

There was an Airborne sticker in the back window and a red Fort Murphy sticker under the Department of Defense decal on the windshield. That fit with the guy's haircut and the way he stood, relaxed but with the feeling that he could snap to attention in a heartbeat.

Dalton really didn't want to visit with a soldier. As much as possible, he avoided everyone and everything having to do with the Army. Not easy when you lived in a military community, but he'd done his best since Sandra...

Thinking of Sandra was another place he definitely didn't want to go—worse, even, than thinking about Dillon. At least his brother was alive, as far as they knew. Someday he might even come home.

Sandra was never coming back.

"Can I help you?" he asked when he was a few yards away. His voice was gruffer than he'd intended, and he was scowling. Noah had told him just this weekend that he was turning into a scary-looking person, what with not cutting his hair or shaving and always glaring like he hated the world.

Only fair, since he did hate it. At least, parts of it.

The man hadn't given any indication that he was aware of Dalton approaching, but he wasn't surprised, either. He straightened but didn't move away from the fence and didn't startle guiltily. "The horses are beautiful. When I was a kid in Texas, my grandparents had a little place out in the country. Most of their horses weren't anything special, just for working, but they had one palomino I used to ride." He got a distant look, as if he were somewhere down south in a good memory.

Sometimes Dalton forgot he had good memories,

too—a lot of them. It was just that the last few years had been so damn hard that he didn't know whether it would be good or bad to remember better times. On the one hand, it might give him hope that things would improve again, but on the other, the way his luck was running, it would be false hope.

The man focused on him again. "Name's Dane Clark. I'm assigned to Fort Murphy."

"I figured." Dalton leaned against a weathered section of fence, almost directly under the arch that identified the Double D. "I'm Dalton Smith. This is my place."

Clark's gaze lifted to the sign. "And here I had visions of pretty female ranchers..."

Everyone Dalton knew, knew the story of the ranch's name. He didn't owe a stranger an explanation and usually didn't give one when asked. But Clark hadn't asked and didn't seem inclined to go beyond the one comment he'd already made.

With a shrug, he said, "My family settled here before statehood back in 1907—two brothers named Donald and Dooley. They thought 'Smith Ranch' was too plain, so they chose to use their initials. Little did they know that someday that would be used to refer to women's breasts, though, from what I hear, they wouldn't have minded the association. Every generation since then that's had sons has named at least two of them to fit."

"There's worse ways to get a name." Clark's gaze shifted back to the horses.

They weren't doing anything—just grazing, a few of the younger ones occasionally kicking up their heels— but watching them was one of Dalton's favorite ways to pass the time. "Do you still ride?"

If he hadn't been looking, he would have missed the stiffness that spread through Clark, the way he shifted his weight and leaned on the fence for support. He freed his left hand and swiped it down the leg of his jeans—new, creased, ending in a crumple above a pair of running shoes so new the white hadn't been scuffed yet. "Nah. Not in a long time."

"I don't think you forget."

"I don't know about that. It was another lifetime." An abrupt change of subject. "You run this place alone?"

Dalton might not know much about human behavior, but if Clark were a horse, he'd say he'd caught a whiff of something fearful. Though he was standing motionless, there was a sense that he'd bolt at the first chance.

But it wasn't Dalton's business why and, more, he didn't care. "My younger brother's in school at OSU. He comes home on weekends to help out, but I do most of the work."

"Is he the other *D*?"

No. That would be my twin brother, who abandoned the ranch and the family because he's a self-centered, irresponsible sonova— Breaking off before he could insult his mother, he smiled tightly. "No."

This time he was the one who changed the subject quickly. "What do you do at the post?"

Clark's smile, if that was what it was, was strained. "Train. Prepare."

"Are you deploying?" There had been a time when Dalton's knowledge of things military was limited to what he'd read in books and papers and seen in movies. Marrying a soldier had changed that. *It's like we're both learning a new language*, Sandra had joked. *Ranch speak and Army speak.*

That was before she'd gotten orders to Afghanistan.

"No," Clark said. "I've done four tours in the desert. I can't go back."

It was hard to tell if that *can't* meant "I'm not allowed to" or "I won't." It seemed to Dalton that one combat tour per person was plenty. Sandra had already finished one round in Iraq before he met her. She'd been assigned to a hospital, more or less out of danger. It was like a baseball game, she'd told him: long hours, even days, of tedious routine interrupted by moments of pure excitement. She'd figured Afghanistan would be the same.

Clark pushed away from the fence, moving carefully over the ditch to the driveway, then extended his hand. "Sorry for keeping you from your work or your time off or whatever."

"No problem." Dalton shook hands with him, then watched as he walked to his truck. Just before he opened the door, Dalton offered an invitation that surprised even him. "If you decide you want to give riding another shot, come back by."

An odd expression flashed across the other man's face, then he nodded. "I'll keep that in mind."

Dalton watched him leave, then shifted to lean on the fence and stare at the horses. They *were* beautiful, and they didn't expect much from him: access to food and water and care when they were sick. Same with the cattle in the other pasture. It was a good thing, because he didn't have anything else to offer.

Was life supposed to be this hard? It hadn't been for his parents or his grandparents, though all of them had been through some tough times. It'd been too easy for Dillon and, please God, it would stay fairly easy for Noah.

But, damn, he wouldn't mind sharing the grief a little. He'd just about had his fill of it.

Tuesdays were Carly's favorite day of the week, and not just because it meant dinner at The Three Amigos with the rest of the gang. On Mondays, the kids were always a little restless, still longing for the weekend that had just ended, and on Fridays, they were anticipating the free days to come. Wednesdays and Thursdays were average, but Tuesdays were good days.

Tuesdays were when they visited the soldiers at the Warrior Transition Unit. Her kids were young enough to accept the injuries they saw with curiosity and concern. They weren't yet self-conscious about hero worship, and they didn't censor themselves. They were blunt, forthright, and open, and most of the soldiers adored being adored.

The school bus pulled into the parking lot at one thirty, and Carly, her classroom aide, and two mothers lined up the kids at the door, then walked them out. All the children were on their best behavior, understanding that acting out could cancel the trip and leave everyone, students and soldiers, disappointed.

The mother who sat across from Carly was new to Tallgrass and Fort Murphy. This was her eight-year-old's third school, and both she and Mom were taking it in stride. Mom asked about restaurants and kid-friendly activities, and Carly answered as if she hadn't spent much of her time in Tallgrass at home alone, but the woman fell quiet when the bus turned into the transition unit parking lot.

"This war is so wrong," she whispered.

Carly gave her a startled glance. Her life, and her friends' lives, had been drastically changed by the war, and they talked about every aspect of it, except whether it was a righteous battle that had to be fought or a tragic waste of American life. Jeff had supported it to the end, and she would like the country to see it through to the end, if that was possible. She didn't want to think his nation might give up on the conflict that took his life.

"My son's kindergarten teacher—her husband died in Afghanistan," the woman went on. "She's younger than me, has two kids like me... It's just so sad."

So did mine, and it is sad, but they died doing something they loved for a cause they wholeheartedly embraced. But the words stuck in Carly's throat.

"My husband's enlistment is up soon, and I want him to get out. It's too dangerous. But he doesn't want to, and with the economy..."

The squeal of the bus's brakes practically obscured Mom's sigh. Grateful for the excuse not to respond, Carly stood and faced the back. "Remember, kids: No running, no arguing, and lots of smiles, okay?"

"Yes, Miss Lowry," most of them chimed. With a gleam in his dark eyes, Paco waited until they were done to energetically add, "You betcha, Miss Lowry."

They filed out of the bus and into the building, down the hall and into the gym. For too many of the soldiers, physical and occupational therapy had become a full-time job. The palpable drive and determination in the room always boosted Carly's spirits but, at the same time, made her just a little ashamed. Some of these guys had lost so much, but they hadn't given up. They were moving ahead.

And so was she. Slowly. She hadn't acknowledged

even once today that it had been twenty-five months, three weeks, and three days since Jeff's death. She wasn't the hermit she used to be. She had a focus in her life now.

She would never stop hurting or missing Jeff, but she could live without him.

The thought brought both incredible satisfaction and incredible sorrow. He was the only man she'd ever loved, the light of her life, but she could live without him.

It was hard to say who was happier to see whom, the kids or the troops. The children flitted like butterflies around sweet blossoms, greeting old friends and introducing themselves to new ones. Robin, the aide, immediately sought out one man in particular. What had started as a class project was evolving into a romance. Carly wished them well and tried to imagine herself in the same place, but it was tough when her heart kept projecting Jeff's face onto the nameless man in the fantasy.

She wandered the perimeter of the room, speaking to everyone, occasionally nudging a shy child or soldier to make contact. She was halfway back to where she started when a tall, lean figure standing next to the seated hamstring curl machine caught her attention. He wore sweatpants and a gray T-shirt and was drinking from a bottle of water while talking to another man straining to maneuver the machine's heavy weights.

It was Dane.

She closed the dozen feet, leaving the machine between them, and lightly touched the second man's shoulder. "Hey, Justin, how's it going?"

"Aw, I'm just playing here. You want me to get up so you can hop on?"

"Are you suggesting that my legs need work more than yours?"

The younger man grinned. "I don't know. Hike that skirt up a few inches and let me see."

She gave him a chastening look before slowly shifting her attention to Dane. "If it isn't the caveman. Fort Murphy is a smaller universe than I thought."

For a moment, he had the same deer-in-the-headlights look that he'd gotten in the cave Saturday when he realized he was trapped with six women. Then he took a breath and his fingers relaxed around the bottle. "Carly, isn't it?"

"Carly Lowry." Hesitation held her motionless a minute before she followed Jessy's lead from the weekend and extended her hand. "Nice to see you again."

His fingers were long, strong, callused, the nails clipped unevenly, and heat emanated from his skin. How could men's hands, so similar to women's on the surface, feel so different to touch? There was strength in his hand, solidity, control, and just holding it briefly sent a hint of a shiver along her arm.

It was just a handshake, one that he ended a few seconds too early, a few seconds too late. Her fingers tingling, she drew her hand back when he released it, then didn't quite know what to do with it. Finally, she wrapped her fingers around the cool metal of the machine.

"Where's Trista?" Justin asked, twisting to look over one shoulder.

"She is…" Carly scanned the room, locating the girl against the far wall, her own hesitant gaze sweeping around, dropping, then sweeping again. "There. Looking for you."

Justin slid to his feet, steadying himself for a moment, then Dane handed him the crutches that had leaned against the wall. "See you guys."

"Abandoning me for a younger woman?" Carly teased.

"Aw, you're sweet, but Trista's got my heart." Using the crutches with ease, he waited until he'd reached the middle of the room to call the girl's name. A smile swallowed her entire face as she launched herself toward him.

Smiling, Carly leaned against the wall. "Trista is as timid as a mouse. Justin paid attention to her the day they met, and she's been attached to him ever since." She gestured toward the machine. "You waiting to use this?"

"Nah. Just talking to Justin. Go ahead and hop on. But I've seen your legs. I don't think you need it."

Did Caveman just compliment her? It was impossible to tell from his expression. He wasn't looking at her—his attention was directed toward the room—but there was a faint hint of pink tingeing his cheeks.

He *did* compliment her—her legs, at least. That was the first time a man had said something flattering to her in…Carefully avoiding the natural thought of Jeff, she finished: in a long time.

She continued to gaze at him long enough that his eyes flickered her way once, then twice. He shifted to lean against the wall as she did and indicated the room with a sweep of his water bottle. "What's the deal with the kids?"

"We come over every Tuesday afternoon to visit. At any given time, half of my class has one parent deployed—a few mothers, mostly fathers. This gives them something to look forward to, a little time with someone like their daddies, and the soldiers enjoy it, too."

"It doesn't scare them?"

"Maybe a few, but we assure them the kids don't bite. Though there was that time JayLo took a nip out of Hannah for making fun of her name. The joys of being named after a celebrity."

He gave her a dry look. "The kids."

"Do the injuries and scars scare them? Not at all. Does it worry them that the same could happen to their dads and moms? On occasion. But they're young. They have blind faith in their parents, in the Army. In their eyes, you guys are heroes who can do anything."

Another bit of pink colored his cheeks. At being called a hero? She believed in heroes—not the popular version of celebrities or athletes, but everyday heroes, who saw a job that needed to be done and volunteered to do it, even when it meant facing danger and death every day. People willing to die for their communities or their country, because someone had to do it.

Because the subject seemed to make him uncomfortable, she changed it with an obvious look at his clothes. "You been PT-ing?" Physical training was a daily part of practically every soldier's life, though in the past few years, it had become just as common for the abbreviation to refer to physical therapy—a daily part of *her* soldiers' lives.

"Yeah. I, uh, just stopped to talk to Justin."

"He's a good kid."

"Kid? You can't be that much older."

She smiled. Justin was twenty-one. She was twenty-eight going on forty some days. Today, maybe going on thirty-five. "What's that movie quote? It's not the years, it's the mileage?" The last twenty-five months had been like dog years: each one stretching into seven.

But time was moving at a more normal pace now. Sometimes it dragged, sometimes it rushed past, but over-all it averaged out. She could breathe. She could think. And if tomorrow wasn't always better, well, the next day would be, or the one after that. Tuesday always rolled around, and she got to come here and to have dinner with the margarita club.

And those two things counted for a lot.

Dane's first impulse was to snort. She didn't look as if she had any mileage on her... though didn't he know how deceiving looks could be? Most of the guys in the gym looked like they'd just started shaving a week or two ago, while a fair number of them were, in fact, learning to do it again with whatever limitations they'd acquired. Justin, at least, still had all his body parts, though his legs were held together with plates and screws. They were surrounded by amputees, burn victims, and traumatic brain injuries, and Carly Lowry seemed to have the least mileage on her of them all.

Kids excepted, of course. He'd heard something about kids visiting but had assumed a couple, related to one of the patients. Not a whole classful. Not accompanied by a pretty teacher with auburn hair and hazel eyes and damn nice legs.

And a wedding ring on her left hand, he reminded himself. As off-limits, even for looking, as a woman could be.

He should get out of the gym before he noticed that her smile was sweet. Before he gave more than a second glance at her breasts. Before one of the therapists asked just how long he intended to make this break.

Before she realized he was a patient along with all the others.

The thought of discovery created a throb in his left leg—not the part that was there, but the rest of it. It was stupid. He couldn't hide the prosthesis forever. People back home knew; his mother had made sure of that. All the regulars in this room knew, along with most of his buddies stationed elsewhere. News like that traveled.

But he'd rather hide. He didn't want sympathy or questions or concern or pity. Hell, he had more than enough pity for himself.

Since Carly didn't seem ready to move on, he would. He opened his mouth to say *I've got to go*, but the words that came out were totally wrong. "So you're a teacher." *Stupid. Obvious.*

She smiled. "Third grade. The kids are big enough to be fun but not dangerous."

"Any of them yours?"

The smile didn't waver. "No. You have any?"

"No." How much worse would that have made finding out about Sheryl's affairs? Wondering if his kids were really his? Believing they were, loving them, then finding out otherwise?

Time for another subject change. "You're not from here."

Her hair swayed in the clasp that loosely held it as she shook her head. "I grew up in Utah. I went to college in Colorado and came here four years ago. You're not from here, either."

"Texas. A little town outside Dallas."

"Do you still have family there?"

"My mother. A few aunts and uncles. Some cousins I

never really knew." His mother had been an only child, his father a surprise born twelve years after the youngest of his brothers. Anna Mae had never had much use for Bill's family, so even though they'd all lived in the same county, Dane had rarely had contact with them. "What about your family?"

"My mom, dad, and three brothers are all happily researching, splitting atoms, and splicing genes in Utah. They have two or three alphabets' worth of letters after their names, and my brothers' wives are raising five little scientists." She shrugged, making her hair sway again. It looked silky, the kind that couldn't hold a tangle if it tried. "I'm the family black sheep. Only one degree."

"But you're using it to teach. A noble profession—isn't that what they call it?"

She gave the snort he'd restrained a few moments ago. "The doctors Anderson believe that those who can, do, and those who can't, teach."

Her gaze settled across the room, and he followed it, watching a little girl with pigtails in red overalls talking with flourishing gestures to a captain whose brain injury made conversation difficult for him. Whether he completely followed the girl's rapid speech was anyone's guess, but his expression left no doubt that he enjoyed her company.

"The doctors Anderson sound a little full of themselves."

Carly's attention jerked back to him. "Oh, they're not so bad. They weren't thrilled when I chose to major in education, but they thought I would get at least one PhD. It was a surprise to them when I got a teaching job instead."

His mother would have been thrilled if he'd gotten a

college degree. He would have been the first in the family. She didn't know that, with the classes he'd taken on post at the ed center and online, he was halfway there. Not that it would matter much. In her mind, it would take more than one degree to make up for being one-legged.

As childish voices rose in the far corner of the gym, Carly sighed and straightened. "I'd better see what's up. Nice seeing you again, Dane."

She stuck out her hand again, and he took it. Odd how soft her skin was. He was used to hands that could cause pain—they didn't call them "physical terrorists" for nothing—but her grip was gentle, better suited to soothing.

He let go the instant he realized he didn't want to and pushed away from the wall, hoping his body hadn't stiffened too much with the inactivity. "Yeah, I gotta go."

With a smile, she went off to referee the fuss, and he headed straight for the door and went to check out with the cadre. In addition to the physical and occupational therapists, physicians, psychologists, and psychiatrists available, each soldier at the WTU was assigned to a cadre with a squad leader, a nurse, and a doctor. As luck would have it, he'd known his squad leader back when they were both stationed in Korea and they'd both lost limbs in the desert. Now the first sergeant was overseeing other soldiers' transitions, and Dane was struggling with his.

After a stop at the commissary for food, he was home within a half hour. Twenty minutes after that, he had everything put away, had done what little cleaning was needed to suit his standards and was considering doing laundry when someone knocked at the door.

It was Justin Stevens—not just a fellow patient but

neighbor, too—leaning more heavily on his crutches than he had at the gym. "Where'd you disappear to?" he asked, limping into the kitchen to get a beer from the fridge and an ice pack from the freezer. Back in the living room, he lowered himself into the chair, propped his right leg on the table and rested the ice pack on his knee before popping the top on the beer.

Dane sat on the couch, propping his left leg up. "I was done for the day." Therapy was never the same. Some days he could push way farther beyond anything he'd done before, and some days it seemed he'd lost ground overnight.

And some days he just had to avoid the people there.

"Did you talk to any of the kids?"

"Not today." And he didn't plan to in the future. He would make a point of being elsewhere on Tuesdays, and not just to avoid the kids.

Justin grinned. "You talked to Carly, though. What was that 'caveman' stuff about?"

"We, uh, met in a cave."

After an expectant moment, Justin scoffed. "Yeah, right. You don't want to say, man—"

"We did. At a park. Last weekend. She was with some friends."

Justin nodded. "Oh, the margarita club."

Dane remembered that moment at the red light in Davis, when he'd seen the women in the restaurant, toasting each other with margaritas. He liked his booze about as much as the average guy, but he'd never considered joining a club to celebrate it.

Aiming for casual, he asked, "Where is her husband assigned?"

Justin's look was long and steady. "She's in the club, man. The Tuesday Night Margarita Club. They meet at The Three Amigos for dinner and drinks every week."

Feeling the way he imagined the brain injury patients did at times, Dane raised his brows. "And what does that have to do with her husband?"

"The margarita club is otherwise known as the 'Fort Murphy Widows' Club.'" Justin paused. "Staff Sergeant Lowry is dead, man. Has been for about two years."

Chapter Three

Dinner was always casual: jeans, a sweater, a little bit of makeup. Carly sprayed on cologne, then closed her eyes and sniffed the shower-warmed air. The fragrance was light, sweet. Innocent, Jeff had said when he'd given her the first bottle. He'd smelled it on a woman at the PX, asked her what it was and gone to the perfume counter to buy it, and Carly had worn it ever since.

She liked the scent well enough, but she'd never loved it the way he did. Maybe it was time for a change. After work tomorrow, maybe she should go to the PX and pick out her own cologne. Something not so sweet and innocent.

Feeling vaguely guilty, she switched off the light, then twisted her wedding band as she went down the hall. It was a little early to leave for the restaurant, but she got her purse and jacket anyway and left the house, driving the mile or so to the strip center where The Three Amigos Mexican Grill sat right in the middle of the parking lot.

It stood out like a canary amidst doves. While the main buildings that enclosed the lot made at least an effort to fit in with the sandstone and brick storefronts of downtown, The Three Amigos' colors were just short of garish: teal, orange, yellow, and lime green. The roof was red tile, and potted silk flowers in bright red filled the planters on either side of the doors year-round. The shaded patio on the east side held wrought-iron tables in a half dozen different styles, a dozen different colors of paint. It marked its little corner of the Tallgrass Center as a Mexican feast for both the eyes and the palate.

The sound of tumbling water greeted her when she opened the heavy door. The first thought that came to mind was the waterfalls from the previous weekend. The cave. Dane. She honestly hadn't expected to see him again.

But it had been kind of nice.

Skirting the fountain in the center of the lobby, she greeted the hostess, then wove through tables to a rectangular table at the rear of the dining room. They never knew how many would join them each week, but there were always at least eight. She was settling in a chair, back to the wall, when Therese joined her.

"Oh, dear heavens, I need a drink."

Carly caught the waitress's attention and held up two fingers. With a wink, the woman headed for the bar. "Let me guess. Jacob is in the fiftieth straight hour of video games without so much as a bathroom break, and Abby has fallen desperately in love with a wannabe bad boy with spiked hair and a nose ring. Any chance she'll run off with him?"

"The way things have been going, she'd probably

move him in with us so I could support him." Therese shuddered, then made an obvious attempt to loosen up. "No, Jacob does take bathroom breaks, at least, and Abby is hating all things male this week. From what I've overheard, the boy she thought liked her asked another girl out, then Mr. Snyder caught her texting at school—giving answers to a test, no less—and took her phone away, plus gave her detention. I had to go pick up her and the phone after work, and I didn't give it back, and she's livid." Therese smiled gratefully as the waitress delivered the two margaritas, then she took a large drink.

Carly's sip was much smaller. In keeping with their group's name, she ordered a margarita every week, but she rarely finished one. She wasn't much of a drinker. She preferred to save her calories for something worthwhile, like chocolate-covered caramels for breakfast.

"Did you ever cheat?" Therese lifted her glum gaze from the glass to Carly. "In school, I mean."

"No." Or anywhere else, unless an occasional white lie counted. She'd never stayed out past curfew, never gotten drunk or used drugs and had tried always to be fair and nice. *Goody Two-shoes*, Jeff had called her.

"Me, neither. I told Abby that, and she came *this* close to calling me a liar. At least she wasn't doing it for herself. She's good at history. She knew all the answers. She was helping out Nicole, who didn't have time to study." After a moment, she sighed. "So how was everyone at the transition unit?"

"Good. The kids were fine, the soldiers were fine." Carly twisted her glass a time or two, leaving wet rings on the napkin, before going on. "I saw Dane."

"Who is—" Therese's brow furrowed. "The guy from the cave? Really? Where?"

"At the transition unit. He was visiting Justin. I told you about him. The surfer kid from California."

"Yeah, yeah, younger than my baby brother. Stick to Dane. Was he as cute as we thought? Did he remember us fondly? Did you find out if he was married?"

Carly blinked, then laughed. "Sheesh, you're channeling Jessy. Let's see...did we even discuss whether we thought he was cute? I don't remember. Did he remember us? I assume so, since he was trapped in a small space with us, though he didn't remark on it." But he *had* remembered her name, she thought with a small rush of warmth.

As to whether he was married...the thought hadn't occurred to her. In her world, there were two kinds of people: those who were widowed and those who weren't. Of course, *those who weren't* broke down into two more groups: those who were married and those who weren't.

Which one was Dane? Face-to-face with him, she hadn't given it a thought, but now she wondered. Was he single, involved, or did he go home to a wife every night?

"I don't know if he's married." She shrugged as if she didn't care. Though he hadn't been wearing a ring. She hadn't realized she'd noticed, but obviously she had. "Why? Are you interested in him?"

Therese's gesture was dismissive. "He's awfully cute, but he's not my type." Then she teasingly added, "I think he might be *your* type."

"I've been alone so long, I'm not sure I still *have* a type."

Reaching across the table, Therese squeezed her hand. "You do. Trust me."

"Yeah, right. Paul's been gone longer than Jeff, and you haven't even looked at another man." She regretted the words almost as soon as they were out, because they intensified the sorrow that was always barely there in her friend's eyes. "I'm sorry, Therese."

"Aren't we all, sweetie." After an uncomfortable silence, Therese straightened, her determination to brighten the mood apparent on her face. "Today the new boy in my class said, 'Miss Twace, the windows are dirty.' I said, 'Yes, they are, Kelvin. I'll give you a dollar to clean them.' He rolled his eyes and said, 'I don't need a dowwar to cwean them, Miss Twace. I need paper towels.'"

Carly laughed, the tension easing in her shoulders. Before the chuckles had quieted, Jessy slid into the chair beside Therese and, without greetings, demanded, "Share the joke. I had a crappy day at the bank, and I need someone to amuse me almost as much as I need a drink."

"What happened at the bank?"

Jessy waved her hand carelessly, the diamonds in her wedding ring catching a bit of sparkle from the overhead light. "People are idiots. Whatever possessed me to get a job where I have to deal with them every single day of the workweek?"

"You're in customer service," Therese said with a snort. "It never occurred to you that meant dealing with idiots?"

The redhead sniffed regally. "I'm an account representative. Which our customers apparently translate to 'complaint taker.' Ugh." Her shudder was delicate, fading as the waitress brought her drink. "Thanks so much, Miriam. One of these every fifteen minutes, and by the time I leave here, I won't care about work."

"Or anything else," Carly retorted.

"Carly saw Dane from the cave again," Therese announced.

"Really. Was he any less intimidated? More talkative? Did he appear to be involved with anyone else? Is he as cute in uniform as he was in jeans?" Jessy sighed. "I love a man in uniform."

Coming up in time to hear the last, Marti Levin and Lucy Hart added their own sighs. "Didn't we all," Marti said softly.

Melancholy settled over the table for a moment before Jessy scattered it with a blunt command. "Sit. Order your drinks. Be quiet. Carly ran into Dane from the cave again. She's going to tell all."

"Ooh. Wait. Here come Fia and Ilena. You can tell us all at once." Lucy shrugged out of her jacket and scooted into the chair next to Carly.

Ilena, round with pregnancy, her center of gravity shifted, looked graceful next to Fia, who limped, favoring her left side a bit. When she noticed them watching, she shrugged and gave them a lopsided smile. "Too much fun Saturday. I must have pulled a muscle."

Once they were all settled and had ordered drinks— iced tea for Ilena—Lucy turned to Carly. "Okay. Tell us all about running into Dane."

With six expectant faces turned her way, Carly laughed. "Guys, it's not like I never see men. I work on post, remember."

"With ankle-biters, which Dane is not," Jessy said,

then mused, "though maybe a gentle nip or two would be fun."

"Ahh, I miss gentle nips," Ilena said wistfully.

Carly gave the details of the encounter—heavens, that sounded so much more significant than it had really been—then finished with a shrug. "Coincidence."

"I don't believe in coincidence," Marti said. "However, I do believe in fate."

"Right." Carly scoffed. "It was a matter of timing. If we'd been five minutes later getting there, he probably would have been gone."

"But he wasn't," several voices chimed together, then Lucy pointed out, "Therese and I work on post, too, but *we* didn't run into him. And he must leave the fort occasionally, but no one else has run into him."

Marti nodded as if that made her point. "Fate."

Carly rolled her eyes, then gestured across the room. "Look, our every-other-weeklies are here."

Everyone greeted the four newcomers and the conversation—thankfully—turned to catching up with them. She didn't need any more talk about Dane. She'd thought about him enough today. And that nonsense about fate...She took her class to the Warrior Transition Unit every Tuesday; he had a buddy there. It was just coincidence that they'd shown up at the same time. Nothing more.

She believed it, too, until after ordering fajitas, then excusing herself to go to the ladies' room. On the way back to the table, she took a shortcut through the bar, where she glanced over a half dozen men, hardly noticing them, before her gaze caught on a lone man at a tall round table. She would have skimmed right over him, as well, if he hadn't looked up at exactly the same moment to lock gazes with her.

You don't believe in fate, remember? Coincidence. A matter of timing. That's all it is.

A tiny doubt-filled voice spoke up then. *Isn't it?*

Once Dane had excelled at stealth, camouflage, and going unnoticed, but it seemed he'd lost more than his foot in Afghanistan. He could have chosen a dozen better tables. He could have taken into account that the clear path through the bar, which allowed him to see the women at the back, also increased the possibility of one of them seeing him. He should have seen that the shortest path from the table to the ladies' room, of course, went right through the bar.

Carly stopped abruptly, still holding his gaze. When a young soldier tried to squeeze past with an apology, she realized she was blocking the way and took a couple of slow steps to bring her to his table. "The world's even smaller than I thought."

He didn't know what a person from Utah sounded like, or if years in Colorado and Oklahoma had made her accent uniquely her own. He did know her voice was quiet, definitely female and, at the moment, lacked the all-business edge he associated with the only women in his life: doctors, nurses, and physical therapists. Only the women shrinks he'd seen back east had ever sounded that soft.

"They tell me this is the best Mexican restaurant in town." Someone had actually told him that, when he'd first arrived. He hadn't paid attention, since he hadn't eaten in a restaurant since he'd come back to the States.

"It is." A group of girls who looked barely old enough to be in the bar swarmed past on their way to the biggest table in the corner, and Carly eased out of their path, practically hugging the tall chair across from him. Her left hand rested on its back, the wedding ring prominent.

He'd taken his gold band off the day his buddies had confirmed his suspicions of Sheryl's affair. Last he'd seen it, it was sinking in the polluted waters of the Bac-chiglione River. Surely by now it had been silted over or had been carried into the Adriatic Sea.

Picking up his beer bottle, he gestured toward her table. "So you guys are intrepid adventurers and connoisseurs of Mexican food?"

She glanced at her friends, none of them watching, then slid onto the stool and folded her hands on the tabletop. "Connoisseurs of margaritas, actually—but yes to the 'adventurer' part, too. We've scaled high peaks, braved dark caves, and hiked until our feet blistered. We even dared to attend the Tulsa State Fair with a group of twenty, rode every ride and sampled every food available. On opening day, no less."

"I'm impressed."

Her smile appeared suddenly, softening the seriousness of her expression. "Don't be. You saw the high peak and the cave, and the hiking trail was paved. But the state fair…it was two thumbs-up until Jessy puked up a funnel cake and a fried Snickers on the Ferris wheel. From the top. The people below were not happy."

"Jessy—the redhead?"

Carly nodded, and a thick strand of her hair, worn down tonight, fell from her shoulder to dangle over a sweater the color of a fine Italian red wine. "Never ride a Ferris wheel with her."

Like that's gonna happen. He'd never been fond of amusement park rides when he had two good legs to escape if he got trapped at the top. Not even a pretty woman like Jessy—or a prettier one like Carly—could entice him to put his life in the hands of old equipment and traveling carnies.

His cell phone rang, and he fumbled it out of his pocket, glanced at the screen, then muted it. Carly moved as if to leave. "You can take that."

"Nah. No name. I don't answer calls with no name."

She smiled faintly. "Afraid the command's trying to call you in to work?"

He made a stab at smiling, too. Caller ID had made it more difficult for first-line supervisors to call people in; most soldiers knew better than to answer a call that likely meant work. The first-line supervisors had started blocking their numbers when they called, so their subordinates had stopped answering blocked calls, too.

He set the phone aside, screen down, and returned to the subject. "Why margaritas? Why not wine or cosmos or lagers?"

"To drown our sorrows, and because not one of us would willingly drink a cosmo or lager."

The face she made showed what she thought of the last two, and he deliberately wrapped his hand around the label on his bottle. The muscles in his neck tightened, a little bit of guilt because he knew something about her of which she wasn't aware. Hell, that was why he'd come here tonight, even after he'd tried to talk himself out of it. He'd known she would be here, and he'd wanted to...just see her. That was all.

The guilt made the next question—the obvious question—difficult to get out, but he managed, sounding relatively normal, he thought. Not like he already knew. Not like he particularly cared. "Do you have a lot of sorrows?"

Her expression saddened, and she fingered the wedding band a moment before putting on a resigned face and answering. "We've all lost our husbands or fiancés in combat. Around here, they call us the Fort Murphy Widows' Club, though not to our faces. We prefer the Tuesday Night Margarita Club. It's a little more frivolous. A little less mournful. And you don't have to say you're sorry. You were there, weren't you? In Iraq or Afghanistan."

He nodded. "Both. Four years."

"You've lost a lot, too."

He wondered for one cold instant if she knew, but she went on.

"Time, hope, illusions. Friends."

His throat narrowed, with both unrealized fears and the sad fact that she was right, and he nodded again. She understood as much as it was possible for someone who'd never been there. She wouldn't ask for war stories, for the retelling of close calls to leave her breathless. She wouldn't ask if he had killed anyone, or how many, or how it had felt. She wouldn't relish the details the way so many people did.

With a fortifying breath he would have missed if he hadn't been watching so closely, she picked up the magazine open in front of him, marked his place with her finger and flipped to the cover. "Ah, motorcycles. Man toys. Do you have one?"

That lump still in his throat made swallowing difficult.

"I used to." Still did, to be honest. The racing bike he'd bought in Italy was in storage with his household goods, waiting for him to land someplace permanently, where he would likely sell it. Like those gorgeous palominos Sunday, the Ducati seemed way out of his league now. His limbs were already 25 percent bionic; he didn't want to take a shot at losing any more.

"I prefer totally enclosed vehicles myself, but you Airborne guys like to fly, don't you?"

"The need for speed." There was nothing quite like going a hundred and fifty miles per hour on the bike, besides free-falling at a hundred and twenty miles per hour. Freedom, exhilaration...and a world of hurt or death if anything went wrong. Kind of like combat. They all got your adrenaline pumping.

The waitress set a steaming platter on the table, then added a plate with the makings for fajitas. Carly inhaled deeply. Then she met his gaze, reluctance in her hazel eyes. "I should get back before they come looking for me and find you. You'd be stuck with eleven of us tonight."

"Yeah." He sounded reluctant, too, that one word all he could say. All he would let himself say. Not *Stay awhile longer.* Certainly not *Can we meet again?*

She stood, but instead of saying good-bye and leaving, she looked at him. "Three times now, and I don't know your last name."

"Clark." He gave a flippant salute. "Staff Sergeant Dane Clark." The same rank as her dead husband whose ring she still wore nearly two years after his death.

Her smile softened, and so did something inside him. "I'll see you around, Staff Sergeant Clark."

It was hunger, he told himself as she wiggled her fingers in the smallest of waves, then walked away. He hadn't had fajitas in nearly two years, and he couldn't remember what he'd had for, or even if he'd had, lunch. Just hunger.

And the hell of it was, it was true.

He just wasn't hungry for food.

His phone beeped while he was finishing the first fajita. He turned it over, pressed view later, and assembled a fajita. He hadn't lied when he'd said there was no name— only the number had shown—but he'd misled Carly into thinking he didn't know who was calling. It was his mother, one of her infrequent calls to check on him that, no matter what was going on, always managed to make him feel worse.

Turning back to the magazine, he ate and read and, way too often, let his gaze wander across the room. Other than the redhead, her back to him, he couldn't identify any of the other women by name, though six faces were familiar. Did the four strangers complete the club membership? Just how many wives at Fort Murphy had been widowed by the war?

Even eleven was too many.

After finishing his meal, he debated having another drink, but had just decided against it when the women in the corner began the readying that signaled departure. He flagged down the waitress, paid his bill and got carefully to his feet. Carly looked up then, and just a little smile touched her mouth as she nodded once. *"I'll see you around."*

He nodded, turning away before any of the others could notice him. From the back, most soldiers looked alike, Sheryl used to say.

It wasn't until he got home, removed his prosthesis and settled in on the couch that he picked up the phone and dialed his mother's number.

"It took you long enough to call me back," Anna Mae said. If he closed his eyes, he could see her face: remarkably smooth for a woman her age, pretty, the natural blond of her hair maintained with chemicals now, her mouth slightly pursed, the usual look in her blue eyes. He'd never been able to decide whether it was disappointment or disapproval. He did know a great deal of it had to do with him, with his father, with the life she'd gotten versus the one she'd thought she deserved.

He didn't close his eyes.

"I was having dinner."

"What, you couldn't have held the sandwich in one hand and the phone in the other?"

His skill in the kitchen didn't extend far beyond sandwiches. She'd never wanted him underfoot when she was cooking, and once he'd gotten married, Sheryl had fixed the meals when they didn't eat out.

"What's up?" Even though these calls were supposedly to check up on him, she never asked how he was, if physical therapy was any easier going, if he'd gotten more comfortable with the new prosthesis. Thinking of his poor leg just made her sad, and she had enough sadness without going looking for it.

"I just got off the phone with Sheryl a minute before I called. I couldn't wait to share the good news. She's pregnant."

Dane stared at the darkened television. What was the right response to that? *Why tell me? Am I supposed to care? Do you expect me to be glad that my ex-wife who always claimed she wanted* my *babies is pregnant by an-other man?* And a last uncharitable thought: *Is she sure her husband's the father?*

"Well? Isn't that wonderful?" Anna Mae sounded as happy and proud as if the baby was her own grandchild.

He cleared his throat. He wanted to growl, *I don't freaking give a damn*, but his father had taught him better. Anna Mae might be pessimistic, perpetually dissatisfied, self-centered, and irritating as hell, but she was his mother, and that had to count for something.

"Uh, yeah," he finally managed. "I guess."

A smile beamed over the distance. "I'll tell her you said so. Not that she asks about you much. Not since...well, you know."

"Not since I came to after an IED detonated and found out my foot was gone?" he asked drily, then immediately regretted the words.

"William Dane! You don't have to *talk* about it."

But the shrinks said he did. So did the therapists and the guys he worked out with. Pretending it didn't happen didn't make it so. It wouldn't grow him a new foot and calf and knee. But if *he* wanted to pretend it never happened, how could he blame her for doing the same?

"Sorry, Mom," he said quickly. "Tell Sheryl whatever you think is appropriate. I, uh, need to go."

"And I need to make some plans. You know, I made crib quilts for each of Sheryl's other kids. I'll have to start one for the new baby. It's so exciting."

Dane mumbled his way through the good-byes, then lay back and stared at the ceiling. Anna Mae had thought her life would be some sort of fairy tale, but instead of the three beautiful daughters she'd intended to have, the only pregnancy she'd successfully carried had delivered him. They'd butted heads routinely, but especially once he'd decided to join the Army. Then she'd been widowed just before her forty-fifth birthday. In divorcing Sheryl, Dane had screwed up the only thing he'd ever done to please her, and he'd had the nerve to come back from the war a cripple. He didn't think that was such a horrible life, but she did, and she was his mother. He could cut her a little slack.

Carly had been widowed a whole lot younger, and under worse circumstances, but she didn't seem to have any of his mother's self-pity. But Carly was a whole different person. He couldn't imagine anyone describing her as pessimistic, dissatisfied, self-centered, or irritating. In fact, a boatload of other words came to mind. Pretty. Warm. Friendly. Generous. Sexy. Sweet. Intriguing. Patient. *Really* pretty. *Really* sexy.

And not married. Still grieving, still attached, but maybe ready to take a step or two forward. Maybe open to spending a little time with another man. Maybe even thinking about more.

But even if she was, could he be that man? Did he even want to?

His snort was loud in the dimly lit room. Oh, yeah, some part of him definitely *wanted*. The other parts of him—the doubt, the lowered self-esteem, the lack of confidence, the shame—sang a line from an old song in four-part harmony.

You can't always get what you want.

After school on Thursday, Carly went home as usual, stopping only to buy a half gallon of soy milk. Cradling the cold container in the crook of one arm, she let herself in and made it halfway to the kitchen before stopping abruptly.

As she stood there in the hallway, she could literally feel her good mood seeping away. It was cold in the house, despite the bright sun and seventy-three degrees outside. Her refuge, her safe haven, felt different. Stifling. Almost like a vacuum.

Letting her bag slide to the floor, she put the milk in the refrigerator, then slowly walked back to the living room. Everything was in its place. Where it had been the day Jeff had left. Truly, the only things different were the wooden box on the mantel holding his awards and the flag that had covered his casket, plus a single plant out of the hundreds that had been sent for his funeral.

She went to the front windows and opened the blinds for the first time in a year and a half. In a rush, she did the same in the dining room, kitchen, and her bedroom. It was too late in the day for sunlight to flood the rooms, but it did ease the gloom.

In the living room once more, she turned in a circle. She should rearrange the furniture. Replace the pastel froufrou rug with something in a bold geometric pattern. Better yet, she should paint the walls. Painting the stunningly boring white walls throughout the house had always been on their list of things to do, but Jeff had put it off every chance he got, claiming he would get to it eventually.

The truth, she'd known, was that he didn't have the patience for painting. He hadn't wanted to bother with taping or drop cloths or prep work. His style had been to slap on the paint quick as he could, and ignore the unfortunate drips, splatters, and thin coverage.

She should paint. Redecorate. Rearrange. Start over.

The momentary rush drained as quickly as it had come. How could she redecorate without Jeff's input? Besides, the bland white on the walls was soothing in a way. It didn't demand her attention or catch her eye. It just faded into the background. And she knew so well where every single thing was located that she could navigate the room in the middle of the night with the lights off and her eyes puffy from crying. And she couldn't begin to move that ridiculous TV by herself.

Feeling as blah as the room, she got the phone, kicked off her shoes and curled up in the recliner. She'd slept there for the first month after Jeff's death, convinced she could feel his presence: the curves where the leather had conformed to his body, the faint spicy scent of his cologne that seemed to have seeped into the cushions, the distant whisper of his voice trapped in the softness.

Now she realized that the curves conformed to *her* body, and the only scent besides leather was her own cologne.

She located Lisa's number in the phone's directory and pressed send, then snagged the fleece throw folded over the back of the chair and tucked it around her.

"I swear to you, Isaac, if you don't leave your sister alone—"

From the other end of the phone came a deep inhalation, and Carly could picture her sister-in-law, eyes closed, mouth thinned, while she did a quick and silent count to ten in at least three of the languages she spoke fluently. The image made Carly smile.

"Hello?"

"Aw, poor baby," Carly teased.

"As he informs me every day and twice on Thursdays, he's no longer a baby."

"I wasn't referring to Isaac. I meant you."

After a moment, Lisa laughed. "In that case, thank you. I need all the sympathy I can get. How are you?"

"Okay." Quickly, before she could latch on to that unenthusiastic answer and run, Carly went on. "How are you and my brother and your adorable children?"

"Isaac is picking on Eleanor because she just wants to play house while he wants to use her Chef Cathy model kitchen to whip up his latest experiment. He's convinced he's on the verge of a breakthrough."

"So much for that cowboy outfit I sent him for his birthday." Carly laughed. "The fun of raising a five-year-old genius. Give them both hugs for me and tell them Aunt Carly misses them."

"I will. I'll do the same with Roger when he comes up for breath. Do you know how hard it is to compete with the latest research in string theory for the attention of a theoretical physicist?"

"Yeah, but you've got your secrets. Those kids weren't conceived in a test tube."

"My secret is Victoria's Secret, including a few skimpy strings of my own."

Memories of her own stash of sexy lingerie flitted through Carly's mind. She hadn't needed it to distract Jeff from work—simply breathing had been enough for that—but it had been fun to dress up from the skin out.

Good thing she had no desire to wear it now, because it probably wouldn't fit her.

"How's the rest of the family?"

"They're fine as usual. Your mom's gone to a conference in China, where she's presenting a paper. Your father actually mentioned the word *retirement* the other day, though apparently the concept struck him as so odd he lost his train of thought. Other brothers, wives, and kids are doing great."

"Great." Everything and everyone was just great... except Carly. Oh, she was better than she'd been a month ago and would be even better next month. She was just tired of the months. She wanted to feel better right *now*.

"How did your last adventure go?"

Ah, see? Thinking of last weekend made her feel better. "I climbed into a cave about eighty feet above the ground and have the pictures to prove it."

Lisa let out an excited whoop. "Good for you! Geez, you've always wanted your feet planted solidly on the ground. Send me pictures so I can enjoy it vicariously."

"I will. So that's the highlight of my week." Absently Carly rubbed her thumb over a scrape on the chair arm, and without thought unbidden words popped out. "I'm thinking of painting the living room."

"No more dull, dreary white walls? Oh, thank God. No one should have to live with white walls. What colors are you thinking?"

"Oh. Um. I actually haven't gotten that far. In fact, I don't even know why I said that because I did think about it, but it's really too big a job for just one person and, really, everything's fine the way it is. It's comfortable and—and familiar."

A moment of complete silence followed her abrupt stop, then Lisa's voice took on what Carly thought of as her mommy tone. "Sweetie, it'll still be comfortable and familiar. Painting the walls and rearranging the furniture or even replacing some of it aren't going to erase Jeff from the place. You've got years of memories of him there, and those aren't going to go away or be diminished if you make a few changes. It'll be good for you. Brighten things up. Make it cozy. Besides, he was going to paint them himself..."

Together they chimed, "Eventually."

After their laughter faded, Carly went on. "I don't know, Leese. It's just...so hard."

"I know, sweetie."

A lot of people Carly had met over the years didn't want anyone telling them *I know what you're going through*, but Lisa did know. She'd been there for Carly every horrible step of the way, holding her, crying with her, feeling, hurting, grieving with her. Maybe she hadn't experienced the death of her husband and their dreams, but she knew from observation and participation how much it had cost Carly.

A wail erupted in the background and Lisa's voice returned to normal. "Uh-oh, junior Einstein just got whacked with a pink plastic skillet."

"Eleanor's got cookware, and she's not afraid to use it. I'll let you go."

"Promise me this, Carly: When we talk next week, you'll have done something, right? Even if it's nothing more than moving the table from one end of the sofa to the other. Okay? I love you."

"Love you, too."

She could handle moving the end table. Maybe the coffee table, too. Maybe even putting higher-wattage lightbulbs in the lamps. Jeff had preferred near darkness for watching TV, but she liked lots of light.

And the room wasn't that big. Painting couldn't be that monumental a job. Therese and the kids would help her move the monster TV if she asked. Jacob might be only eleven, but he was built like his dad.

Before she could change her mind, she pushed herself out of the chair, grabbed her purse from the messenger bag and headed out the door. She would have plenty of time for second thoughts when she was facing the endless paint samples and the wide choice of brushes, rollers, tapes, and cleaners.

She didn't head for the Walmart just south of downtown, but instead followed her morning route to work. Most of the traffic leaving the fort for the day had already done so, and there was little going in. She drove to the huge parking lot shared by the commissary, the PX, a few restaurants, the Class 6 store—better known to civilians as a liquor store—and a handful of boutique shops. She didn't do enough cooking to bother with the commissary these days, didn't eat out by herself, and didn't drink enough to frequent the Class 6 store, but she used the PX, with its combination of a little bit of everything.

After showing her military ID at the door, she walked to the back center of the store, past women's and girls' clothing on one side, men's and boys' on the other. She hardly spared a glance for the display of pricey leather bags or the Bobbi Brown makeup she regularly purchased, but instead made a right at the intersecting aisle and headed for the hardware department.

And not fifty feet after that turn, she got distracted by sweet fragrances mingling in the air. The perfume counter, where she'd faithfully purchased Jeff's favorite scent ever since he'd given it to her.

New paint *and* perfume? Wasn't that a lot to change at once? Besides, she might not love the way her cologne smelled, but she was accustomed to it. How strange would it be, sitting in a repainted, redecorated room smelling like a different woman?

What might she gain from the changes? And how much would she lose?

Chapter Four

Fiddling with a package of picture hangers, Dane turned the corner to head off in search of a hammer. In the days he'd been at Fort Murphy, he hadn't really settled in. He'd unpacked his clothes, but the box of pictures that would make it officially home was still taped and shoved into the back of the closet. It was time to pull them out.

A display of paint samples filled half the next aisle and curved around the end, plenty of colors he could live without ever seeing again, like desert tan, olive drab, and the sterile shades of hospital neutrals. But there were also bright, light colors, the sort that would be okay to look at when he would be staring at the walls for hours on end. When he finally landed somewhere for good— or for three more years, depending whether he stayed in the Army—he just might use every eye-popping color he could find.

"Well, *crap.*" The lone customer in front of the paint

chips sighed heavily and ran her hands through her hair before apparently realizing she'd spoken aloud and looking around to see if she'd been heard.

He would have recognized Carly's voice and silky auburn hair even if she hadn't turned around. He didn't know whether he would have stopped to say hello—the tightness in his gut suggested he would have—but when she smiled in greeting, there was no doubt.

"Hi, Dane."

"Sounds like you're having trouble deciding."

She glanced at the samples and sighed again. "Does there have to be so many choices? Seriously, how many shades of one color can there be?"

He looked at the samples, too, then shrugged. "A whole lot, apparently. But it's just paint. Pick a color, and if you don't like it, do it again with another one."

Her gaze was steady on him, as if she were measuring him in some way. Her conclusion was summed up with an eyebrow lift and one word: "Men." Patiently she explained, "I don't want to do it again and again. I want it to be perfect the first time."

Perfect. What was the thing most of the women he knew had with perfection and getting it right on the first try? Life wasn't perfect. It was incredibly messy and out of everyone's control and sometimes even when you did something a second time, the results still sucked.

Which might be why she wanted perfection in something she could control.

"Okay, so you pick some colors you like, get samples and paint big squares on your wall. Then you look at them for a few days and see which one will be perfect."

"Samples, huh?"

He scanned the paint cans on the opposite side of the aisle, then had to move closer to her to reach the one he wanted. Close enough to smell her perfume, almost close enough to feel the silkiness of her hair. Swallowing hard, he straightened, stepped back and tossed the small can up, then caught it on his palm. "Samples."

She took the can, her nails lightly scraping his skin. Heat flared, traveling halfway up his arm before he managed another step back. He'd already known it'd been way too long since he'd had sex—before the hospitals, before the last rotation to Afghanistan—but if such simple contact could affect him like that, he was in worse shape than he'd realized.

"I don't suppose you would choose the colors, too." The fingers that had just skimmed his hand waved across the display that, he suddenly decided, didn't have nearly enough choices. He could pick a variety in seconds.

"What makes you think you'd like the colors I choose?"

"You're not leaning toward white, khaki, or Army green, are you?"

He shook his head.

"Okay. Me neither. At least you can make a choice. I seem to be paralyzed by the options."

Smiling at her overly dramatic statement, he studied the rows of colors. "What room?"

"Living room."

He took his time moving from the neutrals, though he'd already dismissed them, to the pastels, to the bolder and darker colors, to the neons. In his mind, he was trying to picture his ideal living room, something he'd never given much thought to. Except for the time he was married, he'd lived his adult life in barracks, tents, or plywood structures. A comfortable sofa and a television, the bigger the better, were the only details he could fill in.

Then he glanced at Carly and instead tried to picture her in the room. Not pastels. She was soft enough all on her own. No really bright colors, either. They'd overwhelm her.

Leaning past her, catching a whiff of her perfume again, he chose three colors: chocolate brown, dark green, and a deep burnt orange that would look good with cream-colored trim. Hey, he was from Texas. Go Longhorns.

She took the cards from him, fanning them out. "Wow. When you go for color, you go all the way, don't you?" She flashed a smile. "Isn't that you Airborne guys' motto? 'All the way!'?"

"That's the Eighty-second."

"Oh. Did the Hundred Seventy-Third have one?"

"Officially, no. Unofficially it was 'Stay alive.'"

Emotion crossed her face, too quickly for him to identify, and he dropped his gaze away, unfortunately, to her wedding ring. Her husband hadn't managed to stay alive. Nice of him to remind her of that.

Suddenly hot from the inside out, he cleared his throat, working up the words for an apology, but before he could speak, she did, sounding as normal and friendly as she had two minutes ago.

"Okay, I like these. And since it's a test coat, I don't need to bother yet with tape and rollers and pans, right?"

His breath came a little easier as the heat receded. "Just a brush."

"All right." Picking up two more cans of the base paint,

she moved down the aisle to the brushes. "Do you have any experience at painting, or do you just give advice? You know, men are always great at giving advice."

"When I was a kid, I helped paint my granddad's barn a couple of times, and every time I got in trouble when I was staying with them, my grandmother sent me out to paint the picket fence around the yard. It got painted more often than any other fence in three counties."

"Aw, you had a lot of personality, huh?" Carly laughed, a throaty sound that made him . . . He watched her, searching for the word he wanted, then it came and brought some friends: Warm. Comfortable. Greedy, because he'd like to hear it again. Would like to be responsible for it again.

God. Maybe that IED had taken more from him than his leg, like enough brain cells to make him react like a sixteen-year-old boy to a pretty woman.

"What do you think?"

He focused on her—rather, on the brush she was holding. "Too big, unless you want to pour the paint into a different container."

She switched the brush for a narrower one, then they went to the counter to get the paints mixed. After handing the paint and the sample cards to the clerk, she leaned against the counter, resting her hands on the metal surface. The position kept her ring out of sight, which somehow made him feel just a little easier.

"Are your grandparents still alive?"

He shook his head. "My grandmother died first, going in her sleep, and Granddad passed a month later. He didn't want to live without her."

That emotion came again, accompanied by a sad

smile. Had there been times when Carly's husband died that she'd wanted to die, too?

Probably. She'd loved him and had no children to keep her going. He'd known wives who were convinced they couldn't live without their husbands. He'd known one who hadn't left her husband's casket, even sleeping in the visitation room at the funeral home, until she'd had no choice. He'd known wives who absolutely couldn't process the fact that their husbands were gone. Weeks after the burials, they were still clinging to the hope that they would call and say, _Hey, honey, it was all a terrible mistake. I'm here._

Dane breathed deeply. Though his leg hurt with both real and phantom pain, though his future was nowhere near bright enough to have to wear shades, he was alive. He hadn't felt much gratitude for that until recently.

"You're quiet for a kid who used to do a great deal of punitive painting." She tilted her head to the side to study him. "Must be true that it's the quiet ones you have to watch out for."

"Did people have to watch out for you when you were a kid?"

Another laugh burst loose. "Good heavens, no. Remember, I was an average child in the midst of geniuses. All I ever wanted to do was play or hang out or read, while my brothers were trying to build nuclear reactors or killer lasers or create a new life-form. I learned to get out of the house or take cover quickly any time I saw smoke or smelled chemicals."

"And yet you grew up to be perfectly normal."

The mixing machine went silent, and a moment later the clerk set down the three small cans, a daub of color on each lid. Before she could pick them up, Dane did and together they started toward the front of the store.

"Yeah, I'm the normal one," she agreed, then sadness crossed her face again. "But they've got the wives, the kids, the pets, the white picket fences." Her sidelong glance cleared. "Not that they don't deserve it. My brothers are nice people, exceptionally intelligent, but they have the social skills of rocks—or, as my oldest brother, Leo, would say, naturally occurring solid aggregates of minerals and/or mineraloids."

This time it was Dane who laughed out loud. "Are you kidding?"

"Oh, no. They talk that way. Have since they were four or five. You can imagine the dinner conversations I grew up with, being the only one at the table with an IQ below one-eighty."

"At least you had brothers. There were times I even would have been happy with a sister."

"There were times I would have been happy being an only child. Though that would have made me the focus of my parents' attention, and the weight of their expectations would have been unbearable. As it was, they had three brilliant sons to pin their hopes on. An average daughter could be overlooked."

There wasn't any resentment in her voice, no hint of longing that things had been different. How old was she when she'd realized that her parents couldn't be like other parents and that was all right?

As they joined the shortest line at the checkout, she set the brush down, shoved the paint samples into her purse and removed her checkbook. "I'm sorry. That sounds like I had a bad childhood, and I didn't. My family's eccentric and I love them. I'm average, and they love me, too. We're just different."

"I get it. It's the opposite with my mother and me. She had just the one kid to focus on, and her idea of my ideal life doesn't come close to mine."

"She didn't want you to join the Army?"

He shook his head. "I was supposed to go to college, get a nice boring job in a nice boring office, marry my high school girlfriend, buy a house somewhere nearby and have the kids, the pets, and the white picket fence."

"And instead you joined the Army, went off to see the world and get shot at on a regular basis and...No wife? No kids?"

Dane watched her swipe her ATM card, then thank the clerk with a smile as she took the bag. He paid for his own purchase—the picture hangers—then shoved them into his jacket pocket.

"One ex-wife, no kids." He didn't discuss the marriage with anyone as a rule. When it had imploded, all his buddies had known all the details, since Sheryl had been sleeping with guys in their unit. Hard to keep that sort of thing private. Since then, she'd been ancient history. He only talked about her with his mother, and then only because there was no way to shut Anna Mae down.

So why did he open his mouth and go on? "She was the high school girlfriend. That was the only part I got right."

"I know it's an easy thing to say and not so easy to do, but..." She shrugged as they left the PX for the mini-mall that fronted it. "It's your life. You have to live it. You have to do what makes you happy. If my parents had their way, I'd be married to a nice experimental physicist, having one child every three-point-two years and instead of reading them nursery rhymes, I'd be teaching them Max Born's take on spooky action at a distance."

"Wow. And you do seem perfectly normal."

She turned a bright smile on him that brought back those feelings: *warm, comfortable, greedy.* "*Seem* is the key word." Abruptly she closed her eyes and took a deep breath. "Pizza. It's dinnertime. Want to share a large double everything with me?"

Two meals out in a week—and the second one with a pretty woman. Look at him, seeming perfectly normal, too. His shrinks would be happy, his buddies relieved, his mother disapproving. And him? All he could identify was a funny feeling in his gut—anxiety, he guessed. He wasn't ready to get involved with a woman, especially one still grieving her war hero husband.

Then the part of him that had been dealing with women nearly half his life took over. Spur-of-the-moment pizza at the PX was so far from *getting involved* that it was laughable.

Though he didn't feel much like laughing, because another part of the knot in his gut was longing. He *wanted* to sit at a table with Carly, enjoy a meal and forget at least for a while that that was all he could have for now.

He didn't get to forget very often.

"Does double everything include anchovies?"

She shook her head, her face wrinkled in a delicate gesture of distaste.

"Good. Sounds great."

"I can't believe we ate all that." Carly wiped her hands on her last napkin, then dropped it on the large pizza pan that held nothing but crumbs and a few pieces of crust.

With an overstuffed feeling that stopped just short of un-comfortable, she rested her arms on the table. "It's a good thing I don't go out for pizza often."

"That's the first one I've had that wasn't frozen since I was in Italy. A couple years, at least."

She feigned an incredulous look. "Every time Jeff came back from anywhere, his first meal was steak, his second barbecued ribs, and his third pizza. He couldn't have gone a week without all three."

Dane's gaze darkened before he lowered it and paid more attention to gathering their trash than was needed. "How long ago…"

"Twenty-five months." She drew a breath, then went on. "Three weeks and five days."

"I'm sorry. I shouldn't have—"

"No, I brought him up. It's nice being able to talk about him. For a long time, I couldn't. It hurt too much and, especially here, it makes a lot of people uncomfortable. The men have lost too many friends, come too close to dying themselves, and the women look at me and think *If it could happen to her husband…*" She shrugged.

It *was* nice. Dane understood the war part so he was empathetic, but he hadn't known Jeff so Carly's particular situation wasn't personal for him.

"Why did you decide to stay in Tallgrass? Why not go home to Utah?"

She toyed with the straw in her drink. "I did go home for a few months and stayed with my brother Roger and his wife. Lisa and I are pretty close. But I didn't fit in. I kept calling the grocery store the commissary. When I needed something, I'd say, 'I'm going to the fort' before I remembered there *was* no fort. I couldn't get used to not seeing the base stickers or the people in uniform or the haircuts. I felt even stranger than I had when I'd married into the Army. My job was still open, so I came back. This is where Jeff and I last lived together. It's home."

She hesitated. It was clear his marriage wasn't something he liked to discuss, but he'd touched on a sensitive subject with her, so she felt justified doing the same. If he chose not to answer, she would understand and wouldn't ask again. "What about your ex-wife? Did she go back to Texas or stay where you were?"

His chuckle sounded startled from him. "God, no. She couldn't wait to leave." It seemed he would leave it at that, but unexpectedly he went on. "When your husband's going to work every day with the guys you've been sleeping with, it's best to put a whole lot of distance between you and all of them."

All of them. Carly winced inwardly. One affair was bad enough, but multiple ones must have been so much harder. Or did it work the other way: The first one he'd found out about was such a shock that each subsequent one had less impact?

He left the table, emptying the trash, returning the tray, then came back. When he didn't sit, she lifted her purse and bag to the tabletop and stood.

"Who knew when I left to buy a hammer and picture hangers, we'd end up having a pizza together?" he remarked.

"Who knew you'd forget the hammer?" She smiled when he looked down as if he clearly expected to see a hammer hanging around somewhere. When he rolled his eyes, it gave him a boyish look that needed only a wicked grin to give her a clear image of the mischievous kid he'd been.

"Guess I'll head back inside." He didn't move, though, not right away. "I'll see you?"

"Probably." Four times in less than a week? Very likely. Still…Opening her purse, she pulled out a crumpled receipt and a pen and scrawled her phone number on the back before offering it to him. "Just in case."

He removed his wallet from his pocket, smoothed the paper and tucked it in with the folding money. "Be careful."

She watched until he disappeared inside the store again before heading for her car. The answer Jeff had always given to that admonition echoed in her mind. *Always.*

She was two blocks from her house when she decided she didn't want to go there. It took less than five minutes to reach Therese's. She parked behind the mom van, jogged up the steps, and rang the bell.

The door was jerked open with enough force to make Carly take a step back. Abby Matheson oozed derision from every pore, her lip curled into such a sneer that her cupid's bow disappeared. "Tuh-*reese*!"

Her shout was still echoing in the foyer when she started stomping up the stairs.

And there was a prime example of why Carly didn't teach middle school.

As she stepped inside, Therese came down the hall from the kitchen. Tight lines bracketed her mouth and her hair was tousled as if she'd been raking her fingers through it. No need for television in the Matheson home. They had enough family drama on their own.

A bit of the pinching on Therese's face eased. "Hey,

come on in. I've got fresh tea and warm chocolate chip cookies. Not homemade, mind you, just freshly baked."

Everyone in the Tuesday Night Margarita Club knew Abby's habit of comparing Therese to her mother in every endeavor and finding her lacking. No doubt, tonight it had been, *My mom* always *made cookies from scratch. She would never serve this store-bought crap.*

Everyone in the margarita club thought Abby needed her bottom paddled except Therese. She tolerated stuff that would have yanked Carly's own mother out of her oh-so-important lab for disciplinary action. Just once, Carly often thought, someone needed to remind the child that Therese had taken them in after Abby's mother abandoned her and Jacob, refusing to take them back even after their father had died.

And that always reminded Carly why Abby was so angry and Therese so tolerant.

After closing the door, Carly followed Therese and took a seat at the cozy breakfast table. "Tough evening, huh?"

"Tough week." Therese brought two glasses of ice, a pitcher of tea, and a plate of cookies to the table, then sat down. "She's still on detention, she's still grounded, and I still haven't given back her phone. She's...unhappy."

"I know she is, Therese, but it's not your fault."

"Who else does she have to take it out on? Paul? Catherine? Her grandparents?"

Carly reached for a cookie. That had been Abby's second choice for living arrangements after her father died. All her grandparents had been kind and sympathetic and apologetic, but that hadn't made their refusals any easier to bear.

"Life sucks, doesn't it?" she commiserated.

Therese studied her for a moment, then said, "Not always. You look...lighter. One might even say almost giddy. What have you been up to?"

"Nothing. Just shopping at the PX. Having a pizza for dinner."

Carly wasn't a big shopper, and she knew Therese knew it. Her friend also knew how much she disliked eating out alone, so she locked in on the second part. "With whom?"

Stuffing the last half of the cookie in her mouth, Carly poured herself a glass of tea, chewed a bit longer, then finally washed down the crumbs with a big gulp. "Dane Clark."

Therese's eyebrows practically arched into her hairline. "Dane from the cave? You just happened to run into Dane *again* and had dinner with him?"

"Yeah, I know. Coincidence."

"Or fate. Or an answer to our prayers." Therese shrugged when Carly looked at her. "I pray for you. I pray for all of us to be happy and safe and content." She stared into her tea. "I'm glad God's listening to *some* of my prayers."

Even God needed time to deal with Abby.

"So come on, share. Tell me everything."

That was why she'd come here, Carly realized. She'd wanted to tell *someone*. "I ran into him in the paint section at the PX. He picked out some colors for me to try on the living room walls. I decided this afternoon that I really need to paint, but there were so many choices. The ones he picked are really pretty. Do you want to see—" Automatically she reached for her purse, and Therese playfully slapped her hand away.

"No, I don't want to see the colors. I want to hear how you went from discussing paint to having dinner together."

"It wasn't really dinner. I mean, not like a date or anything."

"Was it the evening meal?"

"Yes, but—"

"Did you sit at the same table and talk?"

"Yes, but—"

Therese interrupted with an imperious wave, her point made. "Tell me. Everything."

Carly related parts of the conversation, feeling like a fourteen-year-old girl with her very first crush. She and her best friend had whispered and giggled for days, until something else had caught their attention.

When she was done, Therese sat back and stared at her. "You gave him your phone number."

Still feeling about fourteen, she shifted awkwardly. "Well, yeah. The way he said it... 'I'll see you?' rather than 'I'll see you.' I just thought...I mean, sure, we've run into each other four times in less than a week, but—"

"Wait, wait, wait. I only know about three times. The cave, the WTU, and today. When was number four?"

Carly's cheeks warmed. "Oh. Uh, coming back from the bathroom at dinner the other night. He was in the bar, and we said hello." And a little bit more.

"And you didn't mention it to us. Hmm, wonder why." Therese tapped one fingertip thoughtfully against her chin before raising her brows again. "Maybe because you didn't want to share him with us? Maybe you wanted to keep him all to yourself."

Now her face burned, as if she stood in front of a blazing fire. "No, it was just...he seemed...as a group, we're a little intimidating..."

Therese's fingers wrapped around hers in a tight squeeze. "Hey, sweetie, I'm glad you like him. I'm glad he likes you. He knows about Jeff?"

She bobbed her head.

"Good. Really, really good."

Carly hesitated over the question on the tip of her tongue, then gave herself a mental shake. She'd asked a virtual stranger about his ex-wife. Surely she could get a little personal with her best friend. "Have you thought about dating again?"

"I like to think I will, but—"

As perfectly as if it were scripted, something sounded directly overhead with enough force to vibrate the light fixture above the table.

"My life is so chaotic, I can't even imagine bringing someone else into it. If the kids hate me for trying to fill in for their mother, how desperately would they hate another man trying to fill in for their father?"

There was such sadness in her voice that Carly's stomach knotted. *"Are we meant to spend the rest of our lives alone?"* Therese had asked last Saturday. Despite having the two kids in her house, she was even more alone than the rest of them. Their hearts had broken in one swift moment. Paul's children were breaking hers every day.

"I'm sorry." Carly maneuvered her hand to give Therese a squeeze. "I wish I had the magic to fix it all—the kids, you, all of us."

"I know. And just knowing helps. Really." Therese took a deep breath and lightened her tone. "So... show me these colors Cave Guy picked out for your living room."

By the time Carly left, Therese was feeling a little better. Her head had stopped pounding, and she'd resisted the urge to get weepy. Sometimes crying helped—all those emotions had to escape somewhere—but usually it just made her eyes red and her nose stuffy and kept her from getting any restful sleep at all.

As she finished cleaning the kitchen, she considered the circumstances that had brought Carly and Dane Clark together so often. If it was fate, Therese would be a little jealous. If it was God's answer to her prayers, well, she would still be a little jealous.

But very happy, too, she hastened to assure herself. Just because her future looked bleak didn't mean everyone else's should. Whatever happiness her friends found would give her hope that she would find it, too, someday.

She shut off the kitchen lights and went into the living room. Abby was in her room, apparently having withdrawal symptoms from the thousand and one texts she sent or received each day, and Jacob was in his, probably playing one last round of video games before going to bed.

Switching off all but one lamp, she curled into her favorite chair and picked up the Bible on the table beside it. Usually she read it in the morning, before the kids were up, with a strong cup of coffee and the energy bar she ate for breakfast. That was when she did most of her praying, too, though there were always short prayers during the day and the regular nighttime ones.

For so many years those prayers had ended the same way: *Please keep Paul safe.* He was forever safe now, and she liked to believe his spirit was with her when she needed more strength than she had on her own. If she could just see him, hear his voice one more time...If he could just talk to his children...

Talking with her didn't help them. She'd lost control of her temper and screamed back at Abby tonight, and that hadn't helped, either. All she could do was pray, and she was about to do that one more time when one of the cell phones in her pockets began to ring, a happy kid-style song. She'd tried just putting Abby's phone away until the suspension ended, but her stepdaughter had proven she wasn't above sneaking in and stealing it back.

Shifting, she pulled the phone out and saw *Mimi M* on the screen. Paul's mother. She should answer and let her know Abby was fine but without phone privileges, but instead she muted the ring and let it go to voice mail. She wasn't up for the subtle criticism Eileen always offered regarding her parenting skills.

She moved to set the phone aside, but her hand hesitated over it. Abby's winning argument for getting the cell had been the ability it would give her to check in with Therese, though she never had. Had she even programmed Therese's number into the phone? And if she had, what ring tone had she given her? Certainly nothing like Eileen's.

She knew she should resist, but now that the question had been raised, she couldn't. She called up the address book, scrolled down to the *T*s. A first quick glance showed no entry for Therese.

A second sharp glance showed she was wrong. She was listed, all right, just under another name.

TheB*tch.

Carefully she set the phone down. She put the Bible beside it, turned off the lamp, drew her knees to her chest, and she wept.

Chapter Five

Saturday morning found Carly running through her usual routine: cleaning, doing laundry, vacuuming. Next she did her grocery shopping for the week, and then the rest of the day was free.

Free had been so much better when there was someone to share it with.

Today, though, she had plans for the afternoon. She was going to move the furniture away from the main wall in the living room, put down a drop cloth and open those three small cans of paint. It had been too late Thursday by the time she'd come home from Therese's, or so she'd told herself, and Friday evening she'd had a headache. The smell of paint, she'd convinced herself, would likely have made her sick.

But she'd slept well last night, and today was sunny and warm, and she felt energetic. Who knew? She might even clean out the cabinets and closets when she was done or organize the mess of her desk or even find something to do in the yard.

After she finished putting away the groceries, including two cartons of her favorite Braum's ice cream—an excellent reason in and of itself for staying in Oklahoma—she ate the fast-food lunch she'd picked up on the way home, then started prepping the living room.

Despite its heft, the couch slid away from the wall easily. The end table, a hand-me-down from Jeff's grandmother, was easy, too. She reminded herself to switch it to the other end when she put it back, so she could keep her promise to Lisa.

With everything in—or out of—place, she pried open the first can of paint and stirred it. It looked like the richest, most luxurious chocolate before it was poured into molds to set, and it flowed over the dingy white with each stroke.

The hunter green was gorgeous, too, peaceful and serene, and the burnt orange warmed the room with a pop of color.

Done, she sprawled in the chair across the room, slumped down, stared at the three rectangles of beautiful change and wondered, just as she had at the paint counter, how she was supposed to decide. She liked all three. Compared to the bland white, she might even love them.

The ring of the cell phone drew her gaze to it. The people who called often had personalized ring tones—the margarita club's was "Margaritaville," of course—but this was the standard ring for not-family, not-close-friends. Still gazing at the wall, she picked it up and absently murmured, "Hello."

"Hey. Uh, it's Dane. Is this, uh, a bad time?"

Pleasure coursed through her with a flare of heat, her lips curving into a smile as she sat straighter in the chair. "Depends on what you want to do. It's not the best weather for sunbathing or building snowmen. It's too early for planting flowers, too late for breakfast, and you've missed trick-or-treating by five months."

He chuckled. "Let me be more specific. Is this a bad time to talk?"

"No. I'm just contemplating my wall, so it's a very good time to talk."

"Have you chosen a color yet?"

"Nope. I like all three of them. It's a shame I can't paint the room in stripes."

"Actually, you could. You just have to—"

"No, no," she interrupted. "You're going to say something about rulers and tape and straight lines, aren't you? And I don't do straight lines. I don't even hang a picture unless it's the only thing on the whole wall. That's how bad my idea of 'straight' is."

There was a moment's silence, then in a low voice, Dane said, "Wow. You're really flawed, aren't you? Your IQ is below one-eighty, you're indecisive, and you're linearly challenged."

"And I eat chocolate for breakfast," she added as she turned sideways in the chair, swinging her legs over the arm.

"Yeah, but who doesn't?"

"I have two nephews whose mother is a postharvest biologist. They're four and five, and they've never had cake or ice cream or a Hershey's Kiss. Their idea of dessert is yogurt with a few berries stirred in."

"That's just sad."

"Yeah. For most of my family, food is fuel, nothing more. My sister-in-law Lisa and I are the only ones who savor it like gifts from God, and *I'm* the only one who shows it." Lisa was a perfect size four, while Carly was...well, not.

There was a sound in the background, the distant blare of a horn, followed immediately by the chiming of a car when the door was opened with the key in the ignition. "Are you out and about?"

"Yeah. I had to pick up some uniforms at the cleaners."

Carly thought of the stiffly starched uniforms hanging in the guest room. Their bedroom closet was so small that only half their clothes fit, so Jeff had volunteered to move his across the hall. *"I'm only doing this,"* he'd teased, *"to keep your clothes from squashing my uniforms."*

They were still there—every uniform item he hadn't taken to the desert with him, including the dress blue uniform he'd worn at their wedding. Dress shoes polished to a high sheen and scruffy but broken-in boots lined the floor beneath the garments. She thought from time to time about doing something with them, but it always seemed too final an action to take.

"Is that a *no*, or are you thinking about it?"

Dane's voice in her ear startled her back to the moment. Whatever he'd asked had sailed past her, blocked by thoughts of Jeff. Giving herself a mental shake, she said, "I'm sorry. I missed that. Can you ask again?"

"Yeah, sure." There was a chagrined sound to his voice. "I was just wondering if you'd like to, um, do something."

"Yes." She didn't hesitate. It didn't matter what or

when or where. The simple truth was yes, she would like to spend more time with Dane.

Jeff understood that. Didn't he?

"Do you want to meet somewhere?"

She thought back to safety advice she'd been given in college—never meet a guy for the first time alone, never go off without telling someone where and with whom, make sure he wasn't a psycho stalker before letting him know where she lived—then looked at the colors on the wall and said, "Why don't you come by? The address is Four-eighteen East Cimarron."

"Four one eight," he murmured, and she could easily imagine him typing the numbers into a GPS. Jeff had used his all the time. No having to learn his way around town when the GPS would guide him to the door.

"I'll be there in a few minutes."

She said good-bye and clicked off the phone, then stared at the vibrant colors on the wall. That was how she would decide: Let Dane do it when he got here. She would be happy with any of the three shades, so it wouldn't hurt to let someone else pick.

When he got here. Dane was coming over. It had been so long since she'd waited for a man to come to pick her up. She'd met Jeff her freshman year in college and, except for one semester, they'd been together since. The idea that a man was on his way over to see her seemed almost impossible. The feelings it invoked were vaguely familiar, long gone but not forgotten. They included anticipation, nervousness, a little guilt, and—

Dane was coming over!

Jumping to her feet, she rushed to the bedroom. Sure, the T-shirt and crop pants she'd thrown on this morning were fine for running errands, but there were lots of things she looked better in hanging in the closet. She'd stripped to her underwear before realizing the blinds were open, twisted them closed, then yanked open the closet door.

Within minutes, she was dressed in khaki trousers and a rusty-colored shirt with chunky shoes that added a few inches to her height, with a suede band holding back her hair. She started to pick up the perfume bottle for a spritz, then put it back. Not Jeff's favorite fragrance. Not today.

A little twinge of regret sliced through her.

When the doorbell rang, she left the bathroom, then hesitated, remembering that old advice in college. Quickly, feeling overly cautious but obligated, as well as just plain foolish, she scribbled a note on the bedside table: *Out with Dane Clark.* Just in case.

Then she went to open the door.

He stood on the porch, hands in his jacket pockets. His jeans were faded, worn through one knee, and his T-shirt fit snugly across his chest. The jacket was brown leather, scuffed and battered. He looked handsome. Just a little hesitant. A whole lot solid. Strong. Someone a woman could lean on.

"Come on in." She stepped back and gestured to the cramped room. "Take a seat if you can get to one."

Instead he stopped in the middle of the room to study the experiment on the wall. She closed the door and stood beside him, near enough to smell his cologne. It was light, simple, no smoky complex fragrances. Just clean. She liked it.

Moving next to the wall, she did a game-show hostess flourish. "What do you think?"

His dark gaze moved from one color to the next, finally landing on her. "You look good."

Self-consciously she fingered the last of the wooden buttons that kept her shirt secured. It had been so long since a man had given her a simple compliment. Likely the last had come from Jeff before his final deployment. "Thank you. But I meant the colors."

"The color looks great on you."

He said it with such seriousness that she couldn't help but laugh. "Thanks. It's one of my favorites. Now... what's your vote? Color number one?" She gestured to the chocolate, waited a minute, then did the same with colors number two and three.

"Why am I picking? I don't live here."

"Remember, I'm flawed. I can't make a decision."

He snorted as he stepped back to the door and turned on the overhead lights before looking at the colors again. "I narrowed it down from a thousand to three for you."

"And I like all three." And she wanted someone else's opinion. She wasn't indecisive, not really. She was just tired of making every decision by herself. At home, everything had had to pass muster with her parents. In college, it had been her roommate, and after college, she and Jeff had made every major choice together. "So which one gets two thumbs-up?"

"I should warn you I'm a Longhorns fan."

Her nose wrinkled automatically. "That's the big game OU has in Texas, isn't it?" At his nod, she rolled her eyes. "When we eventually got pregnant, Jeff wanted to do the nursery in black and gold in honor of the University of Colorado. Football nuts."

After glancing around, Dane picked up a photograph

sitting on the shelves beside the TV. It was Jeff, mugging
for the camera with a couple of buddies, all of them wearing desert camouflage and dark shades in deference to the
bright sun. His hands rested on his thighs, fingers spread
wide, his wedding band glinting.

It hurt her heart that he would never pose for another
picture, never laugh or make her laugh.

Dane didn't comment, but carefully set the frame back
on the shelf before turning away from it.

"So…" Carly went to stand near him again, shoving
her hands into her hip pockets and rocking back on her
heels. "Which of these colors is associated with the
Longhorns? I can see that the brown might reference
something that comes out of a cow, but I'd rather not
think about that if it's going to cover my walls. And the
green, I guess, could stand for the grass they eat. But that
last one…are longhorns orange?"

He gave her a scowl with no heat. "No, but their school
colors are burnt orange and cream. The walls that color,
the cream trim …"

"Ooh, it'll be like a giant pumpkin pie with whipped
cream. I like that." If she'd given herself enough time, she
was pretty sure she would have chosen that color, too. It
was nice that he'd agreed, even if his reason had been as
lame as Jeff's for wanting a black-and-gold nursery.

"Thanks for your help, Dane. Now…" The question
that really mattered. "What do you want to do today?"

Dalton didn't usually need much excuse for being
grouchy, but he had one today. He was having company
tomorrow: his mom and dad were stopping by in their RV
on their way north. His mother had called this morning,

giving him a shopping list for the meals she intended to cook while they were there and informing him that she wanted to sleep in a real bed and use a real bathroom. Her way of saying *Clean the house at least a little.*

He'd sent Noah to do the shopping, and he'd started the cleaning. It wasn't that he was a slob. He just had better things to do, like the ranch work that he, his dad, and Dillon used to do together. The cows and the horses didn't care whether he vacuumed or dusted, but they sure got upset if he didn't take care of them.

The house was big, built mostly from trees harvested off the north acreage and with stone quarried on the property. Too big for one person, though here he was. Downstairs was a living room, dining room, kitchen, and utility room, all oversized, with four bedroom upstairs. His parents had had their own, of course, and so had Noah. Dalton and Dillon had shared the biggest room— twins were expected to share a lot—and the fourth had been for guests. When he was a kid, there had been a lot of visits from aunts, uncles, and cousins.

Now, besides Noah, the only people who'd come for a visit in years had been Sandra's folks, when they'd buried her, and his. It had been one of those odd summer-in-January days that Oklahoma was famous for: eighty-five degrees, only a light breeze blowing across the prairies. The sky had been clear blue, fat clouds drifting slowly to the east. A perfect day for saddling up the horses and riding the trail that snaked along the north edge of the ranch.

Too beautiful a day for a funeral. Even the grayest, dreariest day was too good for that.

Abruptly the vacuum cut off, and he looked around in time to hear Noah's swearing as he untangled the cord from his feet. He carried the grocery bags into the kitchen, then picked up the cord when he returned. "Well, my part's done. I think I'm gonna go outside and check on the horses."

When he plugged the vacuum in again, Dalton switched it off. "Clean sheets for Mom and Dad's bedroom," he said with a nod toward the laundry basket at the foot of the stairs.

"Aw, man...I don't even make my own bed."

"I've noticed." Dalton switched the machine on again to block out anything else Noah might say. He didn't make his own bed, either. Not much point when he was getting right back in it in eighteen hours. It had driven Sandra nuts, so they'd reached a compromise of sorts. Whoever got up last had to make the bed. Since his day always started earlier than hers, that meant she'd always had to make it.

Scowling, he pushed the vacuum across the living room carpet with more force than necessary. He'd already dusted, cleaned both the upstairs and downstairs bathrooms and loaded the dishwasher. The counters and kitchen table still needed scrubbing, but other than that and a load of laundry, the house would be clean to his standards. Not his mom's and certainly not Sandra's, but it would do.

Oh, and the wooden box. It would have to go back above the fireplace. But that could wait.

By the time Noah clumped down the stairs again, Dalton had finished the living room and was wrapping the cord around the vacuum. Noah took a look around, then hesitantly said, "What about the flag? You know Mom and Dad will expect to see it. And the pictures."

His father had made a display box for the flag that had covered Sandra's coffin, a photograph of her in uniform and the ribbons she'd earned during her Army career. He'd been meticulous with the craftsmanship, creating a beautiful piece with Sandra's name and the dates of her birth and death engraved in the rich cherry. It was respectful, an honor, a gift from his father's heart that Dalton could hardly bear to look at. Even so, he'd left it on the mantel where his father had placed it for more than a year before moving it, along with all the other photographs, to the guest room closet.

"I'll get them later."

"When?"

"Tonight. Tomorrow morning." Any time that wasn't *now*.

"Don't forget," Noah warned, then he raised both hands defensively. "I'm just saying."

"I won't forget," Dalton said sharply.

Noah had that look about him, the one that meant he wanted to say something that Dalton didn't want to hear. Dalton set his shoulders, waiting, and Noah opened his mouth, then exhaled, shook his head and went into the kitchen.

Dalton followed him. "Go ahead. Spit it out before you get all sour from keeping it in."

"Like you?" The words burst out as Noah set a can of diced tomatoes on the counter so hard it probably dented the surface, then turned to face him. "You know Mom and Dad worry about you. When they see you like this... When's the last time you got your hair cut or shaved or put on clothes that don't look like they spent a week in the cow pen? Hell, when's the last time you talked to someone without taking his head off? No one expects you to smile and be happy like nothing happened, but at least quit acting like they buried you with Sandra."

Blood turning to ice, Dalton stared at his brother. The list of subjects that were off-limits in this house was so simple even Noah could remember them: Dillon and Sandra. If the restrictions chafed him so much, he could consider the dorm at Stillwater his home from now on and stay the hell away from Tallgrass.

The silence dragged out until Noah shifted his weight awkwardly. "I—I'm sorry. I didn't mean to—" Mouth clamped shut, he picked up the can along with an armful of others and went to the pantry. Before he finished putting the cans away, Dalton left the room and the house. He didn't bother feeling his pockets for the keys he'd left in their usual spot on the counter, didn't turn toward the pasture to catch and saddle one of the horses. He just walked, across the grass that was trying to green up, past the barn, through the gate and across the field.

The temperature fell as he walked from the front moving in that the weather guys had predicted. By ten o'clock tonight, it would be in the low thirties, and tomorrow morning, they were saying, would bring an inch or so of snow. Dalton didn't go back for a jacket, though. His anger at Noah was enough to keep him warm.

But it wasn't Noah he was mad at, he finally admitted. Noah was a kid, not even twenty yet, and he said what he felt needed to be said. It could be worse. He could have been like Dillon, telling people what he thought they wanted to hear, making promises he never intended to keep, never putting himself out for anyone other than himself.

It would be easier to live with a dozen Noahs than just one Dillon.

Finally, deep in the woods, Dalton slumped down on a boulder not five feet from the bank of a sluggish creek. His dad had called this his thinking spot. He must have been about eight when he discovered it, and he'd come here so often in the years since that he swore the sandstone had worn away in the shape of his butt.

He propped his feet on the top edge of the rock, his boot heels leaving marks on the soft surface, and he let his head hang down, his eyes close.

Noah *was* just a kid. How did he know Dalton felt like he'd died with Sandra? Nothing had been the same for him since. He'd kept his distance from his family and neighbors, had given up his friends, had done only what was necessary to keep the ranch running, and for a long time he'd considered giving that up, too. He didn't need much—didn't *want* much. A little place with no memories where he could waste away. Sandra's life insurance would have provided that for the rest of his life and still have money left over.

He'd gone so far as to trailer up the prime of his herd to haul them off to market, but the truck had never made it through the gate. He'd loved ranching. It was all he'd ever wanted to do, not just because he liked the hours and the work, but also because it was a part of who he was. Smiths had been running livestock on this land for more than a hundred years. Being a part of the land, earning a living from it—that was their legacy.

The legacy was what had kept him going the last four years. Not even Noah, who'd lived with him even then after their parents had retired to south Texas, had been enough reason to stick around, but the cows and the horses had. Noah would have been all right on his own, but the animals had needed Dalton. Almost as much as he'd needed them.

So this was what his sorry life had come to. No wife. No kids. No word of Dillon in thirteen years. No friends. No one in his life on a regular basis, unless he counted weekends with Noah. Nothing but a whole world of hurt.

God, he wished he'd learned to like liquor back when Dillon did.

He heard the footsteps approaching long before Noah came into sight. His brother walked up to him, hand extended.

"Here. You left your cell phone."

Dalton took the phone. When a man worked alone as much as he did, the lack of a phone could turn an accident from bad to disaster. He never went out without his. "Thanks."

"I got the groceries put away and cleaned the upstairs bathroom."

"I already did that."

"Huh. Sure could've fooled me. Anyway, I'm going into town to get a burger. Want to go?"

"For what?" He avoided Tallgrass as much as he could.

"I don't know. A haircut? Maybe buy a pair of Wranglers that don't look older than me?" Noah shrugged. "Hell, maybe just for a change of scenery."

Dalton fingered a worn place at the hem of his right leg where the denim was frayed into tiny white threads. He didn't blame Noah for not wanting their mother worried during their visit. When Ramona got worked up, no one got any peace until whatever troubled her was resolved.

If a haircut and a new pair of jeans could keep her from getting worked up in the first place...

"Okay. But I drive."

Noah punched him on the arm. "Aw, man, you drive like an old woman."

"You drive like a NASCAR wannabe. You get one more ticket, and Dad's going to take the keys to the truck back to Texas with him."

Noah grinned. "Yeah, but only the keys, since Mom won't let him park it at the condo. And I know how to hot-wire it."

"Dad can park it here. You come around trying to hot-wire anything, I'll kick your butt."

And that was it. Things were back to normal. No apologies, no talking it out. Everything forgotten.

Except that Dalton never could seem to really forget.

Tallgrass remained a small town despite the increase to its population of fifty-five thousand residents brought by Fort Murphy. People on the sidewalks downtown spoke to everyone they passed. The clerks in the stores were chatty and friendly. Other shoppers didn't hesitate to offer advice or information, solicited or not. It reminded Dane of the town where his grandparents had lived.

Since neither Dane nor Carly had had any particular activity in mind, they had driven downtown, parked the truck in front of the old stone building that housed the county courts and the police department and made their way through the shops, up one side of the street and down the other. He wasn't much of a shopper, but the stores were mostly antique or, more honestly, junk stores, and a lot of the items inside brought back good memories.

As they walked out of the final store on the block, the wind blew a few old dead leaves in a swirl of dust. Carly shivered, pulling her denim jacket tighter. "I've never gotten used to how quickly the weather changes here. At noon it was seventy-something. Now it's thirty-eight."

He glanced at the flashing sign above the bank entrance on the northwest corner. It was a quarter of six, and he could feel the passage of time in his leg. He'd been on his feet for nearly four hours, and he'd already learned that the stump didn't like rapid weather changes. He was thinking about someplace warm, a comfortable sofa, propping up his foot and popping a pain pill when she gestured down the block.

"Serena's Sweets has really good coffee. Can I interest you in a cup and a piece of pie or cake or even dinner?"

He glanced at the shop a few doors down. Condensation on its big plate-glass windows showed it was warm inside, and a padded bench could be as comfortable as a sofa, especially if he could put his foot on the opposite bench. As for a pain pill, who needed that when good pie was available, along with Carly?

"Sounds good," he said, and she tucked her arm through his, pushed her hands into her pockets and began strolling in that direction.

His muscles were taut where their arms made contact. There had been a time when casual touch was so normal a part of his day that he'd never thought twice about it. Brushing fingers with a waitress, bumping shoulders in a crowd, laying his hand on a woman's arm or putting his arm around her shoulders. Simple, everyday stuff. Now it seemed momentous. It made him crave so much, to lean in closer, to run away faster, that it took all his control to do nothing. To act as if it were natural.

"You remember Jessy, the redhead? She lives up there." Carly gestured toward the upper floors of the building they passed. "It's the coolest apartment in town. The ceilings are twelve feet high, and the floors are wood that has this wonderful old glow. The walls are plaster and lath, and the moldings are really elaborate. If Jeff and I hadn't been planning to start a family—"

As she broke off, Dane felt the tension in her own muscles. The only response that came to mind was *Good thing it didn't happen so you're not a single mother and your baby doesn't have to grow up without a father.* But he couldn't say that out loud. She loved Jeff a lot, probably enough to regret that there wasn't a little Jeff running around and giving her purpose.

A bell jingled over the door of the restaurant as she pulled it open. "Some things just weren't meant to be," she finished softly, then smiled at him, her eyes brightening. "Doesn't that smell good?"

"It does," he agreed. Coffee, cinnamon, apples, and something savory. Meat loaf, he thought, and his stomach reminded him that lunch had been a peanut butter sandwich more than six hours ago.

She slid her arm free to make her way through the narrow spaces between tables and booths. When she reached an empty booth against the easternmost wall, she glanced at him, brows raised, then, at his nod, took off her jacket and shivered violently. "Nothing like warmth to remind you how cold it is."

"You went to college in Colorado. This should be a lovely spring evening to you." He sat down and stretched his left leg, rubbing it gingerly, hopefully not too notice-ably.

"I'm a warm-weather girl. My idea of heaven is lots of sunshine, sand, blue-green ocean, a book and something cold to drink."

"A margarita?"

"No margaritas here," the waitress said as she set two menus and napkin-wrapped silverware on the table. "You have to go down the street to Buddy Watson's place for that. But we do have the best coffee in town, no matter what that little froufrou place outside the post gates claims."

"I'd like coffee," Carly said, picking up her menu.

"Make it two." Dane didn't bother with his own menu. A chalkboard on the wall above them listed the evening's specials: meat loaf with mashed potatoes and gravy and pot roast with all the trimmings.

"Dessert or dinner?"

"I'm having meat loaf. I haven't had that in a long time."

"Sheesh, no meat loaf, no pizza…where have you been all this time?"

"Um, in the desert?" Heat rose inside him at the delib-erate lie, but he didn't feel guilty enough to stop it. "In Afghanistan?"

"Oh, right. Sorry. I think I'll have the pot roast." She put the menu down, then settled more comfortably. "Truth is, I don't like margaritas very much. It just seems the right drink to order in a Mexican restaurant. After we became regulars at Three Amigos, they expected us to get them, and then we began calling ourselves the Tuesday Night Margarita Club, and the bartender started making special recipes for us, and..." She shrugged, her auburn hair swinging in its ponytail. "That's why I buy a margarita every week, take a few drinks and leave the rest on the table."

"What a waste of good tequila."

"I know. Jeff had a two-drink limit when we went out together. Mind you, that was *ordering* two drinks. I'd usually get one and take a few sips, then he would finish it. But because he didn't order it, it didn't count toward his limit."

"My ex-wife had a two-drink *minimum*. She liked to party. She's remarried now, has three kids and is pregnant with the fourth, so I'm guessing the drinking days are in the past."

Carly smiled, a full, lush action that made her practically glow. "Ah, you keep up with her."

His own grimace was heavy as her smile seemed light. "Talking to my mother is like watching the national news. You don't want to know what's going on in Congress, but they tell you anyway. You'd think Sheryl was her daughter instead of her ex-daughter-in-law."

"Does that bother you?" She tilted her head to one side, her gaze level on his face, focused on him, giving him the sense that she'd shut out everyone else in the place.

It was a feeling he could grow used to.

He cleared his throat and his mind at the same time before answering her question. "Less every day." It was true, too. Despite Anna Mae's insistence on talking about her, Sheryl was in the past. He would probably never see her again, and if he did, it wouldn't mean anything. They'd had their time together; it was over.

"And what about you? Do you have your alcohol limit?"

He watched as the waitress returned with two cups, a pot of coffee and a dish of individual creamers. "I like a cold beer now and then." In combat zones, liquor had been hard to get, and in the hospitals, he'd had a lot more to worry about than alcohol, to say nothing of all the medications he'd been taking that could interact badly with it.

"Everything in moderation," she remarked.

The words brought memories rushing back, of his father, always easygoing, never settling for less but never asking too much, either. "My dad used to say that."

"Oh, not my parents. They believe in giving everything you do one hundred ten percent—though every one of them would argue that that statement is illogical because a person's maximum capacity is one hundred percent, period. You can't give more than exists." She fingered her napkin a moment before meeting his gaze again, her expression sheepish. "They see things from a totally different logical, pragmatic point of view."

"Geniuses are a different species."

She grinned. "Absolutely."

The conversation broke off for a moment while the waitress took their orders. The restaurant was filling up, the dining room getting noisier. Dane glanced around, noting no familiar faces, not expecting any, either. He'd never had trouble making buddies—an excellent thing since the Army had kept him moving every few years—but since Landstuhl, the hospital in Germany he'd been medevaced to from Kunar Province, he'd had little interest in friends, new or old. Justin, at rehab, was an exception. He was like an overgrown puppy, eager and friendly and impossible to push away without feeling like you'd kicked that puppy.

But Dane wasn't in a place yet where he could be much of a buddy. Wasn't sure he cared enough to want friends. Wasn't sure his future would be worth sharing with anyone.

And yet here he was with Carly. Wasn't she a friend?

Yeah, sure, that was what he'd call it. Though he'd had enough female friends over the years to know that friendship was the least he wanted from this one. But he didn't have a clue whether she was interested in anything more. Her husband hadn't been dead that long. She clearly was still in love with him. She hadn't given any hint she was ready to move on, other than having pizza with him Thursday night. And going out with him today. Suggesting dinner tonight.

All as applicable to friendship as dating.

She knew more about him than anyone else in the state of Oklahoma, but she didn't know he was lying to her with his silence every time they were together. She didn't know that when he should be thanking God every day that he'd come home at all, he was bitter and ashamed that he'd literally left part of himself behind. She didn't know how angry he was, how cheated he felt, how hopeless his future seemed if he didn't learn to deal with his past.

And with nothing more than that to offer, friendship of a sort was the best he could hope for with Carly.

He smiled thinly before easing his gaze back to her. For a long time, he hadn't been able to muster the least bit of hope. Now he'd found some, buried somewhere deep inside him.

It was a start.

Chapter Six

"Dogs or cats?"

Carly pushed a chunk of carrot around her nearly empty bowl, pretending to consider the question, before saying, "Dogs. You?"

"When I was a kid, Mom had a giant orange cat, this big constantly shedding fur ball with beady eyes and a wicked swipe. He always behaved when she was in the room, but when she wasn't..." Dane shook his head. "I've got more scars than I can count from that monster, and I could never do anything about it, or she would have freaked out, so definitely dogs."

She laughed. They'd spent the whole meal trading forced-choice questions. He preferred Coke over Pepsi, hot over cold, and adventure vacations over beach-lazing. He liked his books in paper, his music with an edge, coleslaw on his hot dogs, and mustard-based barbecue sauce over slow-roasted beef.

As if everybody in the universe didn't know "barbecue" meant tomato-based sauce on pork.

"Potato salad," he said. "Chunky or creamy?"

Before Carly could open her mouth, the answer came from above. "Oh, definitely creamy," Jessy drawled, appearing at the end of their table. She wore sweatpants in grungy gray and a tank top fitted so snugly that the only thing left to the imagination was the exact shade of her skin beneath the fabric.

As they turned their gazes her way, she zipped her sweat jacket halfway up before sliding onto the bench beside Carly. "I didn't expect to see you here."

Carly squirmed inside at her friend's probing gaze, but pulled off a pretty good shrug, she thought. "We were downtown anyway, so we decided to stop for dinner." When she continued to stare, Carly gestured across the table. "Dane, you remember Jessy?"

Jessy turned that way, too, leaning across to offer her hand. "Of course he does, doll. No one forgets Jessy Lawrence. And Jessy never forgets a handsome caveman."

His smile seemed forced to Carly, though she doubted Jessy noticed. He shook hands with her, didn't pull away when she held on a tad longer than necessary, and said a quiet hello. Carly would have assured him that Jessy didn't bite, but she didn't know for sure it was true. The girl was bold.

But she was also a solid friend. She flirted with everyone and carried through with no one.

And it wasn't as if this was a date she was interrupting. Hanging out was just hanging out. It didn't imply any interest beyond the general, fun kind. He hadn't suggested dinner; she had. When he took her home, he might walk to the door with her. He might even go inside for a cup of coffee or something. But he wouldn't kiss her good night because this wasn't a date.

But if he did... She hadn't been kissed by a man in so very long.

"—live upstairs and one building over," Jessy was saying when Carly tuned back in. "Between Serena's and all the other restaurants around here, I don't have to ever cook if I don't want to." She elbowed Carly. "And I generally don't want to, do I?"

"She lives on fast food and takeout," Carly agreed.

"So do you, darlin'." To Dane, Jessy said, "It's so nice seeing her outside of The Three Amigos. Before you came along, the margarita club was her only social life. We're fun, trust me, but we are not her type."

Carly's cheeks flushed, and she pinched Jessy under the table, but her friend's grin didn't waver. Bumping her foot didn't bring a response, either. Then she looked under the table. "You're wearing flip-flops!"

Jessy shrugged. "I just finished treating myself to a pedicure. You can't expect me to screw that up by putting shoes on. Besides, I was only outside for five seconds."

A voice called from across the room, and Jessy flowed to her feet in one fluid motion. "That's my food. An Angus burger, extra-crispy fries, a piece of pecan pie with vanilla ice cream, and a slice of carrot cake. Yum."

"I hope your heart doesn't explode," Carly said drily.

Jessy's only response was a wave over her head as she walked off.

"Where does she put it all?"

Carly watched her a moment before shifting her gaze to Dane. His smile was gone, but so was the tension that had made him look so stiff. "She eats, and I put on weight. It's one of the mysteries of the universe."

His smile slowly reappeared. "You know, most guys like curves."

Sweet, innocent pleasure flooded through her. It wasn't just the smile or just the words, but the combination made her feel... She didn't even know what to call it. Appreciated? Reassured? Flattered?

Rather than find the right word, she feigned a forlorn look. "Not fashion-designing guys. Or Hollywood guys. Or modeling guys."

"Maybe not, but *real* guys do."

"Thanks. I'll keep telling myself that next time I go shopping and have to go up a size."

He made a dismissive gesture, then wrapped his hands around his coffee cup. "What's Jessy's story?"

"Sadly, nothing you haven't heard before. She and Aaron got married as soon as he graduated from Basic. He did a tour in Iraq, survived several times when he shouldn't have and came home without a scratch. He was only two weeks from the end of a twelve-month rotation in Afghanistan when he was killed by a sniper."

"Too bad." He stared into his coffee. "What about Jeff?"

"Helicopter crash. Twenty-million dollars or more invested in equipment, weapons, and the training of the crew and troops onboard, and they were brought down by a single rocket-propelled grenade."

"Sometimes that's the way it goes," Dane said softly.

"Such loss. Such heartbreak." But—*sorry, Jeff*—she didn't want to think about loss and heartbreak right now. "Do you know it's supposed to snow tonight?"

He shook his head. "I don't watch the news much."

"An inch or more by morning, then probably in the seventies again on Monday. They say you can't be sure winter's gone here until the last part of April. *Then* I can start working in the yard."

"You like that, huh? My grandmother planted a garden big enough for five families. I can't tell you how many times I've cursed every single weed to ever rise through the Texas soil. I got blistered, sunburned, covered with gnat and mosquito bites and had more than a few run-ins with snakes."

"Aw, and you didn't even get hazard pay for it." It was easy to imagine him as a little boy, in overalls with a straw hat and barefooted, skin turned brown by the summer sun and always on the lookout for an escape from weed duty. Granted, overalls and straw hats were more likely from his father's generation; for Dane, it had probably been a T-shirt, shorts, and disreputable sneakers.

Regardless of how he might have dressed, she liked the idea of him working, however unwillingly, at his grandmother's behest.

"No hazard pay," he agreed, "but there were rewards. The first ripe tomato of the season, still warm from the sun, with a little salt to sweeten it. Grandma's new potatoes and green beans and her zucchini bread and homemade bread-and-butter pickles."

There was an ease to his expression that didn't show up often, but she was happy to see it. For a man who'd been through years of combat, life wasn't as simple as it had been for that young weed-hating boy, but as long as he could remember the simpler times, he was all right. She believed that.

With a sigh that was more wistful than not, she nodded toward the front. "There's a line at the door of people wanting our table. We should probably go."

"And without even a piece of pie."

She grinned as she shrugged into her jacket. "We can get it from Miss Patsy. She's the cashier and Serena's grandmother."

They both reached for the check at the same time, their knuckles bumping. Carly's fingertips were curled over one end. Dane held the other similarly. She tugged, but there was no give. "You paid for the pizza the other night."

"I invited you out today."

"I offered to buy you a cup of coffee."

"But I didn't accept."

"Crossing the threshold into the restaurant and then ordering implies acceptance." Faking a stumble, she grabbed for him with her other hand, then scooped up the bill when he released it to catch her. Swinging the strap of her purse over one shoulder, she gave him a broad grin before heading for the counter, circling around tables to avoid the family making a beeline for their booth.

"Can you add a couple of to-go desserts to the check, Miss Patsy? One pecan pie and..."

"Coconut cream pie."

Carly loved coconut cream pie, and the meringues here rose six inches above the cream in towering peaks. She persuaded herself the pecan pie, so much smaller in volume, was also lower in calories, though sadly that didn't make it true.

After swiping her debit card, then signing, she picked up the smaller foam carton Miss Patsy had retrieved from the counter, and they squeezed their way past patient diners huddled inside the door. As soon as she stepped outside and the wind rushing east down Main Street caught her with a faceful of fat snowflakes, she shuddered.

The snow was starting to stick to the ground. Thankfully, there was no ice under it. Put ice on the streets, and she'd be missing in action everywhere from church to school to the margarita club until it cleared.

When they reached the corner curb, Dane reached for her free hand to steady her on the slushy snow between them and the truck. A tiny smile curved her mouth. Her fingers were safe and warm inside Dane's hand. It felt natural, when nothing between a man and a woman had been natural for her in a long time.

"Did you learn to ski while you were in Colorado?"

"Oh, no. Racing down a slick hill on sticks in the cold is *not* my idea of fun. What about you? Did you learn in Italy when you were with the Hundred Seventy-Third?"

"I did. So close to the Alps, how could I not? I was like an elephant on ice skates. I tried a half dozen times and took harder falls than the worst parachute landings I'd ever had. I decided I would stick with hiking the lower mountains in the summer, when I had relatively stable footing." He walked around to the passenger side and opened the door for her, his hand at her elbow steadying her on the slick running board.

The stiff leather of the seat made her shiver, the chill seeping through her jacket and pants. She set her pie on the console, then pressed her hands together between her knees. She imagined she could feel the warmth from Dane's grip seeping slowly from one hand to the other.

In five minutes, eight tops, they would be at her house.

A small sensation fluttered in her stomach. Her living room was a mess, but there was room to sit on the couch and eat dessert. Would asking him in seem pushy? After all, when he'd invited her to do something, he probably hadn't intended to spend the entire afternoon and most of the evening with her. He might already have plans to meet his buddies at one of Tallgrass's numerous bars or clubs. He could have a date. He could be tired of her.

She couldn't think of anything to say as they drove slowly down Main to the cross street nearest her house. The snow was beautiful in the headlights, thick wet flakes that made the best snowballs and snowmen. She'd hardly blinked, it seemed, and they were turning onto Cimarron Street. Her house in the middle of the block was brightly lit by the lamp she'd left burning and the blinds she'd forgotten to close. It was a pretty place, not just a house but a home.

For one.

Dane turned into the driveway, and for a moment they both sat motionless and quiet. Then, abruptly, he shut off the engine and opened the door. "I'll walk you to the door."

Go ahead and say it, Carly. "You want to come in for some coffee to go with that pie?" But the chill from the open door sapped her confidence. She couldn't get the words out. Instead, with a tight smile, she picked up her own pie and slid from the truck, digging in her bag for her keys as she met him in the headlights.

She climbed the steps and went to the door, sliding the key in the lock.

Dane stopped at the edge of the top step. "Thanks. For dinner. Dessert. Your company."

"You're welcome."

What was the protocol these days for kisses? Second date, third, fourth? Or, rather, meeting, since this wasn't really a date. She'd known once, but that was a long time ago, and life had changed. Societal norms had changed.

But it turned out she didn't need to know the protocol, because instead of moving toward her, Dane smiled politely. "I'll see you."

Realizing he was waiting for her to move, she opened the door, went inside and closed it. After turning the lock, she moved the few feet to the blinds and, as she twisted them shut, watched him walk to his truck.

"Yeah," she whispered to the empty house. "I'll see you."

And they weren't just empty words. For the first time in ages, she was anticipating something other than the margarita club's adventures. Something personal. Something with potential.

One thing she had in common with her family: she *loved* potential.

The snow stopped falling and started melting soon after the sun rose. Carly lay in bed, listening to the drips from the eaves. The lazy part of her wouldn't have minded being snowed in this morning, puttering around in her pajamas and fuzzy house shoes until she got energetic enough to put on clothes and go shopping for paint.

But there wasn't much point in trying when she knew Therese would be calling soon, offering to pick her up for church. Therese knew how much she dreaded driving on slick streets. Having grown up in Montana, her friend had no such qualms. She considered it a challenge: Point the car where she wanted to go, stomp down on the gas, and hold on for the ride.

Besides, even if Carly managed to convince Therese she was perfectly all right, just being a bit lazy, what would she do all morning? Cry over Jeff? Sigh over Dane?

Sliding her feet into her slippers, she pulled on an old sweat jacket of Jeff's that she used for a robe, then shuffled to the kitchen for a cup of coffee and the last bite of pecan pie. It wasn't enough to replace breakfast, so she glanced through the pantry before choosing—surprise—oatmeal, setting the water to boil while the coffee brewed.

She'd gotten little more than a sip of hazelnut-flavored coffee when her cell phone rang. Too early for Therese, so maybe...

It was embarrassingly juvenile how quickly her hopes could get raised.

"Hey, sweetheart, it's Mom. I didn't wake you, did I?"

A person could be forgiven, after a greeting like that, for thinking the caller was actually her mother. It wasn't. For one thing, her mother made personal calls only between eight and nine p.m. on Mondays and Wednesdays. Second, her mother believed everyone should arise at the break of dawn, as she did. Third, the only time her mother had ever used the words *sweet* and *heart* together were in the lab when she'd been given a prime human heart to study.

"No. I'm up," she told Jeff's mother, Mia. Bracing the phone between her ear and shoulder, she took both the mug and bowl into the living room, where the couch still occupied the middle of the room. "Just having breakfast."

"You know, they have these other breakfast foods called 'bacon and eggs' and 'pancakes with maple syrup.' You should try them sometime. You might never go back to bland, tasteless oatmeal."

"I might never go back to a regular-size clothing store again, either."

"Oh, sweetheart, you're beautiful the way you are."

"Thank you, Mama Mia, perfect size two. How's Pop?"

"He's fine."

"And you?"

"Oh, you know that old song. 'Some days are diamonds. Some days are stone.'"

Carly didn't know the song, but she could embrace the sentiment.

"Juanita announced at book club yesterday that her daughter's expecting her third child this summer. That'll make eight grandkids for the old hag, and it just made me feel a little blue."

"I'm sorry, Mia." Carly regretted she and Jeff hadn't tossed the birth control right after she'd tossed the bride's bouquet, but he'd been heading off to Basic, and she'd still had a year of school left. They hadn't been ready to become parents.

Now they could never be parents and Mia and Pop could never be grandparents.

Mia laughed shakily. "Aw, honey, I'm sorry I even brought it up. It's just that Juanita has always gotten on my last nerve, and Phil's out of town until tonight. He invited me to go along, but *seriously*? Three days in a cramped boat fishing, eating what we catch, sleeping in tents, and not bathing? Uh-uh. This girl is way too smart for that. So what's new with you?"

The image of Dane flashed into Carly's mind, and she deliberately pushed it right back out. Mia had assured her she wouldn't be alone forever, that she would find someone else not to replace Jeff but to love just as well. She had promised Carly and her second prince would live long and happily, having pretty little girls and handsome little boys.

But there was a huge difference between a future possibility and *Mia, I've met someone.*

"I'm going to paint the living room."

"Good for you. I hope it's something wild and wonderful. We should be surrounded by bright cheerful colors."

"It is. Burnt orange walls and cream trim."

"Yum, sounds like the holidays. Send me pictures when you're done." A clock chimed in the background, and Mia sighed. "Well, darlin', I'd better get ready for church. Imagine yourself getting a big hug from all of us Lowrys. Love you, girl."

"Love you, too." Carly set the phone down, then wrapped her fingers around the insulated coffee mug. At the moment, she did feel comfortingly hugged. Then she wondered again how in the world she would tell Mia about Dane.

"First," she announced as she stood up, "there's got to be something about Dane to justify telling. A real date? A hug, a kiss, a commitment? Maybe even sex."

Sex. It had been so long. She and Jeff had spent as much as possible of their last few days together, making love, sometimes laughing, sometimes crying. She'd been all out of tears when she'd gone to the post with him that last morning. The unit had loaded up on the buses that took them to Tinker Air Force Base in Oklahoma City for the flight out, then she'd gone to work, pretending that her heart wasn't breaking.

Since then...she had plenty of memories to keep her warm.

And maybe Mama Mia was right. Maybe this thing with Dane would continue to develop. Maybe he would be the man to join Jeff in her heart.

Or maybe he was just the catalyst that would propel her toward that man.

She let herself imagine a future where she wasn't lonely and lost, only to be brought back to the present by the trill of the cell phone. "Margaritaville." "Morning, Therese."

"It's beautiful, isn't it?"

Carly recalled the snow cover she'd seen from the kitchen window while the coffee brewed and shuddered. "I'd rather have sunshine and a warm beach, but it could be worse."

"You're a wuss, Carly Lowry. We'll be by to pick you up in forty minutes. Don't make me wait in the van with two unhappy kids one minute longer than necessary."

Carly could practically see her friend shaking her finger in warning. While science had ruled in the Anderson household, there had never been a time in Therese's life that she didn't attend church. Carly hadn't begun going herself until she'd married Jeff, and neither Abby nor Jacob had gone until Therese had come into their lives. Carly wasn't sure what the two kids got out of it, if anything, unless the tenets of Christianity could be absorbed by osmosis, but she admired Therese for not backing down on her beliefs, no matter how difficult the kids could be.

"I'll be ready. Be careful."

"I do my best."

"That's all any of us can do, isn't it?" Without waiting for a response, she said, "I'll be waiting with my boots on."

"Good. And you can have dinner with us after church and fill me in on your weekend. See you." The last dozen words had a singsong quality.

Uh-oh. Sounded like Jessy had talked. The pint-size tattletale. Carly had better make sure to protect more than just her feet.

Therese loved the peace she felt every time she stepped inside the sanctuary—any sanctuary. It reminded her that she was never alone, that God was always there to help her and to shoulder her burdens when she couldn't. Sometimes, she thought with a sidelong glance at Abby and Jacob, He seemed to think she was stronger than she really was. That was one place she wouldn't mind a little bit more of the shouldering and a little less of the being there.

Then, as the kids split to go sit with their respective friends, she murmured a silent apology. *Don't mind me, God. It's just been a long week.*

Carly slipped into their usual pew, about a third from the rear. Therese took off her coat, but left her scarf and gloves on. The large room was rarely completely warm in winter, but she wouldn't trade its soaring ceiling and high-set stained-glass windows for anything.

"How are the kids?" Carly leaned over and whispered in Therese's ear.

Therese smiled at a neighbor three rows up. "Abby caught Jacob snooping in her room last night. She still hates me, but now she hates him, too."

"Snooping for what?"

"Batteries, he says, and I actually believe him. If his electronics went dead, God forbid, he'd have to check into the real world for a while. Of course, he could have asked me for them, but that would have meant coming downstairs and actually talking to me."

"Do you think it would be easier if they were really your children?" Carly asked, then quickly went on, "Not because they would be of your blood, but because you would have grown up with them. You would have shared their entire history, from birth to now."

"It must be. Otherwise, parents raising their own kids would be about to plunge off the deep end." She nodded toward a family across the aisle and closer to the front. "The McAfees would have long since been committed somewhere." Burt and Joyce McAfee sat together, with their six children, ages eleven to nineteen, filling the row beside them.

The kids were neatly dressed, well behaved. The older ones helped the younger ones with their Bible study, and they participated in everything as a family. Rumor had it that they actually preferred each other's company over others'.

Therese couldn't imagine the instance when Jacob would choose her over his games or Abby over anyone else in the universe.

Sullen. That was about the best behavior she ever saw

from them. And not just the typical teenager sullenness that would pass as they matured, but the traumatic-life-damaged-forever kind.

Please, God, help me with them.

After a moment's reflection, she changed that. *Help me help them.*

As the pastor started the service by greeting everyone, she considered exactly what helping Abby and Jacob meant. She'd prayed for everything to work out when they'd come to live with her and Paul. She'd prayed that they would manage through his deployments. She'd prayed for the patience to love them and the strength to not dump their dinner plates over their heads when they complained yet again about her. She'd prayed a thousand times for God to help them deal with Paul's death, and a time or two, she'd even prayed for Catherine to take them back.

She'd felt oh so guilty for those few prayers, imagining the disappointment in Paul's eyes as he gazed down at her from God's side. But all she'd really been asking for was the best for the kids. Catherine was their mother, after all. Any kids who'd suffered such a devastating loss should be with the mother they loved, not the stepmother they resented.

God answers all prayers, so the cliché went, *but sometimes the answer is no.*

Did that mean He thought the children were better off with her? Did He have a plan for the three of them? Would they ever love her? Would she ever fully love them?

Though she was trying her hardest, it shamed her to admit that what she mostly felt for them was sympathy, along with a connection to Paul. They were young, they were hurting, and they were his kids. She and Paul had never had their own child, but in this way, at least she still had a part of him.

Sunday school, the hymns, the sermon, and the prayers passed in a haze. When she realized Carly was putting on her coat, she gave herself a shake and stood, looking around for the kids. Jacob stood at the back of the sanctuary, listening to the youngest McAfee talk animatedly, and Abby was visible in the vestibule beyond, hands in her pockets, shoulders slumped, looking bored beyond tears while the two girls with her texted on their cell phones.

Paul's children. She'd seen glimpses of the people they really were when he was alive—Jacob's enthusiasm for sports and all things electronic, Abby's wicked sense of humor, their fierce loyalty, the way they blindly trusted their father and loved their mother. If Therese wasn't in their lives, they'd be happy, normal kids.

But if she wasn't there, who would be?

Taking hold of Therese's arm, Carly turned her, then scooted her out of the row and into the aisle. There she hooked her arm through Therese's. "We're not given more than we can bear," she murmured.

"I know a few people who would disagree with that." Sometimes for most, and most times for some, life did seem unbearable. She and Carly had both gone through times they were certain they couldn't survive. How many had given in to grief, anguish, and despair?

She hadn't. She might teeter on the edge sometimes, but she would be strong. Life had left her with no choice.

They shook hands with the pastor, greeted other members, and finally made their way out the double doors into a bright, sunny morning. It was still cold, damp drifting on the air, but the snow was rapidly melting, showing greening grass underneath, dripping from the blossoms on the redbud trees that dotted the sidewalk to the parking lot.

"What about dinner?" she asked as she buckled her seatbelt.

"Anywhere," Jacob mumbled.

"I'm not hungry." That came from Abby with a toss of her blond head.

"What about you, Carly?"

Her friend shook her head. "You know me. I can eat anything."

"One of these days I'm going to take you to one of the sushi restaurants in Tulsa and make you prove it." She was well aware of Carly's aversion to eating anything that lived in the ocean. *"Comes from having a marine biologist for an uncle,"* Carly had said. *"I learned way too much about those suckers to even think of eating them."*

As she maneuvered out of the parking space, Therese feigned a put-upon sigh. "Then I guess it's up to me to choose. How about Zeke's?" The restaurant on the west side of town served a buffet with more salads, side dishes, and desserts than their little group could do justice to. It offered a 10 percent discount to military families, and best of all in the kids' eyes, the tables were small enough to justify splitting into pairs. No eating dinner with TheB*tch.

Three days later, the idea that Abby called her that still disheartened Therese.

She and Carly chatted about nothing as they followed half the church, it seemed, to Zeke's. When they'd circled the parking lot twice before finding a space, Abby heaved a sigh. "You know you have to get here before the church people to avoid the crowd."

"We *are* the church people." Carly's tone was mild, a restraint that Therese appreciated. All the margarita club showed the kids more patience than they deserved at times—and most of them believed that Therese did, too. Not being parents themselves, they just didn't quite understand the situation.

They crossed the lot to the door, the kids trailing behind, and joined the line to pay and gather their dishes before finding tables in the same section, but not too close to deny privacy.

"So many choices," Carly joked as they approached the salad bar. "If I were a good person, I'd stop right here and ignore everything else. But since I'm not, I'm heading straight to the fried meats and the side dishes. See you back at the table."

Therese snorted, then called out before she got more than a few steps away. "From what I understand, Dane Clark seems to think you're just about perfect."

Carly blushed deep pink and, for a moment, looked so young and vulnerable that Therese's heart ached for her. "He does seem...interested."

"Dinner twice in three nights? Make that *real* interested." She staved off Carly's automatic *but* with a shake of her head. "Don't worry. Don't overthink it. Just be happy. I'm happy for you."

And she was. Happy and envious and oh so hopeful.

Chapter Seven

Dane needed only one guess to know who was knocking at his door on Sunday afternoon: the only person who ever visited him at home, Justin. Dane was dressed in sweatpants and a T-shirt and had left his prosthesis in the bedroom, relying instead on crutches to get around. The empty leg of his sweatpants flapped as he opened the door, then headed for the couch.

"Heads up." Justin tossed a paper bag from the fast-food restaurant on post, then set his own bag down on the coffee table.

"What do you want to drink?" Dane asked.

"Water."

Justin returned from the kitchen with two bottles, handed one over, then settled at the other end of the sofa. He leaned his crutches against the sofa arm and, without fail, they slid to the floor in a clatter. "The game's on NBC."

Dane didn't ask what game—just used the remote to

change channels. Though he didn't care about basketball, for the closest thing to a friend he had here and who had brought food, he could sit through a game.

The cheeseburger was big and messy, the fries still warm. He used to grill a great burger, back when hanging around a grill with cold beers, sizzling beef, and rowdy friends had been a regular part of his life. Given the changes since then, fast food was a decent substitute.

Nothing remained but the wrappers and a few burned ends of French fries when Justin gave him a sidelong look. "Bailey said you were out with Carly last night."

Dane fixed his gaze on the TV as if the sport were football and the venue the Super Bowl. "Bailey?"

"Evan Bailey. Skinny guy, red hair, no arms from the elbows down?"

An image of the kid formed in Dane's mind. He was nineteen, maybe twenty, and was learning to use top-of-the-line prosthetic hands as if they were his own. One thing you had to give the Army credit for, when their people got blown apart, they didn't skimp on artificial limbs. Dane's leg was one of the best money could buy.

"Oh yeah, him. Is he a friend of yours?"

"We went through Basic together. He's dating the teacher's aide. Carly's aide. None of which is relevant. Were you out with her last night?"

Carly's aide. Dane vaguely remembered some other women with the class on Tuesday, but once he'd recognized Carly, the rest had pretty much disappeared.

He shifted, sliding low on his spine and propping his feet—foot—on the coffee table. Funny how it felt as if both of them were there.

Funny, too, how he'd rather think about almost anything than talk about his time with Carly. It hadn't been a date. Dates were dinner, a movie, a concert, whatever. Not an impulsive Saturday afternoon spent wandering through antique stores.

Though he couldn't remember having a better time at a dinner, movie, or concert.

Justin crowed. "So it *is* true. I figured Bailey was mistaken. I mean, other than the times she brings the kids to visit us, I've never heard of her ever seeing another guy. Not to say that no one's tried. So, geez, you only met her—what? A week ago? And you've already gone out with her?"

"It wasn't a date. We were downtown. Shopping. She suggested coffee, and we had dinner instead."

"Don't try to rationalize it, man. You were out together. Doesn't matter what you were doing. So...She's okay with...?"

Dane felt the weight of Justin's gaze leave him to return to the television. He was more comfortable staring at the TV himself, though instead of the game, an overly loud commercial touting the merits of one deodorant over its competitors aired. It was followed by a stupid car commercial—press conferences for average people to tell how much they liked their cars? really?—then a beer ad featuring beautiful women and men in possession of all their limbs.

"She doesn't know," he said at last. "She thinks I just stopped by Tuesday to see you."

"But you're gonna tell her, right? If you keep seeing her, she's gonna find out sometime. I mean, you can't *do it* with your pants on."

Another reason it hadn't been a date, Dane thought

morosely. Dates ended with a kiss good night that eventually led to a whole lot more, and Justin was right. You
couldn't get far along the path of *more* without ditching
the clothes.

The dread of that was enough to drown out any anticipation he had about having sex again after so many
months' abstinence.

"Yeah," he said with a sigh. "No. I don't know."

"What do you mean, you don't know?"

"You have a girlfriend when that happened?" Dane gestured to Justin's legs. Covered by denim, they appeared
perfectly normal, one resting on the coffee table, the other
knee bent, foot on the floor. Remove the jeans, though, and
the scars, the deformities, would be clearly visible.

"Yeah. I did." Justin scowled, an expression he normally reserved for therapy and the therapists who pushed
him.

"What happened?"

"She didn't want to be in it for the long haul. After
months, they still didn't know if I was gonna walk again.
They couldn't even say for sure they wouldn't have to
amputate." Justin shrugged. "She was twenty. In college.
She had better things to do than deal with this."

Making excuses for her, when he was only a year or
two older and also had better things to do than rehabbing
an injury that had almost killed him.

Maybe Carly wasn't any different. Maybe she wasn't
a long-haul sort of woman. Maybe she'd lose interest
before sex became a possibility—an issue. Maybe *he*
would.

Yeah. And maybe his leg would regenerate overnight.
Maybe he'd grow a new foot in time for Easter.

Justin unknowingly countered his thought. "But Carly's not like that. She's around guys like us and worse every week. It doesn't bother her."

"Being around it a few hours a week is a whole different thing from living with it." From committing to it.

"Look," Justin went on, determined to make his point. "We both know guys whose wives or girlfriends were just happy to have them come back alive. Every woman's different. And it's got to be easier to go into it knowing that it's happened than having it happen to someone you're already with. Sarah knew me before. We'd dated since we were sixteen. We jogged together, we danced together, we surfed together. Carly didn't know you before you lost your leg, so it won't matter. You should tell her."

Dane shifted again, grimly acknowledging that the discomfort in his joints had little to do with position and everything with the conversation. "We just had dinner. That's all."

"You should still tell her."

He would. Maybe. If things went that far. If it became necessary. If he ever dealt with it enough himself that he could trust someone else to deal with it, too.

Those were some awfully big *if*s.

"I won't say anything to her," Justin said, a tone of finality in his voice that gave Dane hope he was dropping the subject. "But, man, you're gonna have to. Women don't like it when you hide stuff from them."

The kid was right. But in Dane's experience, they didn't like it more when a man was less than he should be. His mother could hardly bear to look at him. His ex-wife could hardly bear to ask about him. In the various hospitals, he'd seen the pity, the morbid curiosity, the shock.

Was it wrong to not want to risk that with the first woman he'd been attracted to in a very long time?

And what did it say about him that he was so self-conscious about the missing leg? Body-image issues were for teenage girls and insecure women—not battle-hardened soldiers. He knew of guys who'd suffered far worse: third-degree burns, leathery scarring disfiguring their faces, ears and noses burned off, right out where they couldn't hide it; blast injuries that blew off part of their heads, leaving doctors to not just rebuild their faces but the skulls themselves; guys who looked like they'd gone through hell and back.

And they were okay with it. They didn't retreat into a dark room. They didn't hide, and for the people who couldn't bear to look at them, so what? They were okay with themselves.

Dane wasn't as strong as they were. As confident. An artificial leg hadn't been part of his plans for his life, and he hated it. He hated the sleeve that protected his stump. He hated putting a shoe on a stupid fake leg. He hated fastening the leg on and taking it off. He was grateful to be alive, but he really, *really* wanted to be alive with his own two legs.

He really wanted to approach Carly, or any other woman, as a whole, intact, normal man. As he'd once been. As her husband had been.

As he rubbed the ache in his left thigh, he thought bleakly that maybe he should look forward to the therapy offered at the unit—not just the physical therapy, but also the shrinks. He wasn't making much headway on this acceptance crap by himself.

He still had a long way to go.

*   *   *

Carly was always the first one at Three Amigos on Tuesday nights, but this week she was even earlier than usual. She'd been unsettled today, not even sure why until the class had arrived at the Warrior Transition Unit and she'd found herself looking around for a particular face. That was when disappointment had settled over her with a weight that matched the dreary gray sky outside, and she'd realized she'd been hoping Dane would be there to visit Justin again.

She hadn't seen him since Saturday night. Hadn't talked to him. Hadn't done much of anything but think about him. She'd tried to casually ask Justin about him, but her young friend hadn't been in the mood to talk to anyone but Trista, and even with the shy little girl, he'd been unusually quiet.

Everyone had those days, she acknowledged as she sipped her margarita, then debated whether to distract herself by getting out her Kindle or the carefully printed book reports she'd brought to read.

She'd decided on the Kindle when a figure approaching the table called hello. Her responding smile faded as Fia limped to the chair across from her and slid in with a relieved sigh. "Are you still sore from the climbing at the park?"

"Oh, no." Fia tucked back a strand of dark brown hair, then shrugged out of her jacket. "I pulled something at work."

"Are you sure it's nothing more serious than that?"

A smile eased the lines around Fia's mouth and eyes. "I'm sure."

Carly's own relief washed through her. If anyone with

a nonmedical background would know, it was Fia. She worked as a personal trainer at a gym outside the main gate at Fort Murphy. She was fit, strong, and healthy and knew her body well.

"How many times have I told you?" Carly teased. "Exercise is dangerous. That's why I avoid it at all costs."

"You can do that because you've got good genes."

With a scoff, Carly corrected her. "Because I don't mind being fluffy." Though she did mind a little bit. When she'd gotten out of the shower Monday morning, she'd taken a long look at her naked body and sworn she could see where every one of those fourteen pounds had grabbed hold. She was softer, her muscle definition blurrier. Jeff would have laughed, called her womanly, and made love to her until every one of her insecurities disappeared.

But Jeff was gone, and he'd loved her in spite of all her flaws. Now it was someone else's opinion that concerned her. Maybe Dane's, maybe not, depending on how things went between them. If not his, then someone else's because she'd learned one thing in the time she'd spent with him: she didn't want to spend the rest of her life alone.

"If I don't work out religiously, within a month I'll need a 'wide load' sign for my butt." With a huge sigh, Fia stuffed a chip dripping with queso into her mouth.

She was joking, of course. Carly would bet food didn't know *how* to turn into fat on Fia's body.

"Wasn't the warm sunny weather Saturday wonderful? And the snow that followed?"

"You know I loved it," Carly replied drily.

"Yeah, me, too. I've never liked the cold, and this winter has kicked my butt."

"You grew up in Florida, didn't you? So why did you stay here after Scott died?"

Fia ate another chip with queso, then brushed her fingers on the napkin and sat back as if she were done. She was. She had the discipline to put the chips out of her mind, while Carly snacked on them before, during, and after the meal.

When Fia spoke, her voice was soft, her gaze distant. Sad. "Me and my mom, we were never close. And my dad...he just came around from time to time, mostly when he was drunk and broke. I doubt he'd even recognize me if he walked in right this minute. I didn't have any brothers or sisters, didn't really know any of my extended family, didn't stay in one place long enough to make many friends. There's really nothing to go back to."

Carly regretted asking the question. She'd known leaving Tallgrass had never been a consideration for Fia after she'd buried Scott in the national cemetery on the edge of town, but she hadn't known how lonely her friend's life had been back home. She whispered a silent apology for the whining she'd done about her own family. Brilliant and socially stunted they might be, but they loved her and they would always welcome her back.

Their usual waitress, Miriam, brought two drinks, setting one in front of Fia and the other beside her. "Jessy's on her way in," she explained with a grin and a wink.

Carly and Fia both watched the redhead breeze through the lobby and toward them. "For someone so tiny, she sure does make a lot of waves when she passes, doesn't she?" Fia murmured.

"She does." She was pretty, bold, sometimes brash, and always blunt spoken. Toss in the red hair and green eyes, and people just automatically paid attention to her—in this case, the hostess, the waitstaff, and all the customers. Especially the males.

Jessy just accepted it as her due. She wasn't smug or obnoxious about it. People noticed. It was part of her life. Carly rather envied her. She'd never been a troll, by any means, but she'd also never been the sort to make a man stop and take a second or third look.

Until Jeff. And maybe Dane.

Who hadn't called or anything since Saturday night.

Jessy claimed the seat next to Fia, raised one hand to stave off conversation, and took a gulp of her margarita, tilting her head back to let it roll down her throat, licking the salt from her lips, then sighing happily. "It's official. I have the crappiest job in the world. I hate it."

Fia grinned at the familiar complaint. "Why don't you come to the gym? They're always looking for people."

Jessy tilted her head as if weighing the option. "Working out with sweaty, half-naked men, a big plus. Having to actually work out? Uh-uh." She maintained her only workouts were the bedroom kind. For a woman who'd been celibate a long time, she liked sex a lot.

So do you.

Shushing the voice in her head, Carly reached for a chip. "We'll pretend we haven't heard this before and play along. What kind of job would you want?"

"One that pays a lot and doesn't require me to expend much energy or accept any responsibility."

"And what kind of qualifications do you have, Ms. Lawrence?"

"Um, I have the best phony smile in the business. I can be polite even when I'm imagining my hands wrapped around your throat. And I can say dirty words in three languages."

"I didn't know you were multilingual," Fia remarked.

Jessy's smile was sultry and sexy. "I'm not. I only know the dirty words."

"So you need a job where you get paid good money to be lazy, where you can smile and not be held responsible for anything you do or don't do. Gee, let's sign you up for the Senate race. I'll be your campaign manager, Fia can be your bodyguard, and Therese can wrangle all the babies you'll have to kiss." Carly laughed at the distaste that curled Jessy's mouth. Even pouting, she was beautiful.

"Thanks for making the bank job look attractive." Jessy drained her glass and glanced around for Miriam, signaling with a nod when she saw her. Turning back, she leaned forward and asked in a singsong voice, "How was dinner with Dane?"

Warmth flowed through Carly, and she let herself pretend the leather jacket was the problem, even when the coat hung on the back of her chair and the heat hadn't dissipated one bit. "It was Serena's Sweets. It was delicious, of course."

"I saw them," Jessy murmured to Fia. "They could have been eating cardboard and not noticed. I practically had to jump up and down just to get them to see me."

"You did not," Carly chided. Pushing aside the margarita, she took a long drink from the glass of ice water, going so far as to consider holding it to her face. She was much too young for hot flashes, wasn't she? Maybe she'd come down with some sort of quick-acting virus that caused her temperature to spike.

Yeah, you did. It's called the you've-got-a-crush-on-Dane-and-he's-ignoring-you syndrome.

Thankfully, she was saved from responding—to either Jessy or that smug little voice in her head—by more arrivals. Therese claimed the chair between her and Fia, while Marti, Ilena, and Lucy settled in the middle. Seven more of the semiregulars filled the last seats after dragging another table to make room.

"You're flushed, sweetie," Therese murmured as everyone took off their coats and stashed bags. "Do you feel okay?"

"I'm fine."

"How's the painting project?"

"I got the paint last night. If I can borrow Jacob for a while tomorrow evening to help me move the big stuff, I'll get started. I'd be happy to pay him."

"I'll bring him over. But no paying. He needs to learn to do favors for people because it's right, not because they offer him money."

Therese's jaw tightened fractionally, something Carly wouldn't have noticed if she didn't know her so well. More trouble with Abby, or just the never-ending stress of their household? If the tension on the ride home from church and dinner Sunday had been any indication, Carly didn't know how Therese stood it.

Spring break was on the horizon. Maybe the kids' mother or grandparents would bother to see them for a few days and give Therese a break.

Once everyone had their drinks, they toasted each other, then ordered their meals before getting down to serious business. They grilled Carly about her date. There were so many snorts when she protested "It wasn't a real date" that it sounded like the hog barn at the fair. Once they'd heard every detail, the subject changed to their various jobs, family issues, health questions, then cooking, quilting, knitting, and other hobbies. Carly even got advice on her paint project from the ones who'd done it themselves.

By the time they began to leave the restaurant in twos and threes, it was eight thirty and Carly's mood was better than it had been all day. She walked to the parking lot with Marti, laughing at a story about Marti's mother, recently divorced from husband number three and already on the hunt for the next one down in Palm Beach. It was a nice, outrageous tale that once again made Carly appreciate her own mother.

They were only a few yards from their cars when Marti caught her breath. "Oh, my," she murmured, then called over her shoulder. "Hey, guys, look who's here."

Carly was aware of her friends' voices, cheers, even a whistle, all sounding more like the hum of annoying insects than words, but her attention was focused on the vehicle a dozen feet ahead of her. More specifically, on the man leaning against it, hands in pockets, shoulders hunched against the chill. She said something appropriate, she thought, to Marti's "good-bye," gripped the purse strap over her shoulder with both hands, and closed the distance.

"I bet they're a lot of fun in a strip club," Dane said.

The image made her laugh, chasing off the butterflies fluttering in her stomach. "We've never been to one together, but I bet you're right."

"Is it too late?"

"For a strip club?"

He shrugged. "A cup of coffee. A glass of tea. A bit of dessert."

The warmth that had so discomfited her earlier returned, but this time it was nothing but pure pleasure. "They make a caramel-vanilla-apple thing here that's to die for."

He smiled. "I like caramel-vanilla-apple things."

He pushed away from the truck, and she pivoted to retrace her steps to the restaurant door. From somewhere behind them came a shrill whistle—Jessy or Fia, she was sure—which she acknowledged with a wave over her shoulder. There would be more talk, more teasing, from the group, but she didn't care.

This time with Dane would be worth all the talk and teasing in the world.

The hostess greeted them, then said to Carly with an overly pleased smile, "Ah, back again," as she led them to a small table in a dimly lit corner. "Enjoy."

The waitress, a slim, sturdy dark-haired woman, brought chips and salsa, along with two glasses of water. "Do you need a minute?" she asked Dane.

"Nah." He'd had a frozen dinner at home while trying to talk himself out of—or into—coming here tonight. "Just bring us the caramel-apple whatever and . . . iced tea?"

Carly nodded.

"All right, two iced teas and one Mexican apple pie with extra caramel sauce and vanilla ice cream. Oh, and *two* spoons." She winked at Carly—*winked*—before leaving them alone again.

"Does everyone in this place know you?"

She smiled tightly. "Pretty much."

They sat in silence for a moment, not the easy comfortable kind but the awkward we're-here-now-what kind. His left leg twinged, and he massaged it. In addition to all the daily aches, he'd found out it didn't react well to cold or damp. Or ironically enough, guilt. Right now he didn't care why it was hurting.

The waitress brought their drinks, and Carly thanked her by name. Like him, she was the type to learn a regular waiter's or waitress's name. Sheryl had always been content to wave or settle for "Hey."

"There were more of you tonight," he said at last.

Carly's smile looked just a little desperate with relief. "Yeah, sometimes we manage to fill that whole section. Only the seven of us at the cave come every week, barring illness or vacation, but there are between fifteen and twenty of us in all."

"Wow."

"Not a good thing to be impressed by, is it?" She emptied a packet of sweetener into her glass, then stirred it a little too long. "How is your week going?"

"Same stuff as always." The voice in his head, sounding remarkably like Justin, mocked the lie. Nothing had been the same in the last months. The blast, the medevac from Afghanistan to Germany to the U.S., surgery after surgery, infection after infection, rehabbing—he hadn't been a soldier in all that time, hadn't had any soldierly duties. He still wore a uniform, followed orders, and called officers "ma'am" and "sir," but the truth was, he was just a patient.

You should tell her.

Yeah, wouldn't that be a wonderful evening? *Here's*

your tea, have a bite of pie, and oh, by the way, did I re-member to tell you I got my leg blown off in Afghanistan?

He'd had an appointment with the psychologist yesterday. They'd talked a lot about adaptability—his relearning to do everything he could—and how increased adaptability increased self-confidence and decreased insecurity. Maybe it was too early in his recovery, but he wasn't sure there was any self-confidence to increase.

This wasn't what he'd signed on for.

And it damn sure wasn't what he'd come out tonight for.

"How's your week going?"

"The usual fun and games. Kids are great. Though there are times when they're so restless and disruptive that I honestly wonder if my parents and brothers didn't have the right idea."

He looked at her, squinting a little, then shook his head. "I can't imagine you in a research lab."

"Thank you. So what exactly do you do? You aren't jumping out of planes here, since Fort Murphy doesn't have an Airborne unit."

His nerves tightened, and his hand trembled slightly so he slid it under the table where he could clench it enough to stop the shaking. "Yeah, no. I—I tore up my leg in Afghanistan. No more jumping. I've got to decide whether to reclassify for another MOS." He tried a smile. "I've got to decide whether I'm even staying in."

She made an expression of sympathy, and his nerves wound tighter. The line about his leg hadn't been an outright lie. What better example of *tore up* than the mangled mess he'd awakened to after the blast? If she chose to interpret it as hurt but still there, it wasn't his fault.

You should tell her.

"What would you do if you got out? Where would you live? Back in Texas?"

The fingers he was massaging his leg with pinched hard enough to hurt. He stopped and folded both hands together, gripping tightly. "Come on, you're a teacher. Don't you know any hard questions to ask?"

She laughed. "Okay, how fast does the Earth rotate over a twenty-four-hour period? No, wait, that's not hard. Can you explain the paradox of Schrödinger's cat?"

"Never heard of it. Can *you* explain it?"

She made a dismissive gesture. "I've got at least three quantum physicists in my family. I've known this one since I was a kid."

When she didn't go on, he prodded her. "No bragging. You can't just claim to know the answer. You have to prove it."

"Oh, you really don't want to hear—"

"Oh, I do. Otherwise, how will I know that you know?"

Her lips pursed, making her look prim and sour, then she leaned forward, resting her arms on the tabletop. "In 1935, Erwin Schrödinger proposed an experiment in which a cat is placed in a closed container, along with a vial of poison and a bit of radioactive material. If the material begins to decay, it triggers the breaking of the vial and the cat dies. The only way to know whether the cat is alive or dead is to look inside the box, so as long as you don't look, the cat is both dead and alive at the same time. Until you look, the cat exists in all possible states. The act of looking causes the other possibilities to collapse and you're left with only one result."

God help him, she could even make quantum physics sound interesting, when the only interest he'd ever had in science had been playing with chemicals.

"So…" He cleared his throat. "Did the cat live?"

"Oh, Schrödinger never actually did the experiment. He was just showing that a random unpredictable event can cause one object, the cat, that is totally unrelated to another object, the poison, to change. To truly accept it, you also have to buy into the parallel universes theory, that we live in a multiverse and every possible outcome to a situation exists in other universes."

He looked at her—the faint pink of her cheeks, the sparkle in her eyes, the corners of her mouth twitching to smile really big—and a line from a TV show popped into his head. *"Our children will be smart and beautiful."*

Swallowing half the glass of iced tea in one gulp—and finding out too late he'd forgotten to sweeten it—helped clear some of the raspiness from his throat. "Was this dinner-table conversation for your family?"

"Science in general was. Schrödinger's cat was more like a bedtime story."

"And did you sleep dreaming of dead cats that had been poisoned that were also alive waiting to be poisoned?"

She laughed. "Of course not. I fell asleep dreaming about fairies and princesses and magic ponies. I was just your average little girl growing up surrounded by geniuses— Ooh."

Miriam brought the apple pie, served steaming on a hot cast-iron platter, and presented two spoons with a flourish. After refilling their glasses, she disappeared again.

Carly scooped up a spoonful of hot caramel sauce and soft ice cream, closing her eyes the instant the sweets touched her tongue, and gave a low, "Mmm."

It was quite possibly the sexiest sound Dane had ever heard. He gulped another big drink of tea, surprised the cold liquid didn't make steam rise from his skin as it rolled down his throat, and realized again it was bitter. Blindly setting the spoon aside, he picked up a packet of sugar and stirred it into the glass.

"Try it," Carly encouraged when she opened her eyes. "It's incredible."

"I might just watch you eat it." He hoped his voice didn't sound as hoarse to her as it did to him. Judging by the way her face pinked, he guessed it did.

She took the next bite almost primly, then nudged the plate a little closer to him. "How do you feel about not being able to jump anymore?"

"Paratroopers have a name for people who aren't paratroopers: legs. It's not said with a great deal of respect. From the time I signed on the dotted line in the recruiter's office, I knew I didn't want to be a legs."

"But it's not by choice."

He shook his head while he carefully cut a piece of pie, staying away from the ice cream puddling on the plate, scooping up the caramel sauce. "No, but it's still disappointing."

"Relieving," she disagreed. "All those jumps—or landings—are hard on your body."

"True. I knew guys who came out of Iraq and Afghanistan without a scratch who then broke a half dozen bones in a training jump in Germany or back here in the U.S."

"Won't it feel strange if you get out? Being a civilian and all? I mean, just those few months I went home after Jeff died, I felt out of place, and I haven't lived the life the way you have."

He was glad she *had* felt out of place. Otherwise, she wouldn't have come back to Tallgrass, and they never would have met. "Yeah. I'd always figured I'd make a career of it. If I don't transition out, though, I'll have to do something else." There was a lot he could do in the Army with just one leg, but he'd never considered any of it. He'd been happy where he was: jumping out of planes, living in combat zones, fighting for his life.

Now he was going to be support. Or out of Airborne altogether.

"But the good side is, if your leg injury keeps you from jumping, it'll also keep you from rotating back to Afghanistan, right?"

"Not necessarily. Other am—" He faked a cough, then took a drink. "Other people with worse injuries have gone back. I've just got a messed-up leg. There was an Air Force pilot in Iraq who'd lost both legs and went back to flying combat missions. Manpower's short. What's an arm or a leg if you can do a job that needs to be done?"

She gave a regretful shake of her head, for the people with worse injuries, he guessed. "I do admire people who do what needs to be done. Jeff was like that. His parents find comfort in it, and I guess I do, too. He always wanted to be a soldier. He believed it was both a duty and an honor to serve, and though it was so wrong that he died so young, he was living the life he'd chosen."

With a shrug, she smiled. "Part of him really wanted to go Airborne, but he had this fear of heights. Flying wasn't a problem because he was inside the plane and he could do a pretty good job of ignoring reality as long as he couldn't see it. But stepping out of it, having to depend on a few yards of nylon—" She shook her head again.

"What was his MOS?" *MOS* was shorthand for "Military Occupational Specialty," a soldier's specific job. Dane's was Mortars.

"Artillery." She shrugged. "He liked blowing stuff up."

"Don't we all."

She returned to the subject of his future. "I'm guessing you intended to make a career of the Army before you hurt your leg. What were your plans for when you'd done your twenty and retired?"

"I hadn't decided. Maybe teach and coach football. Become a scuba instructor. Maybe doing wilderness adventures. I always liked taking eight- or ten-day hikes to nowhere. Pack in everything you need, eat what you can trap, sleep under the stars." He could still teach, once he finished his degree, and coach—not the kind of hands-on coaching his own football coach had done, but he could give advice.

He could still dive, too, but making a career of it, getting in and out of the water...He couldn't climb a ladder onto a boat, wouldn't be able to walk out or back in for a shore dive, and in a pool, he could lift himself onto the side, no problem, but unless his prosthetic was right there, he couldn't go any farther without help.

There was just so much he couldn't do without help.

Carly was wrinkling her nose when he refocused on her. "I never liked eight- or ten-*minute* hikes. I can't imagine spending a whole day doing it. When I first saw you in the cave, I was out of breath in part because I was scared, but mostly because I'm so out of shape. My idea of out-doors time is working in the yard or strolling through a park." She added unnecessarily, "I'm a girly girl."

"I noticed that," he said drily. Soft, sweet voice, curves in all the right places—all things that made a man feel…well, like a man. Even if he spent too much time feeling less so these days.

"My father's done some research into the theory that we were all hermaphroditic at one point, probably around the time we crawled out of the primordial ooze, but a genetic mutation led to male and female chromosomes, which then led to single-sex organisms, which eventually developed into us. Frankly, he didn't see the point to the development. He would have been perfectly happy being a self-contained unit. Other than for its research value, he doesn't appreciate things like differences in genders." She smiled. "I, on the other hand, am very grateful for them."

"You're very well adjusted for having been raised by robots."

"I am, aren't I?" She took one final bite of pie, then set the spoon on the far side of the plate. "What would you teach?"

"History."

"Ah, nice and unchanging for the most part. What area?"

"U.S. World. The Civil War is my favorite period, then the World Wars."

"Times of turbulence. Were they always your favorite, or just since the war on terror?"

"Nah, people trying to kill me didn't influence it. I've always been interested in those eras."

"So you can teach something you enjoy and maybe

help the future leaders of the world avoid a few mistakes."

Those that fail to learn from history are doomed to re-peat it. Dane didn't have a bad history to repeat where she was concerned. The only serious relationship he'd ever had was with Sheryl. If she'd been less inclined to sleep with other men, they would probably still be to-gether...or would have been, at least, until the IED. Like Justin's ex, that was something he didn't quite see her tak-ing on for the long haul.

Not wanting to continue thinking along those lines, he changed the subject. "How were the soldiers today?"

"They were working hard and happy to see the kids. Except..." Her brow wrinkled in a frown. "Justin seemed kind of distant. He didn't have much to say."

Given a choice, Dane would rather discuss his all too uncertain future, because he had a pretty good idea why Justin hadn't been talkative with her. He'd had plenty to say to Dane on Sunday, and he hadn't been at a loss for words this morning when he'd found out Dane had deliberately scheduled an appointment during the kids' visit. All those words had ended with *"Man, you're a frickin'—"* Then he'd dragged his hand through his hair, muttered something and hobbled away.

Jerk? Idiot?

Coward.

He had medals for bravery—two Bronze Stars and three Army Commendation Medals, all with combat "V" device—but his courage must have bled out in Kunar Province before his buddy had gotten a tourniquet tied off on his leg. He was more afraid of telling Carly what had happened to him than he had been of getting shot at on patrol.

No, not afraid of telling. Afraid of her reaction. Afraid of everyone's reaction. Her friends wouldn't be so enthusiastic about the two of them if they knew his physical and psychological limitations. *She* wouldn't be so willing to spend time with him.

Given everything else he was trying to deal with right now, that was a possibility he didn't want to face.

Chapter Eight

"Liam's family is going skiing on spring break."

Startled out of her thoughts by Jacob's voice, Therese glanced across the van at him. He rarely spoke to her when he didn't have to, and then it was usually responses to direct questions or something he couldn't avoid. *Teacher says you have to sign this. Coach wants us to stay late.* She couldn't remember the last time he'd initiated an actual conversation.

"I never learned to ski. It must be fun."

"I dunno."

She waited for more, but nothing came. As she turned onto Carly's street, she was about to write off the brief exchange as an aberration, until he suddenly blurted, "Abby wants to go see Mom on spring break."

Almost as an afterthought, he added, "Me, too."

She'd known spring break was coming up soon. The post schools fell under the Department of Defense rather than the local school district, but they kept pretty much the same schedule. Because she didn't want to imagine an entire week home with the kids, she'd let the break slide from her mind. Easier to ignore than to anticipate the unpleasantness ahead.

The instant she stopped in Carly's driveway, Jacob opened the door and lunged out. His cheeks were red, his brows knitted in a scowl. Therese was slower to slide out of the van, and her expression, she was sure, was no happier than his.

Of course he and Abby wanted to see Catherine. She was their mom, and since Paul's death, they'd had only short visits when Catherine breezed through Tallgrass on her way somewhere else. The last time had been right after this school year had started. More than six months ago.

An entire spring break. What were the odds Catherine would agree? And if she did, it would be the first break since Abby and Jacob had come to live with her and Paul that Therese hadn't spent the five days off in a continual state of tension.

At the front of the van, Jacob scuffed his feet before asking, "Are we going in?"

"Go ahead. Tell Carly I'll be there in a couple minutes." Sliding back into the seat, she removed her cell phone from her purse, then watched as Jacob covered the sidewalk in three huge strides, took the steps in another, then knocked at the door. He was a big kid for his age, all arms and legs, and awkward like a gangly newborn colt, and he reminded her so much of his father that her heart hurt.

Carly invited him in, leaning out to wave, and Therese returned the wave before scrolling to Catherine's number in her cell.

Her finger hovered over the call button. Current wives and ex-wives weren't supposed to get along, and she and Catherine hadn't bucked tradition. They'd never come to words, but only because Therese had bitten her tongue so often the teeth marks would probably never fade. After Catherine had made it clear that she wasn't taking her children back after Paul's funeral, Therese had limited her contact with her to only the absolutely vital.

Did spring break count as vital? Probably, to Abby and Jacob, or he never would have brought it up. How would such a visit affect them? How hard would it be for them to spend time with their mom only to have to return to Therese and Tallgrass when the week was over? Would it make their living situation even harder? Would they be hostile with renewed feelings of abandonment, or just possibly, if God took pity on Therese, would they appreciate the visit for what it was and, maybe, her for setting it up?

"Lord, I don't know," she murmured. "This could go wrong in so many ways."

But time with the mother they loved so loyally could also be very right, couldn't it?

Hoping she was making the right decision, she pressed the button, and a few seconds later the phone began ringing. It was two o'clock in Los Angeles. Catherine should be at her job as an executive assistant. She would probably glance at caller ID, then let the call go to voice mail. That was what she'd done with each of the other rare calls Therese had placed to her. Was Catherine avoiding her ex's widow or really that busy?

"Hello."

Therese needed an instant to realize she was hearing a

real voice and not the beginning of a recorded message. She wasn't prepared, so she stumbled for a greeting. "Oh. Hey. Um, hi, Catherine. This is Therese." Then she added, "Matheson."

After a long silence, Catherine said drily, "I remember your last name since, gee, I happen to share it. Remember? I was married to Paul first."

A marriage that had ended before Therese had even met him. Yet somehow the woman still made her feel as if she had somehow been responsible for it.

"What do you want?"

The kids are fine. Thanks for asking. But Therese bit the tip of her tongue before replying. "Spring break is coming up in a couple weeks, and Jacob and Abby would like to spend it with you. Could we do that?"

She expected an argument, with a list of all the supporting reasons: it was too little notice; Catherine would have to take time off work or find someone to watch them; the timing wasn't good; how would she entertain them?; wasn't it better not to disrupt their routine?; it was too hard on her, still grieving, to see their father in them. Therese had heard them all.

"It's short notice. The airfare would be outrageous this close to the flight date."

"I'd pay for the tickets." Every dime she'd spent of Paul's life insurance had been on the house or the children. She would be more than happy to shell out a chunk of it for them to see their mom. "And spending money, of course." Since it wasn't as if Catherine had contributed to their support once she'd sent them to live with Paul.

But that was okay, Therese hastened to remind herself. Any money Catherine did send would have gone into the kids' college funds. Between her own salary, their military benefits, and the life insurance, she was perfectly capable of supporting them herself. Thank God.

"When are you talking about?" The skepticism in Catherine's voice didn't bode well.

"Two and a half weeks." Fumbling in her bag, Therese found her wallet and read the dates off the calendar tucked inside. She was only vaguely aware of a car door closing nearby, then footsteps passing her on the way to the house. Dane, she thought distantly. Probably come to help Jacob with the heavy lifting.

"Hm." A fingernail, usually unnaturally long and red, tapped the phone. "I do have some time on the books, and it's been a few months since I've seen them. I guess..." Catherine sucked in a breath. "Why not? It'll be a great chance for us to catch up. I'll take a few days off, and we can do the whole California thing. The beach, Disneyland, Hollywood..."

As she warmed to the idea, Therese chilled inside. Abby and Jacob were so young, and Catherine had fallen far short of good mother material. *What do you think, Paul?*

He had let the kids visit their mom before, with no qualms. If he were here right now, he would be fine with it. He probably would have thought of it himself, then suggested with that sly, sexy grin she'd loved that he and Therese use the time to start working on kid number three.

"...me know once you get the reservations. They can come in on Monday and go back on Saturday. Not too early on the return flight. It's about an hour to the airport from my place."

Aching lungs forced Therese to breathe. "Okay," she managed. "I'll call you."

"I didn't know you had real muscle coming in to help."

Carly, standing in the hallway, glanced up as Therese joined her. "I didn't know, either. I mentioned last night that you'd volunteered Jacob, and I guess he decided you and I weren't adequate assistants."

The *he* she was referring to was Dane, of course. She'd been surprised when he showed up at her door, and... happy. Not only did she appreciate his consideration, but she also more than appreciated watching him work. His biceps bulged under the short sleeves of his T-shirt, the muscles in his back rippling, as he and Jacob maneuvered the bookcase from the wall and into the center of the room. She'd always enjoyed looking at a fine male specimen, as her mother might have put it, and Dane was definitely that.

Therese stepped past Carly and went to the kitchen. "A woman could get used to having him around," she remarked as Carly followed her into the room.

Oh, yeah. But outwardly she tried to play cool. "Yeah, I guess so."

Taking a bottle of water from the refrigerator, Therese snorted. "Yeah. He gets credit for coming to the restaurant last night when he knew we would all be there."

"He thought you guys would be fun at a strip club."

Her friend almost choked on the drink she'd taken. After the coughing subsided, she raised her brows. "I wouldn't be surprised if a few of our bunch have been thrown *out* of strip clubs."

"Jessy." Carly scrunched up her face in thought. "Maybe Lucy."

"And Fia."

"And here the only man I've ever seen strip was Jeff."

"Really."

Carly gazed out the window above the sink at the greening yard, the blooming clover and a bed of sunny yellow daffodils, swaying with the light breeze. "I was only eighteen when we met, and I came from a home where physical displays of affection weren't exactly the norm. I'd never even kissed a boy until college. In fact, he was the one who introduced Jeff and me."

Therese came to stand beside her, gazing out at the same view. "Paul and I met when my car quit running in the middle of a busy intersection. He and some of his buddies pushed it into a parking lot for me. They went on. He stayed and fixed it, then I took him out to dinner as thanks. I got home three and a half days later."

Wow. Carly hadn't imagined that Therese might have had a wilder side before she married, was widowed, and became sole caregiver to two less-than-appreciative kids. Therese just *looked* like exactly what she was: wife, mom, kindergarten teacher, regular churchgoer.

"Aw, now I've shocked you, haven't I?" Therese laughed before her expression turned a little dreamy. "I think I was in love with him by the time our 'date' ended. I was already planning to marry him, have babies with him, and make a wonderful little family that would only be enhanced when Jacob and Abby came for their regular visits. I was going to be the new wife who was friends with the ex, the stepmother whom the kids adored, and everything was going to be happy and shiny and perfect."

She hadn't gotten any of that, but Carly knew she'd loved Paul with all her soul and had hoped with all her heart. Carly wasn't sure she could have coped nearly as well in the same situation. For starters, she'd have muzzled the kids, especially Abby, until they learned to behave. Maybe Therese hadn't earned their love or affection, but she darn well deserved their respect.

With a big sigh that encompassed her entire body, Carly said, "Jeff was perfect, you know. I do love perfect." In spite of the fact that he'd dropped his clothes where he took them off and left his dishes where he set them down. He hadn't shared her passion for yard work, never grasped the concept of sorting laundry, and hated to call a professional to fix something around the house even if he couldn't fix it himself.

Still, he'd been perfect for her.

A sound came from behind them, and she turned to see Dane in the doorway. His expression was so blank, she knew it was by design, and she wondered how much he'd heard about Therese's meeting Paul and her unrealized dreams.

"We're ready to move the television," he said, the same blankness there. "We need you two to move the cabinet for us." Turning, he was halfway back to the living room by the time either of them took a step.

Because some of the living room pieces were bulky and heavy—and she had no handy empty room waiting to hold them—they'd decided to huddle the big stuff together in the middle of the room, then she could drape drop cloths over them to catch any wild splashes of paint. The giant television Jeff had loved so much, along with the solid piece that held it, was the last thing to go.

"Jake and I will hold the TV while you slide this over there against the couch," Dane said. "You'll have to lift it up over the edge of the rug. Can you do it?"

"We are women. We are strong." Therese positioned herself at the far end, where Jacob stood, ready to test his young muscles with the weight of the TV.

That left Carly the end where Dane waited. She slid in close to him, catching the scents of cologne and faded cotton, laundry fresh. Add in a little bit of sweat from all the work he'd done, and the combination was almost heady. Definitely sexy.

"Okay, Jake, one, two, three."

As they lifted the television six inches into the air, Carly bent in, half under Dane's arms, to get a good hold on the china buffet Jeff had inherited from his great-grandmother, and together she and Therese slid it toward the center of the room. They had to grab the lip of the top to get the front feet onto the rug, then they slid it again until it bumped the sofa.

Looking a lot less exerted than she and Therese, Dane and Jacob carried the television the six or seven feet and carefully lowered it back into place.

"You know, the newer flat screens aren't nearly this heavy," Jacob remarked.

Carly blinked. She couldn't remember ever hearing him speak unsolicited. Of course, his comment was directed to Dane, not to her or Therese. Come to think of it, she'd never heard anyone call him Jake, either. *"My name is Jacob,"* he'd coolly announced to Fia once when she'd shortened his name. But he didn't seem to mind it from Dane.

Maybe he had more respect for Dane, being a soldier

like his dad. Or maybe he thought Dane would be more likely to react unfavorably if he complained.

"Well, I think this deserves a treat," Carly said. "I stopped at CaraCakes on the way home. Come on into the kitchen so we can sit."

Therese and Jacob automatically turned that way, but Dane held back. "You know, I'd probably better get going."

Her stomach knotting, Carly stared at him. They hadn't even had a chance to talk, and she'd been hoping his unexpected arrival meant he would help her get started with the painting. He didn't even need to actually do anything; moving the furniture had been enough. Maybe just give her a little advice as she worked. A little assurance.

Though the tiny can of burnt orange paint had been beautiful, buying two gallons of it had raised her doubts.

Did he think he was intruding? That maybe she and Therese had things to discuss? Or that three were company and four were a crowd? It was too awkward to say *Don't mind them, they're leaving soon.*

Instead, she swallowed and said, "Oh. Well…"

Therese, bless her heart, didn't feel any such hesitance. She looped her arm through Dane's and pulled him along with her. "You've never had anything from CaraCakes, have you? Because no one with a taste bud on their tongue would ever pass up CaraCakes, especially when it's free."

Dane didn't seem overly convinced, but he wasn't rude enough to forcibly free himself from her grip. With a silent sigh of relief that did nothing to ease her confusion, Carly followed them.

The bakery was a full-service place filling a small

space downtown just off Main Street. On Sundays when she and Jeff had eaten dinner at home, they'd stopped there for a loaf of fresh-baked bread to go along with the meal and whatever sweets caught their attention for dessert. This afternoon, she'd gotten fruit tarts, tiny pecan pies and, her favorite and the bakery's specialty, carrot mini-cupcakes.

By the time she reached the kitchen, Jacob had already claimed the dining chair closest to the window, and Therese was settling Dane in the chair opposite. Carly opened the pastry box on the counter and transferred the sweets to a serving tray while Therese took drink requests.

"He's kind of like a skittish horse today," she murmured when she reached to get glasses from the cabinet next to the one that stored the plates. "Spooks easily. You just have to show him who's boss."

Carly winced. To Therese, who had grown up with horses, showing an animal who was boss was probably a simple thing. Carly, on the other hand, had never met a horse that didn't try to take a bite out of her.

Once everything was on the table, she and Therese sat across from each other. With the enthusiasm of a growing boy, Jacob didn't require any nudging to move one pecan pie and two mini-cakes to his plate and start eating. Dane was a little slower, but no mortal could resist two heavenly bites of carrot cake topped with a dollop of cream cheese frosting.

"Cream cheese is the best food ever invented," Therese said with a sigh. "Appetizer, entrée, dessert, and it's pretty darn good all by itself for a snack. I bow at the feet of whoever discovered it."

"I'm sure multiple members of my family can tell

/you," Carly said before biting into her own mini-cake.

Therese finished hers with a grin, reached for another, then said, "So, Dane, Carly says you think we'd be a lot of fun at a strip club. You tell us your experiences, and we'll tell you ours."

The only person at the table who wasn't surprised by Therese's offer was Therese herself. Jake's mouth had dropped, Carly's eyes were popped wide open, and Dane was pretty sure his own expression fell somewhere in between.

"Um, yeah, I just meant—"

Therese's grin widened. "We know what you meant. The margarita club members can be a rowdy group."

Especially with a few margaritas in them. He kept that observation to himself, though. No need to add to the stunned look her son already wore.

"You go to strip clubs?" Jake demanded, his cheeks red, his voice cracking on the final words.

"No," Therese replied.

"But you said you'd tell your experiences—"

"My experience is that I've never been to one. But he didn't know that."

Jake swallowed hard, peeled the paper from another cupcake, and shoved it in his mouth.

"I would've figured Jessy as the one to say things for the shock value," Dane said.

"It got you talking, didn't it?" She finished a fruit tart, delicately wiped her fingers on a napkin, then slid her chair back. "Finish up, Jacob. We need to get home so you can do your homework."

The boy stood, took a swallow of pop, grabbed a pecan

pie, and headed toward the hall. There he turned back and grudgingly said, "Thanks, Ms. Lowry."

"Thanks so much for your help, Jacob," Carly said. "We couldn't have done it without you."

"You mean, Dane couldn't have done it without him." Therese touched his shoulder briefly as she passed, stooping to give Carly a hug. "Invite us over to see the paint job when it's finished, and we'll help you put it all back."

When they were gone, the room seemed half its size and twice as quiet. Dane ate another cupcake, then shifted in his chair, making it squeak faintly. He couldn't think of much else to say, so he focused on Therese and her son. "Jake doesn't look anything like his mother."

"He looks like his father, she says. Anyway, she's his stepmother. Jacob and Abby came to live with them when Paul got transferred here."

"Where's their mother?"

"In California." Carly's nose wrinkled. "She needed time to find herself."

He frowned. "If you don't do that before you have kids, you don't *get* to do it until they're grown."

A faint smile eased some of the tension from her face. "I agree. Even after Paul died, their mother wouldn't take them back. She claimed she was grieving too much."

"And they weren't?" Dane shook his head. "My mother drives me crazy, but lately I keep getting reminders that she could have been a lot worse." Anna Mae was overly critical and too quick to show her disappointment, but at least she hadn't abandoned him until he was well past his teenage years. One visit to the hospital for his first surgery, then she'd never come again.

But it had been for the best. He'd had enough of a negative attitude himself. He couldn't have handled hers, too.

She hadn't wanted a son with only one leg. Just as Carly likely wouldn't want a man with only one leg. *"Jeff was perfect, you know. I do love perfect."*

Hearing the words again, even if only in his head, tightened his gut and made uneasiness shiver down his spine. It would be kinder to her if he just stopped coming around. He could avoid her until he transitioned. The only places he had to go were the WTU and, occasionally, to the commissary, PX or dry cleaner's. It wouldn't take any real effort to be elsewhere every Tuesday until he left Fort Murphy.

If he had the courage.

If he didn't mind being alone and lonely again.

If he didn't care about giving up the only relatively normal part of his life.

Feeling the weight of her gaze, he glanced up and found her watching him, a question in her eyes. Had she said something he'd missed, or was she wondering why he'd been so quick to try to say good-bye this afternoon?

He figured it was the second, since she didn't repeat a question but instead stood and carried the dishes to the sink.

"I guess I should get started with the painting since I have no place to sit in my living room for the near future."

Go ahead. Say, "Yeah, good luck with that" and walk out the door.

But his conscious mind all too willingly ignored his subconscious mind. "I'll start the taping while you change clothes."

The smile that flashed across her face was relieved,

and most of her awkwardness vanished. "You think I'm too messy to wear pants and a silk shirt?"

"I think you're too smart."

She tilted her head to one side. "What about you? Your clothes look new."

"Everything I have here is new. I haven't gotten my household goods yet." It wasn't unusual for a shipment to be slow to arrive, especially coming from overseas. Personal belongings came by boat, and more often than not, it was a slow one.

Though the only reason his stuff hadn't reached Fort Murphy was because he'd had it all put in storage in Bethesda and hadn't made any effort to retrieve it yet. Furniture, the Ducati, electronics—everything he'd left in Vicenza when he went to Afghanistan and everything he'd taken to the desert—waited for him to land somewhere.

Carly accepted his statement at face value. "We had friends who got orders to Schofield Barracks. Their stuff had to be trucked from Fort Carson, in Colorado, to the coast, where it was loaded onto a ship, and halfway to Hawaii, the ship sank. They lost everything except the couple of suitcases' worth of stuff they'd taken on the flight over."

"Tough. I've got a lot of buddies who sell everything when they get orders and just keep whatever will fit into the suitcases they can take. That's what I had planned to do."

"What changed your mind?" she asked as she emptied two plastic bags onto the table: rolls of painter's tape, drop cloths, trays, rollers, and brushes.

He'd had more important things on his mind, like the

infections and the three successive amputations that had taken more and more of his leg.

If someone had told him two years ago that so much of who he was was tied up in his leg, he would have thought they were crazy. Turned out, he was the one who was a bit crazy.

"I got sentimental, I guess," he said at last. "I didn't want to leave any more behind than I had to."

Her forehead wrinkled, but she didn't pursue the comment. "I'll be back in five."

Once the sound of her steps had faded down the hall, he grabbed three rolls of wide blue tape and went into the living room. He started with the door frame, precise in his placement of the tape. He'd never needed to tape anything; he was good at putting the paint only where he wanted. But Carly didn't have his experience with a brush, and as she'd said several times, she liked perfect.

Which he wasn't. Which her husband had been. Like it wasn't hard enough to compete with a dead man's memory, Jeff Lowry just had to be a perfect memory.

Maybe she wouldn't care, once she got to know Dane better. It was one thing to know a person's flaws right from the start and accept him anyway. But when she knew him for the man he was inside, maybe the outside wouldn't matter so much.

Or maybe it would. It came down to a matter of how much he was willing to risk. Stop seeing her now and be alone again, or wait until he cared a whole lot more than he already did and find out that she couldn't bear the reality. By that time, it wouldn't be just loneliness he had to deal with. There would be pain, too, and whatever self-confidence he'd managed to recover would bleed out again.

It wasn't so hard a decision, though, he realized when she came into the room. She'd put on denim shorts that showed an awful lot of long, sexy legs and a sleeveless T-shirt that couldn't have fit tighter if it'd been painted on. With her feet bare, her toenails polished pale pink and her hair pulled back in a ponytail, she looked young and happy and beautiful enough to make his mouth dry and his hands unsteady. A strip of blue tape went wild of its mark, a downward slash across the plain white wall.

She didn't seem to notice as she picked up her own roll of tape. "Should I start with the window frame?"

"Uh, yeah, sure." He wished he'd brought his pop in with him. He could use a drink before his tongue stuck permanently to the roof of his mouth.

She was very careful with the tape, too, aligning the edges so the wood was completely covered but not blocking the Sheetrock, either. She started about three feet off the floor on the near side of the double window and worked her way to the bottom, then straightened again to finish the top part. When she stretched to reach the very top, her shirt pulled up with the movement, revealing soft golden skin and something he hadn't expected: a pale blue stone nestled in her belly button.

He didn't even bother to tear loose the tape he'd just applied, but left the roll hanging there and covered the distance to the kitchen in record time—at least, for him. Grabbing his glass from the table, he downed the contents in one gulp, emptied the rest of the can into it and drained it just as fast.

He'd known women with piercings almost every-where. It wasn't anything new or shocking. He was used to it.

He just hadn't expected it of Carly.

He'd seen a lot more skin than that, too. In fact, he'd seen more women naked than he wanted to remember. Truthfully, more than he did remember. Those months after the divorce, he'd dulled his pain with booze, sometimes without complete recall of what he'd done under its influence.

But he hadn't seen Carly's skin. Hadn't seen Carly naked.

And as long as there was a chance that might happen, he wouldn't be walking away.

"All right. Are we ready for paint?" Carly stood back from the wall, hands on her hips, and scanned the room. Lines of blue tape circled the doorway, windows and baseboards, and white tarps were draped across the furniture. She'd guessed two would do it and had bought four; it had taken three. The other would come in handy to protect the floor.

"Let's say the *room* is prepped. Are *you* ready?"

She took a deep breath. "Yeah. Let's start."

While he set the first can of paint on a stack of newspapers, then pried it open, she spread the last tarp along the wall where she intended to start. It was the long one, nothing but Sheetrock, no openings to paint around except the electrical outlet at each end, also taped in blue.

"You want to use the cutting brush to cut in along the ceiling," Dane said, pouring thick rich paint into a disposable tray. "That's the two-and-a-half-inch brush you bought. Do you have a ladder?"

Carly brushed her hair back. "Oh, yeah. Been used once. One day Jeff decided to replace the ceiling fan in the dining room. He climbed up, overstretched, and crashed onto the dining table and sprained both wrists. I never let him try it again."

She headed to the utility room, where the ladder had occupied the narrow space between the dryer and the wall since Jeff's fall. She hefted the bright yellow metal and half carried, half dragged it back to the living room. "Where do you want it?"

Dane looked up, his gaze traveling the length of the ladder. His expression was measuring, his mouth in a taut line. "Sorry, Carly, you'll have to do the climbing."

She was thinking she liked the way he said her name when their conversation the night before crept into her mind. *"I tore up my leg."* No more jumping from airplanes, or riding motorcycles, she guessed, and the injury probably restricted him from other activities as well, like climbing ladders.

Smiling to hide her empathy—and her curiosity—she said, "Good. I like climbing." It was totally a lie. Climbing and heights were the reason behind her leading the hike up to the cave the weekend they'd met. But the ladder was only six feet, and she didn't have to go all the way to the top.

She placed it along the middle of the wall, climbed up, then accepted the quart plastic container Dane offered, along with the brush. "Okay. I'm ready."

He waited, watching. She dipped the brush into the paint, swiped off the excess and stopped an inch from the wall. "Tell me I'm gonna love this."

"You're gonna love it," he said obediently, then went on. "If you don't, you'll pick another color and do it again."

"Okay." She repeated the dipping-swiping process, but this time she actually made contact with the wall, leaving a narrow swath of paint that didn't quite reach the ninety-degree angle of the ceiling. She dabbed a little and covered the wall but got a few dots on the ceiling, too. She was frowning at it when the ladder steadied a bit under her.

Dane braced the ladder with one hand. "It's paint. It doesn't have to be perfect. Not a whole lot in life is."

She knew that firsthand, of course. So did he.

Following his instructions, she cut in a length, then swapped the ladder and brush for a roller. As she painted big Ws on the wall, then rolled back and forth to fill them in, she realized she was going to love it. The color glowed with warmth and welcome and transformed the boring old white into a dramatic statement.

That statement might be *My boyfriend's a big fan of the University of Texas*, but at least it wasn't *I'm a bland and boring room for bland and boring people*.

She paused in her rolling, glancing over her shoulder where Dane was cutting in around the window. *My boyfriend*. Was she allowed to call him that, or did they need some sort of agreement first? She was so clueless on the whole dating thing, with so little experience so long ago that it was meaningless.

My boyfriend. She liked the sound of it. Like the paint, it made her feel warm and glowing, as if the sun had finally come out after a long gray winter. The living room was popping with life, and she wanted to, too.

Her pleasure with the painting started to fade by the time she finished the first wall and moved on to the shorter unobstructed wall. Her knees weren't used to climbing up and down the ladder or crouching to get the bottom few inches, and her shoulders ached. She was thinking of ibuprofen, cold water, and something easy for dinner when Dane broke the quiet.

"Looks like that's it for the first coat."

Blinking, she looked and saw he was right. Every inch of the walls matched the saturated roller in her right hand. She lowered it back onto the tray, placed both hands in the small of her back and stretched. She was warm, sticky, splattered with paint from fingertips to shoulders and probably had it in her hair as well, but none of that stopped the sense of accomplishment welling up inside her.

"I do love it," she said as she slowly turned. "It's so..."

"Burnt orange?" he provided drily.

"Dramatic. When everything's finished and I get a new rug and new lamps and maybe a smaller TV, it'll be perfect." Her energy renewed, she swiped her hands on her shorts. "Now, about dinner—"

"Now, about cleanup."

"I know it's not environmentally correct, but I bought roller covers that weren't so expensive I'd feel obligated to clean them, and I bought quite a few. I was thinking I could just throw them out..." She let her voice trail off. Even a stranger could tell from his look that he wasn't finding it a good plan.

Finally he asked, "Are you offering to cook dinner?"

"I can do that." More or less. Her freezer held chicken breasts, microwaveable bags of mashed potatoes, and several loaves of CaraCakes' take-and-bake bread, and there were canned green beans and jars of gravy in the pantry. It wasn't exactly home cooking, but it was close.

"Then the least I can do is clean the rollers and brushes."

"Deal," she said quickly, handing the tray, its roller and leftover paint to him. "I do like a man who compromises. Come on into the kitchen when you're done."

Carly hadn't cooked a meal for anyone but herself since Jeff had shipped out, and the prospect pleased her more than she'd ever expected. Too many breakfasts and dinners alone, she decided. Next time, she would cook a real meal. Though her parents had employed a housekeeper-cook who hadn't wanted her underfoot, Carly had discovered that learning to cook was like learning any other subject: If a person could follow directions, she could cook.

Though lessons from Jeff's mom, Mia, had helped.

Her prepackaged meal was simmering, baking, and radiating along when Dane came in. He washed his hands before taking up position against the island.

"Do you cook?" she asked as she removed a tub of margarine and a Dr Pepper from the refrigerator. For her own drink, she grabbed a bottle of water to mix with a packet of mandarin-mango tea powder.

"I do a great burger and a steak. I learned to fry eggs from the master—my grandmother—and I make a decent pasta sauce."

"What's your favorite meal?"

"Hm. Turkey, dressing, sweet potatoes with marshmallows, and pecan pie." He smiled at her look. "What can I say? I missed too many Thanksgiving and Christmas dinners."

Wow. That was a bit ambitious for her first attempt at cooking for him. She and Jeff had been lucky in that they'd always managed to make it to her family's or his for the holidays. She'd never roasted a turkey or made a pecan pie.

"Can I help?"

"Um, yeah. If you'd get the glasses and ice."

"What's your favorite meal?"

"Depends on the season. In winter, I love beef and cabbage stew or chicken stew. When it's a hundred and ten in the shade, salad with crabmeat and avocado is perfect. Any time I feel in need of comfort, it's pasta with lots of cheese." And there were those times when she went all sweets, but he didn't need to know that. If he hadn't stayed, she would have stuffed herself with the rest of the fruit tarts, carrot cupcakes, and pecan pies and called it supper.

She cooked the chicken with a generous hand on the spices, seasoned the mashed potatoes with salt, pepper and garlic, and sliced thick slabs of hot bread, adding margarine and honey to the table. When everything was ready and Dane was seated, she took her own chair, closed her eyes for a brief, silent blessing, then filled her lungs with fragrant air.

The scene was achingly familiar: her in her usual seat, hot food on the table, a man she cared about across from her. The only significant difference was who that man was. For an instant, it hurt that it wasn't Jeff, that she would never share another meal with him.

But it was a fact. She could regret it all she wanted, but his life had ended and hers was still going on. And she thought maybe, just possibly, she wanted it to go on with Dane in it.

"Am I sitting in his chair?"

Startled, she blinked. "Hm? Oh, um, yes."

"Do you want me to move?"

"Move? Oh, no, of course not. It's okay. I was just thinking... You're the first person I've cooked for since Jeff." A piece of chicken quivered on her fork, and she lowered it to the plate. "I haven't cleaned out his closet yet. I haven't packed up any of his stuff. I got rid of my car so I could keep his." Abruptly she offered him a shaky smile. "I'm sorry. You don't want to hear this."

Dane set his own fork down and picked up a slice of bread, spreading it heavily with butter. "There's no proper schedule for dealing with loss."

Her second smile was even shakier. "That's what the chaplains and the grief counselors say." With a loud breath, she said again, "I'm sorry. Let's talk about something... anything else."

His dark gaze held hers a long moment before he carefully spoke. "I know what it's like to... lose and... and feel like you're never going to get past it. Any time you want to talk, I don't mind listening."

Something inside her warmed, and an earlier thought bloomed back to life. She wouldn't give up one second of her past with Jeff, but she was pretty sure she wanted Dane in her future.

Chapter Nine

Yet one more uncomfortably silent meal was nearly over in the Matheson house when Therese finally pushed her plate a few inches away and rested her arms on the table. "You know, spring break is two and a half weeks away."

Jacob made a startled sound and fixed his gaze on his food as if he couldn't get it to his mouth without extreme concentration. To his left, Abby stopped shredding a roll to pieces and put all her teenage obnoxiousness into a sigh. "Yeah, like that hasn't been the only thing *everyone* talks about. Even the teachers are excited about ditching their stupid classes for a week."

Please, God, don't let me stuff that roll in her mouth. "I talked to your mother this afternoon, and..." With a silent request for forgiveness, she told a bit of a lie. "She wants you two to spend it with her. We got your reservations. You'll fly out that Monday and come home on Saturday."

Jacob's gaze jerked to Therese's face, his cheeks pink-ing, then to Abby, as if to base his reaction on hers. Therese watched her, too—watched the emotions flash unguarded through her expression: surprise, excitement, an instant of pure joy, then annoyance.

"Oh, my gosh, I can't believe this! You think you can just get rid of us for the week without even asking? What if I'd had plans with my friends?"

"Do you?"

Abby rolled her eyes. "*No*, but that's not the point. What if I did? They'd be ruined and I'd have to cancel them and everyone would be ticked off at me. The least you could have done was ask if we even wanted to go see her. Right, Jacob?"

"I-I, uh, well—" Now his face matched the red hue of the apples filling the bowl on the counter.

"See?" Abby gave her hair a flip as she shoved her chair back and stood. "We don't have any say in anything 'cause we're just kids, and we're not even your kids, so you think you can make us do whatever you want. I might not even come back from Mom's. I bet that would make you happy." With that, she flounced from the room, her steps forceful enough that Therese imagined the pictures on the hall wall vibrating. A moment later, her bedroom door slammed.

In the silence that settled, Jacob stared at his plate again, though he gave up any pretense of eating. After a moment, his voice barely audible, he said, "I want to see Mom. Abby does, too. She said so. She's just..."

How often had Therese heard those words applied to Abby? Starting with Paul: *She's just angry, she's just scared, she's just disappointed that Catherine and I aren't getting back together.*

From her pastor: *She's just grieving, she's just lost, she's just so unsure of her place in life.*

From the grief counselor: *She's just trying to cope and she doesn't have the skills.*

And once from Jessy: *She's just a brat. Don't cut her so much slack.*

"I know, Jacob." Therese suddenly felt tired. She'd hoped this trip might ease things between her and Abby, at least a little. After she'd prayed, after she'd talked to Catherine and made the reservations, she'd hoped...

One thing it seemed she would never run out of: hope. Was she a fool?

She began gathering dishes, ordinarily a job the kids shared. "You know I'm not trying to get rid of you, don't you, Jacob?"

He was still for so long she thought he wasn't going to answer, then he stood and took the dishes from her hands. "Yeah, I know."

As he headed for the sink, she stood, too, and picked up the serving bowls. "You and Abby are always welcome here."

"Yeah." Lower, practically under his breath, he murmured, "Just nowhere else."

Therese's heart hurt. How sad was it that an eleven-year-old child felt he wasn't wanted anywhere except the one place he didn't want to be? Desperately she wished she could wrap her arms around him and hold him until all their aches were gone, but she'd been pushed away so many times in the past, the most she dared was a hand on his shoulder after she set the dishes down.

He flinched away from even that.

Therese left the kitchen. She would put on her pajamas, brush her teeth and scrub her face, then settle into her favorite chair to read. Surely she could find a soothing verse or two in the Bible.

It took every bit of her energy to climb the stairs. She knocked on Abby's door, intending to tell her to take her temper downstairs and help Jacob with the dishes. Abby's voice from inside stilled her hand in pre-knock position.

"—trying to take credit for all of it, of course. '*I* talked to your mother,' '*We* got your reservations.' Yeah, right. It was Mom's idea, I know it. Tuh-reese doesn't ever think about us. She doesn't care what we want. She just wants us to get out of her house and her life. I told her maybe I'd just stay with Mom, and you should've seen her face. She'd like that."

Therese lowered her arm to her side, then backed off a dozen feet. "Abby, Jacob's started the cleanup. Go down and help him." Without waiting for a response, she went into her room and closed the door. Wearily, she sank down on Paul's side of the bed, letting her head rest on the pillow. For a long time, the scent of him had remained. She wasn't sure if it had eventually faded, or if she'd cried the fragrance right out of it.

She wasn't going to cry tonight.

Rolling onto her other side, she gazed at the large photo of Paul on the opposite nightstand. "Why, Paul? Why didn't you come home? You promised you would. You promised all of us."

There was no answer, of course. Just that dear smile on that dear face. Jacob was growing to look more like him every day, and Abby had every bit the stubborn jaw. How different their lives would have been if he'd kept his promise and returned home. Oh, Abby would still be a pain and Jacob would still be moody—they were kids, af-ter all—but there would have been so much more. They would have been a family.

Her inhale was shaky. "Jacob helped moved the furni-ture at Carly's so she could paint," she whispered. "He's so big and strong. You'd be proud of him, Paul. And Carly's got a boyfriend. He seems like a very nice guy, and he makes her smile. You'd like him. He reminds me of you in ways. Nothing physical. He just has the same sense of honor and decency about him that you do."

She paused to trace a pattern on the floral coverlet. "I miss you so much, sweetie…and I'm so jealous of Carly. She and the other women in the margarita club are the best friends I could ask for, but sometimes…I'm so lonely. If I could have just one more hug from you, just one more kiss…"

The hot dampness seeping from her eyes proved she'd been wrong earlier. After a few more nights like this, she might find hope in short supply, but she had absolutely no shortage of tears.

"How are you today, Staff Sergeant?"

It was Friday afternoon and Dane had taken all he could in the gym. Sweat dampened his shirt, and his leg hadn't decided if it was going to throb or tingle, so it was alternating between both. The last thing he wanted was to get in a conversation with anyone, but when Captain Rush fell in step with him, he nodded a hello, then shrugged. "Can't complain."

"Aw, there hasn't been a man born who can't com-plain." The cadre nurse smiled to take the sting out of her words. She was a beautiful woman, with sleek black hair, ebony skin and a terminally positive way about her, no matter how grim the job. Half the guys under her care had fallen for her, but she never took it seriously, so it never got awkward.

If Dane hadn't already fallen for Carly, he could have tumbled for Captain Rush, too.

"Where are you headed?" she asked.

"Home, for a carrot cake cupcake with a chaser of hydrocodone."

"You had me until the chaser. CaraCakes?" She waited an instant for his nod, then made a dreamy face. "They're the best. I don't even let myself drive by there more than once a week or the smell lures me in. How's your leg? Any problems?"

"Just the main one. It's still gone."

"And the prosthesis? You're walking good. You doing okay with it?"

"As long as I go in a straight line at an old lady's pace."

"Ha. And you said you couldn't complain."

He gave her a sardonic smile as they approached the main entrance. "Word around the gym is that you were some hotshot pediatrics nurse practitioner before you came here. Isn't that a big change?"

"Kids to wounded adults? Not so much as you'd think." Her laughter was full, the kind that made people look her direction. "You have plans for the weekend?"

"I'm helping a friend paint her living room."

"Hm. A girlfriend?"

"Uh, she's a girl and she's a friend, so yeah."

"Playing with words, Staff Sergeant. You say 'friend.' I say 'sweetie pie.'"

He chose the steps that led to the sidewalk rather than

the ramp; he could use the practice. Then, for some perverse reason, he returned to the subject. "You don't think men and women can be just friends?"

"Sure, they can. I just prefer to think that everyone's happily matched with a significant other."

"We haven't even been out on a real date."

She laughed. "My husband and I have been married nearly twenty years and have four kids, and we've never had a real date, either. We just did stuff—impromptu meals, running into each other around town, spending time together—and before we knew it, we were in love and getting married. I guess you could say our wedding was our first formal date, with both of us dressed up, a fine meal, and wine."

His hand sliding along the railing, Dane eyed her. Even in her loose-fitting ACUs, it was clear she was lean and muscled. Better yet, he'd seen her in PT shorts and a T-shirt that was a size too small and couldn't look better. He wouldn't have guessed her to be mom to four or old enough to have been married twenty years.

"So is your friend who's a girl significant?" Captain Rush fished.

"Aren't we all?" he countered.

"We are, at least in God's eyes." Then she smiled. "And this woman is pretty significant in yours, too, isn't she? Good for you, Staff Sergeant."

Stopping in front of his pickup, Dane beeped the lock open. "Yeah," he agreed, shooting for sardonic again. "Good for me." He figured at best he and Carly were on the road to disappointment. At worst, he was going to find out that the divorce from Sheryl no longer held its place as the worst time in his personal life.

"Don't overdo the painting," Captain Rush said. "Have a good weekend. And consider taking that girl out on a date."

He responded with a nod, then climbed into the truck. For a moment, he sat there, rubbing the stump of his leg, watching until the captain disappeared into the building next door. *"Don't overdo,"* she'd said, and he'd been careful of that. No way he was going to show weakness in front of Carly. She did all the climbing, all the crouching on the floor, while he painted what he could reach standing up. She never asked him how he'd "torn up" his leg, and he was grateful for that.

He was pretty sure, if things continued the way they were, the question would come sometime. Unless he made her forget about it by doing the stuff a normal man would do. If he could climb stairs, he could climb a ladder. If he could get down on the floor, maybe not kneel but sit on his butt, then he could get back up again. It would be graceless, but he could live with that.

He went home, parking near the building since most of his neighbors were still at the WTU. On the way to the door, he realized he was limping and he amended his chaser to a pain pill and a muscle relaxer. Maybe a bath instead of a shower. Some deep heat would feel nice.

In the bathroom, he set the tub to filling, went back to the kitchen for the cupcake and a fruit tart as well as a bottle of water and two pills. Back in the bathroom, he pulled off his T-shirt, removed his right shoe, then took off his sweats and boxers. Pressing in the button near the knee, he released the prosthesis and set it aside, then pulled off the liner and laid it next to the sink.

His legs were so pale, anemic even. He'd always spent

a ton of time outside in the summer, usually in shorts or swim trunks, and always turned a deep shade of brown. Even in Afghanistan, he'd spent enough time in shorts to get dark.

Now his entire body was white. His upper body strength had improved in the months in the hospital, and his right leg was stronger, too, but that made the nine inches or so of his left leg look even punier. It *was* punier, he thought as he swung his leg over the side of the tub, then slid in. After each surgery, there had been a lot of swelling, but after that went down, eventually the stump got even smaller as the muscles atrophied.

Which did he hate more—the sight of his leg or the prosthesis? He couldn't decide as he washed down the pills, then reached for the cupcake. Right now he could hate them both equally.

But if they cost him a relationship with Carly...

The water had cooled, and his pain had eased as well by the time Dane finally hauled himself out of the tub. He'd forgotten to bring in clean clothes, so he dried his left leg thoroughly, pushed the liner into the limb until it locked into place, then pulled it on, adjusting the pliable material until it conformed to his leg. Avoiding the mirror, he went to the bedroom to dress.

His cell phone rang with Carly's tone—nothing sappy, just an old-fashioned ring that reminded him of his grandparents. He really needed one that said, *Danger, danger.*

Propping the phone between his ear and shoulder, he said hello, then went on with the process of zipping his jeans.

"Are you still willing to help tonight?"

"Yeah, sure. I was just getting cleaned up."

"I guess we're ready to start the trim, right? Since I'm not great at making decisions—"

"Gee, imagine that."

"—how about I pick you up and we go to the PX together?"

Uh, yeah, no. If she didn't already know for whom the squat barracks had been built, the big sign at the curb left no doubt. Let her think he lived in regular housing. "Let me pick you up. We'll get the stuff, and when we've done that, we can—" With Captain Rush's farewell words ringing in his ears, he finished. "We can go out to dinner. You know, like a date. If you'd like."

Carly's silence lasted too long to be comfortable, but the warmth in her voice when she did speak made up for it. "I would like that. I'll see you..."

"Fifteen minutes?"

"Sounds great. Bye."

Maybe Captain Rush was right. Maybe he did have a girlfriend.

At least for a while.

Jeff had hated to shop for anything besides electronics or tools he would rarely use. If it didn't come with a plug or a USB connector, he wasn't interested. Carly couldn't say for sure that Dane enjoyed it, but he didn't give off any of the disinterested guy signals Jeff had excelled at. He picked out the trim paint, estimated how much they needed, got a tub of caulking and a scraper to fill in any imperfections.

"Knowing how you like perfection," he said drily with a glance her way.

"Aw, come on." She bumped him with her shoulder.

"Doesn't everyone want things as close to perfect as possible?"

"You know perfection rarely exists."

She rolled her eyes. "Of course it does. You just have to have a realistic view of it."

Now he mimicked her eye-roll. "Perfection by definition is perfect."

"But who defines *perfect*? We do. My vision of perfect might not match yours, but to me, it's still perfect."

"I bet your family would have a few arguments for that."

"Oh, yeah. But it's not their life or their perfect, so their opinion is just that."

As they left the hardware department, Carly saw the perfume counter ahead and remembered that she hadn't replaced her fragrance yet. She hadn't worn Jeff's favorite again, though. It was excellent support for her argument: He'd thought it the perfect perfume and she hadn't been wild about it.

She wondered what Dane would find perfect, then immediately discounted the thought. A fragrance that *she* wore every day had to meet her approval, no one else's.

And she wasn't ready yet. It would be kind of like packing up Jeff's clothes or selling his car or taking off his wedding band. It would be saying good-bye and moving on in a way that she couldn't take back.

She paid for her purchases, and they went to Dane's truck, so new it still had that new smell. She gave him a choice of restaurants in town, and he chose Luca's, a small Italian place that occupied an old house just a block away from CaraCakes.

Though it wasn't even six o'clock, most of the dining

rooms the hostess led them through were full. They got a table for two in the corner of what had once been a library. Dark paneling still hung on the walls, and dark velvet drapes at the windows. It was her favorite room, especially when a fire simmered in the small marble fireplace. Now only a trio of candles burned there.

"You lived in Italy," she commented as she spread the damask napkin on her lap. "Do you still like American Italian food?"

"Lasagna is good pretty much wherever it's made."

"There's a town a few hours southeast of here, just a little bit of nothing where there are a half dozen well-known Italian restaurants and a great Italian market."

"Krebs." A smile warmed his eyes. "I've been there. When I was a kid, my dad liked to take Saturday trips every couple months. I think we visited every out-of-the-way restaurant with a reputation within half a day's driving distance of Dallas."

"The margarita club went a few months ago. We got there in time for lunch at one restaurant, then did some antique shopping in McAlester, then went back and had dinner at a different place. Luca is from there, so good food runs in his soul."

Dane glanced up from the menu. "Are we going to run into any of them tonight?"

She shook her head exasperatedly—but affectionately. "You never know. Jessy lives just a few blocks away, and she has to take a break from Serena's once in a while. None of us do a lot of cooking, except Therese, since she's got the kids. For the rest of us, though, cooking for one..."

His movements precise, he closed the menu and laid

it on the table. When he lowered his hands to his lap, she wondered if he was rubbing the ache in his bad leg. "Yeah, I know. I think I've got some beer, some water, and maybe some ketchup in my refrigerator."

"That would be sadder if you lived in a house. But you're in the barracks. You're excused from cooking. If it weren't for frozen and canned stuff, I'd starve." So very not true, given her stash of chocolate-covered caramels. But she certainly wouldn't get any real nutrition if she didn't eat in the school cafeteria five days a week.

The waitress set a basket of warm bread, along with small dishes of softened butter, on the table, then took their orders: lasagna for Dane, eggplant parmesan for Carly.

Dane broke a slab of dark bread in half and took a bite before changing the subject. "I heard someone at work mention spring break. You have plans?"

"My sister-in-law, Lisa, wants me to come and stay with her family for a few days, but I don't know." There was no way, face-to-face, that she'd be able to hide the fact that she had a boyfriend—it was official now, wasn't it, with this date? The rest of her family would think nothing of it; some of them studied people who felt the need for other people in their lives, but their personal experience was limited. Only Lisa would recognize it for the major development it was.

"Is Lisa a genius, too?"

"Pretty much, but she has all the social skills the rest of the family missed out on. She's a great mom and wife, and I love her to pieces. I just don't think I want to go to Utah this break." After resisting as long as she could, she chose a piece of crusty garlic bread from the basket and took a heavenly bite before musing, "Maybe I'll get some more work done on the house or get my yard ready for summer. I didn't even clean out the beds last fall."

"Is that something you did with Jeff?"

A wave from the doorway caught Carly's attention, and she nodded a greeting to the parents of one of her students. The mom volunteered a few hours at school every week. The dad had just come back from Afghanistan. They were among the lucky ones.

Then she glanced back at Dane. The navy of his shirt was a great color for him, and with it tucked into hip-hugging denims, the neat-casual style was enough to make most women look twice.

For the first time in a long time, she was feeling pretty lucky herself.

He cleared his throat, and she remembered the question he'd asked. "Um, Jeff's idea of yard work was lying on the chaise while I worked. His only interest in grass was playing football on it, he couldn't have cared less about flowers, and while he loved vegetables, he associated them with grocery stores, not gardens."

The waitress brought their salads, a spring mix of lettuces and grape tomatoes dressed with Luca's special vinegar and oil. Dane waited until she'd left again. "Do you stay in touch with his family?"

"His mom mostly, though she puts Pop on the phone from time to time. They still live in Colorado, where he grew up. He was an only child, and Mia and I were— are—pretty close. What about you? Do you ever talk to your ex-mother-in-law?"

"God, no. Sheryl's mother hated me, all the way back

to the eighth grade when Sheryl and I started going steady. She didn't see me ever getting rich and giving them the life she wanted."

"Them?" Carly echoed.

His smile was crooked. "Rhonda believed in the trickle-down theory. If her daughters married well, naturally some of their prosperity would pass on to her. It worked for her, I guess. Last I heard, she and her husband were living in their new son-in-law's vacation home on the Gulf Coast."

"Better for the son-in-law than actually having them live in his regular home." She took a bite of salad, savoring the tang of the balsamic vinegar with the mellowness of the olive oil, and almost sighed in appreciation. "Just think, if you'd chosen a different career path, that could be you supporting them."

He faked a horrified expression. "With all the downsides to the Army, especially during a war, it's been a much better life than living in the same state as Rhonda."

She toyed with her fork, pushing a crouton around the plate, before setting it down and looking at him. "Would you do it again? I mean, enlist in the Army. If you knew you'd be in combat, that you'd lose friends and your marriage would end and you'd hurt your leg?"

He looked back at her, but his expression was so distant that she doubted he was actually seeing her. He didn't hesitate, though, and there was no uncertainty in his answer. "Yes."

Then, as they both had a habit of doing, he turned the question back on her. "Would you do it again? Marry Jeff if you knew he was going to go to war and not come back?"

Her answer was just as swift, just as certain. "Yes. I have regrets, but loving him is not one of them."

Lord, she hoped falling for Dane wouldn't become one.

They ended their dinner by sharing a dish of Luca's incredible torta barozzi, then went to Carly's house, where she changed into the paint-stained shorts and T-shirt she'd worn the last two nights and they worked in a comfortable silence until the first coat of trim was completed. Her body was aching, the paint fumes were making her eyes water and her nose twitch, and she was tired enough to expect a decent night's sleep.

And her living room was gorgeous.

They were sitting on the edge of the drop cloth, the sofa at their backs, studying the contrast of the colors, when Dane broke the silence with an exhale. "Mind if I borrow a patch of floor for the night? I think I'm too tired to get up."

"I'll help you." But she didn't move. She was too comfortable. "Or maybe I'll just share it with you." Wouldn't the club think that was a hoot, if her first night with another man passed in sleep because they were both too worn out to do anything?

"Do you like the colors?"

"Love 'em. Go, Cowboys."

"That's Oklahoma State. Or Dallas. UT is the Longhorns." He yawned, then stretched, and she tried not to notice too obviously the muscles straining the T-shirt he'd changed into to paint. "I'd better clean the brushes, then go."

"I'll clean them." She stood, her back protesting, and

offered him a hand. He studied it a moment before taking it, and she pulled. Favoring his left leg, he got to his feet, and there he stood. Close enough that she could feel the heat radiating from him. His breath touched her forehead in little puffs, and his eyes…She could get lost in his eyes.

In fact, she thought she might have. It seemed forever when his fingers squeezed hers, then he started toward the door, pulling her along behind him. There he picked up the navy shirt hanging on the knob with his free hand, then asked, "You have plans for tomorrow?"

She moistened her lips with her tongue. "Just the usual. Cleaning, laundry, groceries. I'll be done by noon."

"I'll call you."

"I'll answer." Inwardly wincing at the sappy response, she seized an impulse, one she hadn't felt in a long time, leaned forward, and brushed his mouth with hers.

Again his fingers tightened around hers, and his gaze turned dark with emotion—surprise, uncertainty, temptation, desire. Finally he smiled, just a little one, and let her go as he opened the door.

Almost immediately, though, he stepped back, slid his hand into her hair, dislodging her ragged ponytail, and he kissed her back. It was innocent—no tongues—and sweet and hinted that he wanted so much more. Her fingers were raising, curling, to grab hold of him for support, and a breath later, he stopped kissing her.

"Good night," he murmured, his voice husky, color in his cheeks, as he pivoted and walked away.

"Good night," she whispered as he climbed into his truck, then backed out of the driveway.

She wasn't sure how long she stood there watching—long after his taillights had disappeared from sight—when a breeze sent shivers through her. She closed and locked the door, walked to the living room doorway, let her gaze sweep over her beautiful new walls and trim, then laid her fingers on her mouth.

Experience came slowly but surely. She'd kissed her first boy at eighteen, and now ten years later, she'd kissed the third one.

And it had been nice.

That warm happy feeling carried her through the best night's sleep she'd had in a while. When she woke up Saturday morning, her usual first thought came—twenty-six months, four days—followed by a new one, part wonder, part brag: *Dane kissed me.*

Still in her pajamas, she wandered down to the kitchen, started a cup of coffee and boiled water for oatmeal. Once those were both done, she carried them into the living room, climbed around the end table and into the seat of Jeff's recliner. When the phone rang, she snagged it from another table and said, "Good morning."

A moment of silence followed before Lisa spoke. "Is this a bad time?"

Carly snuggled deeper into the chair. "Of course not. Why do you ask?"

"You sound so...cheerful. I thought maybe you had company."

"This early in the morning?"

"Actually, I meant overnight company."

In the background, three-year-old Eleanor asked, "Does Aunt Carly have slumber parties like me and Missy?"

"Kind of," Lisa said. "Eat your pancakes."

"But I wanted eggs."

"Then you should have *asked* for eggs," Isaac pointed out. "That's what I did, and that's what I got."

"Hush now, kids, while Mom talks to Aunt Carly."

"Okay," Eleanor said with a sigh. "But I still wanted eggs."

Carly laughed. "Some mom you are. You can't even read their minds about breakfast."

"Ah, but I'm impossible to distract. Did you have a slumber party?"

"No, I did not."

"So why the cheerfulness?"

"It's spring, the sun is shining, it's Saturday." *And Dane kissed me.*

"Same thing here, but no cause for joy."

"Well, I'm enjoying my morning sunshine in the middle of my newly painted living room." Before Lisa could ask the inevitable, Carly went on, "Burnt orange walls and cream trim."

Lisa shrieked. "Whoa, when you make a change, you go big. It must be gorgeous when the sun's shining in."

"It is." They'd had to take the blinds down to paint the window trim, and she decided in that moment that she'd leave them down. She didn't need any more privacy than a pair of medium-weight curtains could provide.

"I'm proud of you, sweetie." Lisa's voice took on a wheedling tone that sounded much like her kids when they wanted something. "So who helped?"

"Helped?"

"Last week you said it was too big a job for one person. Who helped?"

"Oh, um, well, Therese and her stepson came over to help move the furniture, and, um, another friend helped with the moving and the painting."

"Male friend or female?"

"What does that matter?" Carly's voice cracked, and she cradled the phone against her shoulder while she wrapped both hands around the coffee mug to warm her suddenly chilled fingers.

Silence, then... "Carly Marie Lowry, do you have a boyfriend?" Lisa whispered excitedly.

Was she ready to tell? The margarita club members all knew something was going on, but that was different. They were everyday friends. Lisa, on the other hand, was family, and if she told her family about Dane, then sooner rather than later she'd have to tell Mia, and that was going to be so hard.

But Lisa was a friend, too, and she would keep any secret Carly entrusted with her.

"It's kind of early to say," she hedged. She didn't want to jinx anything.

"Have you seen him more than once?"

"Yes."

"Told him about Jeff?"

"Yes."

"Have you participated in a physical manifestation of your feelings?"

Carly smiled in spite of the anxiety inside her. "You're going to have to use bigger words than those if you don't want Isaac to understand what you're saying."

"He might understand the words but not the meaning. So... any slumber parties without the slumber?"

"No." Honesty—and the giddy desire to share her newest experience—pressed Carly on. "But he kissed me last night. After I kissed him, granted, but still—"

Another shriek pierced her ear. "Was it wonderful?"

Carly gazed around the room and realized that no matter what happened, now it would always remind her of both Jeff and Dane. Her first love...and maybe her next.

Maybe her last.

"It was," she agreed softly.

"Sweetie, I'm so glad." That was one of the great things about Lisa: Her emotion came through so clearly in her voice. She really was happy for Carly, and she didn't diminish her own pleasure or Carly's by offering warnings.

Lord knows, Carly could provide herself with more warnings than a woman needed.

"One thing, though, Leese. Don't tell anyone about this, okay?"

"Not a word. One more thing from you: What's his name?"

"Dane."

"Dane. I like that."

"Staff Sergeant Dane Clark."

In the moment of silence before Lisa responded, Carly could hear her sister-in-law's reservation: *Oh no, another soldier who could get sent into combat.* But quickly Lisa said, "Sounds handsome and strong. I hope I get to meet him someday."

"I hope so, too," Carly murmured, and she really meant it. She hoped it lasted long enough. She hoped it wasn't one-sided. She just hoped.

"Leese? You don't think..." She breathed deeply.

"Sometimes when I think of me with any other man but Jeff, it seems impossible. Disloyal."

"Oh, sweetie, no one would ever consider you disloyal. We know how much you loved Jeff, how much you still love him. We're so sorry he died and left you alone. But we also know he was the last person on earth who would want you to stay alone, grieving him forever. Carly, you have the capacity to love two men in your lifetime without diminishing either one."

Silence settled for a moment. The only sounds on the phone besides Carly's and Lisa's soft breathing were Isaac and Eleanor arguing over who could eat the most. It was such a normal scene for Lisa, and one Carly had thought she'd never get to experience herself.

She could never have Jeff's babies.

But that didn't mean she couldn't have someone else's babies. Maybe Dane's.

"You're a good friend, Lisa."

Lisa's laugh was warm. "I know. Your brother and family got a great deal when they got me."

"We certainly did. Make sure Roger never forgets that."

"One of the things I live for. I'll let you go, Carly. I've got to clean up this disaster that passes for a kitchen and get these kids over to their grandparents' house before I hit the grocery store. Keep me filled in on all the juicy details with Dane."

"You bet." Fingers crossed that there would be more juicy details. "Love you."

"Love you, too, sweetie."

Slowly Carly set the phone down. *"Love you more"* had always been Jeff's response to her words. Sometimes they'd argued like kids. *"I love you more than anything in the world."*

"I love you more than that."

"There is no more than that."

Her sigh echoed in the room. "I'll always love you, Jeff."

But she prayed Lisa was right, that it was all right for her to love again.

Chapter Ten

Dalton roused long enough to roll onto his side and was about to drift off again when the light outside registered. Sitting bolt upright in bed, he checked the clock, then swore. He hadn't slept until ten since he was a kid, if even then. Life on a ranch didn't allow for lazing around in bed.

He found a clean, ragged pair of jeans in the closet and tugged them on before shoving his feet into socks and boots, then dragging on a work shirt and buttoning it on his way into the bathroom.

Five minutes later, he was taking the stairs two at a time, smelling coffee, bacon, and—he sniffed deeper— Mom's fresh bread. She'd filled the freezer with loaves of it before she and Dad had left again Tuesday morning.

He expected to see Noah sprawled at the table with a heaping plate of food in front of him, but the kitchen was empty. There was a plate on the back of the stove, though, covered with foil, and another on the counter. Leaning

against the coffeemaker was a piece of notepaper, covered
in Noah's scrawl.

Take the day off. I've got things covered here.

His first impulse was to crumple the note, gulp down
some food, and head out to the barn. But as he filled a
travel mug with hot coffee, he tried to remember the last
time he'd taken a day off.

Not even Sandra's funeral had been a true day off.
He'd fed the stock that morning before the service and
had been back out there afterward, leaving his parents to
deal with hers. Noah had come along uninvited, helping
with the chores and saying nothing.

There hadn't been anything worth saying.

A day off. Twelve hours or so with nothing to do except what he wanted. The problem was, what did he want
to do?

He mulled that question as he ate the still-warm eggs
and bacon between two thick slices of Mom's bread. All
in all, not a bad breakfast, especially considering Noah
fixed it. His younger brother didn't have many more skills
in the kitchen than Dalton did, which was why they lived
on sandwiches most of the time.

The problem with an unexpected and unasked-for day
off was that there was nothing he wanted to do, no place
he wanted to go. Maybe Tulsa. He wouldn't run into anyone he knew there, that was for sure. He could see a
movie, eat at a restaurant, maybe buy some new clothes.
He hadn't done any of that since Sandra deployed.

It was a little early, but he could buy some flowers and
go to the cemetery.

Noah would make no secret of the fact that anyone
else in the world could find something better to do on his

one day off, but since he didn't get a vote on it, it didn't matter.

Grabbing a pen, he added a note to Noah's—*Back later*—then got his keys from the hook next to the door and headed out to his truck.

The miles into town passed without Dalton really noticing. Before Sandra, he'd found two dozen things to appreciate on the four miles of dirt road and another two dozen reasons to be grateful for where he lived once he'd turned onto the paved road.

Before Dillon had taken off, both those numbers would have been doubled.

Pansy's Posies was the first flower shop heading into Tallgrass from the north, the primary reason Dalton used it. The owner was a woman about his mother's age and twice as round, with hair the red of a Hereford only a dozen times more intense. She'd come to Tallgrass with her husband when the Army assigned him there thirty years ago, and they'd chosen to stay when he retired. And she was usually a big talker. He'd experienced that.

All she knew about him was that he bought flowers every three or four weeks and paid cash. She teased him about his girl, and he found it easier to let her believe that than tell her the flowers withered on a grave.

There was one other customer inside the shop when he went in, a slender woman whose red hair was as natural as Pansy's wasn't. Waiting at the counter, she gave him a polite smile. He intended to return it but honestly couldn't say whether his mouth had cooperated or not.

He looked around at arrangements to welcome babies, celebrate birthdays and anniversaries, to say thanks or sorry for a loss, winding up at the refrigerators that held fresh flowers in buckets of water along with premade bouquets.

"Pansy will be out in a minute," the redhead said.

"Okay." He slid the cooler door open and chose a vase with flowers the shade of a child's sun. Sandra had liked yellow. Practically half the clothes in her closet had been that color, a bright contrast to the camouflage, green and khaki uniforms in the other half. Had she found much of the color to cheer her in the drab of the desert?

"Those are beautiful," the redhead said. Her gaze flickered to his left hand. "For your wife?"

"Yeah."

Thankfully Pansy chose that moment to return from the workroom, an arrangement of deep red flowers in her arms. "Morning, young man," she greeted Dalton, then showed the bouquet to the customer. "You want me to deliver this?"

The redhead delicately touched one flower, her hand pale against so much color. "I think I'll take them myself this time, Pansy." She settled up, picked up the flowers and gave him another polite nod on her way out.

Pansy chatted as she rang up the yellow flowers, but few of the words registered with him. "Lovely weather...busy around here with Easter coming... daisies...carnations...lucky woman."

If Sandra had been truly lucky, she would have lived to see her twenty-eighth birthday.

He said as little as he could without being rude, paid thirty dollars and carried the heavy-duty plastic vase to the truck, along with a cardboard box to hold it upright in the seat.

Fort Murphy National Cemetery was on the east side

of Tallgrass, its main entrance half a mile past the Fort Murphy gate. He tried not to look at the statues, the flags, the neat rows of marble headstones as he drove to the section where Sandra's marker stood.

He'd visited her grave at all hours of the day and didn't think he'd ever seen the place empty. Today was no exception. Probably half a dozen vehicles were parked alongside the roads, including one right where he always parked. Its driver was bent over at a gravesite, placing deep red flowers in the grass, a mix of straw yellow and spring green. The sunlight danced on her hair when she straightened and swiped her cheek.

His muscles tight, he collected his own flowers and cut as wide a path around her as he could without going into the next section.

Though as a kid he'd accompanied his mother to the area cemeteries on Memorial Day, when he couldn't wriggle out of it, he'd never seen much sense in visiting graves. If you couldn't take time for a person when they were alive, what did it matter when they were dead?

That was before he'd buried anyone really important to him.

He didn't stay long. She was dead, after all, and he didn't talk to the dead...or to most living people these days. He put the flowers down, stared at the name, rank, and dates inscribed in the marble, said his thousandth mental good-bye, then took a deep breath and headed back to his truck.

He was almost there, head ducked, hands shoved in his pockets, when a shadow shifted across the ground in front of him. It was the redhead, leaning against her car, watching him.

"Hi again," she said.

It was too late to avoid her and too rude to ignore her. Whatever faults he had, rudeness wasn't usually one of them. His mother had taught her boys to be polite when they could and respectful when they should.

If a cemetery didn't require respect, what did?

"Was Sandra your wife?"

Frowning, he looked over his shoulder and could barely make out the writing on the stone, and then only because he knew what it said. The grave bearing the red flowers was nearer so he could read the name easily: Aaron Lawrence.

"She was," he said at last, then nodded toward the red flowers. "Your husband?"

"Yeah. He died two and a half years ago. What about Sandra?" She raised one hand to brush her hair back. "I've got great vision, but the dates are smaller."

It was strange, someone talking openly about Sandra's death. His family tiptoed around it, probably because he'd taught them to do so by his responses. "Nearly four years. She died in Afghanistan."

"Aaron, too." She sighed, turning to gaze across the cemetery. "So many people..."

Dalton looked, too, at the nearby sections with their obviously newer stones. Rows of them, and this was just one cemetery. Just one very small group of the service members who had died in the most recent conflicts.

Before the full impact of that could sink in, the redhead moved again, coming closer, extending her hand. "I'm Jessy."

He looked at her hand as warily as if it were a copperhead. He hadn't really talked to any woman besides his mom since Sandra's death—hadn't touched any woman besides his mom once he'd tolerated all the hugs of condolence at the funeral or here at the graveside.

"Dalton," he said, finally accepting her hand. Her fingers were soft, her nails a ridiculous shade of purple, not a pale Easter-y shade but loud, bright.

"Nice meeting you, Dalton." She drew her hand back, then suddenly seemed as if she didn't know what to do with it. Sliding it into her pocket, she took a few steps backward before turning to circle her car. There, she looked back at him. "Hey, I'm headed over to Aaron's favorite bar to get a burger and drink a beer in his honor. I don't suppose...I wonder...Would you like to join me?"

A burger and a beer; Sandra's favorite combination. He could get it at any of a number of restaurants between Tallgrass and Tulsa, eat it by himself, and wish he'd stayed home. At least around here, he wouldn't be far from home when he needed it.

"Yeah. Sure. Where?"

She perked up, her green eyes flashing with a smile. "Bubba's on Main Street. You know it?"

"Yeah." He and Dillon had been thrown out of it often enough back after high school. The burgers and fries were the only things on the menu, and they were greasy. The beer was cold, the country music loud, and the clientele mostly oilfield workers or cowboys. Even though she wore jeans and boots, he wouldn't have figured her for a Bubba's fan. She looked too classy for cowboys and beer-crying music.

"Then I'll meet you there."

He climbed into his truck and followed her to the

cemetery exit. There she caught a break in traffic a couple minutes before him. It would be easy for him to turn off anywhere along the street and head on to Tulsa or back home. It wouldn't be a disappointment to Jessy. Within five minutes of her walking into the bar, Bubba's regulars would be hitting on her. She wouldn't be lonely.

But he didn't turn off the street and head to Tulsa or back home. He kept driving west, through downtown, past the fringe of businesses as Main Street turned into a highway. More than a mile outside the town limits, he turned into Bubba's parking lot. The bar was a log building, with a porch that ran the length of the front. Steps climbed both ends and in the middle, and a split-log rail did its best to keep patrons from pitching headfirst into the gravel lot. Even in midday, neon beer signs glowed in the windows.

And the redhead waited at the top of the stairs. For him.

Maybe for a little while, he wouldn't be lonely, either.

"You heading anywhere special?"

Dane stopped at the sound of Justin's voice and turned to watch him swing out his front door on his crutches as naturally as if he'd been born with them. Carly was expecting him to pick her up in fifteen minutes, but she wouldn't mind if he was late, especially if Justin was the reason. "You need to go anywhere special?"

"Nah, not really. I was just thinking about maybe catching a ride downtown—go to the movie or something. It's one of those days, you know?"

Dane knew those days: When the pills weren't enough to knock down the pain, or when you would give anything you owned just to be like you were before, or when you wondered if you were working your butt off for nothing, if you were ever going to get better. Times that on occasion left you so tired, so down, that you started wondering if you wouldn't have been better off dead.

According to the shrinks, most guys in the program went through it sooner or later. The cadre was always watching for signs of depression, the inability to cope or anything remotely suicidal. Those guys could go downhill really fast—*not them, us*—from fumbling along, trying to find their way, to dead in no time.

In the early weeks after being wounded, Dane had caught himself sliding on that slope a few times.

"Forget the movie," he suggested. "Carly and I are going to Tulsa to do some shopping and have dinner. Come with us."

Justin's look was skeptical. "Man, you've been out of the dating world too long. You can't invite another guy to tag along on a date unless you're looking to dump her on him or you're just weird. And I know you ain't looking to dump Carly."

"I'm not weird, either. At least, not in that way. She's just looking for a new rug and a few lamps or paintings or something. It's a shopping trip with dinner thrown in. She wouldn't mind at all."

Justin came a few steps closer, leaning on his crutches. There were lines at the corners of his eyes and his mouth. He was always so positive that sometimes Dane wanted to punch him, but now he just looked tired. "You ever tell her you're missing one leg?"

"Not yet. And if you do, I'll beat you with your crutches."

Justin scoffed and slowly started toward the parking lot. "You've got to get 'em away from me first. Even in this shape, I bet my sorry ass can outrun yours."

It wasn't a bet Dane was willing to take.

When they got to his truck, Justin passed the passenger door for the rear door. "What? Am I your chauffeur now?" Dane popped off as he got into the driver's seat.

"Carly should sit up front, and it's easier to get in once than twice." Justin carefully eased himself onto the running board, then into the backseat, stowing his crutches across the rest of the seat.

This was good, having Justin along. It would ease any awkwardness from the way they'd said good-bye the night before. Dane hadn't expected her to kiss him, and he really hadn't expected to kiss her back. It was normal, considering how much time they'd spent together, but not given who they were: Carly who loved perfection and him, hiding his imperfection.

Besides, the guilty voice in his head pointed out, he wouldn't have to find a reason to slow her down on the shopping or else push himself so that his leg throbbed all night. She would take it easy for Justin's sake, and the fact that Dane would benefit from it as well would be just between him and Justin.

When he got to her house, he went to the door to get her, partly because his father had raised him that way and partly to judge if those kisses had changed anything. *How* they'd changed it.

She opened the door before he had a chance to knock, wearing jeans, an eye-popping orange print top, and a smile that could make him and Justin both weak in the knees if they weren't already. Her hair hung loose, and her lips were tinged a faint pink, and he wanted to kiss her again more than he wanted to breathe.

"Hi," she said softly. "Let me get a jacket and my purse."

He stood in the doorway, watching her until the closet door blocked his view, then shifted to look in the living room. Even with the furniture still clumped in the middle, the colors made it a whole different room.

Would Jeff have been happy with walls so orange?

"I'm not a big shopper," Carly said as she came back down the hall, a buttery gold leather jacket over one arm, "but I'm looking forward to this. I haven't bought anything new for the house since . . . ages."

Since before Jeff died.

"Um, I asked Justin to come with us." Dane stepped out onto the stoop again and waited while she locked the door. "He's having kind of a tough day, and . . . Do you mind?"

"Of course not. Poor baby. He's always so cheerful and determined. I knew he had to have some down days, but I've never seen them."

"Poor baby? He's eight inches taller and forty pounds heavier than you."

"He's an overgrown kid." She smiled innocently. "Most men are."

Dane opened the door for her, closed it, then walked back around the truck while she greeted Justin. Sheryl's temper tantrums whenever their plans changed unexpectedly—especially if he was the reason for the change—had been legendary among their friends. Carly was one-eighty different. She really didn't mind having Justin along. Just one more of the things Dane liked about her.

Many things.

Tulsa was about an hour southeast, the road running past pastures growing anew, redbuds and fruit trees in bloom and fuzzy yellow tendrils signaling the arrival of leaves on the oak trees. It wouldn't be long before the bluebonnets were in bloom down in Texas—just about the only thing in the state that Dane missed. They'd been his grandmother's favorite flower, and he was pretty sure from the way Carly pointed out various wildflower patches that she would love them, too.

Maybe, when he got around to telling her the truth, if she stuck around after that, they could drive down one weekend, see the flowers and eat at a couple of his father's favorite old places.

That was a big *if.*

Once in Tulsa, they hit a couple of furniture stores, where Carly picked out an area rug, mostly light brown with a few squares of bright color, and two lamps made of wrought iron and stone. Dane and Justin were happy to test a sofa she kept returning to, but in the end she decided to think about that and bought a small square table instead to use as an end table.

With the rug and table in the bed of the truck and the lamps sharing the backseat with Justin, they headed to a Mexican restaurant on the north side of town that one of Carly's friends had recommended.

"Lucky we're early for dinner," Justin said as they squeezed inside the door. "If we'd waited another hour, we'd probably be standing in line somewhere around the corner."

"My friend says the food is that good," Carly replied.

There were a dozen tables in the dining room and half

that many small booths. The only place to sit was in the booth farthest from the door, requiring a zigzag through spaces barely wide enough for Justin's crutches.

A booth—and Justin—meant Dane sat next to Carly, closer than they'd ever been, including in the cave the day they'd met. He felt like an inexperienced kid sitting close for the first time to his latest crush, not quite sure how to sit, where to put his hands, if it was okay to lay his arm along the back of the seat.

You're thirty years old. You've been with plenty of women. You were married. Act like it.

But none of those women had been Carly, and he'd had a pair of matching legs at the time. He'd had plenty of confidence and a healthy sense of self-worth. At the moment, he had little of either. Geez, he didn't even know how well the mechanics of sex would work for him now. He knew it *would*, just not what would be the same, what would be different.

Just that it wouldn't be perfect.

While looking over the menu, he wasted a moment wishing he'd met Carly before his last deployment. But she'd been married then, and before that, back when she'd been single, he had been the one with the ring and the vows. She wouldn't have broken hers, and he'd never broken his.

Life's timing sucked.

The sound of a cell phone woke Dalton from sleep. He frowned, unable to recognize anything about the tone beyond the fact it was splitting his head in two. His own phone just had regular rings, and Noah kept "Ride 'Em Cowboys" on his, like any good OSU student.

Abruptly, the sound stopped, followed by a murmured curse and the rustling of covers. Dalton stiffened, barely able to drag a breath into his lungs. What the hell...Where...Who...

His memories returned in bits, pushing through the ache in his head and the bass drums that boomed around it. The cemetery, red hair, purple nails, dark red flowers. A burger and a beer, in honor of her husband and his wife. Switching to harder stuff, trying to keep up with her, stumbling out of Bubba's together and almost taking a header over the split rail. A laugh, a kiss, and—

Oh God, he was in bed. With Jessy Lawrence. Naked.

After rousing enough to silence the phone, she'd gone to sleep again, lying on her stomach, the sheet slipped down to her waist. Her skin was creamy gold—a redhead with a tan—and her hair tumbled over her face, blocking it from his gaze. Her breathing was deep and slow and just almost a snore.

Carefully he eased from under the covers and to his feet. The where, he decided, must be the motel at the far end of Bubba's parking lot. It wasn't the sort of place he would choose to take a woman. But then, he'd never taken any woman to a motel, except for Sandra on their wedding night, and that had been a suite at the Bellagio in Las Vegas.

He found his clothes scattered across the room, along with two condom wrappers. Not his. Nice to know that Jessy Lawrence went prepared for a good time when she visited her dead husband's grave.

The sarcasm faded as he quickly, quietly dressed. If he was going to get so drunk he didn't know what he was doing—and that was the only explanation he could think of for his being there—it was good to know that she, at least, had been prepared.

Should he do something? Wake her up and say something? He picked up her clothes, his face turning hot as he handled the skimpy bra and panties, and left them more or less neatly on the dresser. He located one of her boots under the bed, the other across the room, and he set those together in front of the dresser.

That was it for doing. As for saying something? The only thing he could think of was *God, what a mistake. Let's forget this ever happened. I hope I never see you again.*

He figured since she was a stranger that could go unsaid, so he let himself out of the room, closing the door softly behind him, and headed into the dark to his truck.

When Therese got home Tuesday afternoon, she was greeted by the sound of video games from Jacob's room, muted by the floor and carpet. Abby's voice became audible a few steps inside the door, coming from the kitchen, likely a rehash of the day with Nicole, whom she'd just left five or ten minutes earlier.

Therese knew the instant Abby became aware of her: When she said, "Gotta go. *She's* home."

Lord, grant me patience. It had been a difficult day at school, with the kids wound up, both her aide and her volunteer parent absent, and a headache throbbing dully right between her eyes. It didn't look as if the next few hours were going to be any more fun.

Thank God it was Tuesday.

She walked into the kitchen and laid her bag and coat on the table. "How was your day?"

"Eh." Abby hadn't changed from her school uniform yet: navy plaid skirt, hem brushing the top of her knees until she rolled it four times at the waist; white shirt, sleeves unbuttoned and cuffed; navy blue vest. Add kneesocks and a ponytail, and the look was so classic, it was a stereotype.

Add black hiking boots and the scarlet streaks in her hair, and it was just a bit twisted.

"You had a math test today, didn't you? How did that go?"

"Eh." Abby opened the refrigerator and tossed sandwich makings onto the island. The bread landed with a whoosh of plastic, and the stoneware plate bumped a time or two before settling.

"'Eh' isn't an answer. How did the test go?" Therese asked as she circled the other end of the island to start a mug of coffee brewing. A couple of aspirin tablets washed down with caffeine would go a long way toward easing her headache.

Along with the anticipation of an evening out.

"I'm not stupid. I aced it."

Her jaw clenched, Therese ran the grinder, scooped coffee grounds and measured water, then shoved a mug into place and turned the machine on. In seconds, the fresh aroma of coffee filtered into the air, encouraging her to breathe deeply. "Good for you."

"Oh, yeah, good for me for passing a stupid math test. Big deal." Abby squirted big gobs of mayo and mustard on each slice of bread, slapped ham on one side, cheese on the other, then mashed the two sides together and started from the kitchen.

"Hey, don't forget to put everything up."

Abby whirled back around. "Why should I clean up? That's your job."

Could you hurry with the patience, Lord? Mine's about to slip through my fingers.

The coffee finished dripping, and Therese concentrated fiercely on stirring in two packets of sweetener to offset the real cream she put in. "You're part of this family, and that comes with responsibilities, such as not leaving meat and cheese on the counter once you've made your sandwich."

"Well, I didn't ask to be part of this *family*, so you can put it away yourself."

Abby started toward the door again, but so did Therese. Catching the kid off guard, she managed to block Abby's path, her fingers curled tightly around her coffee mug, her jaw aching with tension. "I know you'd rather live anywhere but here, Abby. You've made that clear. But you do live here, and I expect at least a minimum of courtesy. Put the meat, the cheese, the mustard, and the mayo back in the refrigerator." Her voice was steady, her tone firm, not angry at all—amazing when the only name she could put to the emotions roiling inside her was anger.

Abby backed up a few steps and set the plate on the island. Thinking she was giving in, Therese forced her muscles to relax at least a little, but they tightened again when Abby placed both hands on her hips.

"Make me."

Oh God, how had her life come to this? When she was growing up, disobedience, defiance, or disrespect had never been an option. Her parents simply hadn't tolerated it. Their disappointment would have been enough to dissuade her if she'd even thought about acting up.

But Abby didn't care about disappointing her. She didn't respect Therese and didn't want her respect in exchange.

Therese's chest tightened. What was she supposed to do if Abby refused to obey? If she just pushed past and went on her way? She had no emotional ammunition to use, and she couldn't use physical force. She could only ground her—again. Take away her cell phone—again. Consequences that didn't seem to have any effect besides making Abby angrier.

The girl—Paul's daughter—was staring at her with such disdain, such stubbornness that Therese's impulse was to walk away. Give in. Give up. Then the thud of footsteps sounded in the hallway and Jacob came into the room.

He headed straight to the counter, apparently not noticing the tension in the room. "Oh, good, you got the sandwich stuff out for me." He playfully shoved his sister with his shoulder when he passed, grabbed a plate and started putting together a sandwich twice the size of hers.

"Don't forget to put it away when you're done." Picking up her own plate again, Abby smiled maliciously at Therese all the way to the door.

She'd won. Therese had lost.

No, the truth was, they'd both lost. There weren't any winners in this game—none of them, not Catherine, certainly not Paul. It was just sorrow and regret and bitterness.

And that was no way to live.

Aware of the numbness in her fingertips from holding so tightly to the cup and with a deep weariness in her heart, Therese went down the hall to the living room and

curled up in her favorite chair. She sat there, coffee growing cold, head still hurting, staring at the largest photo of
Paul on the mantel until her sight grew blurry.

She was tired of pretending everything was going to be
okay, of living without Paul, of living with his children,
of being lonely and stressed, of not having anyone to love
and love her back.

She didn't know how long she would have sat like that
if Jacob hadn't stopped in the doorway. "Aren't you going
to the Mexican place tonight?"

Startled, she looked his way and saw so much of Paul
in him that tears came to her eyes. She swallowed and
blinked them away before checking her watch. It was a
quarter to six. "Yes. I am. I was just thinking…"

"About Dad?"

That surprised her even more. Jacob didn't talk about
his father, not to her. He didn't initiate any conversation
with her if he could avoid it. Gingerly, half afraid he'd
startle if she moved too quickly, she smiled. "I was. I miss
him a lot."

That was one of the many holes in her life: Someone
to talk to about Paul who'd known him. Her parents
had loved him, but they'd only seen him a few times a
year. His parents were more interested in criticizing her
parental skills than reminiscing, transfers had kept their
Army friends on the move, and she'd never felt comfortable bringing him up with the kids.

Jacob shuffled his feet, his gaze locked somewhere between them, and muttered, "I do, too." Then, before she
could say anything, he rushed on: "You should go."

She should. She was rarely late, a quality well suited
to the regimentation of school and Army life. She stood

and walked to the doorway, pausing there long enough to look up at him. *Up.* He was so tall, no longer the little boy whose head hadn't even topped her shoulder when they'd met.

"I'll be back around the usual time. If you need anything, you can call Liam's mother or—or me."

He nodded, then went into the living room and sprawled on the couch, turning on the TV with the remote. When she passed by the room after retrieving her jacket and bag from the kitchen, he gave no sign that he heard her good-bye.

Chapter Eleven

"Human contact," Lucy announced. "That's what I miss most."

"Intimate contact," Marti added, and Lucy nodded.

"Not just the wild monkey sex, but a hug. Holding hands. Warm legs to put my feet on in winter. Snoring."

"Does Caveman snore?" Marti asked.

All eyes turned Carly's way, and she blushed. "I have no idea." When they feigned disappointment, she teasingly added, "But he's a great kisser."

He'd kissed her again Saturday night, after they'd dropped Justin off at his quarters, then unloaded her new stuff at her house, and on Sunday night. She hadn't seen him Monday or so far today, but she was cooking dinner for him tomorrow. A turkey breast in the slow-cooker and all the traditional side dishes. She was nearly giddy with anticipation.

"At least you're getting that much," Jessy said, drawing one fingertip around the rim of her empty margarita glass. "The only intimacy in my life is with my gynecologist."

"And not being preggers like Ilena here, you can only see him every so often." With a shiver, Marti drew on her jacket. Cold? Or remembering what it was like when Joshua was alive?

"I miss having someone who knows what buttons to push to make my blood pressure redline." Fia sighed. "I never thought I'd wish for a fart joke or cans of flat pop in the refrigerator or huge lint balls in the dryer because Scott never remembered to clean the trap."

Lucy's snort jiggled her round cheeks. "Mike never put a load of wet clothes in the dryer. It could mildew in the washer for all he cared."

As the others joked about their husbands' faults, Carly stirred the melted contents of her weekly drink. Jeff had liked jokes about bodily functions, too, and he'd been perfectly happy to put one shirt or pair of pants in the dryer while leaving the washer full of wet clothes. It was a guy thing, she supposed, and they'd all been married to such *guys*.

The conversation faltered after a moment, silence settling at the table like a soft quilt on a cold night. Jessy broke it by reaching across and taking the glass from under Carly's straw. "Every week you come in here and waste perfectly good tequila. Being environmentally conscious, I'm going to put it to good use."

"Environmentally conscious?" Marti snickered. "You use paper napkins, eat off foam plates *all the time*, and drink from plastic cups. You don't recycle, you don't reduce, and you don't reuse."

Jessy tossed back the drink, then smirked. "Then how

about fiscally frugal? Try saying that three times fast with three and a half margaritas in you. But who's counting?"

No one pointed out that she'd had four and a half. But they weren't counting, right? And Jessy could handle liquor way better than Carly. *She* would be unconscious before she could drink that much in one evening.

Life was too precious to lose even one evening to unconsciousness.

"So." Ilena rested her hands on her stomach and fixed a curious gaze on Carly. "Where exactly do things stand with you and Dane?"

Six expectant faces looked her way. "Well...I guess we're dating."

"We know that, sweetie." That, along with a shoulder nudge, came from Therese. "We want to know how serious it is. How often do you see each other? Are you the only woman he's seeing? What do you talk about? What do you do?"

"Has he copped a feel yet?" Lucy's words were followed immediately by a blush. "Oh, great, now I'm sounding rude like Jessy."

"I'm not rude," Jessy protested. "I just cut through the bull—"

Ilena clamped her hand over Jessy's mouth. "Not in front of Hector Junior, please. Besides, we're putting Carly under the microscope now, not you."

"Thank God for small miracles."

Carly looked from one woman to the next, ending with Therese, then quietly said, "I like him. A lot. He's...special. And I think he likes me, too. A lot. I think." Growing warm under their gazes, she twisted her wedding ring in slow circles. "It's all pretty new, you guys. I don't know where we'll be in a month or six months or even next week. It's kind of scary to look that far ahead. When I married Jeff, I thought it was for the rest of eternity. I didn't know 'forever' was going to be four years."

Four years was no eternity. She'd been anticipating sixty or more.

At least, however pitifully few, their years had been happy. They'd had fights, of course, and there'd been a few times when they'd gone to bed mad, but oh, the making up had been sweet.

Blinking back the moisture that stung her eyes, she deflected the conversation away from herself. "Ilena, you're not really going to call that child Hector, are you?"

The blond faked offense. "I am, after his father."

"But his father went by Juan," Fia pointed out.

"Well...I *am* naming him Hector. Hector Juan Lewis Gomez. For his father, his father's father and my father. But his daddy insisted we would call him John."

His daddy who'd never known of his existence. She and Dane had talked about so much, but she had no clue how he felt about kids. Did he like them? Want them? Was it too early for her to even be wondering?

As she'd said earlier, it was all so new. She could be investing way too much hope in this relationship...but that was the way her heart worked.

Please, God, don't let it get broken again.

It was Therese who moved to leave first. "Wish I could stay longer, but kids at home and school tomorrow."

Carly gathered her things, then hooked her arm through Jessy's as they strolled to the door, a few steps behind the rest. "You okay?"

Jessy gave her a sidelong look. "Sure. Why do you ask?"

Should she mention the drinking? It wasn't as if she'd ever seen the redhead tipsy or stumbling. She never slurred her words, didn't miss work, didn't drive after having a drink or two.

Was it up to Carly to even decide what was too many? She readily admitted she wasn't a drinker. Even Mia imbibed more than she did. Heavens, her own mother enjoyed a glass or two of wine with dinner on a regular basis.

She chose to let it slide. "Just wondering. Can I give you a ride home?"

Outside the door, Jessy paused, face tilted to the night sky, eyes closed. She took a few deep breaths, then looked at Carly, her gaze as clear as could be. "Thanks, but I like the walk."

"I'm not brave enough to walk alone at night."

"Night? See all these lights? And there are restaurants or clubs on every block. If I screamed once, a whole company of soldiers would come racing to my rescue." Jessy's grin was quick and lascivious. "Hey, that's not a bad idea."

Carly laughed. She'd never had a bit of the other woman's boldness and never would.

"Go home, kiddo," Jessy said, tugging her into a hug. "Call soldier boy and tell him good night. Better yet, invite him over and show him a good night. Then tell me all about it, would you?"

Carly watched her head off west on Main Street before turning to the eastside parking lot and her car. Calling Dane and telling him good night... Hey, that wasn't a bad idea.

She drove home, letting herself in, then stopping

abruptly in the doorway to the living room. Therese and Jacob had helped her and Dane put all the furniture back in place Sunday afternoon, along with laying the rug. It still surprised her every time she saw the new room, as if the turn in the very familiar hallway had taken her to a very unfamiliar place.

She liked it.

She was ready for bed, warming a cup of milk in the microwave and debating what changes to make next, when the cell phone rang. Recognizing the number on the display, she answered with a smile. "Hello."

"Do you ever get tired of Mexican every Tuesday night?"

Tilting her head to hold the phone, she stirred chocolate sauce into the milk, then licked the leftover bit on the spoon. "No. I'm just a routine sort of person, I guess. I find it comforting to know that a few things in my life are carved in stone."

Dane's voice was thoughtful when he replied. "Yeah, I can see that. How are the margarita girls?"

Taking her milk and a magazine from the day's mail, she padded down the hall to the bedroom. Maybe the dimly lit corridor should be her next project. Sunshiny yellow or pure bright white. She'd have to ask Dane's opinion.

She settled in bed, sliding her feet under the covers, and gave him a quick update on the six regulars.

"And how about you?"

"Good." It wasn't her usual automatic response, the one that had become standard after Jeff's death, the answer most people hadn't really wanted to hear to a question they felt obligated to ask. *I'm fine. I'm doing okay.*

I'm all right. People showed they cared by asking, and she acknowledged it by not burdening them with the truth.

Tonight she really was good.

"What are you up to?" she asked.

"Seeing how long I can lie on the couch flipping through the TV channels and eating potato chips."

She laughed at the image. "Wow, strenuous work. What's your record?"

"Forty-seven hours if you don't count bathroom breaks and switching to cookies when the potato chips ran out. That was in Italy."

"After the divorce?" She couldn't imagine the woman who'd chosen affairs over him, especially being so indiscreet. If Carly ever had an affair, it would have to be the most closely guarded secret in America and she would have to be certifiably nuts. She didn't *believe* in breaking vows.

"Yeah, but that wasn't why. We'd just gotten back from three weeks' training in Germany and had a long weekend off. That was how I spent half of it."

She echoed his words back to him. "Yeah, I can see that. I'd certainly need forty-seven hours vegging out on the couch after three weeks in Germany."

"Hey, it was work. Mostly." His yawn came through the phone. "Want me to bring anything tomorrow night?"

Just yourself. "Um, no, I've got it covered." Mia's recipe for the turkey, Lisa's for the dressing, Therese's foolproof gravy. She'd figured out the sweet potatoes and the pecan pie on her own.

"Okay." This time his yawn triggered the same in her. "I'll see you around six."

"Good night."

The instant she laid the phone down, she missed him. It had been that way with Jeff. He could have been 7,500 miles away, but while they were on the phone, it was as if he were right next to her, and when he hung up, she felt so alone.

This time there was a certain comfort, though, in the fact that the solitude wouldn't last long. She would see Dane in about eighteen hours, and instead of dwelling on the time apart, she was anticipating tomorrow's dinner. As she settled pillows behind her back and opened the magazine, her brain warned that she was expecting too much too soon.

But her heart didn't care, and it hadn't led her wrong yet.

The last thing on Dane's schedule before leaving work Wednesday was meeting with the first sergeant, his cadre squad leader, about his upcoming thirty-day assessment.

"You haven't decided yet what you want to do," First Sergeant Chen remarked. "You know, this is just a preliminary report. No one expects you to be a hundred percent about anything yet. Are you leaning one way or the other?"

Dane shifted in his chair. "Depends on when you ask. After physical or occupational therapy, I'm pretty sure the answer is transition out. Some days I think I might as well stay, and others I wonder..." He gazed at the framed commendations on the wall, thinking of his own collection on his own wall. "I always thought I'd make a career in the Army, in Airborne. I wasn't prepared to put in twelve years, then not be able to jump anymore, not be combat-ready anymore."

And there was one more thing to factor into his decision now: Carly. Obviously she didn't mind dating a soldier, but how would she feel about getting serious with one? A lot of women were like Army groupies, going from one soldier to the next, but Carly wasn't that kind. She'd been through the training, the deployments, the separations. Worse, she'd had to deal with Jeff's death: the casualty notification; the days waiting for his body to return; the dignified transfer home to Colorado; the funeral arrangements; the funeral itself; living without him.

If Dane stayed in, he wouldn't likely be sent back into combat, but he was still deployable. There would still be separations, and there were still hazards inherent to the job. Would she *want* to be with another soldier, not just dating but on a permanent basis? Would she want even the slightest risk of being an Army widow not once but twice?

God, was he really thinking about getting married again? Falling in love again?

Not so much thinking about it, he was afraid, as verging on doing it. Getting involved. Caring. Wanting a lot from a woman who still didn't know exactly the man she was dealing with.

"You know, there's a lot you can do besides Airborne," Chen said. "You're an Eleven-Charlie. You could reclassify without too much trouble and teach at the artillery school at Fort Sill. You could be an instructor at TRADOC at Fort Polk, getting units ready to deploy. If you have any interest in medicine, you could go to Fort

Sam." A wicked grin spread across his face. "If you want to go back home, you could do recruiting."

Dane snorted. "Yeah, I'd be a great one to sign up new recruits. *Join the Army, get shot at, and get your leg blown off.* No, thanks, First Sergeant. Recruiting's tough duty."

And the worst place he could possibly be stationed was back home, where he would almost certainly run into his ex-wife and her happy family, where his mother would make sure not a soul in the county was unaware of her poor crippled son. *I told him not to join the Army, but no, he wouldn't listen. And there he is, not even a whole man anymore. Good thing his wife left him before this happened. Can you imagine how hard this would have been for her?*

"You got any particular reason for getting out or staying in?"

"Besides the body parts I lost?" Dane asked drily.

Chen laughed. "Yeah, but lucky for you, the Army had replacement parts in stock."

"Yeah. Lucky me. Lucky *us.*"

Dane had met First Sergeant Chen eight years ago, when they were both stationed in Korea. They'd been friendly enough, though not the kind of buddies who hung out together. They'd been through a lot since then. Chen had gotten married, Dane divorced. Chen had three little girls no more than a year apart in age, their photos decorating the desk. Dane wasn't sure kids were in his future. They'd both gone to Iraq twice.

Chen had lost his left arm from the elbow down and his left foot on his first tour in Afghanistan, and Dane had lost his leg on his second tour.

Chen was coping. Dane wasn't.

"There's a woman." Dane blinked. He'd intended to say no, nothing pulling him either way, but the words had come out on their own.

"Isn't there always."

"She doesn't know."

"About your leg?" Chen waited for him to nod. "Yeah, I've noticed you tend to avoid any unnecessary display of the prosthesis."

"I can't pretend it's not there if I have to look at it all the time." Though at the moment, even with his pants leg and boot covering it, he couldn't forget it for a second. "She's got this thing about perfection."

Chen's chair squeaked as he rocked back, hands folded across his stomach. His left hand was so similar in skin tone and he was so comfortable with it that people who didn't know it was a prosthetic wouldn't notice the difference. "Is *she* perfect?"

Wishing he hadn't started this conversation, Dane managed a weak grin. "Pretty much, yeah."

"Is she pretty? Smart? Nice?" After Dane muttered "yeah" to each question, Chen grinned again. "Then what's she doing with you?"

Getting over Jeff? Taking a step back to some semblance of a normal life? Maybe falling for him, too?

"There comes a point where she's got to know. *Seriously.* I mean, you can't"—he shrugged—"without her finding out. If she's smart and nice, it's not going to matter. If it does make a difference, better to find out before it's too late, right?"

That all sounded good and logical. But... "How can I ask her to accept something I haven't gotten used to yet?"

"I'll tell you something my wife told me back at Walter Reed, Staff Sergeant. There's only two ways to look at the situation you're in. You can be grateful for what you've still got and make the most out of life, or you can mourn what you've lost and miss out on the rest of your life.

"I know it was hard losing your foot. I know it was even harder when they had to take you back and do the second amputation, and I can only imagine how tough it was when they did the third one, because they're not just cutting off tissue and bone then, they're cutting off hard work and hope. But you're *alive*. You can still do just about anything you want. You just have to make adjustments, and the mental adjustment is the hardest one of all. But do you want to guess how many people buried in those cemeteries all across the country would have loved to trade places with you?"

"Yeah," Dane murmured. "One in particular." At the first sergeant's look, he went on. "Carly's a member of this group in town. They call themselves the Tuesday Night Margarita Club."

Recognition flashed across Chen's face. "The widows' club. How long has it been for her?"

"A couple years. A helicopter crash in Afghanistan."

"Any kids?"

"No."

"You've got to tell her at some point, Staff Sergeant, even if you don't know where things are going. Like I said, better to find out if it matters before it's too late."

"Before it's too late." The words kept echoing in Dane's head long after he'd gotten home, showered and dressed for dinner. How was he supposed to tell her? It

wasn't something he could just drop into casual conversation. *This is a great meal. The paint job in the living room looks really good. By the way, when I mentioned I'd torn up my leg, what I meant was they amputated three-fourths of it. Mind if I grab another Coke?*

Yeah, that would go over well.

He was kicked back on the sofa, the television on but muted, when his cell phone rang. He glanced at the screen to make sure it wasn't Carly, then silenced the phone. Two minutes later it rang again, and once more two minutes after that. Anna Mae didn't give up once she decided to do something, and apparently today she was determined to talk to him.

With a sigh, he answered.

"You know, you should really keep your phone with you all the time," she said in place of a greeting. "I mean, in your condition and all, having so much trouble getting around, it would be easier if you kept it in your pocket. And what if you fell or something? How would you call for help?"

"Funny thing about the Army. They keep tabs on us soldiers who need extra help—you know, the brain-injury patients, the ones with PTSD, and the people missing arms and legs."

Anna Mae's response was what his dad had always referred to as her "miffed sniff." Bill had been good at teasing her into a better mood, but Dane had never had the gift. "As they should, considering they're responsible for crippling all of you."

"Mom, I'm not crippled." Like First Sergeant Chen had pointed out, a lot of people would rather have lost a limb or two than died. And a whole lot of people would have thanked God to get their child, spouse, or parent back in his condition.

Another sniff. "Disabled, then. Do you prefer that?"

Closing his eyes, Dane rubbed his temple with his free hand. It was the place where his patience resided, he decided, and Anna Mae could drain it empty with laser-guided accuracy in a matter of seconds.

How many times had he told her he wasn't disabled or handicapped? A dozen, at least. His brain still worked fine, and so did most of his body.

So why did he care so damn much about the part that was missing?

"I'd prefer not to be labeled at all." Not that he expected her to listen, much less hear. "How are you?"

"I'm just doing the usual stuff. Oh, and I've started volunteering at the church with the preschool program. I figure since I'm never going to get grandkids from you, I'd better find substitutes somewhere. Though, of course, there's always Sheryl's babies. They're practically mine." Her tone turned a hundred shades lighter, more enthusiastic. "She's just *glowing* with this pregnancy. Her doctor's got her doing yoga, and she's looking more beautiful every day." She heaved a longing sigh. "I do wish you would have tried to work things out with her."

"Sorry. It wasn't meant to be." Sheryl hadn't liked monogamy, and he wasn't cut out to ignore her affairs. His dad would have understood, but his mom had a different outlook. Yet Bill had loved her until the day he died. Some mysteries were never meant to be solved.

"When can you come for a visit? You know, the baby's due—"

Startled by the question, Dane tuned out the rest. Sure, he'd have to go home sometime before his mother died, but he was figuring on at least another ten years before he had to worry about that. He didn't *want* to go home. Didn't want to stay in the house he'd grown up in, where he'd had such big plans. Didn't want to see his ex-wife and her children.

Didn't really want to see his mother, not until he had a better grip on his life and his future.

"We-ell?"

He knew that voice: *I asked you a question and I want an answer.* Though he'd blocked out everything after "baby's due," he knew the question hadn't changed. It never did with Anna Mae. "I don't know when I can get time off."

"Texas and Oklahoma are neighbors, you know, and we're talking about a weekend. You can't spare a weekend?"

"It's still kind of hard for me to travel." That was true. More than a few hours on the road, and he began hurting in places that hadn't even been injured.

"You managed to travel from Washington, D.C., to Oklahoma just fine."

"Mom, I flew here on an air evac flight. There were nurses and medics on board. I could lie down if I needed to." *I could take drugs if I needed to.*

"Well, if you can't make even one short trip to visit your mother..."

He noticed she didn't offer to come here to Fort Murphy. She hadn't bothered to fly to Washington, either, beyond one two-day visit right after he'd arrived. The other months, nothing.

"I've got to go, Mom."

"Me, too. My quilting club meets tonight, and I need to put some work in on the baby quilt. You take care of yourself."

That was the closest she ever came to voicing any good feelings about him. The last time he'd heard *I love you* from her, he'd been about twelve years old and sick with the flu.

The last time he'd said it back to her had been at least that long ago.

"You, too." After sliding the phone into his pocket, he stood up, pain spasming through his leg. The stump had looked a little chafed when he'd showered—not unusual, but something that tended to freak him out since the infections that had led to the second and third procedures had started with a little chafing.

Tired, annoyed, and more than a bit ashamed of his own cowardice, he limped toward the door. He really needed a quiet evening with Carly tonight. No confessions, no dwelling on the negative, no confusion.

Just Carly, dinner and, if he was a lucky man, a few kisses.

Carly heard Dane's truck pull into the driveway, the finely tuned engine a quiet rumble before he shut it off, and she smiled. That was a sound she could become used to—someone coming home to her. Though some snotty little voice in her head warned her not to be so anxious, she opened the front door before he had a chance to knock, and her smile stretched ear to ear. "Hi."

"Hi." He wore jeans as usual with a faded T-shirt that she thought had once pretty closely matched the burnt orange of her walls. He stepped inside, shut the door, then closed the distance between them and kissed her. It felt like a quick kiss that suddenly decided to linger, and she was glad it did.

When he finally lifted his head, his expression was dazed and hers was unsteady, along with her entire body. She wanted to wrap her arms around him for a moment, just to regain her balance, but he took her hand and walked down the hall with her to the kitchen. "I was going to bring a bottle of wine, but since you're not much of a drinker, I got this instead."

She hadn't even realized he had something in his hand. "You didn't have to—"

Reaching inside the bag, he pulled out a tub of ice cream. Braum's vanilla-caramel, wonderful on its own and way better on pecan pie than Cool Whip. "Ooh, thanks. My favorite."

He opened the freezer to put it inside, then slowly turned back, two plastic-wrapped items and an incredulous look on his face. "You froze the paint brushes?"

Her cheeks warmed as she slipped past him to check the sweet potatoes in the oven. The marshmallows were melted and starting to brown nicely. "I sealed them in plastic wrap first," she said in her defense.

"That is not how you clean brushes."

"I read somewhere that if you seal them in plastic, it would keep the bristles from getting stiff for a while. I also read that if you froze them, the paint wouldn't set up so you could clean them later, at your convenience. And I was tired when we finished painting. So were you. So I put them away to clean later." She swallowed. "At my convenience."

He tried to wiggle the bristles. "Look how stiff they are."

"Well, of course. They're frozen."

He stared at her a moment longer, the corners of his mouth twitching, before he gave in to the laughter. "Before we start our next paint job, I'll buy my own brushes and you won't be allowed to touch them."

Tossing her head, she sniffed. "I bet mine thaw out to be just as good as your new ones." As he returned the brushes to the freezer, she changed the subject. "If you'd get the glasses and drinks, I'll get the food on the table."

She removed a package of CaraCakes yeast rolls from the top rack of the oven and emptied them into a napkin-lined basket, then carried the sweet potato casserole to the table with silicone mitts. She unwrapped the foil from the turkey, moist from the slow cooker, then blasted it in the hot oven to brown the skin, and pulled the dish of dressing from the microwave where she'd stuck it to keep it warm.

"One of these days, I want to remodel the kitchen, and the top thing on my list is a double oven," she said on a trip back to the kitchen for serving utensils. "Both Mom and Mia have them. Mom's never touched hers, but Lisa uses it when the family gets together, and Mia loves hers. She's a big-time baker. She used to send more cookies, brownies, and candy to Jeff than his entire company could eat."

She turned back to the table to find Dane staring at it. The expression on his face was odd—surprised, pleased, intense with something she couldn't recognize.

"You made Thanksgiving dinner."

If she hadn't been standing close, she might not have

heard the words at all. She certainly wouldn't have caught the tiny tremor at the end of the words.

Her smile was shaky. "You said it was your favorite meal—turkey, dressing, sweet potatoes with marshmallows, and pecan pie. I added the bread because, well, you have to have bread with gravy or what's the point? And it's just a turkey breast because there are just two of us, so again, what's the—"

His mouth cut off her words, his arms sliding around her waist, his body hard against hers. Warmth bloomed through her as she wrapped her arms around his neck, one hand sliding up to stroke his hair. She'd almost forgotten that the best thing about a high-and-tight haircut was the velvety smoothness of the bottom part, where the hair was clipped impossibly short. She loved that feel almost as much as she loved the sensation of strong arms around her, of a strong body to lean on, almost as much as she loved the idea that she had someone to care for who cared back.

Dane drew his hands along her spine, back up to her face, where he cradled them to her cheeks. His tongue dipped inside her mouth, and a faint whimper of need and hunger and satisfaction echoed in the air around them. It had been so long, and she had been waiting for this practically since the day she'd seen him in the cave. It made every other kiss they'd shared seem insignificant, made her want...

Dane lifted his head, just enough to break contact, and stared at her, that intensity still in his brown eyes. "You're amazing."

Suddenly, unexpectedly, she had the strangest need to cry, to curl up tight and weep—for Jeff, for Dane, for herself. She'd been so lost for so long, and though she dearly regretted Jeff wasn't here to ground her, she was so very grateful Dane was.

Blinking rapidly, she forced a wobbly smile. "You'd better taste everything before you say that."

He gave her a look that confirmed he wasn't talking about her cooking abilities, then pulled out a chair for her at the table. She said a silent prayer that everything tasted as good as she hoped, only to get confirmation a moment later as Dane took his first bite of turkey. "Hmm," was all he said, along with a thumbs-up, and she sighed gratefully.

"Did you have a good day?" she asked before sliding a spoonful of crusty browned marshmallow into her mouth.

"I've had worse."

"Wow, that's a ringing endorsement."

"I talked to the first sergeant about whether or not I'm staying in the Army, then had a call from my mother. She wanted to know if I could plan a visit home around the time my ex-wife's newest baby is due."

Luckily, the marshmallow and bits of sweet potato were too soft to choke her. "What fun that would be. Was she serious?"

"Dead serious. She's convinced she's not getting any grandkids from me, so she's glommed on to Sheryl's as if they're her own."

Carly cut a piece of tender turkey with her fork, dipped it in gravy, then suspended it, over the dressing. "Do you not want kids?" She hoped the question didn't sound as serious to him as it did to her, that he would think she was asking out of simple curiosity, not any real need to know.

His response—spooning another serving of dressing onto his plate—was as casual as she could have hoped for. "I always just figured that I'd have a couple at least. I mean, that's what people did where I came from—grew up, got married, had children. Sheryl and I talked about it some, but it was never the right time for her. Of course, eventually I found out why. Hard to attract boyfriends when you're obviously pregnant."

"I'm sorry about that."

His smile was faint and lopsided. "It happens. In the long run, it was best. She's happier. I'm happier. And where would *we* be if I were still married to her?"

"Certainly not having dinner alone." Something fluttered in Carly's chest—sharp and sweet and almost painfully tender. He counted her a good thing in his life. She made him grateful for his divorce.

He *cared* about her.

"So…" She cleared the huskiness from her voice. "Back to the baby question. If you always planned to have kids, why is your mother convinced it isn't going to ever happen?"

He set his fork down, took a long drink of pop, then reached for another roll from the basket. The sweet yeasty fragrance drifted over the table, made even more mouthwatering by the warm butter he spread over it. Finally, he looked up, not quite meeting her eyes, and shrugged. "I don't know. Maybe she thinks I was such a lousy husband that I'll never find anyone to marry me again. Maybe she thinks women have better choices than settling for me."

Carly smiled though she didn't feel like it. How sad that his mother apparently had such a low opinion of him. Granted, he had disappointed her by going for the life he'd wanted rather than one she'd picked for him, but children did that all the time and parents got over it. *Her* parents loved her in spite of her lonely little degree, and if they ever thought no one would want to marry her—an idea that seemed impossible because, despite her one degree, she was still an Anderson—they had the decency to keep it to themselves.

"Maybe your mother is just...gee, how do I say this politely? Crazy."

He laughed. "Yeah, that's one way of looking at it." Then he sobered. "She's...disappointed, not just in me but everything. She expected more out of life than she got."

"Don't we all? But you either deal with it or you lose out completely." She couldn't spend the rest of her life with Jeff, but she could fall in love and grow old with another man. She couldn't have Jeff's children, but she could have that other man's. She couldn't have her happily-ever-after with Jeff, but there were millions of happily-ever-afters out there. No law said a person was limited to just one.

She could be grateful for the time she'd had with Jeff and still live a happy, loving life without guilt.

They talked about little things through the rest of the meal, nothing memorable or important but special for its very ordinariness. She treasured moments of pure ordinariness.

After putting away the leftovers, Carly dished two slices of warm pie and topped each with a scoop of vanilla-caramel ice cream. They settled in the living room at opposite ends of the sofa, and she kicked off her shoes, then tucked her feet under her so she could face him. "What would you do if you got out of the Army?"

Though he'd brought up the subject over dinner, the

question seemed to surprise or maybe discomfit him. "I don't know." He attempted to change the topic. "This pie is good. Is it from CaraCakes or did you bake it?"

"I baked it. It's Dear Abby's recipe. You remember, the advice columnist back when we were kids? Mia makes it all the time, and she gave the recipe to me in a family cookbook my first Christmas with them." Just as easily, she switched back. "You had plans for after the Army. Teaching, coaching football, scuba diving, and hiking as torture."

"Yeah, but that was before..."

He'd injured his leg. How had it happened? Had it been painful? Other than occasional stiffness or a limp, did it still bother him? She was curious, but she wouldn't ask. Too many soldiers got questioned too avidly about their war experiences. Jeff hadn't liked to talk about it. He hadn't wanted to worry her about the close calls he'd survived, hadn't wanted to relive the fear and the danger and the loss. He'd mourned for every guy or girl he'd worked with who'd been injured or killed, and chatting casually about them struck him as disrespectful.

When Dane was ready to talk about it, he would let her know.

"So that was then. This is now. If you got out of the Army, say, in six months, which one of those careers would you most like? Or have you thought of something else?"

"You like tough questions, don't you?" He finished his pie, leaned forward to set the plate on the coffee table, then sat back, his left hand dropping automatically to his leg. "Those were just possibilities, for sometime in the distant future. Things I would have to prepare for in some way—finish my degree, get more certifications, save money for the investment. I figured on making a decision and having all that stuff in place by the time I did my twenty."

"How close are you to the things you need?"

His gaze settled on the wall behind her. "I'm about sixty hours from finishing my degree. For scuba, I'd need to get through the rescue diver, dive master, and instructor development courses, which with my schedule would take a couple years. And I'm pretty sure I've crossed 'hiking as torture' off my list."

"Aw, that's a shame." She stretched her legs out, socked feet resting on the coffee table. "I was thinking that could be a great adventure for the margarita club. You, me, and my six best friends." Her grin was wicked, his expression akin to aghast. "It could be a real family thing. Therese's step-kids could come, and of course Ilena would have to bring the baby, since she plans to nurse him. Doesn't that sound like fun?"

With a look so dry it could sear paint, he said, "I've spent eight days in the wilderness with people like your friends. It's called war. I bet your group's idea of roughing it is a hotel without room service. I can't see any of you being happy humping a forty-pound pack for even one day."

"Not even me?" she teased.

He reached forward, his strong fingers snagging the hem of both pant legs, and swung her feet onto the couch. "Imagine wearing hiking boots with these socks. Sheesh, they don't even match."

She wiggled her toes to better display the socks: definitely made to be worn together, same hues but wildly different patterns. "I know better than to wear these with boots. These are for cute. Boots are for work. I know the difference."

Slowly he wrapped his fingers around her right ankle, circling them until his thumb and forefinger touched, then tightened his hold until his entire hand was in contact sliding down over her heel, to the arch, to her toes, then back again. Her eyes practically rolled up in her head, so she closed them and tilted her head back. Such attention to tight muscles and tired feet left her incapable of speech. A huge, relieved "Ahhhh" was all she could form.

"You're on your feet too much."

"Teachers do that." She opened her eyes a slit to study him. "So do soldiers."

That day they'd met, when she'd studied the photograph Lucy had sent of him, she'd thought his jaw was strong, his nose nice and straight, his eyes intense and his mouth sensitive. She'd thought those features had added up to a good face, but not a particularly handsome one.

Silently she snorted. Even a blind woman could have seen how gorgeous he was. But she'd still been mourning Jeff deeply at the time. She had rarely looked at male members of the species as men, but rather mere people.

She had also thought then that there was something haunted in his eyes. When he grinned or, better, smiled, his gaze was clear and deep, bottomless rich brown. But sometimes there was still a look…He'd been through things that had changed him. Loss of innocence, illusions, friends. Injury. Fear. Courage in spite of the fear. Was he a better man for it, damaged by it or simply different? Still good, honorable, decent, but with a different outlook on life and death and sacrifice.

He gave her foot a last squeeze right beneath the toes, then set it aside to pick up the other one. "Did you hear me?"

"No, I was just admiring your face."

"Yeah, women do that all the time." He grinned smugly. "I asked if redoing this room had taken care of your need to paint."

"Oh, no. The hallways are next. I was thinking yellow. Then the dining room. I can actually move the computer out of there and use the room for its intended purpose. Then the bathrooms. One of them is Pepto-Bismol pink. Then that would leave just the bedrooms and the kitchen...oh, and the outside."

His fingers continued squeezing long and slow the length of her foot before he finally spoke. "Give me a pen and paper before I leave."

"To make a list of supplies?"

"To make a list of my favorite foods. You'll have plenty of chances to cook dinner again before we finish all that."

She gave him two thumbs-up. "Sounds like a plan."

One she could eagerly embrace. If he stuck around as long as there were projects to help with, the work on her house would never be finished. She would make sure of that.

When he finished rubbing her right foot, she groaned. "That feels so good. Kick your shoes off and stick your feet up here. I'll return the favor."

The strangest expression crossed his face—panic, she might have thought—and he shook his head. "Thanks but no, thanks. I'm fine."

He wouldn't get any argument from her about that.

Chapter Twelve

Y ou want to go into town for dinner?"

Noah looked as if Dalton had suggested they flap their arms and fly to the moon. Quickly he adjusted his expression, though, and said, "Sure. I like Mom's casseroles, but I sure wouldn't mind having a big greasy burger hot off the grill. Get changed and let's go."

Dalton's first impulse was to ask why he should change, but he knew the answer without even looking. There was a time his mother would have swatted him if he'd even thought of leaving the house looking like this. His jeans were the rattiest, oldest pair he owned, with both knees worn clear through and jagged rips along one leg where he'd gotten caught up on a nail in the barn. His T-shirt was pretty old, too, from a trip he'd taken his sophomore year in high school. The writing had flaked until only a letter here or there was legible.

Upstairs in his room, he shucked the boots and clothes in exchange for his newest jeans, a plain white shirt and his good boots. He tucked the shirt into his jeans, slid a leather belt through the loops and went into the bathroom to comb his hair and take a look.

The image gazing at him from the mirror was painfully familiar: brown hair, brown eyes, skin tanned from so much time outside. The lines around his eyes and mouth made him look older, wearier, much more like his father than he should look at this age.

Was Dillon out there somewhere, staring into a similar version of the same face? Did he ever look at himself and think about home, about Mom and Dad and Dalton and Noah? He could have come back any time in the first couple years after he'd left, and everything would have been okay, but he was too selfish. Too irresponsible. Maybe too ashamed.

As he should be.

Dalton rubbed one hand across his jaw, feeling the stubble there, wondering for just a moment if he should have shaved when he'd showered. It was Saturday night, after all, and he was fixed up every other way.

But he was only going into town to eat. Not to have fun. Not to do anything that might require him to look more reasonably presentable.

Damn well not because of his last trip into town.

Scowling, he flipped the light switch and headed down the hall to the stairs. That last trip had been a major mistake. He'd spent the first twenty-four hours feeling sick over it, and the six days since pretending it hadn't happened.

He hadn't taken flowers to Sandra's grave.

He hadn't met Jessy Lawrence.

He hadn't gone to Bubba's with her.

God, he wished he hadn't gone to bed with her.

But he had. He'd done all those things. And even now, as he took his Stetson from the hook beside the door and clamped it on his head, as he locked up behind them, as he and Noah climbed into the truck and started the drive into Tallgrass, he couldn't help but wonder if he went to Bubba's again, would she be there?

And if he did, if they shared a few drinks again, would they wind up in the same place?

Brutal honesty forced him to admit that the knot in his gut wasn't entirely disgust for what they'd done. Four years was a long time to go without sex. Man wasn't meant to be celibate, Dillon used to say.

Granted, in Dillon's mind, man wasn't meant to be faithful, either. He'd had no boundaries, not in his own relationship or anyone else's.

"You heard from Mom and Dad?"

Dalton glanced at Noah, so quiet on the other side that he'd practically forgotten he was there. "They're in Wyoming. Mom said tell you to listen to your voice mail from time to time."

He could practically hear the eye-roll in Noah's voice. "Everyone knows if you want me to notice, you should email or text."

"I don't text."

"Yeah, well, you don't call, either."

That was true. Dalton couldn't remember the last time he'd made a phone call that hadn't involved ranch business. It probably would have been a few months after Sandra's funeral, when he'd called her parents just to . . . to connect with someone who'd known her even better than he had. Her mom had started crying so hard the moment he'd identified himself that her father had taken the phone, and he'd cried, too. The call had put Dalton in a bad place, when he'd already been barely functioning.

He hadn't reached out to anyone since. That was a long time to be so alone. No wonder he'd screwed up so bad with Jessy Lawrence.

The highway was widening into a street, better paved and better lit, when Noah spoke again. "Where we going?"

"What do you want?"

"How about that little café downtown? The one with the pot roast like Granny's?"

Their grandmother had died when Noah was ten, but it wasn't a surprise that he thought of food when he thought of her. Pot roast had been a Sunday routine, with no exceptions but Christmas, along with meat loaf on Fridays, snow ice cream with every heavy fall and oatmeal-raisin cookies any time her grandchildren visited. Food had been her way of showing she loved them. Not many hugs or kisses, but lots of homemade treats.

Dalton responded with a grunt as he turned east a block before Main. On a Saturday night, the only parking near Serena's was going to be on the side streets. He parked in the sole spot in front of the newspaper office, blocked on each side by driveways running back from the street, and they headed toward Main.

It was a nice night, warm early for the season but with enough of a bite to make Noah's jacket comfortable. Dalton didn't mind the chill, though. Just the air from his brother who'd suddenly decided to fill him in on his last week at school was enough to keep him warm.

Tallgrass's downtown didn't close up and go dark on

Saturday nights, at least not all of it. There were restaurants, a gym, a couple clubs, and a few small shops that
stayed open late to benefit from the others' business.
Muttering "uh-huh" in the appropriate places in Noah's
monologue, he glanced in the store windows as they
passed, almost stumbling when he caught a glimpse of a
redhead at the back of the gym.

She disappeared behind a machine, then reappeared an
instant later: tall, muscular, hair too short. Not Jessy.

His heart thundering in his chest, he reminded himself
of why he'd stiffened. He never wanted to see her again.
Wanted to forget he ever *had* seen her.

"So what do you think?" Noah asked.

"About what?"

Noah's sigh was heavy with impatience. "Me going to
summer school. Do you never listen to anything I say?"

The desire to grin cut through Dalton like wind-driven
fire across a dry prairie. It seemed odd and felt odder, as
if the muscles in his face had forgotten how to make that
action. He popped his brother on the back of the head,
just hard enough to let him know he'd been popped. "You
sound just like Mom. 'Do you ever listen to anything I
say? No, of course not, and then you come whining wanting your father and me to get you out of trouble.'"

"I didn't get into *that* much trouble," Noah muttered
before catching sight of Dalton's grin. He stared, first in
surprise, then narrowed his gaze. It stayed that way until they'd been seated against the back wall at Serena's.
They'd asked for a table. The booths were close quarters and they always wound up kicking each other for
space underneath because of their long legs and Noah's
big feet.

"So what's up with you, man?"

The grin was long gone, and Dalton's face had settled back into a more comfortable scowl. "What do you mean?"

"You were weird last weekend, and you're weird this weekend. Wanting to come to town for dinner? Smiling like you used to?" A light lit Noah's eyes. "Did you meet someone last Saturday? What did you do while you were gone all day?"

Dalton flipped through the menu though he would order what he always did: the pot roast that was, like Noah said, the closest they would ever get to Granny's. After a moment of silence, he met his brother's gaze. "I took flowers to Sandra's grave."

There was a time when Noah's response would have been predictable: *For all frickin' day?* Unbelievable as it sounded, he knew Dalton had done just that a time or two in the beginning. He also knew of plenty of times when Dalton had visited a bar after the grave, when someone had called him hours later to drag his brother's sorry ass home.

He and Noah might not be the twins in the family, but Noah knew him as well as—better than Dillon.

The waitress came to take their orders, then brought pop for both of them. "It's a shame they don't serve beer here," Noah remarked. "That's my favorite drink with a burger. It makes the finishing touch to the meal."

"You're not old enough to legally drink."

Noah shrugged. "Minor technicality."

"Yeah, *you're* the minor."

"And you're a major pain. Sorry to not tiptoe around you for once, but I'm gonna say it anyway. You need to get laid, Dalton. Maybe then you wouldn't be moping around all the time acting so tortured."

Noah looked defensive, obviously expecting something major from him—a blowup, maybe even walking out and leaving him to find his own way home. There was a minute of anger where Dalton considered doing just that. But the earlier words stopped him. *"Sorry not to tip-toe around you for once."* Noah had been doing that, and so had their parents, for a long time. They'd given him space and time to grieve, and he was still taking both all these years later. It had come to feel natural to him, but it wasn't, not really.

He was the adult, the older brother to Noah's kid. If anyone should be doing any caretaking, it was him, but instead he spent his time dwelling on Sandra and himself.

It was okay to grieve. He didn't need anyone to tell him that. But it wasn't okay to wallow in it to the point that his family had to change who they were to accommodate him.

Aware that Noah was waiting for a response, Dalton breathed deeply. "I don't recall ever asking you to tiptoe around me." No doubt, though, his behavior had demanded it. He'd been on the edge for so long, refusing to talk about Sandra, refusing to talk, period. "But feel free to go back to being the pesky little brother you always were. I wouldn't want you to fall off those tiptoes and hurt something. I've got enough critters to take care of already."

Noah continued to stare at him, still a little challenging and a little confused. After a long silence, he finally said, "Right. For your information, if I fall and hurt something, I don't need you to take care of me. Two of the most gor-

geous women I've ever seen live in the apartment across
the hall from me, and they are both just aching to take me
on. Let me tell you..."

His smugness was familiar—a perfect mimic of their
missing brother. Dalton wondered if Noah had always
had the attitude and he just hadn't seen it because everyone had been treating him like fragile glass, or if Noah
had picked it up from Dillon. The kid had been barely
seven when Dillon took off. For the two years before
then, Dillon had been too busy letting every girl in the
county catch him to spend much time with the rest of the
family, and he'd had no patience for a little kid.

What other things, Dalton wondered, had he missed
seeing in Noah because he'd been too absorbed in himself?

Noah was a ladies' man, he learned when they went
to pay. There was a crowd at the door, people waiting
for seats or to pick up carry-out orders, others trying to
pay. While Dalton settled the bill, he heard Noah talking
a few feet away. He didn't need to understand the words
to know his little brother had met a pretty woman. That
came out in the tone, his laughter, hell, in the air that surrounded him. Dalton was probably in for a drive to the
house alone, with the rest of the evening on his own. That
was fine with him.

Then, after shoving his wallet back into his pocket,
he took the few steps to reach his brother, getting close
enough to see around Noah's broad shoulders to the short,
slender woman the kid was charming: abbreviated clothing to show lots of smooth golden skin, a mouth worth
kissing, green eyes, red hair.

Dalton's gut tightened. It was Jessy Lawrence.

She glanced up at him—he was hard to ignore, loom-
ing over her and Noah, surprised and embarrassed and,
someplace where he didn't quite have to admit it, pleased
to see her again—then her gaze slid back to his brother as
if he weren't there. Not even the slightest flicker of recognition, good or bad, crossed her pretty face, and her words
flowed without so much as a hitch.

Anger built inside him, knotting his fists, creeping
across his face in a steel-cold scowl. Either she was deliberately ignoring him or she didn't recognize him. Was
she embarrassed by what they'd done? Didn't appear so,
not the way she was touching Noah's arm and smiling at
him as if she were parched and he was a long tall drink.
Could she have been so drunk that she didn't remember
Dalton even though she'd been sober when they met?

Either way he was relieved, or so he told himself. Last
Saturday had been a huge mistake. The best thing either
of them could do was pretend it had never happened.

But all this heat and tension didn't feel like relief.

"Come on, Noah." Dalton didn't care that he'd interrupted Jessy midsentence. "Let's go."

"Hold on." Noah's expression was his usual charm-the-
girls smile with a heaping helping of I-can't-believe-I-got-
this-lucky excitement. "Jessy was just suggesting—"

"We've got work to do." Dalton clamped his fingers on
his brother's arm and pulled him toward the door. He'd
be lucky to make it five feet out the door before Noah ex-
ploded and demanded to know what the hell was wrong
with him, but Dalton didn't care.

He wasn't sharing another woman with either of his
brothers.

* * *

After work Tuesday, Carly stopped at Walmart to pick up Easter gifts for her nieces and nephews. Buying for Eleanor was easy; she liked what any little girl liked. The four boys would much prefer chemistry sets, equipment or possibly a little yellow-cake uranium for their latest experiments, but they'd accepted there was only so much their aunt Carly could or would do.

After gathering toys, sweets, games, and cards, she was on her way to find shipping boxes when she passed a display of plastic storage tubs. Her feet slowly came to a stop as she looked at them. Big, tight-fitting lids, decent protection for whatever they held, like clothes. Uniforms. Jeff's uniforms.

A gasp tried to escape her, but the tightness of her throat strangled it into nothing more than a small sound. It was too early to pack away Jeff's things.

It had been twenty-six months.

But he'd left them in the closet, right where he wanted them.

And he wasn't coming back. He had no need of them. And it didn't matter whether the clothes stayed in the closet. *He* was in her heart and always would be.

She was wiggling an orange tub from the stack when a thought occurred to her: Had this idea suddenly come into her head because it was time...or because of Dane?

She yanked hard on the tub, and it popped out, sending the rest of the stack tumbling to the floor. When she whirled around, she hit the pile of lids and they fell, too, scattering across the tile.

"And here I thought I was the only one who created messes like this in public." Ilena pushed her cart out of the way among racks of sales clothes, then bent to pick up a few lids. "Thank you for assuring me I'm not the only klutz in the world."

"Happy to serve." Carly picked up the rest, balancing four tubs and lids on her shopping cart before straightening the rest. "Why aren't you at work? Are you and Hector okay?"

Ilena patted her stomach. "We're fine. Dr. Madill just said so." She wiggled her fingers in the direction of Carly's cart. "Easter shopping. What fun. I'm spending this Easter with Juan's family in Broken Arrow. They color about ten dozen eggs. Of course, they have five dozen grandchildren."

An exaggeration, Carly knew, though she did remember some mention of Juan's eight siblings and more than twenty grandkids. Quite a change for only-child Ilena.

Ilena eyed the bins. "Doing a little spring cleaning?"

"I, uh, I'm packing up Jeff's uniforms. Maybe. I think. Soon." Her voice trembled on the last few words. "Do you think it's too soon?"

Ilena's smile was tinged with sadness. "We all have to figure out what our own 'too soon' is. I gave Juan's uniforms to his brother who's in the Army about a month after the service, and his other brothers and nephews took the rest of his clothes. My mother said it was too early, but like Juan's mom said, he doesn't need them anymore."

Carly had still been pretty much nonfunctioning a month after Jeff's funeral. She'd barely been able to dress herself. Dealing with his clothing would have been impossible.

"It depends on what brings you comfort, Carly. I have a friend whose husband died in 2004. She's still got his stuff everywhere. Marti's and Lucy's husbands died together, and Marti still has Joshua's things while Lucy cleaned out Mike's on the first anniversary of his death." Ilena shrugged. "You do it when it feels right for you, not because someone else thinks it's right."

After a moment's hesitation, she asked, "Is Dane pushing you?"

"No. Oh, no. He's never mentioned... He understands..." *Any time you want to talk, I don't mind listening,* he'd told her. He would never pressure her. She was sure of that. "I just thought... it occurred to me..." She blew out her breath, then combed her hair back. "I'm dating another man. Maybe it's time." Self-consciously she twisted her wedding band. "It's not like I'm sleeping with one of Jeff's shirts or—or standing in the closet with my face buried in his coat. The clothes are there, just like the furniture and the light fixtures. I don't need them to remember him."

Ilena clasped Carly's hands in hers, stilling the ring-twisting. "I kept some of Juan's stuff—his dress uniform, a couple of his favorite shirts, a pair of the god-awful holey socks that he wouldn't let me throw away. And you know what, Carly? Giving away the rest didn't make a big difference. It didn't make me miss him any less or any more. It didn't make the house seem any less empty. There wasn't any closure, but there haven't been any regrets, either."

Regrets. Carly echoed the word silently after saying good-bye to Ilena and continuing to the aisle that contained shipping material. She had plenty of sorrows, but not many regrets. Other than putting off having a baby, she wouldn't change anything she'd done.

She finished her shopping, checked out, then battled the afternoon wind across the parking lot to the car. One thing she could say for Oklahoma: no matter how hot it got, there was usually a breeze. Unfortunately, that went for no matter how cold it got, too.

At home she carried the storage tubs into the guest room, then spent the next hour divvying the Easter goodies, signing cards, stuffing pastel gift bags, and packing them into shipping boxes. Tomorrow after work, she would mail them to Lisa, letting her play Easter Bunny on the big day.

That done, she stood at the kitchen table a long time before slowly walking down the hall to the guest room. It wasn't particularly inviting: a small room with two windows facing the street and a closet behind louvered doors. The walls and ceiling were white, dingy after so many years without touch-ups. The double bed was inexpensive, the night tables hand-me-downs from Jeff's uncle. Only one thing hung on the wall, a needlepoint Mia had given them, and a plain spread in pale blue covered the bed.

The bright orange tubs popped against such drabness.

She opened the closet doors, clasped her hands and stared at the uniforms. Old fatigues in woodland green and desert camouflage and newer digitized ACUs hung next to Class B and dress uniforms. Pushed to one end by itself hung Jeff's dress blue uniform that he'd worn for their wedding. She fingered the material, remembering how handsome and impressive and *happy* he'd been that day. He'd never had a moment's nervousness or doubt, no last-minute jitters.

He'd been that certain about everything—even going

to war. He'd been so positive everything would turn out just fine that she had, too.

She'd just never thought that *fine* could mean his dying. Granted, he was in heaven with God. That was about as *fine* as life could be for him. But for her...

She was doing okay. She was healthy and hopeful and falling in love again. She was way better than okay.

Carefully she closed the louvered doors, turned off the light and left the room and the house, heading for The Three Amigos. This time she wasn't first to arrive. Fia sat at the table, her back to the wall, eyes closed, head down. Carly slipped into the chair beside her and gave her shoulder a gentle squeeze. "Hey, kiddo."

Fia was smiling when she looked up, but the lines of fatigue etched at the corners of her mouth and around her eyes lessened the impact. "Hey yourself. How are you?"

"Good," Carly said. And she truly meant it. "How about you?"

Fia's smile weakened as she straightened her shoulders, then shoved her hands through her hair. "I've been better." Quickly, though, she went on. "I just have a headache, and my shoulder's sore. It's nothing. It'll go away."

For a personal trainer who could outrun, outlift, and outlast just about everyone, Fia had had some tough days in the past month, Carly reflected. She'd always been slender—body fat around 18 percent—but this evening she was looking a little gaunt. The healthy glow to her skin was gone, and there was a faint tremor in her hand when she picked up her margarita.

"When's the last time you had a checkup?"

Fia's laugh sounded as genuine as ever. "Don't worry,

Mom. I saw the doctor last week, and he said there's nothing to worry about. I've just had a run of bad luck with pulled muscles. That happens to active people, you know."

"Actually, I'd—"

Fia chimed in. "You don't."

They both laughed. "What can I say? If God had intended me to be athletic, He wouldn't have birthed me into a family of scientists. My family would never set foot outdoors if it wasn't necessary to get to their labs."

They chatted until the rest of the group drifted in, two and three at a time. Once everyone had arrived and their dinners had been ordered, Marti called for attention. "Don't forget Lucy's birthday dinner this Saturday at KariOkie. We'll be leaving here at five thirty. I'll drive, and if we have more than my truck can hold, Therese will take her van, too."

Jessy raised her hand. "I've slept since we decided this. Refresh my memory. It's a karaoke bar without the bar, right?"

Carly hadn't forgotten. It was one of the few notations on her practically empty social calendar. The restaurant, located south of Tulsa and named for its owner, Kari, who was, of course, an Okie, was known for its food and incredible desserts. Lucy had heard raves about the caramel cake and thought the whole Saturday-night karaoke thing would be too much fun.

It would be the first Saturday night Carly had spent without Dane since they'd met. She would have a lot of fun, as she always did with the club, but she would miss him.

It was a nice feeling—missing that was temporary.

*   *   *

Pizza, mozzarella, hot pepper shaker, pop, napkins, and crutches. With everything in place, Dane sat down on the sofa, unfastened his prosthetic, set it aside and began eating while his laptop booted. There'd been a time when he was technology obsessed. Television, cell phone, computer, game systems—he'd had the latest and best. With combat pay, he'd made good money, and without Sheryl, he hadn't had anything else to spend it on.

For months now, he'd rarely bothered with the computer. Whatever buddies had still emailed him after he'd come back to the States had pretty much stopped when he never answered. He should have—he knew that. No one had so many friends that he could afford to lose them for no reason other than self-pity.

But he'd gotten pretty good with self-pity.

There was more spam in his mailbox than actual mail. He deleted the junk, opened a few brief *how are you* and *where are you* notes from friends, then paused the cursor over the last one.

On the surface, it looked like two dozen others he'd received over the past year: same sender, same subject line. It was from Ed Rowan, one of his buddies in the 173rd. Ed kept in touch with other buddies, some still in the Army, some back in the civilian world, and shared news with them all. The first email Dane had gotten had been an update on a friend's injury. The second had detailed Dane's own injury.

Guys had called him, sent him emails. One had driven with his wife from Fort Bragg to Bethesda to visit him a couple times. More than his own mother had visited.

The emails were usually encouraging, sharing good

news, offering shoulders to lean on, ears to listen. Ed firmly believed there was no problem so great that Sky Soldiers and hope couldn't deal with it together.

A lot of times Dane had thought hope was a fragile thing—when he'd first seen his leg, each time the doctors had said *"We're going to have to amputate,"* when physical therapy had beaten him down, when his mother had looked at him with revulsion.

But if the past year had taught him anything, it was that there was nothing fragile about hope. No matter how many times he'd thought he'd lost it, it was still there, the most resilient thing in his world.

Ed understood that.

Finally Dane clicked on the email. It wasn't the same as the others. It was short, to the point, written by a stranger.

I'm Ed's brother, Lenny. Ed shot himself last night and died at 3:22 this morning. You guys meant the world to him. He wanted to help you all, but he couldn't help himself.

The service will be Friday in Bangor, Maine.

Dane stared at the screen, tears seeping into his eyes. His mother had done her best to teach him that men didn't cry, not for anything, but his first combat experience had undone that. If a man couldn't cry while he helped gather the remains of what had been a friend a few minutes earlier, or while he tried to hold pressure on a wound so devastating that the guy's face was unrecognizable, if he couldn't cry at the loss of lives that had meant something to him, he wasn't a man, just a machine.

Hands shaking, he tried to type a response to the email, but he kept hitting the wrong keys. Finally, swiping one arm across his eyes, he closed the computer and tossed it aside, then reached for his cell.

The phone rang twice before he realized it was Tuesday night. His finger was on the end button when Carly's voice came through. "Hey, how are you?"

If he hung up now, she'd just call him back, so he cleared his throat. "Sorry. I forgot it's Tuesday."

She was silent a moment, but the noise level in the background changed, the women's voices fading, replaced by the soothing splashing of water. He could imagine her sitting on the edge of the tiled fountain in the restaurant lobby, and he felt a little soothed himself. "They won't miss me. Are you okay? You sound..."

He cleared his throat again. "Yeah. No. I just found out...a friend of mine..." The lump in his throat wouldn't let him continue.

"Where are you? I'll come over."

He glanced at his crutches, leaning against the coffee table, and his prosthetic, standing on the sofa cushion as if it were a guest. "Thanks, but no. You're busy. I know you look forward to this time with them. I really did just forget. I'll talk to you—"

"Dane." Her tone was sharp to get his attention. "I'll tell them I have to leave early. It's not unusual. People do it all the time. Do you want to tell me where you are or would you rather come to my house?"

He became aware of some emotion, warm and comforting, settling through him. Sure, people left the Tuesday night dinners early, but not Carly. She had no other claims on her time, no other priorities greater than her friends. But she was making him a priority.

He hadn't been anyone's priority for a long time.

"I'll see you there."

"Be careful."

Maybe he'd been too careful, he thought as he replaced his leg. Maybe if he'd talked more, if he'd been more open and receptive to Ed's emails, maybe he would have known Ed needed help. Maybe—

Grimly he shut down that part of his mind. The rest—putting away the leftover pizza, putting on his jacket and driving—could be done on autopilot, exactly what he did. When he found himself in Carly's driveway, he couldn't remember the route he'd taken there, if traffic had been light or nonexistent, if he'd caught a single red light.

She wasn't home yet, but a light shone in the hallway. He sat down on the top step, the concrete rough and chilled, and he closed his eyes and waited.

He couldn't remember the last person he'd turned to for comfort. His wounds, other friends' deaths, the end of his marriage, his father's death—he'd been pretty much on his own. There had been people around: doctors, nurses, fellow soldiers, his mother, Sheryl. He just hadn't gotten much comfort from any of them.

An engine cut into his thoughts seconds before headlights flashed across him. He watched Carly get out of her car and walk toward him with long strides. She didn't give the sense of rushing, but she closed the distance between them quickly.

She sat down beside him, resting her arms on her knees, then gently bumped her shoulder against him. She didn't ask for details or even say anything at all. She just waited.

It seemed a long time before he found any words to say. "His name was Ed. We were in Iraq and Afghanistan together. He was six, maybe eight years older than me. Practically a father figure to the young kids. Real concerned with keeping his people safe. He did more tours than anyone I know because he felt obligated to see these guys through."

Dane talked on, about Ed's family in Maine: parents, a brother, a sister, two daughters, and a son. His marriage had ended between the first and second tours. Something about the military and combat tended to have a bad effect on marriages. But his kids were well cared for and well loved, and when he'd retired after his last round in Afghanistan, he'd intended to make up to them for all the time missed.

He told her about the emails, always optimistic, like Ed himself, passing on information about guys doing well and not so well. He'd included resource information—for counseling, for jobs, just for connection. He'd talked about not being too proud to ask for help, about how any problem could be resolved if you just asked.

"He sounds like a great guy," Carly murmured when he finally fell silent.

"Yeah. Except he didn't follow his own advice." He stared into the darkness a long time. Lights illuminated the houses across the street, and the streetlamps added their own yellowish glow. Most of the people on the block were families, most of them Army. Probably all of them had done at least one year in Iraq or Afghanistan. Except for Jeff, they'd all come home, maybe truly okay, more likely not so much. The worst wounds, Ed had always said, were on the inside, where no one could see them, but God, you could feel them.

For a long time, Dane had believed otherwise. He was

one of the few among his buddies who hadn't been diagnosed with post-traumatic stress disorder. Sometimes he'd thought, given a choice, he would prefer PTSD over amputation. Psychological wounds could be resolved with the right help; he couldn't regenerate a limb.

But a missing leg wasn't going to kill him.

"In the hospitals, the medical holding companies, the transition units, everyone keeps a close watch on us. They say these guys—us guys—can go downhill really fast, from coping and even improving to suicidal in no time. There's just something about the combination of the trauma to the brain and the body and the loss of hope. The suicide rate of returning veterans is high. So is PTSD, homelessness, joblessness, depression. Everybody's lost something—friends in combat, wives who got tired of waiting, parts of themselves. The thanks of a grateful nation is nice, but it's not enough when you need jobs, health care, places to live, understanding, help."

He glanced at her and laughed weakly. "Sorry. Thinking about Ed seems to bring out the soapbox in me."

"Don't apologize. You're absolutely right."

"Soldiers are supposed to be tough. Our job is protecting our country and its interests, which means witnessing and committing a lot of acts of violence. Combat's not for the faint of heart or stomach. When your friends get killed in battle, you can't even take a moment to grieve because the guys who killed them are looking to kill you. You've got to be able to compartmentalize and be strong and professional and deadly."

"And it's not easy to be all that one day and then admit that you need help holding it together the next."

He sighed deeply. He hadn't even been sure where he

was going with that topic, but she'd arrived at the destination with him. She understood. His relief was huge, but at the same time, he felt fragile. Exposed. And all he really wanted to do was withdraw into himself until he was firmly back in control.

It had gotten uncomfortably cold, he realized when she shivered beside him. He slid his arm around her, and she did the same, her small hand resting at his waist on his right side.

"Ed was good at protecting and looking out for his guys," she said quietly. "He was encouraging and passed along advice that he failed to take himself.

"'Ask for help,' he always said. 'When you're down, when you don't know what to do, when you can't do it by yourself any longer. Don't see it as weakness. Be strong enough to say "I need help." '" He bitterly finished. "He shot himself last night. He died this morning. All that damn preaching he did to us about asking, and he wasn't strong enough to do it himself."

Chapter Thirteen

Carly could make excuses for Ed's behavior. Sometimes when you were the one with all the answers, it was really hard to admit that you were hurting just like everyone else. Maybe he hadn't wanted the guys who looked up to him to know that he was fallible. Maybe the despair had just been too deep.

Instead, she stood, moving in front of Dane, reaching for his hands. "Come inside. I'll fix you some coffee. I'll even share my chocolate caramels."

His smile was thin and sad. "Coffee and candy don't solve everything."

"No, but they make it easier to deal with. Mia says so, and she's had some troubles in her life, too." She tugged, and he reluctantly stood, then followed her into the house. She led him into the kitchen, then removed his jacket and hung it on the back of a chair with her own.

He sat at the table, the overhead light showing the sorrow etched on his face. Swallowing hard, she turned to the task of making coffee and setting out cups, saucers and caramels.

Poor Ed and his family. His poor children. He'd retired. They must have thought they were safe because *he* was safe. No more deployments, no more combat. But the battle waging in his head was the one he couldn't win.

She said a silent prayer for them, then carried the plate of candy to the table. "Feel honored that I'm sharing my Mags' Mojos with you. They're made by a woman in Tulsa who started them as Christmas gifts, and they were so popular that she began selling them. I order a box about every month to test my willpower and see if I can make them last longer than three days."

"Do you succeed?"

"Most months. Though when I ordered the sea-salt caramels, the entire pound was gone in a day and a half. They're dangerous to my health."

She served the coffee, too, in sturdy, summer bright mugs, before sitting next to him. "Are you going to Ed's service?"

He was still a long time, as if the thought hadn't occurred to him, then he shook his head. "With most of my friends who died, I was still in the desert so I couldn't attend their funerals. Even if I could have... The idea of lying cold and stiff in a casket, being lowered into the ground and covered with dirt..." His shudder finished the sentence eloquently enough.

She laid one hand on his. "That's just the body. You know the spirit is someplace so much better." At least, she prayed so for Ed's family's sake. "Jeff's funeral was huge. Kalitta Charters made the dignified transfer from Andrews to Fort Carson. There were hundreds of Patriot

Guards on their motorcycles, police officers, sheriffs' deputies, and highway patrolmen in the caravan, and people with flags and signs lined the road for forty miles to the funeral home. There were so many names in the guest books for the visitation and the funeral itself—family, friends, veterans, dignitaries, strangers. It meant a lot to his parents that for those few hours, he was front and center in people's thoughts.

"Most of his Army buddies weren't there, though. Some were still overseas. Some sent flowers or cards. Someone, we never knew who, dropped off an envelope at the church that was full of pictures taken over there with him in them. Some guys we never heard anything from. Everyone has their own way to remember and honor those who have passed." She picked up her coffee cup, warming her hands, but didn't drink. "I can tell you from experience that it would mean a lot to Ed's parents and especially his children if you'd write them a letter. Let them know he won't be forgotten."

She knew Jeff would never be forgotten, not by the people who'd known and loved him. But there were times she wondered if his sacrifice would be remembered by anyone else, or if he would become just one more casualty of a war that a lot of people had long since grown tired of. He'd given his life for his country, and she didn't want everyone besides his family and friends to forget that. She didn't want it to be for nothing.

Dane's expression was grim, but he nodded. "I'll do that."

Silence settled for a moment as they drank their coffee and indulged in the chocolate-caramel candies. She did have willpower, Carly decided, limiting herself to only two a day. Just not enough to lose the extra pounds she was carrying.

"I'm sorry to take you away so early from the club."

Carly glanced at the clock. The group would be breaking up about now, heading home to empty houses or hypertension-inducing stepchildren. She'd never missed a minute of their fun, had always met the end of the evening full of pleasure competing with regret that it was over. Tonight, when she'd heard Dane's voice on the phone, she hadn't given a second's thought to regret. She'd had to go to him, plain and simple.

"Jessy and Marti were in top form, trading stories about their families and themselves. No one missed me." Not entirely true. She hadn't told them why she was leaving, just that she was meeting Dane. Therese, of course, figured something was wrong and told her to take care of him, and everyone else had said good-bye, but there'd been a few looks, a you're-choosing-him-over-us sort of thing. It wasn't that at all. He'd sounded so vulnerable, and they'd been laughing nonstop. It was a simple choice: who needed her more.

While she would give anything if his friend hadn't killed himself, there was something awfully satisfying about being needed.

"Jessy's always in top form, isn't she?" he asked drily. "And Marti...black hair? The one who announced that Ilena is preggers?"

"That's her. She can be a real drama princess, which is fair, I guess, since her mother is the East Coast's reigning drama queen."

"How are they all doing?"

She blinked. Most people assumed that because they

had each other, they were fine, all the hurts were healed over and life was moving on. They were better than they'd been six months ago, but instead of healing, some of the hurts had merely formed scabs, and scabs could break.

"I worry sometimes," she said honestly. "Therese's stepdaughter is a major pain—sorry, Therese says she's *in* major pain, which makes her behavior okay. Fia's looking worn down, and Jessy seems to...to drink too much." She hesitated. Of all the problems people didn't talk about, substance abuse headed the list. It seemed disloyal to even think the thought, much less say it aloud, but she went on, curious about Dane's impression. "I don't know, maybe she doesn't drink the rest of the week, but she has three or four margaritas with dinner every Tuesday, and you'd never guess it. She never slurs, stumbles, or anything. And maybe that's because it's all right. Because I'm imagining a problem where there's not one."

She didn't realize she was looking hopefully at Dane until he shook his head and disappointment welled inside her.

"I spent too much time drinking too much booze after the divorce. If she's drinking that much and not showing any effects, my guess would be either the drinks are pretty weak or she's pretty tolerant—and places popular with soldiers tend not to sell watered-down drinks."

She sighed. "I hate to say anything, but how can I not? I'll just have to figure out what and how and when. Fia says she saw her doctor last week and he says there's nothing to worry about, so hopefully she'll be better soon. And poor Therese...I don't think her situation's going to get better until she smacks some manners into that brat,

Abby. We tell her she needs to make both Abby and Jacob behave, but none of us are parents, so what do we know? And it's tougher since she's just their stepmother and she feels really, really sorry for them."

"Jacob seems like a good enough kid."

"He was with you. He's just sullen and rude with Therese. He locks himself in his room with his video games and ignores the world."

Dane grinned. "You just described half of the ten- to eighteen-year-old guys in this country."

"I know. But when it's *your* kid, like it is for Therese, it's just one more thumbs-down on your parenting skills."

"I take it she's tried counseling."

"She has. Abby hated it so much that the therapist actually suggested they take a break. She's grieving her parents, of course, but on top of that, she's spoiled and self-centered and the most obnoxious child I've ever known."

"Maybe Therese can get her a new stepfather. One along the lines of a Marine Corps drill instructor."

Carly chuckled. "Oh, I'd hate to see a Marine cry." After a moment's silence, she laid her hand over his. "I'm glad you called tonight."

His smile was faint and awkward. He lifted her hand to his mouth and kissed it, right in the palm, then wrapped his fingers tightly around hers. "So am I."

Therese was carrying an armload of hanging clothes to her room Saturday morning when a rustle inside caught her attention. She frowned at the reflection of blond hair, streaked with turquoise at the moment, in the mirror over her dresser but didn't say anything, instead waiting for Abby to notice her.

There wasn't even a hint of guilt when the girl did. Her upper lip curled and her nose wrinkled, but she continued rooting through Therese's jewelry box.

"What are you doing?"

"Looking for some earrings."

Her movements tightly controlled, Therese laid the clothes on the bed, then walked to the dresser, nudged Abby's hand away and closed the lid on the wooden box with a thud. "No."

Abby tried to open the lid again, but Therese refused to move. Heaving her well-practiced sigh, Abby clenched her hands on her hips. "What's the big deal? It's not like you have anything expensive. Most of it's just junk."

Buzzing started in Therese's head, right in the spot where her temples always hurt, then spreading outward. Some of the pieces in the box *were* expensive, and none was junk. More important, they all held sentimental value for her. And even more important, that wasn't the point. "No," she repeated, half surprised by how deadly calm her voice remained. "It's my jewelry, and you're not taking any of it."

Abby scoffed. "I don't want to *take* any of it. I wouldn't be seen in most of it. I just want to borrow a few pairs for the trip. I need something to wear with that red shirt, and I need those long dangly silver ones for my—"

"*No.* Don't come into my room again without permission, and don't ever take anything of mine—*borrow* anything—without asking first. Understand?"

The anger in her stepdaughter's eyes was breath stealing, turning her from a beautiful pale angel of a girl to a raging mass of emotion. "You can't order me out," she said petulantly. "This is my father's house, not yours! I have as much right to come in here as you do!"

"Your father and I bought this house together, and we invited you and your brother to live here. You have your own room, and you're welcome to use the other rooms, but you respect Jacob's privacy and mine. Do you understand?"

Abby's shriek was so shrill that it made Therese's ears ring. "You can't tell me what to do! You're not my mother, you're not even my dad's wife anymore! You're just a stupid woman who married him for his money and I hate you! I hate you more than I hate him!" Her gaze darting wildly, she gave a sudden violent shove to the jewelry box and everything else on the dresser.

The box slid from Therese's grip, crashing to the floor and spilling its contents, while perfume bottles, photographs, and other odds and ends tumbled down.

"Abigail Catherine!" Therese snapped, and Abby glared at her, then gave her a shove, too.

Therese caught her arms, both to stop her and to catch her balance, and Abby responded by jerking her right arm free, then swinging it back, her open palm connecting with Therese's face.

Shock ripped through Therese. She stared, wide-eyed, her hand automatically rising to her stinging cheek. Her thoughts were a jumbled rush: *I can't believe... oh God, that hurt... no one's ever... I should slap her...*

From the open door came a low, horrified gasp. "Abby! What did you— *Abby!*"

Her gaze jerked from Therese to Jacob, then back again as her eyes filled with tears. "I hate you! I hate you all!" she cried, running across the room, shoving past her brother, slamming her door a moment later.

Slowly Therese sank down on the bed, her hand still hovering a millimeter above her cheek. She felt the heat and knew she must have an imprint in the shape of Abby's delicate palm. She was horrorstricken, furious, shocked, stunned and hurt. Oh, God, she hurt so much, not her face, but deep inside.

"Are you—" Jacob came a few steps into the room. "Are you all right?" Instead of coming to her, he went to the dresser, kneeling to pick up the items scattered in front of it. The jewelry box lid hung crookedly, and bits of gold, silver, gems, and enamel nestled in the carpet nearby.

Therese couldn't answer him. All she wanted to say was *Dear God*, and all she wanted to do was cry. For the first time since Paul's death, she was grateful he wasn't there. Seeing his precious baby girl whom he'd adored so thoroughly strike his wife would have broken his heart.

She stared at nothing, nerves taut to the point of exploding, tears in her eyes. Her heart pounded in her chest, and the shock echoed like a rush in her ears.

When Jacob's lean, strong hand touched hers, she flinched, and he hastily drew away. Just as quickly, she caught hold of his fingers. "I'm sorry. I—I—"

He was kneeling on the floor, having undone the mess created by Abby's fury. "She didn't mean— She's just nervous about seeing Mom— She didn't mean to do that, any of that, I swear. She's— She's—"

"I know, Jacob."

He was out of words to describe—defend his sister's actions. For the moment, so was Therese.

She was also out of empathy, sympathy, and everything else. Abby had threatened not to return from this visit to Catherine's, and dear God, Therese hoped she didn't. She prayed for it now, and intended to pray for it every hour of every day she was gone.

She didn't care what Abby wanted, what Catherine wanted, or even what Paul would have wanted. As of this moment, she was done.

The Princess of I Hate You had created her last disturbance.

"I wrote the letter."

Dane felt the instant Carly's gaze moved from the tomato plants she was inspecting to his face, though he didn't meet her gaze. He pretended not to notice, more comfortable with looking at the pots filled with bell pepper plants instead.

After a moment, she went back to the tomato plants. "Good." Then . . . "Did you mail it?"

"I did. This morning on my way to your house."

"Good." She picked up a large Better Girl tomato plant, started in a greenhouse and already loaded with tiny fruit, and added it to the ones already in the cart.

They were two aisles over, looking at cucumber plants, when he went on. "I just mentioned the good things about him. How he took care of everyone. How he was responsible. How he missed his kids so much. But I kept wondering if they'd think, 'If he missed us so much, why didn't he come home sooner?'"

"They might," she agreed. "They're too young to understand that sense of duty."

He nodded as she bypassed a spindly plant for another greenhouse start, one with a few yellow blossoms already formed. "I also found all the pictures I had of him and printed those out to go with it."

"They'll appreciate it. I know Mia and Pop and I did." She looked over the plants in her cart, then smiled. "Time to get down to the real shopping."

"What? Tomatoes, cukes, and peppers aren't real?"

"These are for just one small bed. I need flowers. Lots of them." Grinning, she led the way to the other side of the nursery.

Also grinning, he followed. When she'd told him the margarita club had an out-of-town birthday dinner tonight, his first thought had been that this would be the first Saturday in five weeks that they hadn't spent at least part of together. Then she'd invited him to lunch and the nursery, and he'd been happy to accept. Better than not seeing her at all, right?

The thought made him feel about twenty. It had been so long since he'd cared whether he spent time with any particular woman. Even in the last few years of his marriage, time together was a given, not a gift.

Time with Carly was definitely a gift. She made him feel normal and satisfied and hopeful. Little things, but, as Ed's death had pointed out, so necessary when you'd already lost so much.

He'd sent flowers to the service, too, taking the advice of the clerk at Pansy's Posies on what to send. The message on the card had been lame—*Sorry for your loss*—but hopefully the letter would make up for it.

"Do you know how to do any wiring or plumbing?"

He brought his attention back to Carly, motionless for the moment, surrounded by water fountains. "I do. I look in the Yellow Pages under *Plumbers* and *Electricians*. I'm very good at dialing numbers and scheduling appointments."

She laughed. "Ah, a man who thinks the way I do. I like that. Jeff considered calling a professional an affront to his manhood."

That quickly his good mood dissolved. He managed to mumble, "My manhood doesn't reside in my ability to fix things I know nothing about." But heat was rushing through him to the accompaniment of his snide inner voice smirking, *No, it resides in your missing leg. The blast and the amputations missed the vital organs by a good nine inches, but you can't tell it by the way you act.*

He should have told her already. It wasn't fair to lead her on, not letting her know right up front that he was damaged goods. He'd had no right to pursue her—and that was exactly what he'd done, whether he admitted it— no right to kiss her or do anything else with her until she knew what she was signing on for.

He excused his silence: *The time's never been right.*

To which he could hear everyone else—Justin, the cadre, her friends—saying, *So make it right.*

And he would. As both Justin and First Sergeant Chen had pointed out, they couldn't *do it* without her noticing. And he really wanted to *do it* with her. Just as soon as he found the courage to tell her.

If it didn't matter to her.

If she still wanted to bother with him.

It was scary how much he wanted her to bother.

She picked enough flowers to fill one flat cart, then sent him back to the entrance to get another. He didn't recognize most of them, but the colors were like a bright pop of sunshine in the middle of a black night: orange, yellow, red, hot pink, white, purple, blue. By the middle of June, her yard was going to look like the lushest of oases on the Oklahoma prairie, and he had a deep need to see it for himself. To see it this June, next June, and ten Junes later.

After she'd paid the bill and they'd loaded the miniature Eden into the back of his truck, they stopped at Subway for a couple of sandwiches to go, then went home. Just carrying most of the flats and pots from the driveway to the backyard was enough to make his leg twinge. He wasn't sure how well he would endure the bending and kneeling that came with planting, but he damn well intended to try. To show her that he could do anything a whole man could do—almost. That he might be missing a leg but he tried harder.

The reasons made him uncomfortable. They didn't sound like a guy who was making progress at accepting the changes in his life.

While he moved the last of the flowers she'd designated for the backyard —there were still a half dozen flats plus pots for the front—she pulled two lawn chairs to flank a small iron-and-stone table where she set out their lunch and cold drinks.

"It's a perfect day, isn't it?" she asked after they'd made a good start on their food.

There was that word again: *perfect*. Still, he forced himself to look before responding at the sky, deep blue with hazy clouds drifting slowly. The temperature was in the mid-seventies, a light breeze was blowing from the northwest, and the air smelled clean, fresh, fragrant with mown grass and new green. As weather went, yeah, it was just about perfect.

"If you want to watch TV while I plant, you can go in-

side, or you can bring my laptop out if there's anything
you want to do online."

He frowned at her. "I came to help you." Well, to see
her. To spend time with her. But planting was third on his
list of reasons for being there.

She looked pleased. "Trailing after me at the nursery
was the best I could expect from Jeff. He hated even the
idea of getting down and dirty with flowers."

Dane forced a smile, but Lord, it was hard. "I'm not
Jeff," he pointed out.

He half expected a flash of sadness to cross her hazel
eyes, but it didn't happen. "No, Dane," she replied.
"You're not."

And he would have sworn, with her sweet, warm,
perfect smile, that the fact didn't disappoint her in the
least.

There were twelve for dinner, so Carly rode with Therese
and Ilena, plus two of their semiregulars, Bennie Ford
and Leah Black. Conversation never lagged on the drive,
though she was fairly certain the others were a tad more
boisterous in Marti's Suburban.

"If this were school, they'd be the naughty girls," Ilena
said, "while we'd be the good ones."

"They're probably discussing sex as we speak," Leah
agreed.

"Not that we're boring," Bennie said. "At least five
men in the world appreciated good girls."

There was a sigh from the backseat at that, and Carly
joined in. Therese didn't. She'd hardly spoken since
they'd met at The Three Amigos parking lot, other than
saying hello and smiling a smile that didn't reach her

eyes. More trouble with the Bitter Princess and her faithful follower?

At Highway 97, their little caravan turned south. In the parking lot, Marti had debated taking the freeway into Tulsa, then traveling south, but had decided to save a few miles and get a more scenic drive. They drove through part of Sand Springs, then reached Sapulpa, a small town located on Route 66 whose business district, with its two- and three-story buildings and large murals painted on the walls, reminded her of Tallgrass.

A few miles south of Sapulpa, they reached Kiefer, then turned east. Soon they were parking in front of Kari-Okie in a small strip center. "I hope they can seat us all together," Leah said as she got out and stretched her legs.

"I called ahead," Lucy said. "I didn't want to have to rearrange the dining room without permission."

Jessy fisted one hand on her hip. "Hey, we had a reservation at that place, and they weren't going to put us together. When Fia and I started moving tables, they got their butts in gear and managed to seat us where they should have in the beginning."

As the others started across the parking lot, Carly linked arms with Therese. "Dane's right. Life's never dull with these guys."

"Sometimes I wouldn't mind a little dull," Therese murmured with a grimace.

"What's up, sweetie? The kids stirring things up at home?"

The grimace deepened, and she raised one hand to her face. "Kids? Oh, you mean the sullen boy and the self-absorbed brat?"

The response so startled Carly that she tripped over

the curb and grabbed Bennie's shoulder to catch herself. "Sorry."

"Any time, doll." Bennie pulled her up for a hug, not releasing her until they'd filled the small lobby. "I wish I could make it to these things more often. I miss you guys so much."

Bennie was a nurse's aide at a local hospital while attending nursing school part-time and taking care of her elderly grandmother, who'd raised her. Tuesday nights were class nights most weeks, but she joined them when she could.

"We miss you, too. But you'll be graduating before long, and we'll all be there to cheer you on."

Bennie pulled a long face. "Before long? Doll, I've got another eighteen months to go. I'm gonna dance across that stage."

Eighteen months could be an eternity...or the blink of an eye. Bennie knew that better than most. It had been eighteen months ago that J'myel died in combat, eighteen months before that when they'd gotten married.

"We'll form a conga line with you," Jessy offered. To demonstrate her willingness, when the waitress led the way to their tables, she hooked her hands on Bennie's waist and danced, with Fia and Lucy joining in.

Carly fell back beside Therese again, snagging the two chairs at the end for them. If the others got noisily distracted—no bookie would offer odds against that—she wanted to probe a bit more. She hated seeing her friend look so...defeated. Down and depressed—any of them could handle that in their sleep. But defeat...that was just scary.

They'd hardly gotten settled when music started and a

young man with a microphone stepped onto the stage and started singing a country tune. "Boots, jeans, and a belt buckle as big as my head." Halfway down the long table, Fia swooned. "I love Oklahoma."

"And a voice better than most that come out of Nashville. Happy birthday to me!" Lucy clapped delightedly.

They ordered iced teas and lemonades, laughed and talked, ordered meals and laughed and talked more. At least, all of them but Therese. She was morose—trying to hide it, but failing. Carly didn't have a chance to talk to her until they'd eaten, enjoyed a half dozen songs from other diners, and three of their own—Fia, Jessy, and Marti—were approaching the stage for their own performance. She leaned close and whispered, "Is Abby pregnant? Did she start a live website where she talks to pervs in her underwear? Did she pierce her girl bits?"

Therese didn't smile at any of her suggestions. As the opening bars of Shania Twain's "Man! I Feel Like a Woman" started, she shifted her grim gaze to Carly. "She slapped me."

"Oh." A knot formed in Carly's gut, pushing her back into her seat. *No.* That was wrong on so many levels. Thirteen-year-old girls just didn't get to turn violent with their parents, no matter how unhappy or bratty they were. It simply wasn't allowed.

"I'm sorry," she said at last, then fiercely added, "I hope you smacked her into next week."

Therese's voice was an unemotional drone. "You can't respond to violence with violence. It's a lose-lose situation."

Carly snorted. "I beg to disagree. 'Walk softly but

carry a big stick.' Remember that from history class? Some things can't be tolerated, Therese, and that child getting physical with you is at the top of the list. How dare she touch you?"

Therese stared at the stage, where their friends were belting out the song on key and with practiced moves. Had they choreographed it in anticipation of tonight, or did it come naturally to them? Carly wondered vaguely while waiting for a response.

The song ended to rousing applause and great bows and waves from the singers. In the moments while the next scheduled act moved to the stage, Therese finally whispered, "I've tried, Carly. I've tried so hard. She's Paul's daughter, his baby, and I promised him I would take care of her and Jacob, but I can't do it anymore. I don't care anymore. I'm miserable and stressed out and sick of it all. I've survived deployments and Paul's death and I've managed to live nearly three years without him, but this child has forced me to give up. I surrender. I'm done."

"Oh, Therese," Ilena said with a small gasp, and Carly realized the others nearby were straining to listen in.

"What did the snot do?" Jessy demanded, still standing after her triumphant performance. Her stance was aggressive, her jaw jutted forward. If Abby were present, just one look from those angry green eyes would be enough to scare her straight, at least for a while.

Therese's face flamed. "Guys, I'm sorry. Let's not discuss this. It's Lucy's birthday. We're here to have fun with her."

Lucy came to the end of the table to hug her. "Honey, don't worry about me. I've had a great time. I'm just thrilled to be with all of you. It doesn't matter what we do. It's all important. *You're* important. We take care of each other, right?"

"Go on," Marti encouraged, and Therese sighed, then related the incident in low tones. Eleven stunned faces stared at her when she was done, all with varying degrees of other emotion.

Therese ducked her head, shielding her face with her hands. "You all told me I was being too lenient with her—"

"Ah, I believe what we said was you were taking too much sh—crap from her," Jessy interjected, making Therese drop her hands and smile faintly.

"I just thought she needed time. That was what the counselors and the chaplains and my parents and Paul's parents all said. Do you know I got through the first year after Paul's death with nothing more than an occasional sleeping pill? But since then, I've had to take antianxiety medication. Every time I walk into the house, my chest tightens, my heart races, and I can't breathe."

Carly had known about the medicine. She didn't know it was directly tied to the kids.

"Send her to stay with Auntie Bennie for a few weeks." Bennie pointed at herself with a grand gesture. "She'd be so happy to get away from all the rules that Mama Maudene raised me with that she'd be a whole different person when you got her back."

"Rules don't mean anything to her," Therese muttered. "That's part of the problem."

"No, doll, rules without consequences don't mean anything to her. Getting grounded or losing her cell for a week don't mean nothing. Mama Maudene's rules—

they've got *consequences*. And that scrawny little girl of yours ain't about to go toe to toe with Mama Maudene and win."

"She's right, Therese," Marti spoke up. "There were never any consequences in our family. As long as we stayed out of our mother's way, we could do anything we wanted. We thought it was cool at the time, but she didn't do us any favors. And it wasn't fun when I moved out of the house and found out that other people had expectations, even if my mother didn't."

"I have expectations," Therese said quietly. "I expect her to be living somewhere else when the school year is over."

That stunned everyone into silence again. They all knew, as Carly did, about her promise to Paul. They knew she felt as if she were failing him every day things weren't all happiness and light. Carly couldn't even imagine the number sending them away would do on Therese's self-esteem.

Surprisingly, it was Jessy, who'd never shied from stating her blunt opinion of Abby and Jacob, who spoke up. "You don't have to make any decisions right now, Therese. The kids are going out of town for a week, then you've got more than a month before school is out. That's plenty of time to figure the right thing to do." She looked around the group. "I think it's time for cake and ice cream, and then another go-round on the stage. How about it, GI sisters?"

The others cheerfully agreed, and Lucy waved their waitress over as they all resettled. While their attention was on the list of desserts the woman recited from memory, Therese softly said to Carly, "My mind's made up.

But, hey, there's never a bad time for cake and ice cream, right?"

Back in Tallgrass, Therese dropped everyone off at their vehicles in The Three Amigos lot, hugging Lucy and wishing her happy birthday, accepting hugs and promises of prayers from everyone else. By the time she parked the van outside her house, she was bone-tired.

The only lights on were the ones she'd left in the kitchen and the hallway. The kids were spending the night with Nicole and Liam. Jacob probably hadn't said a word about this latest showdown, while Abby had surely spun it into some great drama where she was the victim of her evil stepmother's evil ways.

Was she evil for wanting to send Paul's daughter away? Was she selfish?

"I'm not their mother, their grandmother, their grandfather, their aunts, or their uncles," she said fiercely as she climbed the steps and let herself inside. "I'm not their family *at all*."

But she was their legal guardian. She would have to check with a lawyer at the judge advocate general's office on post to find out how to go about finding them a new home.

A line from an old hymn ran through her mind. *And there will be peace in the valley for me.*

Dear God, she needed peace.

She left the light burning in the kitchen, shut off the one in the hallway, and switched on the bulbs that illuminated the stairs. The house was quiet, but not peaceful yet. That wouldn't come until long after it had been cleansed of Abby's presence.

She'd just shut off the stair lights and reached her bedroom door when a sound below froze her: the front door
opening, then softly closing again. She fumbled in her
pocket for her cell phone and slowly forced herself to turn
back the way she'd come. "I'm calling nine-one-one," she
said, her phone a bright spot in her hand.

The tall, lanky shadow stopped a few steps up. Even
without the faint light from the kitchen, she would have
recognized Jacob: his height and leanness, the way his
head was ducked and tilted to one side, his shoulders
hunched, his hands shoved in his pockets. "It's me."

Relief settled with a whoosh in her chest. "Does Mrs.
McRae know you've sneaked out of the house?"

"No. If it comes up, Liam'll tell her I'm in the bathroom or something." He shifted his weight uncomfortably
before looking up at her. "Abby didn't mean to do—what
she did." He indicated the bedroom with a jerk of his
head. "She was wrong, but... Are you all right?"

"I guess." Putting the phone away, Therese sank to the
top step, her arms folded across her middle. "Am I so horrible to live with, Jacob?"

She didn't need to see to know his face had turned
bright red. Talking with adults who weren't coaches
wasn't one of his favorite or most comfortable things. He
shifted back and forth a couple times, then, in stops and
starts, climbed until only six steps separated them. There
he slumped down, his back against the wall. "No. It's
just— She wants to live with Mom and Dad."

"That's impossible."

"I know. She knows. And if she can't have both of 'em,
then she wants to be with Mom."

Mom, who'd given her up like a hobby she'd grown

tired of. Heedless of her mascara, Therese rubbed her eyes wearily. "Do you want to live with your mom, too?"

He was silent a long time, though not still. His knee bounced and his fingers drummed a beat on the carpeted step. "I love my mom," he said at last. "But she didn't want us when we were little. Why would she want us now?"

He's eleven, Therese reminded herself, her heart aching, *and already so cynical*. And so right. Catherine wouldn't want them unless they came with some real benefit to her. Maternal love and accepting responsibility for the lives she'd brought into the world weren't enough for her.

Wishing he was close enough to touch—not a hug, she wouldn't try that, but maybe ruffling his hair—she smiled sadly. "You know your dad wanted you. He was so thrilled when he found out you were coming to live with us."

"I bet you weren't."

"I wasn't thrilled, no, but I thought…I thought we could be a family. I never wanted to replace your mom…or your dad," she added even more sadly. "But I thought we could be friendly and respect each other and even come to love each other."

"So did…so did Dad. He told us that when we came."

"He had such hopes for us all."

Jacob grunted, then shifted on the steps to stare off into the living room. A little light filtered in the blinds, not enough to show the details, but she imagined his gaze was directed right at the fireplace where Paul's photographs and the medals he'd earned were displayed.

After a long time, he made a choked sound, then demanded, "Why did he have to die?"

Hesitantly Therese moved down a few steps, then laid her hand gently on his arm. He didn't relax or move toward her, but he didn't flinch away, either. "I don't know, Jacob."

"Liam's dad went and came back. All the kids at school—their dads and moms went and most of them came back. Why didn't our dad? Our mom already didn't want us. Why did we have to lose him, too?"

Her own choked sound escaped, and she raised one hand to find tears had slid from her eyes. "Sweetie, that's probably the only question in the world that has absolutely no answer. No one knows why this person lives and that one dies. When I was six and my grandfather died, my grandmother told me it was because God needed him more than we did, and even then I knew that absolutely was not true, because no one needed him more than me. No one needed your dad more than us. We'll never know why it happened. We just have to live with the fact that it did."

"I don't want to!"

"Me, neither."

They sat that way a long time, her hand lightly on his arm, until he abruptly shuddered and pushed to his feet. He swiped at his face and said without looking at her, "I'd better get back over to Liam's."

"I can call and tell his mom you decided to stay here."

"Nah. It's not that far." He took a few steps. "You can see from your bedroom window."

At the bottom of the stairs, he called back, "I'll lock up," then let himself out and did so.

Therese stood and went to the bedroom window, watching him jog across the street and down two houses before disappearing into the shadows. For a long time she stood there, gazing out at their peaceful neighborhood, breathing deeply, feeling a little peaceful herself.

Maybe Abby hated her and was a lost cause, but Jacob...For the first time in a long time she had reason to be hopeful about Paul's son.

Chapter Fourteen

When she got home, Carly set a big foam take-out box on the kitchen table, pulled a bottle of water from the refrigerator, then dialed Dane's number. He answered on the third ring, the sound of a baseball game in the background. "Hi, is it too late?"

"Depends on what you want to do. To find shapes in the clouds in the sky? Yep. To catch the after-Christmas sales? Yeah."

She made a miffed sound. "To share a piece of the best caramel cake I've ever had."

"Not at all. How was the dinner?"

"Good. Fia, Jessy, and Marti do a mean take on 'Feel Like a Woman,' and Bennie—you haven't met her yet— had the place in tears with her version of 'Amazing Grace.' The food was wonderful, and we had a really nice time."

"But?"

She carried the water into the living room, kicked off

her shoes, and curled up in the recliner. How was he able to hear that *but* in her voice when she barely heard it herself? "Therese had a really tough day, so she was really down. She made a difficult decision, and I'm afraid it's the wrong one, but she's got to live with it, you know." She dragged in a deep breath. "Are you coming over?"

"I'm leaving right now."

"Good." *Maybe this time you'll spend the night.*

Surprised by the words, she blinked before awkwardly tacking on, "I'll be, uh, waiting."

Where had that come from? They'd kissed—a lot—but mostly hello and good-bye. They didn't sit around and make out, but they weren't hormone-driven kids. They were adults proceeding at their pace. They were in no rush. They could take their time, as if they had their entire lives ahead of them.

Besides, she hadn't done a thing about losing those fourteen pounds. She wasn't sure she was ready to be seen in her bare skin by anyone besides her gynecologist. She doubted her underwear even matched tonight, confirmed by a peek: cream-colored bra, pink bikinis with blue and purple dots.

She wasn't sure she was ready to see another man in the bed she'd shared with Jeff. And she was nervous— more than nervous—about making love for the first time with only the second man ever.

All perfectly reasonable worries...*if* Dane had ever hinted that he wanted to have sex with her. *She* had invited him over, remember? Because she'd wanted to see him tonight if only for a few hours. Because she'd brought back that huge slice of cake as an excuse.

But if things happened to move that way...One thing

she and Dane both knew too well was that life was short.

And a wise person lived accordingly.

She considered turning off some lamps and lighting some candles, changing underwear to something prettier and a bit sexier, refreshing her makeup or even putting on some perfume. Anything that might tempt him to do more than kiss.

In the end, she was making coffee when he knocked at the door. There was nothing special about tonight. She would see him tomorrow and probably the next day, too, and several more times before next weekend. And she would start a diet tomorrow.

When she opened the door, he greeted her with a sweet, satisfied smile. She imagined it was the way she greeted him each time. There was just something so *right* about being with him, some contentment and gratitude: *He's here again and he's happy to see me.*

He stepped in, closing the door behind him, and rested his hands on her waist. "This is how you dress to go out with the girls?"

"Hey, I could wear this to work." But she didn't. The white denim skirt was long by a lot of standards, nearly reaching her knees, and hugged her hips and butt more snugly thanks to the fourteen pounds. Her shirt was orange, sleeveless, the top button just low enough to reveal some cleavage. Sandals and a wood-bead belt, along with dangly wood earrings, finished the outfit. A little more length, a little less boob, and *then* she could wear it to work.

He eased her closer, his hands skimming along her spine, bending his head to nuzzle her ear, the day's growth of beard prickling and tickling. "You smell good."

"I probably spilled some of that incredible beef gravy somewhere." Her eyes fluttered shut when he reached her mouth and for an instant, she thought, yes, she *was* ready to be naked with this man, extra pounds, Jeff's bed and all.

Then she simply stopped thinking for a while.

She experienced a moment of utter silence when he finished the kiss—no sound, no thought, no sensation, while she found her way back to reality. Looking as dazed as she felt, he turned her toward the kitchen and gently pushed her that way. "Show me this cake," he said, his voice husky and heavy. "I want you to know that while you were enjoying incredible food with your friends, I was eating cold Bueno all alone in front of the TV."

"Hey, the only Mexican fix I got before the club formed was Bueno. Besides, don't you have a microwave?"

"That's cute," he said as he took out coffee mugs and began fixing their drinks. "You think a microwave is a substitute for fresh, hot food."

"Don't tease or I won't share." Using a pancake turner and a fork, she transferred the wedge-shaped slice of cake from its box to a dinner plate, then showed it to him. It was two huge layers, slathered with caramel frosting between, on the outside and on top.

They carried dessert into the living room and settled on the couch, mugs on the coffee table, plate balanced on his right knee. After totally agreeing with her how good the cake was, he asked, "What's up with Therese?"

Carly repeated the story with a little knot in her gut.

"The kid slapped her. Wow."

"I know. I'd be furious. I am furious. But Therese..."

she's just...hollow. She says she's not letting Abby live there anymore, that when school's out, so is Abby."

"And you think she's acting in the heat of the moment."

Carly took a last bite, then set her fork down, too stuffed to consider even another swipe of frosting. "Isn't that obvious?"

"And you think she's wrong."

"Well, yes. Don't you?"

He shrugged. "I can't tell you how many heat-of-the-moment decisions saved my life or someone else's."

"But you're talking combat."

"Sounds like that's what Therese and her stepdaughter are engaged in." He ate another bite, too, before setting the plate on the table between their coffees. "We all get that the kid's had some bad breaks, but has it occurred to you that, putting all the grief aside, she's an angry, self-absorbed, bitter person who likes to make other people suffer?"

Actually, no, it hadn't. Now she considered it. It was easy to blame Abby's problems on her mother's abandonment and her father's death—wasn't that enough to turn any sweet angel into a screaming banshee? But from what Therese had said, Abby had been no ray of sunshine before Paul died. She'd been happy when she got her way, sullen when she didn't, and sometimes just plain mean. Was Therese bending over backward to accommodate not a grief-stricken child but a common-variety mean girl?

Dane took her hand, drawing her attention back to him. "I always figured I'd have kids, but I never wanted to be a father to someone else's kids. I could have done it, for the right person, but it's a hard job when they're your own flesh and blood. You see with Therese how hard it can be when they're not."

She watched as he gently bent the fingers of her right hand back and forth. When he held her hand, it was always the right one. Just coincidence? Or was the reminder of her wedding ring on the left hand too much?

"So if there was a little Jeff Junior, toddling around here, you wouldn't be here?"

Was he slow answering, or was it only her sense of time that suddenly crawled? Only hers, she decided, watching the seconds tick past on the clock.

He folded his fingers over hers, then slowly tugged her toward him. When they were so close she could smell the intoxicating mix of caramel and coffee on his breath, so close that his mouth brushed hers as he spoke, he responded, "Like I said, I could do it. For the right person."

She wanted to bounce, to clap her hands with delight as Lucy had done at the restaurant, to chant, *I'm the right person, I am!* But it was impossible to do anything at the moment because he was kissing her, deep and sweet and hot, his hands pulling her closer, her own hands clutching his soft T-shirt, trying to get as close as two people could be without absorbing into each other.

His tongue was in her mouth, his fingers fumbling with the first, then the second, button on her blouse when she snuggled a little too close and lost her balance. He fell back against the sofa arm, and she landed on top of him with a soft but satisfied grunt. He was strong and solid, and she'd missed strong and solid for so long. She'd missed contact with a man's body, missed that feeling of completeness and safety and belonging. She belonged with Dane, and he knew it. He wanted her, and

she wanted him, Lord, more than she could remember
wanting.

Vaguely, though, she realized that the tenor of their
kissing and touching had changed. He wasn't thrusting
his tongue into her mouth any more but twisting his head
to avoid her, and his hands weren't fondling her breasts.
They'd moved to her shoulders, pushing her back, lifting
her away almost in a panic.

Confusion bloomed through her, along with embarrassment and hurt, and she scrambled to her knees,
clutching the undone fabric of her blouse while he
straightened to sit, practically hugging the sofa arm. The
expression on his face was stark, but she couldn't identify
it. Panic? Dread? Mortification? Had she misunderstood
his words or his kiss? Had she jumped to conclusions
about being the right one? Had he meant the kiss to be
just like the others they'd shared—incredible and needy
but nothing more?

He was aroused. She'd felt it, could see it despite his
rigid posture.

Aroused by need. Not necessarily by her.

She sank back on her butt, leaving most of the couch
between them. Her fingers eased on the handful of fabric
they held, then tightened spasmodically. Looking down—
far easier than looking at him—she refastened the buttons, then tugged the neckline higher, as if it might cover
more now than it had before.

They spoke at the same time. "I, uh—"

"I should—"

Clamping her lips to keep them from quivering, she
smiled tightly and nodded to him to continue. Avoiding
her gaze, he did. "I should probably go."

"Yeah. It's late." All of eleven ten. And here she'd had fantasies about him spending the entire night.

She felt foolish and small and sad.

He didn't move for a moment, but when he did get to his feet, his leg buckled and he nearly lost his balance. She reached out a hand, too late and too far away to be of any use, of course, but he steadied himself on the sofa arm, then carefully circled the coffee table and headed to the front door.

She stood, hugging herself, walking to the door but keeping her distance.

They stood there, not close enough to touch, neither looking at the other. The door creaked when he opened it, then immediately he closed it again and turned back. From her peripheral vision she saw him drag one hand through his hair—not much there to tousle—then he sighed heavily. "Listen, Carly—"

Though she'd rather clap her hands over both ears and sing *lalala* to block out his voice, she didn't move, hardly breathed and listened, but he didn't go on. How hard was it to say *I like you but not that way* or *not that much*?

Fearful that he would find the words, she spoke in a rush. "It's okay. Don't worry about it." When she finally found the courage to look at him, he looked as pained as she felt.

"It's not okay. And it's not you, Carly, honestly. It's just—"

She cringed inside. The old *It's not you, it's me*? Granted, she'd been out of the dating game for a long time, but did men even still use that line?

He reached out, but clearly not with the intention of actually touching her. "I didn't— I just— It's been so damn long…but not long enough. I can't…not yet…not until…"

Before she could say anything—not that she had a clue what to say—he leaned forward, pressed his mouth hard against hers, only long enough to steal her breath, then he was gone.

Carly slowly raised her fingers to her mouth, the closing of the door echoing in her brain, the emptiness creeping in around her. How had things gone from so toe-curlingly good to—to this in a matter of minutes?

Despite the hour, as soon as she was ready for bed, she crawled under the covers with her phone and dialed Lisa. Her sister-in-law sounded wide awake. "Is everything okay?"

"Yeah, Leese. Sorry about the time. Dane just left a bit ago, and— I needed to talk to you."

There was a click over the phone, then the background noise on Lisa's end disappeared. "Is that man trying to get you into bed?" She feigned outrage, then laughed. "Good for him."

"I wish. I thought maybe tonight, but…" Though heat flooded her face, Carly went on. Lisa knew every moment in her life, good or bad. "For whatever reason, he didn't want me."

Lisa uttered one succinct syllable that made clear what she thought of that. "He's a guy, right, and he's breathing. If I were a guy, I would so find you hot."

Despite her mood, Carly couldn't help but laugh. "Oh, Leese, if you were a guy, I would so find that awkward. After all, you're married to my brother."

She laughed, too, then sighed. "Aw, Carly, who understands the minds of men? It's like trying to explain the nuances of m theory to a rock. But one bump in the road tonight doesn't mean things are over. You two have been seeing each other, what? Four, five weeks? It hasn't been that long."

It's been so damn long…but not long enough, Dane had said. Then he'd kissed her.

Too long for him? Not long enough for her?

"It's just…I really like him a lot." *A bit of an understatement.* "And I want…more. You know Jeff is the only guy I've ever been with, and I'm not exactly brimming with a lot of confidence, and Dane started this tonight and when it got hot, he looked so mortified and mumbled something about it not being long enough and left. He even used that old line, *It's not you, it's me*. But he kissed me before he left."

"Did you consider, Carly, that it's true—it's not you, it really is him?" Lisa paused. "Obviously, I don't know the guy. I only know what pitiful little bit you've chosen to share with me." Her voice carried a bit of a pout. "But the guy's a soldier. He's been to war, multiple times, I'm guessing. Maybe he's got some sort of hang-up with that. Maybe he's worried about competing with Jeff's memory."

"He *was* a paratrooper," Carly acknowledged, "and he hurt his leg badly enough on the last deployment that he can't jump anymore." But what were a few scars? He was alive and healthy and whole. As far as competing with Jeff's memory, he'd been extraordinarily understanding about Jeff. Surely he understood there wasn't any competition going on. She'd loved Jeff, still did, always would, but he was gone. And she loved Dane, who was here.

"For whatever reason, he just needs a little time. Don't go all insecure on yourself and think it's somehow your fault. You remember how much trouble I had getting Roger to realize that I was even a woman? Trust me, if I hadn't been patient and stubborn as hell, Isaac and Eleanor wouldn't even be motes in the cosmos. And I'm talking a lot more than four or five weeks."

She was right, Carly admitted. Roger had admired a great deal about Dr. Lisa Varner for a very long time before her gender or beauty or personality had registered. But Lisa had the advantages of being a genius, beautiful, and a perfect size four.

Not that Dane would care whether Carly was a genius. And he seemed to think she was pretty enough. And if her less-than-perfect size bothered him, it never showed.

Maybe Lisa was right: It *was* him. And all Carly had to do was be patient and stubborn.

Luckily for her, she excelled at both.

Dane couldn't sleep.

He'd taken a long shower. He'd sworn—and regretted—a lot. He'd blamed his leg and taken pain pills. But still, there he lay, wide awake and pissed with himself, at three in the morning.

When had he become such a damn coward? When had he lost his ability to deal with a situation like a grown man?

Unfortunately, he could pinpoint it to the day, hour, and approximate minute.

He punched his pillow a time or two, rolled onto his side, then, after a moment, turned to his stomach. Bracing his arms, he rose onto his knees—make that *knee*—like he was doing a push-up. Like he was leaning over a beautiful woman. Over Carly.

His balance was shaky, his stump falling well short of the mattress. He had the upper body strength to hold the position, but it was awkward and unfamiliar and uncomfortable as hell.

With a grunt, he lay facedown, half wishing he'd fall asleep and suffocate in the pillow. Remembering Ed immediately made him regret even the thought.

So the first time he had sex, he could lie on his back. It wasn't his favorite position, but it was doable. He wasn't likely to fall on his face and make a fool of himself. And maybe sometime later they could try different stuff. There wasn't anything he couldn't adapt to, the cadre preached.

Even if he hated the idea.

Shifting back onto his side, he stared into the darkness until finally he drifted off. When he awoke again, the sun was up, his head felt like he'd been on a binge, and the first clear memory to come to mind was the hurt, stunned look on Carly's face when he'd pushed her away.

Damn.

He should call her, but it was Sunday. She always went to church on Sunday.

He could go, too—see her there. God knew, it'd been long enough since he'd attended regularly, and a sermon might do him a world of good. But he didn't know which church she attended, and if he went—*Sorry, God*—he wanted more than just a sermon for his efforts.

In the end, he got dressed, washed down a couple of aspirin tablets, grabbed a protein bar, and headed to his truck. Within minutes, he was on the highway heading out of town, no particular destination in mind. The windows were down, there was good music on the radio, and he wanted to just *be*. Not think, not talk, not do anything but find a little peace if he could.

He found that peace in the pasture full of palominos. Leaning against the board fence and watching the animals move took him back to his grandparents' place and the horse he'd kept company on his visits.

Life had been easier then. He'd known he would join the Army and see the world. He'd even expected to see combat at some point, but to a little Texas kid, that had seemed like a big adventure. It had never occurred to him that he would lose so many buddies or a part of himself. He'd never dreamed that at thirty, he'd be self-conscious, scarred, and scared about what the rest of his life would hold.

Hell, back then he'd never thought about even being thirty. That had been so far away, and he'd had so much living to do first.

He'd been standing there so long and so still that three of the horses grew curious enough to approach, watching him with big somber eyes, the smallest eventually pushing close enough to nuzzle his hands.

"They'll eat pretty much anything, but they especially like these."

Dane startled at the voice, and the horses reacted in kind, dancing back from him. He looked up to find Dalton Smith offering him a handful of peppermint candies, the fat puffy kind. Picking up the smell, the horses immediately returned, pushing each other aside to reach him first.

Dane fed the first one to the smallest horse. "I would have stopped at Atwood's for some treats if I'd known I was coming here."

"There are treats in the barn. On the shelf to the right of the door." Dalton leaned against his own section of fence. "Nice day for a drive."

Dane grunted in agreement as the animals jockeyed for the remaining candies. It was a nice day to have so many beautiful females eating out of his hand. Too bad Carly couldn't be placated with peppermints.

Though maybe a few boxes of sea-salt caramels would make her more forgiving.

"You change your mind about that ride?"

Dane looked at the horses and recognized the longing to be on one of them. Logic said he could ride as well as ever. On the back of a horse, there would be no worrying over his own weakness, no fears that any other rider didn't share. They could cover a lot of ground with minimal effort on his part, and he would feel...free. Normal.

Though there was that small problem of mounting and dismounting. He used to have more confidence when he did something for the first time. He hadn't needed anyone to talk him out the C-130 door for his first jump, hadn't needed any urging on his first hundred-and-fifty-kilometer-per-hour ride on the Ducati. Now he wanted—needed—to know he could succeed before trying, or he didn't want to try.

And, as last night had proven, that was too damn bad.

"Thanks, but not today," he said, wiping his palms on his jeans.

Dalton nodded toward the barn. "I was just headed out to doctor one of the cows. Want to have a look around?"

For just a moment Dane hesitated. Spending a little time in a place that reminded him of his grandparents had its appeal, and something about Dalton Smith told him they had a lot in common. Besides, the longer he delayed returning to town, the longer he could put off facing Carly, apologizing for his behavior the night before and telling her the reason.

The longer he could put off finding out whether she wanted to see him anyway.

"Sure. I'd like that."

They drove the long lane that ran between pastures to its end, where he parked behind a dusty Ford pickup. He followed Dalton a few hundred yards to the barn, in need of a coat of paint but looking as strong and solid as when it had been built more than a hundred years ago.

The doors stood open wide, and the sweet scents of leather and hay filled the air. Sunlight showed dust motes drifting lazily on the air, and the lone cow inside made a soft sound as Dalton approached its stall.

"You said your brother helps out on weekends. Doesn't that still leave a lot of work for you?"

Dalton maneuvered around the cow. "It's more hours than I'd want if I didn't live alone, but..." He shrugged. "It gives me something to do."

"Seems like hiring some help and sleeping once in a while would give you something better to do."

"I'll sleep when I'm old and retired." Dalton finished with the cow and came out of the stall, latching the gate behind him.

"When you've got your own D-named kids running the show?"

"Got no kids, no wife, and no desire for either. The place will probably end up with my brother Noah, if he wants it. If not..." He shrugged again.

"It'd be a shame to let that kind of history pass out of the family."

"I notice you're not running your grandparents' place down in Texas."

Dane shook his head. "They passed when I was twelve or thirteen. No way my mother would have lived out there, and anyway, all I ever wanted to be was a soldier."

"You making a career of it?"

Dane considered the question as they went back out into the sun. He'd never gotten around to talking to Carly about that. He was just full of omissions, wasn't he? "I don't know. Things have changed."

"Isn't that the truth," Dalton said flatly. Like his changes hadn't been any happier than Dane's.

They did a quick tour, checking out the Oreo-striped cattle, looking over the horses that had refused to be tempted by peppermints, glancing into the small out-buildings. The conversation was exactly what Dane needed—interesting and impersonal. He wasn't about to pry into Dalton's business and vice versa.

They finished at the corral on the north side of the barn. "This is my project for today. You're welcome to hang out if you want. Maybe even pick up a hammer, or did they not teach you how to do that in the Army?"

Dalton's gesture took in the fence, the stacks of boards and the paint on the ground. The corral had taken some hard use, the paint little more than flakes, the fence patched apparently by whatever means had been easiest at the time. Some boards were nailed crookedly across gaps. In some a few lengths of broken wire had been stapled to form a bridge. Some of the boards were just flat worn out, sagging where the nails in the ends gave way from the posts.

Dane grinned. "I've done more fence work than you can probably imagine. To be more technical, fence painting. Grandma believed that if a boy had time to get into mischief, then he certainly had time to make himself useful with a paintbrush."

"Then let's get started."

There was something amazingly soothing to it: The sun shining; the screech of nails pulled loose from their anchor; the rhythmic pounding of the hammer, along with the occasional curse, as Dalton replaced the boards; and the familiar swipe of fresh paint over thirsty wood, a movement he'd made so many times that it came naturally, like muscle memory.

By the time they took a break, Dane's muscles were also remembering the fatigue of that familiar back-and-forth swipe. He rested the brush across the top of the paint can, stretched both arms over his head for a resounding pop in his shoulders, then leaned against the section where Dalton was finishing up the last board.

Nails clenched between his teeth, Dalton looked at the fresh paint and grunted. "You must have gotten into a lot of mischief."

"I did." Idly he moved closer to steady the end of the board while Dalton pounded the nails home at the other end. When he stepped away to give Dalton room to finish, his jeans leg caught on a protruding nail down near the ground. His own forward momentum sent him stumbling until, with a sharp rip, the denim gave way and he twisted, trying to catch his balance. *Trying* being the operative word.

As he landed flat on his back with a bone-jarring thud, the thought flashed through his mind that at least he hadn't fallen on his face. It wasn't as much comfort as he would have expected.

A shadow fell over him as Dalton stepped up beside him. "At least you didn't hit anything on your way down," he said in that rough way of his. "You all right?"

"Yeah. I'm Airborne," he said drily. "I've fallen much farther and landed much harder than that."

Dalton offered his hand and pulled him to his feet with so much power that he could have heaved him over the fence into the corral with no extra effort. Dane was about to make some crack when he saw that Dalton was staring at his leg.

The rip of denim had been the left leg of his jeans, a long tear that flapped to either side of his bionic prosthesis. Heat flushed through him, turning his hands clammy, knotting his gut. He stared at Dalton, searching for some reaction, some hint of something that *he* could react to.

After a long silence, Dalton walked to the shade of a massive blackjack oak and pulled two bottles of water from a cooler there. He offered one to Dane, sat down on a boulder and asked, "You got giant springs in there so you don't make any hard landings when you jump out of those perfectly good planes?"

Dane sat on the second boulder, breathing, taking a long drink and letting the tension ease from his shoulders. "That's not a bad idea. But since I only have the one, I'd pull to the left."

"I didn't mean to stare."

"I didn't mean to let it show."

Dalton tilted his head, staring deliberately now. "Why not?"

The question surprised Dane, and he stared back. "I'd had the original for twenty-nine years, until that IED went off. I was kind of attached to it."

"Until you weren't. But you can walk, you can work, you can drive a truck, and you're pretty useful with a paintbrush. Figure out the mounting, and you can ride a horse again. In fact, have you found anything you *can't* do?"

The heat returned to Dane's face. He would rather be celibate the rest of his life than discuss his concerns with any man who wasn't wearing a caduceus on his collar. But, totally unexpectedly, something even more important came out of his mouth.

"Yeah. I can't find the nerve to tell my girlfriend about it."

Chapter Fifteen

It was none of Dalton's business. He wasn't in the habit of giving advice or playing counselor. Truth was, he just plain didn't give a damn about anyone's problems when his own had damn near suffocated him. He didn't have to change the subject smoothly or politely. No one expected much in the way of manners from him these past years.

Still, the question came out without regard for any of that. "You serious about her?"

Dane stared off in the direction of the cattle that had wandered behind the barn. "I think I want to marry her."

Dalton stared in the same direction. "You think it'll make a difference to her?"

"It damn sure made a difference to me. And to my mother. I'm known around my hometown as Anna Mae's poor crippled son who's so damaged he'll never find a woman to want him." The words were accompanied by a laugh, but it was bitter.

Dalton understood bitter. "I always knew they weren't as smart down there in Texas as us Oklahomans are."

The surly loner inside him spoke up again. This wasn't a conversation he should be having. He hardly knew Dane Clark. Today was only the second time they'd even spoken. But he liked him. He knew Dane was a good guy, in the same tug-at-his-gut way that he knew with everyone he met. It took only a couple seconds to know, and as far as he knew, he'd never been wrong.

"You don't give the woman much credit, do you?" He sighed heavily. It seemed the words were going to keep coming, and he feared, with chills down his back, where they would go before they stopped. Maybe getting them out would be good, and getting them out with a stranger had to be better than someone he knew. Maybe.

"She thinks I'm a normal, healthy man. She didn't sign up for dealing with this."

In his peripheral vision Dalton saw him gesture to his left leg, but he kept his gaze trained in the distance. "That's because you didn't give her a chance by telling her."

Before Dane could respond to that, Dalton drew a breath and went on. Once he started, he was sure he would have to say it all at once or lose his nerve. "I told you I'm not married, but I was. She was in the Army. A medic. We met one week and went off to Las Vegas to get married the next. We didn't tell anyone. Didn't even think we'd really go through with it, but we did.

"She loved the ranch, riding the horses, working the cattle. She talked about getting out of the Army when her time was up and the two of us running this place together. She had big plans. Then, two years after we were married, she got orders to Afghanistan. About six months in, the convoy she was in got hit by a roadside bomb. She lost both legs. She was alert, awake. She knew she'd lost her legs, and she told another medic, one of her buddies, she didn't want to live that way. They had a lot of badly wounded soldiers to transport, and somehow, between the blast site and the field hospital, she managed to loosen the tourniquet on her right leg. It took only seconds for her to bleed out. By the time they realized what she'd done, she was dead."

Tears clogged his throat, but his eyes remained gritty and dry. "No one knows. Not her parents, her sisters, my parents, my brother. They think her injuries were just too severe for her to survive. I don't ever plan on telling them that she chose to die. That her legs were more important to her than leaving everyone who loved her. But I know, and every day I hate her a little for it. For not believing she could handle the amputations, for believing we couldn't love her that way. For not giving us credit."

There. That was the first time he'd ever told the truth.

He waited to feel better. It didn't come. He didn't feel worse, either. Just...kind of unburdened. A little. Now someone else knew that Sandra hadn't loved him enough to give him a chance.

"I'm sorry." Dane's voice was quiet, sincere in a way that a lot of people couldn't be. Dalton didn't doubt his neighbors and friends were sorry Sandra had died, but they didn't understand it the way Dane did. He'd seen what Sandra had seen. Hell, he'd *experienced* what she had experienced, but had chosen to live. Sort of.

Realizing the water bottle he held was empty, Dalton crumpled it, then screwed the lid back on as he stood.

He walked halfway back to the hammer atop the pile of boards, then turned again. "I lost my wife because of an IED. There's no point in you losing your girlfriend over one."

They worked another hour, not talking much, before Dane put the lid back on the paint can, cleaned the brush and straightened. He faced Dalton, hands shoved in his back pockets. "Carly's part of a group in town. They've all lost their husbands in the war. They meet every Tuesday at six at The Three Amigos to talk and eat and just...understand. If you're ever interested..."

Join a support group? Dalton couldn't begin to imagine it. Before today, he'd never talked to anyone about Sandra's death beyond a few sentences here and there with his parents and Noah.

"I'll keep that in mind." But it wouldn't go any further than that.

"I'm going to clean up and...go talk to her."

"Good luck." Before he turned back to his work, he called, "You don't need two legs to sit on a horse. Next time we'll get you on one."

If Sunday morning's service had been less than inspiring, dinner was the epitome of unappetizing. Therese was silent and withdrawn, Abby touchy and more defensive than ever. Only Jacob seemed anywhere near his usual self, which didn't mean he was good company.

Carly was so happy when Therese pulled into the driveway to let her out that she felt giddy—and guilty—about it. Before closing the door, she turned to the kids in the backseat and said, "You guys have a good time with your mom," then gave Therese a tight smile. *You have a good time, too, and come out of this funk. Things will get better.*

It came to pass, it said in the Bible. *To pass*. Nothing stayed forever—not happiness, not peace, not joy, not anger, not spoiled brats. Life would go on with its ups and downs and maybe, just maybe, a few higher ups and a few shallower downs.

As she let herself into the house, her gaze fell across the couch and embarrassment flushed her cheeks. She was looking for a few higher highs and lesser lows in her life, too, and the start, she decided, was to act as if nothing had happened last night. It wasn't unusual for her to call Dane and invite him over, and that was exactly what she intended to do today. They had to address whatever had gone wrong last night, or they'd never get anywhere, and she so wanted to get somewhere with him.

She changed from her dress and heels into a T-shirt, shorts, and sandals, put her hair up in a clip, then dialed Dane's number. It went to voice mail, and not even the kind where she got to hear his voice. She left a cheerful message—*I'm fixing lasagna for supper. Want to come over?*—then went to the kitchen and downed a Mojo.

The next call went to voice mail, too, and so did the third and fourth. Was he avoiding her? Was whatever stopped him last night more of an obstacle than she'd thought?

Would he let whatever it was be the end of them?

After the last call, she dug around the mess on the dining table until she found Justin's phone number. While she dialed, she practiced tones, wanting to sound just curious, maybe a little concerned, but not needy or clingy in any way. When he answered with a sleepy "Hello," she said, "Hey, Justin, it's Carly. Is this how you spend your Sunday afternoons, dozing your life away? You should be out with your friends, charming a few girls, maybe breaking a few hearts."

He yawned, then said, "I'm sleeping because I was out all night, charming at least one girl. I didn't get in until after the sun came up. Never let it be said that bad legs and crutches stand in the way of Justin Stevens's love life."

Her smile hurt a little. He'd told her about Sarah, who'd dumped him after his injury because she couldn't deal with it. He was okay with it, he'd insisted, but Carly had seen the pain in his eyes. She'd wanted to smack the girl.

"Hey, I made a joke there. Bad legs and crutches? Standing in the way? The least you could do is laugh."

She managed a chuckle before getting to the point. "I'm sorry I interrupted your recuperative nap, but I've been trying to get hold of Dane and he's not answering his phone."

"I still don't get why you choose him over me. I'm a lot better looking. More fun, too. I wouldn't be wasting time going shopping and painting. I'd be showing you how much more there is to life."

When she just sniffed, he laughed. "You want me to go over and bang on his door? See if he's home?"

"Go over?"

"He lives next door."

Carly blinked. Neither of them had mentioned that before. Of course, it explained how they knew each other and why Dane had visited Justin at the gym that day.

With something niggling in the back of her mind, she

said, "No, that's okay. I think I'd rather go over and bang on it myself. Which barracks do you live in?"

There was a sudden stillness on Justin's end. "Uh, I should probably...you know, he's probably not home. Just let me go see and, uh, I can tell him to, uh, call you or something if he is there."

The niggling got worse, and something cold seeped down her spine. "Justin, what's the building number?"

"You know, Carly, I can't just—"

"Justin."

Reluctantly he gave her the building number, the name and Dane's room number. She picked up a pen, poised to write it down, but there was no need. She recognized both number and name. She passed it every Tuesday on her way to the transition unit with the kids. Except for a few lucky ones with family in Tallgrass, every patient she knew at the WTU lived in the barracks just down the street.

Dane lived in the wounded warrior barracks.

"Don't you go over there and warn him," she said quietly.

"Carly— Man, he'll kill me if I don't— Just wait. Let me go see—"

She hung up on him.

He'd told her he'd torn up his leg in Afghanistan. It didn't take a life-changing injury to bar a paratrooper from any further jumps. Those guys suffered back and knee injuries all the time and went on living a relatively normal life, no different from any hard-charging athlete. Injuries were part of the job.

But it pretty much did take a life-changing injury to end up in the wounded warrior program. He didn't show any signs of a traumatic brain injury or post-traumatic stress disorder. Was his leg injury worse than he'd admitted?

But he didn't use crutches. He limped only on occasion. He'd hiked into the falls at Turner Falls and climbed to Wagon Wheel Cave. His only limitations seemed to involve kneeling and climbing ladders, and he'd done plenty of kneeling helping her plant yesterday.

She realized with a start she was standing at the front door, her purse strap over one shoulder, her keys in her hand. By the time she'd reached Main Street, she'd managed to tamp down her curiosity and hurt into a sort of wait-and-see numbness.

She followed the familiar route onto post, pulling into the barracks parking lot and, first thing, noticing Dane's truck off in a distant corner. After parking, she sat for a moment studying the buildings. They were modeled after Tranquility Hall at National Military Medical Center in Bethesda: small apartments that allowed the recovering soldiers to adapt to regular life. Some had extra bedrooms so family could stay, give emotional support and help when needed and practice the responsibilities they would face at home.

Her aching fingers made her realize she was gripping the steering wheel. She was delaying.

Slowly she forced her fingers loose, then opened the door. It took only moments to cross the parking lot to the building, to locate Unit 6. Her hand clenched, and instead of knocking, she banged on the door, just as she'd told Justin she would.

There was a moment's silence, then Dane's voice filtered out. "For God's sake, Justin. Can't a guy take a bath without you calling and pounding—" The lock clicked, and the door swung in, and he stood there, leaning on crutches. He wore a T-shirt and sweatpants, the left leg swaying gently from midthigh down. His right foot was bare. The left...

Wasn't there.

The expression on his face was stark, color draining, eyes widening. His hands clenched the crutches, the muscles in his arms bunching and rippling, then his face turned a mottled red and he took an awkward step back, as if to shield himself behind the door. He wanted to *hide*. From *her*.

Carly wanted to do a dozen things. Hold him and hug him until everything was all right. Demand to know everything. Ask why he hadn't told her. Plead to know why he hadn't trusted her. Beat him with one of the crutches for being so...so...

Striving for a cool, even tone, she politely asked, "May I come in?"

His hesitation was so long that she thought he was actually going to tell her no. Finally, though, he stepped aside and nudged the door open wider. She walked into the apartment, her gaze taking in the institutional feel of the furnishings, the lack of personal items...and the lifelike prosthetic leg sitting on the couch. She couldn't help but stare at it before turning her gaze back to Dane.

"This is what you call 'tearing up' your leg?" She gestured toward the prosthesis without taking her attention from his face, from the embarrassment that still bronzed his skin, from the mortification still in his eyes.

"It was pretty damn well torn up before the doctors cut it off." His tone was flat, edged with dark emotion. Anger. Bitterness.

"Why didn't you tell me?"

"When would have been a good time for that?"

"The first time we met. The second. The third. Or the first time we kissed, or the second or the third, or, hell, last night when we were on the couch with my blouse half undone." Tears welling, she swallowed hard and tightened every muscle in her body to stave them off. "That day in the cave, when you told me you were stationed at Fort Murphy, it would have been so easy to add 'at the Warrior Transition Unit.' That second time, in the gym, when you pretended you'd just stopped by to visit Justin, you could have been honest instead."

He closed the door, then leaned against it. "Like that wouldn't have changed things?"

"Changed things how?" Slowly his meaning dawned, and the desire to give him a whack with his own crutch returned. "You think it would have mattered to me? That I wouldn't have been interested? You think I'm so shallow that I wouldn't get involved with a man missing a leg?"

The bitterness that had been in his voice earlier returned. "You do have this thing about perfection."

Her own eyes doubled in size. "It's a word I use, for God's sake! The weather is perfect, my flower beds are perfect, the colors in my living room are perfect. You're perfect, too, Dane. You're a perfect ass. You didn't even trust me." Finally a tear slipped free. "How can you care about someone you don't even trust?"

"Carly—" He dragged his hand through his hair, not as easy to do when he was using crutches to hold him upright. "I meant to tell you. Really. It's just... I was... The doctors say I have body-image issues. I'm not adapting well to my new reality." He snorted. "I hated losing my leg. I hate the prosthesis and the sleeve and the stump and the crutches and the pain and everything else, so I don't tell anyone. I figure if I don't have to see it or talk about it, and no one else does, either, then I can pretend it didn't happen."

Her chest tightened, making air difficult to take in. "You should have told me. You should have given me a chance, Dane. I wouldn't have let you down."

Heat flared in his voice. "My own *mother* let me down. She only came to see me once in all those months in the hospital. She calls me crippled and says no woman would want me like this."

Carly tried to imagine Mia or her own mother ever saying such things to their sons, and the image wouldn't form. No loving mother could ever be so insensitive and cruel. "Then your mother's a fool, Dane, because *I* wanted you!" *Want you, will always want you*, was what she meant, but she used the past tense in a petty effort to transfer a little of her hurt to him.

He noticed. His mouth thinned, the muscles in his clean-shaven jaw working. "Do you want to know now?"

She had to swallow a couple times to get the answer out, steeling her nerves, steeling her heart, because she knew his story wasn't going to be easy to tell, easy to hear. "Yes."

He walked smoothly, as if he'd used the crutches long enough for them to become a part of him, and moved the prosthetic from the sofa to the chair. Though he looked as if he wanted to throw it, he set it down with restraint, then went to sit at the other end of the sofa. She eased onto the cushion farthest from him, turning to face him.

When he began, his voice was blank, an emotionless recitation of what must have been the worst day of his life. "It was my fourth tour in the desert. We were stationed in Kunar Province. Routine day, routine patrol, until it got blasted all to hell. IED. One minute, we were driving along, arguing about the best place to find pizza back in Vicenza, and the next, I was lying facedown twenty-five feet away. I guess I blacked out for a moment. When I opened my eyes, I saw my boot about twelve feet away. I knew it was mine because it had this oil stain that I couldn't get rid of. There was dust settling all around, people yelling and running, and that damn boot was just standing there.

"And then I realized my foot was still in it."

Carly's throat swelled, and she clamped her jaws together, pushing her tongue hard against the roof of her mouth. Thanks to the media embedded with American troops, she could too easily imagine the scene: the chaos, the urgency, the fear. Injured buddies, probably one or more dead, feeling exposed as if the enemy might pick them off one at a time while they tried to save their friends' lives.

"By that time in our deployment, some of us were routinely wearing tourniquets when we went out, loosely cinched on our thighs. I didn't even think to tighten it. I just kept looking at that boot, the sock, the ragged flesh, and wondering how was that possible. It was my *foot*. It was supposed to be *attached*." A note of wonder, of confusion, came into his voice before the monotone returned. "One of the guys from the vehicle behind us tightened the tourniquet on my leg, and they got us out of there and to the field hospital. I don't know how it happened, but we all survived."

It happened by the grace of God, Carly thought, because he was meant to come into her life. Meant to change her life.

God, did it make her ungrateful that she would prefer change without pain?

"I got evacked to Landstuhl, where they did the first amputation, then sent me to Bethesda. But the force of the blast blew debris into my leg, damaged muscles, tissue, and bone, and caused an infection. I'd just gotten relatively ambulatory with my new foot when they said they had to do a below-the-knee amputation. But the infection wouldn't go away. They treated it aggressively, because having a knee is always better than not having one, but after a few months, they had to go in again."

He smiled weakly. "And here I am."

And here he was. Carly didn't know what to say. She understood in her head that the loss of a limb was traumatic, though she couldn't begin to know just how traumatic it was to *him*. But he was *alive* when so many others had died. He should celebrate that, he should be grateful every day, not embarrassed, not trying to hide what his service had cost him. Jeff would have been so thrilled to come home that he would have danced her through the streets of Tallgrass, prosthetic leg and all.

But Dane wasn't Jeff, and Jeff had known she loved him.

Jeff had trusted her totally, completely, utterly.

And Dane didn't.

He stared toward the television, and she followed his look to a photograph standing beside it. It had been taken in the desert, a bunch of guys in khaki T-shirts and DCU pants, all with high-and-tights, some wearing dark glasses, some holding weapons that seemed almost as big as they were. She wondered on which deployment it had been taken, which of the men in it had come back, which hadn't, how much loss they had suffered.

Realizing her cheeks were wet, she raised one hand to swipe away tears. "I'm sorry," she whispered, then spoke louder. "I'm very sorry."

Then... "Is that why... last night...? It really wasn't me, it was you."

He gave her a dry look. "We couldn't have gone much further without having to take our clothes off. I may be an ass, but even I know that dropping my pants with a surprise like that is going to put one hell of a damper on the mood."

Yeah. Even with her limited sexual experience, she knew shock wasn't exactly a great turn-on. She would have been horrified—not by the prosthesis but by everything he'd gone through.

On the other hand, her fourteen extra pounds didn't seem so worrisome in comparison.

"I've been celibate a long time, but I think I remember a lot more to foreplay than what we did last night," she said, trying to match his dryness.

His response could have been a laugh or a cough. "I've been celibate a long time, too. Trust me, I don't have the self-control to wait much beyond what we did last night." His glance her way was awkward, self-conscious. "I was going to tell you today. Honestly. I want—I want *you*. I want to—to be with you. To spend the future with you. I was just cleaning up before going to your house." He gestured toward the prosthesis. "I was even going to wear the pretty leg."

She believed him. She just wished it had happened the way he'd planned.

She really just wished he'd told her right up front. Even if he'd been uncomfortable telling the truth the first time they'd met, at some point after that, after he'd gotten to know her, hadn't he realized she wouldn't care? Hadn't he had a little bit of faith in her, just enough to know that she was a person of substance? That she was honest and genuine and would never, ever judge him on his physical limitations?

If he hadn't learned that much about her, had he learned anything at all?

She didn't realize how long the silence had gone on until he broke it, his words little more than a whisper. "This makes a difference, doesn't it?" Grimly, he grasped a handful of his pants leg in the middle of his thigh, bunching the empty fabric.

"It doesn't. I don't care that you don't have a leg." She swallowed hard, then took a couple deep breaths for strength. "I care that you didn't trust me, Dane. That you didn't think enough of me to give me a chance."

The words hung in the air between them, heavy and sad and accusing. She imagined she still heard their faint echoes when she stood. "I need...time."

The bleakness in his eyes when he nodded just about broke her heart. Instead of walking to the door, she wanted to go to him, wrap her arms around him, convince him that her feelings for him didn't have anything to do with the number of body parts he had or lacked, that it was the man he was inside that she loved.

But the man he was inside was ashamed of himself and unsure of her.

She stopped at the door, but didn't look back. "I—I'll call you." She opened the door, stepped out into the warm afternoon air, then closed it quietly behind her.

As she crossed the parking lot to her car, she thought about how good she'd become at keeping herself under control. Army widows were expected to show restraint in public. They rarely sobbed through their husbands' funerals. They didn't collapse with grief at the grave sites. They maintained control, then fell apart in private.

That was what she did on the drive home: maintained. Her jaw was clenched, her fingers taut, her muscles stressed to the max to keep her erect and composed. She would cry when she got home, with the door securely shutting out the world, letting her grieve and get as sloppy sad as she wanted.

But when she got home, she didn't throw herself on the couch and sob. She didn't seek the shadowy sanctuary of her bedroom. She stood in the hallway for a very long time, lost and confused and heart-sore but, to her surprise, still hopeful.

"Every journey starts with one step," Jeff used to tell her. She and Dane had taken a hell of a lot of steps on this journey. Was she going to throw it all away because of one misstep early on? Was she going to stop loving him, wanting him, needing to be with him because of something he hadn't said when he should have?

Of course not. She just needed time to get over the hurt

that he hadn't confided in her, that he hadn't trusted her with information that was such a part of him.

Twisting the band on her fourth finger, she realized that she also needed time to say good-bye. Jeff would be in her heart forever, but it was time to move on from parts of her past and to open herself fully to the possibilities of the future.

With one last twist, she removed her wedding band, then stared at her hand. Every moment, waking or sleeping, she'd worn that ring, ever since Jeff had placed it on her finger at the minister's behest. It left a groove at the base of her finger, pale, shiny skin so rarely exposed.

Her hand felt naked.

Her heart felt lighter.

She slid the ring onto her right hand, then clenched her fingers. "I love you, Jeff," she whispered. But she loved Dane, too.

Jeff was all right with that. She knew it deep down in her heart.

Sighing out a bit of heaviness and stress, slowly she went down the hall to the guest room, where she opened the closet and took out an armful of Jeff's uniforms. Gently, reverently, she began packing them away.

Chapter Sixteen

The first day of spring break should have meant sleeping in late, lounging around in pajamas with a cup of coffee and something truly decadent for breakfast, like sticky, cinammony, nut-laden monkey bread, but instead Therese had gotten up at her usual seven a.m. She showered, dressed, and put on makeup, adding extra concealer under her eyes to cover the shadows there. Before heading downstairs for coffee and yogurt, she knocked sharply on the kids' doors, getting a grunt from Jacob, nothing from Abby.

Granted, she and Abby hadn't exchanged five words since the incident Saturday.

The reason Abby hadn't answered was apparent when Therese reached the kitchen: The girl was sitting at the island, dressed and ready to go, her luggage next to the doorway. She'd gotten a bottle of pop and a yogurt from the refrigerator, but didn't seem to be making headway on either one, instead running her hands restlessly over her hair, her clothes, her cell phone.

Therese stopped in the hallway before Abby saw her and just studied her. She was so pretty, so delicate. There was much of her mother in her, but Therese could recognize a lot of Paul, too. *Baby girl*, he'd called her, and *Scooter pie.* She'd loved the first and rolled her eyes at the second—the reason he'd done it, of course.

Where would she go if Therese insisted on giving her up? Catherine and both sets of grandparents had already made clear they didn't want custody of her, but that was when they'd known she had a home with Therese. If they knew her only option was entering the foster system, surely—maybe—they'd change their minds.

Considering Catherine had called yesterday to try to weasel out of this visit—*"I don't know that I'm ready for this"*—Therese wasn't hoping for help from her.

Clunky steps plus the *thud-thud* of a bag being dragged sounded from the stairs, forcing Therese into motion. She walked into the kitchen, avoiding Abby as studiously as Abby avoided her. By the time she'd filled a travel mug with coffee and adjusted it to her tastes, Jacob was coming into the room. He tossed his lone backpack onto the floor next to Abby's two suitcases, then headed for the refrigerator.

Weren't they a cheery family?

When her nerves were strung as tightly as she could take, she put her coffee down and got her purse. "Here's your IDs." She laid the Department of Defense dependent ID cards that entitled them to medical care, among other benefits, on the island. "Spending money." Two equal piles of cash. "And a power of attorney allowing your

mother to get medical care for you if you need it." After
a moment's hesitation, she laid the folded piece of paper
with Jacob's things.

Abby's eyes widened, then her entire face narrowed
in a sneer. "Oh my God, you're giving her *permission* to
take her own kids to the doctor? She's our *mother*. She
has that right. She doesn't need your okay for *anything*."

Therese was debating whether to respond or bite her
tongue until it bled when Jacob matter-of-factly said,
"Yes, she does." He stuck the money and ID in his left
pocket, then folded the power of attorney into a small
square and stuck it in his right pocket. "Therese is legally
responsible for us. Mom doesn't have the right to do anything. She gave up those rights when she gave us up."

Abby glared at her brother as if he'd betrayed the family bond by speaking up. Therese turned away from them
to hide her sad smile. She fully believed siblings should
be raised together whenever possible, but if no one in
Abby's family stepped up to take both of them, surely it
would be all right for Therese to keep Jacob, wouldn't it?
He didn't deserve the foster system just because his sister
was out of control.

Guilt turned the coffee sour in her stomach, but she
stubbornly pushed it away. She *wouldn't* take the blame
for this. Yes, it was her decision, but Abby had made it
for her. She'd pushed Therese into a corner where giving
up custody was the only hope for her own future.

She was *not* at fault.

And she would keep repeating it until she believed it.

A grand gesture. Justin had spent the rest of Sunday, all
day Monday, and most of Tuesday telling Dane that was

what he needed. Something seriously romantic, to make Carly swoon, to make her go all soft and warm and forget that he hadn't been open with her. Trouble was, neither of them had a clue what kind of gesture would sweep Carly off her feet, and Dane wasn't any good at gestures anyway. They seemed phony to him—an insincere attempt to make up for what he'd done wrong, when he'd never been so sincere in his life. Like he'd told her, he wanted her, wanted to spend the rest of his life with her.

Like he hadn't told her, he loved her.

And he was pretty sure she loved him, too, even if he wasn't perfect.

It had been hard, but as of five Tuesday afternoon, he hadn't called her. She'd said she needed time. He'd given her that. She'd said she would call him. He'd waited. He'd kept his cell phone right next to him all day; he slept with it in his hand at night. He'd had a couple calls from his mother that he let go to voice mail, and a couple from Justin with more suggestions for grand gestures. But not one from the only person who mattered.

The only person… He hadn't treated her that way. Yeah, he'd been scared, but she was right. That day at the cave, it should have been so easy to say, *I'm at Fort Murphy at the WTU.* She would have known what that meant. All Army people did. Little words, big meaning, awkwardness avoided.

Either she would have cared and they wouldn't be where they were right now, or she wouldn't have cared and they wouldn't be where they were right now. Either way, heartache avoided.

When his phone rang, jerking him out of his thoughts, for an instant his heart pounded and his palms grew clammy, even though in the next instant he knew from the ring tone that it wasn't Carly. Since Anna Mae didn't give up easily, he might as well get this over with and get a head start on a little peace until the next time she called. He settled more comfortably on the couch and said, "Hello."

"Did that accident cripple your dialing finger, too, that you can't even pick up the phone and press return?"

He smiled faintly. The only thing accidental about his injury was that the enemy had intended to kill him and instead they'd just maimed him.

Just maimed him. The thought made him go motionless. His heart was still beating. His brain was still functioning. His spirit was beaten but intact.

His future was still ahead of him, not buried in the losses of his past.

He believed that as completely as he believed the sun would rise tomorrow. Too bad, though, it had taken him so long to get to that point.

"Hello, Mom. How are you?"

"Wondering if my son's still alive. What keeps you so busy you can't call me? And don't say physical therapy. You've been using that excuse for months. If you're not walking good by now, it isn't ever going to happen. You should just settle for what you've got and be happy with it the best you can."

Something was different this time, but it took him a moment to realize what: His muscles hadn't gone tight the way they usually did when Anna Mae said something rude or insensitive. The bitterness wasn't seeping through him. *"Your mother's a fool,"* Carly had said, and in the ways that mattered, she was right. He'd known that even as a kid. He'd never turned to his mother for approval or advice or anything else. All that had come from his father, his grandparents and coaches because his mother simply wasn't capable of it. Never had been.

Why, in the toughest situation he'd ever faced, had he begun accepting what she said as fact? Because he'd been weak. Well, hell, he'd had all the weakness, cowardice and self-pity a man could stand. Like the slogan said, he wasn't just strong. He was Army strong.

"I'll tell the doctors you said that."

Of course she missed the irony in his voice. "They're just delaying the inevitable, if you ask me. Instead of all this rehabilitation, they should help you find a job you can do and put all this behind you."

"I have a job, Mom. And when I'm ready to get out of the Army, there are plenty of other jobs I can do. Pretty much anything I want." With the right attitude, the right adaptations, and a little support. He'd never get that from Anna Mae.

But he'd get it from Carly. Had gotten it already from Carly just by knowing her.

"How's your baby quilt coming?"

Anna Mae hesitated a moment. He could picture her, the prettiness that was steadily giving away to bitterness, eyes narrowed the way they always did when she suspected him of mischief. "I've picked the fabrics—the most adorable stripes and polka dots and prints in pastels. They remind me of the cotton candy you used to get at the fair when you were little. I never did figure out how sugar crystals ended up in your ears and down your back and even inside your shoes. Anyway, I showed the fabric to Sheryl today, and she thought it was just beautiful."

"How's Sheryl?"

Another silence, this one potent enough to make him smile. He *never* asked about Sheryl, not once since the divorce, and said little more than grunts when his mother brought her up.

"She—she's fine. Doctor said she's the healthiest mama-to-be in town." Anna Mae cleared her throat, then cautiously asked, "How are you? Is everything okay?"

Mark this day on the calendar: Mom finally *asked how I was doing.* "The docs say I'm the healthiest amputee in town." And he had the opportunity to be the happiest.

Anna Mae made her usual shushing sounds. It was her philosophy of life. *Ignore the ugly, and it will go away. Never stop wishing for what you want. Pretend for all you're worth.*

It was sad. He hadn't wanted to be part of that when he was a kid, and he didn't want to now. She wasn't about to change. She'd always gauged life—success, happiness, love—by her own standards. No matter what she had, it was never enough.

He'd spent his last day pitying himself for the leg he'd lost. From now on he would be grateful for the life he'd kept and the future he'd gained.

He waited until she took a breath, then said, "Hey, Mom, I'm sorry to cut this short, but I've got to change clothes, then go ask a girl a question. I'll call you."

She snorted. "You haven't called *me* since your last Mother's Day in Afghanistan."

He'd missed a Mother's Day in between, and another one was coming up in a few weeks. He would make a note on the calendar. "I'll call you," he repeated. "I love you."

Before she could respond to that, he hung up.

* * *

When Dane had mentioned the support group Sunday, Dalton had pretty much brushed him off like he brushed off everyone who wanted him to talk. *I'll keep that in mind.* Usually he said the words and immediately put whatever it was right *out* of his mind.

That hadn't been the case this time. At odd moments while he was working, showering, trying to sleep, the thought came unbidden into his head: A group of people who'd been through what he had, who'd felt what he felt.

More or less, he added with a scowl. It wasn't likely any of those women's husbands had chosen suicide over coming back home to them. It wasn't likely they'd meant so damn little to their husbands.

Still, they knew what it was like to plan to spend the rest of their lives with someone and have that plan blown all to hell. They knew how it felt to wake up in the middle of the night and forget just for a moment, to reach to the other side of the bed expecting to find their spouses' warm body, only to suddenly realize they were alone. They knew how to live with the loss and the anger and the despair and the loneliness.

He wanted to know how to live.

The clock on the kitchen wall showed five twenty-five. He'd knocked off work early, showered, shaved, put on his newest jeans and best boots. And still he paced the kitchen.

This group of Dane's girlfriend was all women. Though Dalton had paid nearly zero attention, Noah had even mentioned them before—the Fort Murphy Widows' Club. How the hell was he supposed to approach a bunch of women he'd never laid eyes on and bare his private sorrows to them?

He wasn't. It was unnatural. There were other ways to deal.

Like letting a pretty stranger pick him up in the cemetery, for God's sake, and getting so drunk that he barely remembered having sex with her?

Grimacing, he snatched his keys from the hook near the back door and headed for his truck. He would drive in to The Three Amigos. Have a drink, maybe dinner. Maybe even look up an old friend to join him. There must still be a few of them around. If he spoke to the women, that was fine. If he didn't, well, that was fine, too.

The miles passed in a blur, his stomach knotting. It was six o'clock when he passed Pansy's Posies. Six oh five when he caught the red light at Main downtown. Six ten when he walked through the door of The Three Amigos.

"How many?" the pretty hostess asked.

"One."

"Bar or table?"

"Bar." The way his gut felt, booze would go down easier than food.

She flashed a smile. "Inside or out? Our patio is officially open for summer."

He glanced around the dining room and saw no more than four women in any group. "Out."

The patio was on the east side of the restaurant. Dining tables filled three-fourths of the area, with a small portable bar at the north end providing seating for five. Three of the stools were occupied. Dalton chose the one nearest the building and ordered a beer before slowly turning his attention to the women who dominated the area.

There were seventeen or eighteen, ranging in age from very young to mid-fifties. They were white, black, Asian, Latina, underweight to overweight with a stop at every ten pounds on the scale in between, with hair that was blond, black, brown, gray, and red, and they—

His gaze jerked back to the redhead just as she tilted her head back for a throaty laugh. Jessy Lawrence.

Damn, she was beautiful.

Then it hit him: Jessy Lawrence was one of the women he'd thought might teach him how to live again. Jessy Lawrence, who picked up strange men in the cemetery and got drunk enough to have sex with them. Jessy, who'd looked him right in the eye a week later and had no clue who he was.

Hell, he'd rather stay exactly as miserable as he already was.

It was a perfect evening—belatedly Carly caught herself and substituted *beautiful*—for the margarita club to move their meal outside. The sky was a lovely shade of blue, the air was warm, the chimes around the perimeter tinkled sweetly, and even the traffic forty feet away on Main Street seemed slower, in tune with the evening.

Picking up her sweating margarita glass, she savored a drink, though she grimaced just a little when the liquid hit her throat. Even so, tonight she might drink the entire thing. She was celebrating, after all.

Leaning close to Therese, she asked quietly, "Did the kids get to their mother's okay?"

Therese stirred from her funk. "Yeah. Jacob texted me from Abby's phone. I know it was Jacob because it didn't end with, 'Drop dead, bitch.'" After a moment, she took a slug of her own drink. "I've got an appointment at JAG on Thursday. Just to ask some questions and get some information."

Though the thought of her giving up custody of Paul's kids made Carly's stomach hurt, she forced a smile. "You know whatever you decide, we'll back you all the way."

"I know." Therese tilted her head to one side, gaze narrowing. "What's going on with you? You look...different." She looked Carly up and down, then her mouth formed a silent *oh* when she came to the band on Carly's right hand. "Is this because of Dane? Or for him?"

"For. I packed up Jeff's clothes, and I—I called Mia this afternoon. She answered, 'Ah, daughter-in-my-heart,' and I almost lost it then. But I managed to tell her about Dane, and then we both lost it." She touched the corner of her eye with her pinkie, careful to blot away the moisture without disturbing her makeup. She had plans for after dinner tonight. She'd even shopped for the event: a sundress in tropical shades that exposed way too much leg for school, strappy sandals, and even a little sexy lingerie.

If Dane was willing. If he was, she wanted to look all that willing and more.

She wasn't going to call him until after dinner. She'd finished packing Jeff's clothing, both military and civilian. She'd boxed up mementos from his youth and college and a few places the Army had sent him. Where the guest closet had held hanging clothes, now it held orange tubs.

Not everything was gone. She'd kept all the photographs, his dress blue uniform, his ribbons and awards. The small pottery dish on the dresser that held all the challenge coins he'd collected in the Army remained. She'd kept a few notebooks filled with his big loopy writing, his favorite pair of aviator shades and a few other sentimental items.

And then she'd called Mia, who insisted she was happy for her, but sobbed all through the call. Carly had no doubt Mia really was happy she'd met someone else, but she had to be going through a lot of sorrow again. It had to be a tangible reminder that all her dreams for Jeff and Carly were over.

Not that Carly would ever quit being part of Mia and Pop's lives, unless it was too painful for them.

That call made, now she was free for one more, and the time was soon.

"So." Therese drew her attention back. "You're really ready to move on."

"Yes. I am."

"I hate you. Here you're falling in love and being really happy again, and I'm...I'm just falling apart." Therese lifted her margarita. "But I'm also unbearably happy for you. I hope you and Dane live a long, long life together."

Carly clinked glasses with her, then gazed around the table at their friends, wishing she had a camera that could capture them all. In that moment, everyone, every single one, was smiling, even Therese. Everyone looked happy, as if they'd found some small measure of peace on this perfect Tuesday evening. It was enough to make her throat tighten and tears well in her eyes.

She was trying to surreptitiously wipe her eyes when Jessy's voice arose above the others. "Oh, my God." After a moment, in a less surprised tone, she said, "Carly, tell soldier boy he needs to get out in the sun. He's way too pale for my fantasies."

Her gaze jerked to Jessy, then past her to the parking lot. Beside her, Therese gasped and whispered, "Bless his heart." Understanding barely registered as Dane came toward them. He wore a T-shirt, as he nearly always did, and cargo shorts that ended at his knee. His right leg, as Jessy had pointed out, was too pale to match the rest of him. His left leg wasn't the pretty flesh-toned one, but a mechanical robotic prosthesis that looked futuristic and efficient.

His stride was nearly perfect, but his face was red with self-consciousness. That was when the enormity of it hit her: He was *wearing shorts* in public. He was putting himself and his prosthetic leg on display for anyone who wanted to look—and everyone on the patio was looking. Not because they'd never seen a soldier with a prosthesis before, but because this soldier was special. He was worth looking at.

And he'd done this—come here like this—for *her*. He wasn't ignoring his leg, covering it up, pretending it didn't exist so no one else would know it did, and he was doing it for *her*.

He walked through the gate that led directly onto the patio, passed off a grimace for a smile and murmured a few names as he passed. "Ilena. Jessy. Marti."

Carly was about to rise from her seat when Therese stopped her. "This is his show," she murmured. "Let him play it out."

He circled the table to her seat. Space was tight, so Fia, Lucy, and Bennie scrambled to slide their chairs back and give him more room. At the same time, Therese, with help from someone unseen, pulled Carly's chair back from the table so he could face her. He stood there in front of her, gazing down at her, his dark eyes nervous and comfortable and calm. A serious calm that she'd never seen on him.

Everything on the patio had gone dead-silent. Even the strangers at the bar had stopped talking to watch.

His voice was husky but steady, low but strong. "You said you needed time, and I waited more than forty-eight hours. But if there's one thing you and I both know, it's that time is precious. I don't want to wait any longer, Carly. I *can't* wait."

"Oh, Dane—"

A round of shushes went up from the table, and the anticipation level tripled. Carly felt everyone's attention riveted on them even though she didn't once let her gaze shift from him.

Resting one hand on the arm of her chair, he started to move, then stopped for a wry grin. "You realize I may need a little help here in a minute?"

All she could do was bob her head. Her heart was pounding about a hundred times a second, and if she didn't get a breath in her soon, she was going to slide down into an unconscious heap at his feet.

Awkwardly, carefully, he lowered himself to one knee, the prosthetic resting on the tiled floor. "You were right that I should have told you about my leg. I wasn't in a place where I could do that. I was too angry and bitter and... afraid. I'd lost so much, and I didn't want to lose you, too. In the beginning, I didn't know if it would make a difference, and later... You had a right to think it was because I didn't trust you. I should have. I knew the first time I talked to you that you were special. I just didn't know how special."

A tear rolled down her cheek, and he raised his hand to wipe it away. "I don't like gestures, Carly. That's not why I'm doing this here, now. But I want you to understand that I'm not going to hide anymore. So I lost a leg. For a long time that was the worst thing I could imagine. But I've got these great fake ones. I can walk. I can do anything, with a little help and imagination. But losing you..." His voice quavered, then steadied. "There aren't enough adaptive skills in the world to get me through that. I love you, Carly. I want to marry you. I want to have little Jeff Juniors and Dane Juniors and Carly Juniors to chase after with you."

He stopped, swallowed hard, glanced around, then locked gazes with her again. "I don't need a leg to make me whole, Carly. I just need you."

Soft sighs swelled around them, and she swore she heard a sniffle or two before she realized it came from her. Tears filled her eyes, her heart actually hurt with joy, and wonder made her hand tremble when she laid it on his cheek. "Dane, I love you," she whispered.

"Speak up, Carly, we're having trouble hearing at this end," Leah said.

She laughed, and the tears began seeping away. Her voice as strong and certain as she could make it, she said, "I love you, Dane, and I would dearly love to marry you."

There were voices then, cheers, applause, but she was only dimly aware of it all because he was kissing her with every bit of the need and hunger and love that welled inside *her*. For one instant, she thought of Jeff, smiling with approval, before his image faded. He was happy for her. She had no doubt.

When Dane ended the kiss, he gave her a look so perfect that she knew she would remember it always. "Can you miss dinner just this one night? I'd really like to be alone with you."

Thinking of his words just a moment before—*I can do anything, with a little help and imagination*—she smiled and whispered in his ear, "I'd really like to be alone with you, too. I've got *tons* of imagination."

"I figured you did." He released her and steeled himself for the process of standing.

"Tell me what you need," she said, unsure what kind of help to offer.

He grinned, pushed to his feet with grace and strength, then offered his hand to her. "Only you, Carly. Only you."

Ever since she lost her husband, Paul,
to the war in Iraq, Therese has struggled
to raise her troubled teenage stepchildren on
her own.

But when Paul's old Army buddy Keegan
suddenly shows up in Tallgrass, he sparks
feelings Therese isn't sure she's ready to
face.

Is Keegan really the man she needs?
Or is he the man who will push Therese's
fragile family over the edge?

Please turn this page for a preview of

A Man to Hold on To

Chapter One

The first thing Therese Matheson did when she arrived at Tulsa International Airport was head to the bathroom and blot her face with a damp paper towel. She should have taken an extra antianxiety pill this morning or skipped the pancakes and blueberries for breakfast. Maybe she should have stopped off somewhere for a fortifying drink, even though it wasn't yet noon, or guilted one of her friends into coming along.

"It's not that scary," she whispered to the pale reflection staring wide-eyed at her. "You're just picking up the kids after their spring break trip. Paul's kids."

Usually, reminding herself that Abby and Jacob were Paul's kids helped calm her. Paul had been the love of her life, and when his ex-wife had sent the kids to live with them nearly four years ago, Therese had embraced the opportunity for a ready-made family. When he'd deployed to Afghanistan not long after, she'd promised to keep them safe for his return. When he didn't return, well, she'd been shocked that their mother didn't want them back, but she'd done her best. They were his kids, after all.

Now, she'd used the time they were gone to seek advice about giving up custody of them.

Shame crept into the reflection's eyes. She'd promised Paul. She'd wanted to love them. She'd tried, God help her, but in the end, it had come down to two choices: keep them or find some much-needed peace. Break her promise to their father or break her own spirit.

She was surviving Paul's death, but she wasn't surviving life with his angry, hostile, bitter children.

Child, she corrected. Before they'd left for the visit with their mother, Jacob had shown her some sympathy, even some respect.

It was Abby who was breaking her.

With a deep breath, she forced the shame from her gaze, then left the bathroom and took the escalator to the baggage area above. There weren't many people waiting for the incoming flights. She missed the happy reunions that once were common in airports. Getting off the plane and finding someone waiting for you had been part of the fun.

Someone who was happy to see you, she amended when passengers started appearing in the skywalk from the main terminal. She wasn't happy to see Abby, already texting on her cell, strolling lazily, mindless of the people who dodged her snail's pace, and the swell of pleasure brought by the sight of Jacob wasn't really happiness. It was a start, though.

Tall and broad-shouldered, Jacob had a pack slung over one shoulder—his only luggage for the six-day trip—and buds in his ears. A person could be forgiven for thinking him six or eight years older than his eleven, not only because of his size, but also the look in his eyes, the air of having lived about him. He looked so much like his father that most days seeing him made Therese's heart hurt.

Next to him Abby looked even more petite than ever—and less angelic. For once the bright streaks that sliced through her blond hair were gone, and the blond was platinum instead. It had been cut, too, in a sleek but edgy style, sharp angles, short in back, longer in front, no bangs but a tendency for the entire left side to fall over her face—her *made-up* face.

Her clothes were different, too. Therese had seen swimsuit bottoms that covered more than Abby's shorts, and the top looked more like a beach cover-up than a blouse except that it was too short to cover anything adequately. The bright print was semitransparent and kept sliding off one shoulder or the other, revealing the straps of her new black bra.

Therese's efforts to breathe resulted in a strangled gasp. Another pill, two more pills, and definitely a drink, or maybe she could borrow a sedative. Surely someone in the Tuesday Night Margarita Club still had a stash of sedatives somewhere.

She couldn't pull her gaze from her stepdaughter even when she had to move left or right to maintain line of sight. Abby's skin was darkly tanned, a startling contrast to her white shorts and platinum hair and her shoes—

Another strangled sound escaped. White leather, heels adding at least four inches to her height, skinny straps crisscrossing her feet and wrapping around her ankles to end in bows in back.

Oh, my God.

Beside Therese, the conveyor belt rumbled to life and people began nudging her aside to get prime spaces for reclaiming their bags. She took a step toward the kids as they neared, digging deep to find a neutral expression and to stifle the shriek inside her. *What was your mother thinking?*

Abby barely slowed when she reached Therese. Recently manicured nails didn't pause in typing as she said, "My bags are pink. I'll be waiting at the door."

Therese turned to watch her go, then whispered, "Oh, my God."

Jacob stopped beside her and pulled the buds from his ears. "Scary, isn't it?"

Forgetting Abby for the moment, she studied her stepson. He looked exactly the way he had the day he'd left. He might even be wearing the same clothes. Whatever effects the visit with Catherine had had on him, they weren't as painfully obvious as with Abby.

She wished she could hug him or even just lay her hand on his arm to welcome him back home, but he kept enough distance between them to make it difficult. "Did you have a good time?"

He shrugged. "It was okay. We didn't do much."

Of course not. By the time Catherine had bought new clothes and shoes for Abby, taken her to a tanning salon and gotten her hair cut and colored, there probably hadn't been much time left over for Jacob.

"If you want to go on and get the car, I'll get her bags."

"Okay." Therese took a few steps, then turned back.

"Why are her bags pink? She left with black luggage."

He grimaced. "Mom bought her new ones. She said only—"

After a moment, Therese said, "It's okay."

"Only boring people use black luggage."

She forced a smile. "Well, I never aspired to be exciting. She did bring them back, didn't she?" Black though they were, the suitcases were sturdy and still had a lot of miles left on them.

At the hopefulness in her voice, he grinned. "I did."

"Thanks." This time she did touch his arm, just for an instant. "I'll meet you guys out front. Make her carry her own, will you?"

He grunted as he stuck the earbuds back in.

A warm breeze hit Therese as she walked out of the terminal, then crossed the broad street to the short-term parking lot. Her flip-flops keeping familiar tempo, she pulled out her cell and dialed her best friend back in Tallgrass.

The call went straight to voice mail. No surprise since Carly had gotten engaged just a few days ago and was still celebrating. After the beep, Therese said in a rush, "I know you're probably busy with Dane, so don't call me back. I won't be able to talk for a while anyway. I'm at the airport, and oh, Carly, I sent a wholesome sweet-looking thirteen-year-old to visit her mother and got back a tarted-up twenty-three-year-old streetwalker-wannabe! Makeup, high heels, platinum hair! I'd be afraid she's got tattoos or piercings or something even more inappropriate except that there's not enough of her clothing to *cover* anything like that!"

She drew a deep breath. "Okay. I'm breathing. I'm

in control. I'm not going to explode. Yet. I'll call you later."

Once she reached the mom van, she buckled herself in and practiced a few more breaths. As she flipped down the visor to get the parking ticket stub, her gaze landed on the photograph of Paul she always kept there. He'd been in Afghanistan, smiling, full of life, in a khaki T-shirt and camo pants, with dark glasses pushed up on top of his head. He'd emailed the photo to her, then followed it up with a print copy, where he'd scrawled on the back, *Major Paul Matheson, Helmand Province, counting the days till he sees his beautiful wife Therese again.*

"Oh, Paul," she sighed. "I wish you were here. You were the only person in the world who loved both Abby and me. Maybe you could negotiate a truce, because, sweetheart, we are facing a major battle. Send me some strength, will you?"

She sat there a moment, wishing she would actually feel *something*. Just some small sign—a bit of warmth, encouragement, hope.

The only thing she felt was sorrow.

It took a few minutes to exit the lot and circle back around to the loading lane in front of the terminal. She was breathing normally, and a glance in the rearview mirror showed her shock was under control. It also showed the grimness in her eyes, dread for the upcoming skirmish.

The kids were waiting, Jacob with the suitcases, Abby still texting. She did pause long enough to open the rear passenger door, slide inside and fasten her seatbelt, then she ducked her head and went right back to it.

Therese got out and helped Jacob load the luggage.

The black one was easy to lift, since it contained nothing but the other empty black one. His muscles bulged as he hefted the matching pink ones inside. "Thank you, Jacob."

He started to go around to the other passenger side, then stopped. "Can I ride in front?"

Her first response was a blink. For years, she'd chauffeured the kids nearly everywhere, with emphasis on the hired-driver concept. On the rare occasions it was just her and Jacob, he sat in the front seat, never talking to her but listening to music and playing video games, but if she had both kids, they always sat in back and pretty much pretended she wasn't there.

"Sure. That's fine." It wasn't much, but as she'd thought earlier, it was a start.

Jessy Lawrence rolled onto her side with a groan and opened one eye. All she saw was pale aqua with a strip of brown on one edge. Closing her eye again, she digested that bit of information. She was lying on the couch, and it was daytime. Late morning, judging by the light coming through the south-facing windows of her apartment. It was Saturday, so there was nowhere she needed to go, nothing she needed to do.

She did a little shimmy, just enough to realize she was wearing clothes and not the tank top and boxers she normally slept in, and a flex of her feet revealed she still wore the heels she favored to disguise the fact that she was vertically challenged.

That little movement was enough to make her aware of the queasiness in her gut and the throb in her head. She hadn't felt so bad since she'd gotten the flu last winter.

She'd stunk of sweat then, too, and had been certain that the slightest movement would make her puke.

Slowly she nudged the pumps off, and they fell to the floor with a thud muffled by the rug. Her arches almost spasmed in relief. Next she rolled onto her back and opened her eyes, then oh, so slowly she sat up. Her stomach heaved, the sour taste of its contents making its way into her throat, making her clamp her hand over her mouth, and *that* movement sent daggers through her head. She could only hope the brain tissue they destroyed was nonessential, but she wouldn't count on it. After all, this wasn't the first time she'd done this to herself.

The absence of sound in the apartment both soothed and pricked at her. It was always so empty, and it made her feel even emptier. She lived there alone. Slept there alone. Got sick there alone. Grieved there alone.

Home was the second floor of an office building in downtown Tallgrass. Originally, an abstract company and a dentist had shared the space, then a dance school, but after it had stood empty for twenty years, the owners had converted it into residential space. It was the first place she and Aaron had looked at when the Army had transferred him to Fort Murphy, and the last. She'd loved it on sight, with its high ceilings, tall windows and ancient wood floors. She'd loved the old architectural details of the moldings and the couldn't-be-more-modern kitchen and bathroom and the convenience of being within walking distance of restaurants, shopping and clubs.

Aaron hadn't loved it so much. He had wanted an extra bedroom or two for kids and a yard to mow and play in, but he'd loved her so he had agreed to the apartment. It wasn't like it was permanent, he'd said. They could always move as soon as she got pregnant.

She hadn't gotten pregnant.

He had died eleven and a half months into a twelve-month tour in Afghanistan.

And she was so sorry that she was drowning in it.

It was too early to start feeling bad—worse—so she carefully pushed to her feet, swayed a moment, then headed toward the bedroom. She was halfway there when the doorbell rang, the peal slicing through her. Cursing the day she'd given her friends keys to the downstairs entry, she reversed direction and went to the door, opening it without looking through the peephole.

Ilena Gomez stood there, blond hair loosely pulled back, face pink from the exertion of climbing the stairs. Her hands were in the small of her back, and she was stretching, making her pregnant belly look huge compared to normal. She greeted Jessy with a smile, all white teeth and pleasure, and said, "Hector and I are starving. Are you ready?"

Jessy tried to erase the dull look she was certain glazed her eyes while searching her mind for a clue. *Starving* meant food; obviously she had agreed to go to lunch with Ilena today. She must have been insane at the time—or as fuzzy as she was right now—because Saturdays were never her best days.

But she couldn't renege. Sure, Ilena would understand, but that was rule number one in Jessy's life these days: never fail to be there for any member of the Tuesday Night Margarita Club, also known around town as the Fort Murphy Widows' Club. Without them, she wouldn't have survived the past year, and by God, she would return the favor.

"Give me ten minutes. Come on in and sit down." As quickly as her stomach and head would bear, Jessy went into the bedroom, then the bathroom with an agenda. First: Take aspirin. Second: Brush horrible taste out of mouth. Third: Shuck clothes and give sigh of relief that everything was fastened properly and she still wore her underwear. Fourth: Shower, dress, and apply makeup. Fifth: Avoid looking in mirror until absolutely necessary.

Missing her target by only four minutes, she returned to the living room. She wore one of her girl-next-door outfits: cargo shorts, T-shirt, sandals with a thin sole. Her red hair was short enough that all it needed was a finger fluff, and her makeup was minimal to go along with the nice and innocent look.

She would feel nicer and more innocent if she could remember what she'd done last night.

Ilena was sitting on the couch, holding the digital picture frame from the end table and gazing at some of the photographs Jessy had taken over the years. "You take beautiful pictures. Majestic. Haunting."

"Sometimes I feel like a queen," Jessy said flippantly.

"And sometimes like a ghost?" Ilena's look made it clear she found that odd. That was okay. A lot about Jessy was odd, and no one had stopped loving her because of it yet.

She found her purse on the dining table instead of hanging from its usual hook near the door and slung the strap over her shoulder, then went to help Ilena up from the too-comfy couch. "What does Junior want for lunch?"

"My boy may be here by way of Guadalajara, but we

need some pasta and cheese today. How about Luca's?"

"Sounds good." Comfort food, and she definitely needed comfort.

"You should take her with you."

Keegan Logan secured the duffel that held his clothes, then rummaged through an olive-drab backpack to check its contents: laptop computer, power cords, paperwork, a handful of CDs. After zipping it, he finally met his mother's gaze. "It's a nine-hour drive."

"You can stop every few hours to give her a break."

"That would make it an eleven- or twelve-hour drive." When that didn't faze Ercella, he made another excuse. "She's not comfortable alone with me."

Ercella gave him a dry look. "You mean you're not comfortable alone with her. You could fix that if you just tried. Get down on the floor with her. Play with her. Talk to her. Bounce her on your knee. Lord, Keegan, you know how to act with babies. I've seen you with your sisters'."

"Yeah, you saw me ignore their existence until they were old enough to be fun. Besides, they're boys." Both his sisters lived in Shreveport, so he didn't see their kids that often. And he was good at doing boy things. And his nephews didn't look at him like they'd summed him up and found him lacking. They didn't narrow their eyes into little squints and let out shrieks that could shear metal.

They didn't look lost and alone, the way Mariah sometimes did.

"Besides," he went on before Ercella could speak. "I want to check this guy out. I want to see..."

His mother's eyes narrowed into little squints, and she

held the baby a little tighter. "Are you sure...Have you really thought about this?"

Hell, he'd done nothing but think about it for the last month. He woke up wondering what to do about Mariah, and he fell asleep considering the same thing. He'd been going into work late and taking off early, talking to social workers and even the chaplain in his unit at Fort Polk. He hadn't had a date, hadn't done a damn thing besides think about Mariah.

And regret the day he'd ever met her mother, Sabrina.

He'd loved her, he'd hated her, and since she'd abandoned Mariah with him, he'd been furious with her. Not that she knew or cared, since he hadn't heard from her for more than a year before she'd decided to take a vacation from being a mother. He hadn't even seen the nearly three-year-old Mariah until the day the social worker had led her by the hand to him and performed the introductions.

If he could get his hands on Sabrina...

He risked a look at the little girl, settled into his mother's arms as if she belonged there, blond hair curling delicately around her chubby cherub face. Her brown eyes watched him with a seriousness no two-year-old should ever know, and he wondered for the hundredth time what was going through that little brain of hers. Faultfinding? Her mother had certainly excelled at that. Disillusionment? Sabrina had that in spades, too. Wariness that, like her mother, one day he and Ercella would disappear from her life without notice?

Guilt prickled his neck because that was exactly what he planned. If everything checked out in Oklahoma, she would be going to another family. Another man would get on the floor and play with her, talk to her and bounce her on his knee. Another man would fall in love with her and do his best to protect her and keep her safe.

Keegan wasn't meant for that role. He wasn't father material. Especially for another man's daughter.

Deliberately he shifted his attention from Mariah and that line of thought. "When are you guys going home?" Home for Ercella was Natchitoches, fifty miles from Leesville, half that again from Shreveport. She had more or less moved in with him when Mariah had come, but with him out of town, she was happy to be returning to her own place.

"Soon as I get her stuff packed. I'm going to show her all the places my other grandkids—I mean, my grandkids—love and all the places you grew up and got into trouble." Regret pinched the corners of her mouth. He'd warned her before she'd come here that Mariah's presence in his life was just short-term, and she'd insisted that she understood. Still, it hadn't taken her more than about five minutes to get totally charmed by the kid. Left to her, he would be Mariah's father, despite proof to the contrary, and Sabrina's daughter would be a Logan forever.

But it wasn't just for himself that he was heading off to track down her father. She deserved to be with real family. She deserved to know who her people were, and they *weren't* Logans.

"Okay. Well. Guess I'll take off." He circled the dining table and hugged his mother, inhaling the scent of bacon lingering from breakfast, perfume and clean laundry and recently bathed baby.

Ercella squeezed him tightly, then forced a big smile

for Mariah. "Sweetie, want to give Keegan a hug good-bye?"

As usual, the girl studied him, fingers stuffed in her mouth, as if he were an alien creature. She wasn't going to give him a hug, say good-bye or anything else but look at him and judge him, and he and his mom both knew it.

This time, she surprised them both. Just as he started to step back, she pitched forward, tumbling out of his mother's arms and landing in his, her chubby arms wrapping around his neck.

Keegan froze, not quite sure what to do. Her solid little body felt foreign—too soft, sweet, innocent. He'd never held her, not once, because she hadn't allowed it, because he hadn't wanted it. She'd never spoken to him, never touched him, never done anything but watch him warily, and now she was holding on as if she might never let go.

It felt…nice.

Aw, hell, he really needed to get on the road.

He was about to tug loose and return her to Ercella when she reversed her earlier move, leaping into his mother's more familiar embrace. His throat tight, he forced a smile. "Gotta go. I'll call you."

"Be careful."

He nodded, picked up his bags and left the apartment.

His destination was programmed into the Garmin: 724 Cheyenne, Tallgrass, Oklahoma. He felt bad about leaving Mariah, though she was happier with his mom than she was with him. It was necessary, though. Since Sabrina had named him as father on Mariah's birth certificate, no one else was much interested in finding her real father. Besides, like he'd told his mother, he wanted to check the guy out. He wanted to make sure he was a good fit for

Mariah. Wanted to be sure she would be welcomed into his family.

And if he decided she didn't belong there? Then what?

"I'm not her father."

Too bad that didn't solve the problem.

And way too bad that saying the words aloud didn't ease the guilt still prickling at the back of his neck.

On the hour's drive northwest to Tallgrass, Therese asked the kids if they wanted to stop for lunch. Jacob declined, and Abby ignored her. She asked if they'd taken lots of pictures. Jacob said no, and Abby ignored her. She asked how their mother was. Jacob grunted and Abby ignored her.

Once they got home and she told Abby that she would *not* be wearing those clothes or that makeup for at least another few years, Abby would no longer be pretending Therese didn't exist. Therese half wished she could do the ignoring and just close her eyes to what the girl did, but there was no way any child in her care was going to leave the house looking like *that*.

Tallgrass was a small and lovely old town, dating back to Oklahoma's pre-statehood days. Its early purpose had been to provide for the area ranches and the settlers brought there by the land run. Later it had supported the oilfield workers, as well. For the last sixty years, it had been home to Fort Murphy, which more than tripled its population.

Paul had been transferred there four years ago, and she'd fallen in love with the place. They'd bought a house big enough for his kids and the babies they'd intended to have together, with a manicured front lawn and a big backyard for play and family cookouts. But there hadn't been any babies, his kids weren't interested in outdoor play, except for Jacob's football and baseball teams, and Abby never missed a chance to remind her that they weren't a family.

Someday the kids would be gone, Therese thought as she pulled into the driveway. Either their mother would take them back, or her parents, or maybe Paul's parents. Or maybe Abby would miraculously start behaving like a human being, or Therese would find peace with the idea of putting her in foster care. Failing all that, maybe she could hold herself together for five more years of misery, and then she could be free.

Freedom had never sounded so good...or seemed so impossible.

As she shut off the engine, she said, "Abby, put the phone away, take your stuff inside and unpack."

Abby either didn't think Therese saw the face she made or simply didn't care, but she tucked the phone into her tiny purse before sliding to the ground and stalking to the back of the van. The high school boys sitting on the porch across the street came to sudden attention, eyes popping, mouths gaping.

Oh, Lord, please not that. Therese had enough worries without adding males to the list.

Abby dragged her pink bags into the house, leaving the door standing open, and the boys slowly sank back into lethargy. Therese wanted to yell at them, *She's thirteen!* She wanted to go upstairs to her room and march back down with the .40 caliber handgun locked in Paul's gun safe and warn them what would happen if they even *thought* about his baby in that way.

She settled for scowling at them, then jerking the black bag out, slamming the hatch and following Jacob inside. He went to the laundry room off the kitchen, unzipped his backpack and dumped the contents into the hamper there. After grabbing a bottle of water from the refrigerator, he headed past her with a grunt on his way upstairs. Within minutes he would be on the computer, headset on, jumping into the game he'd last played six days ago with both feet. He wouldn't make another appearance until hunger drove him to it.

Therese put her purse and keys in the kitchen, blew out a breath, and much more slowly climbed the stairs. Abby's door was open, and she was reclining on the bed, one sandaled foot on the white spread, the other stretched high so she could admire the shoe. As usual, she was talking on the phone to Nicole, her BFF and, until very recently, the coolest kid in town. No doubt, Abby now felt that title belonged to her.

"—*so* much fun," she was saying when Therese stopped in the doorway. "I can't wait till you see my hair and all the clothes she bought me. And the shoes! They make me taller than you. We spent a whole day at the spa, and I've got the best tan ever, and the cutest outfits! It was the best week of my life."

Therese waited, hands hanging limply at her sides. She really wanted to fold her arms across her chest and scowl as hard as she had at the boys outside, but there was no reason to start off openly aggressive. They would get there quickly enough.

Tiring of admiring her right foot, Abby lowered it to the mattress and raised the left one, twisting her ankle this way and that. It was a pretty ankle, a pretty leg, all bronzed and lean and leading to a compact lean body. She was more assured at thirteen than Therese had been at twenty, more aware of the attention she received from others. The teenage girl Therese had once been envied her; the woman who was charged with overseeing her welfare was cringing in the corner with her hands over her eyes.

Trying to feel more like that woman, she moved into the room and picked up the larger of the suitcases, set it on the foot of the bed and unzipped it.

Frowning at her, Abby said, "Gotta go, Nicole. See you tomorrow." She set the phone on the nightstand, then sat up, arms folded over her middle. "Those are *my* bags. They're private."

"You live in this house. Nothing is private beyond your journal, if you keep one, your purse and, to some extent, your room, so long as you don't give me a reason to reconsider that." She flipped open the suitcase and saw nothing but unfamiliar clothes inside. She shook out the top garment. "Is this a dress or a shirt?"

Abby rolled her eyes. "A dress. Duh."

With a nod, Therese laid it to one side. Next came a pair of jeans so skinny that only through the miracle of stretch fibers could they possibly fit her stepdaughter. They were the start of a second pile. The tiny shorts that measured barely the width of Therese's hand from waistband to crotch joined the dress, along with a couple of tops too fitted, too revealing or too trashy for any child.

"What are you doing?" Abby finally demanded.

"Sorting out what you can wear and what's going into storage."

Abby surged from the bed and nearly lost her footing.

She wasn't quite as accustomed to those four-inch heels as she'd thought. "You can't do that! They're mine! My *mother* bought them for me."

Therese reached the bottom of the suitcase and picked up a handful of undergarments. No, not undergarments. *Lingerie.* Matched sets. Bikinis. Thongs. Push-up bras. Black, royal blue, red, purple. They were cuter, sexier, and more revealing than anything she owned, including the lingerie she'd bought for her honeymoon.

Struggling to keep her hand steady, she began repacking them in the suitcase. Out of the twelve garments and the lingerie, she left only two or three pieces on the bed.

"You can't do that!" Abby repeated, grabbing for the bra in Therese's hand.

Therese shot her a look so hard that Abby should have fallen backward from the impact. Sullenly, she let her hand drop, then took a few steps away, her bottom lip poked out.

After a moment's stare, Therese looked at the bra. Catherine hadn't bothered with Victoria's Secret, judging from the padded cups, red lace edging black satin and breakaway front clasp. She'd gone straight to Frederick's of Hollywood. For her *thirteen*-year-old daughter! She dropped it into the suitcase, closed the flap and zipped it before reaching for the smaller bag.

Quivering with anger, Abby went to the closet. "You have to let me wear them." She threw open both bifold doors, then clenched her fists. "I have nothing else. I left all my other clothes there because I knew you would do this. I told Mom so."

She wasn't exaggerating by much. Except for her school uniforms and the dresses she wore to church, her closet was practically empty. A few pairs of jeans, a couple of old T-shirts that had sentimental value but no fashion sense, two hoodies. There were gym shorts and underwear in her dresser, plus socks, but she'd taken practically everything else with her.

"You'd better call your mom and ask her to ship them back, then, or you're going to get awfully tired of wearing the same things all the time." Therese sorted through the second bag, confiscating three more pairs of ridiculous heels, two more bags of cosmetics and—she gulped silently—two of the skimpiest swimsuits she'd ever seen. She was surprised thunder didn't roll across the plains from Paul's roar of disapproval.

"I can't do that because we threw them away."

Therese hoped she was lying, but it sounded like exactly what she and Catherine would do. Catherine might be Abby's mother, but she didn't want to be. Occasional friendship without real responsibility better suited her nature, and conspiring with Abby to thwart Therese would be an easy way to cement that friendship.

"If that's the case, you'll have to buy new clothes from your allowance."

She expected another roar, but the girl just stared at her. In that moment, there was nothing of Paul's baby in her, just quiet fury. Malevolence. Sheer hatred. Her eyes were like chocolate ice, her rage unflinching, but when she spoke, her voice was far calmer than the shriek Therese was used to.

"You know, I don't pray very much because I don't think God really listens, but I do pray for one thing every night. I pray for you to die."

THE DISH

Where Authors Give You the Inside Scoop

♥ ♥ ♥ ♥ ♥ ♥ ♥ ♥ ♥ ♥ ♥ ♥ ♥ ♥ ♥ ♥

From the desk of Jennifer Haymore

Dear Reader,

When Sarah Osborne, the heroine of THE DUCHESS
HUNT, entered my office for the first time, I thought she
was a member of the janitorial staff and that she was there
to clean.

"I'm sorry," I told her. "I'm going to be working for a few
more hours. Can you come back later?"

Her flush was instant, a dark red suffusing her pretty
cheeks. "Oh," she said quietly. "I'm not here to clean...I'm
here as a potential client."

Now it was my turn to blush. But you couldn't really
blame me—she wore a dark dress with an apron and a
tidy maid's cap. It was an honest mistake.

I rose from my seat, apologizing profusely, and offered
her a seat and refreshments. When she was settled, and
neither of us was blushing anymore, I returned to my own
chair and asked her to tell me her story.

"I'm the head housemaid at Ironwood Park," she told
me. Leaning forward, she added significantly, "I work for
the Duke of Trent."

I'd heard of him, and of the great estate of Ironwood
Park. "Go on."

"I want him," she murmured.

I blinked, sure I'd missed something. "Who?"

"The Duke of Trent."

"You are the *housemaid*."

She nodded.

"He is a *duke*."

She nodded again.

I shook my head with a sigh. The housemaid and the duke? Nope. This wouldn't work at all. The chasm between their classes was far too deep to cross.

"I'm so sorry, Miss Osborne," I began, "but—"

Her dark eyes blinked up at me and she held up her hand to stop my next words. "Wait! I know what you're going to say. But it's not as impossible as you might think. You see…I am His Grace's best friend."

I gaped at her, for that was almost more difficult to believe than the thought of her being his lover. Dukes simply didn't "make friends" with their maids.

"We have been friends since childhood. You see, the duke's family is quite unconventional. The dowager raised me almost as one of her own."

Now this was getting interesting. I cocked my head. "Do you think he would agree with your assessment?"

"That the House of Trent is unconventional?"

I chuckled. "No. I know the House of Trent has been widely acclaimed as the most scandalous and shocking house in England over the past several decades. I meant, would he agree with your assessment that you are his best friend?"

She folded her hands in her lap, and her dark brows furrowed. "If he was being honest?" she said softly, and I could see the earnest honesty in her gaze. "Yes, he would agree."

I leaned back in my chair, drumming my fingers on my desk, thinking. How intriguing. Friends to lovers, to…*love*. What a delightful Cinderella story this could make.

My lips curved into a smile, and I flicked open the lid of my laptop and opened a new document. "All right, Miss Osborne. Tell me your story. Start with the story of the first time you laid eyes upon the Duke of Trent…"

And that was how my relationship with the wickedly wonderful family of the House of Trent began. I've loved every minute I've spent with them, and I hope you enjoy Sarah and the duke's story as much as I enjoyed writing it.

Please come visit me at my website, www.jenniferhaymore .com, where you can share your thoughts about my books, sign up for some fun freebies and contests, and read more about the characters from THE DUCHESS HUNT and the House of Trent Series.

Sincerely,

Jennifer Haymore

♥ ♥ ♥ ♥ ♥ ♥ ♥ ♥ ♥ ♥ ♥ ♥ ♥ ♥ ♥

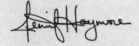

From the desk of Marilyn Pappano

Dear Reader,

One of the questions authors get asked most is, "Where do you get your ideas?" I've gotten inspiration from everything—music, news stories, locations, weather, simple thoughts or emotions, from events going on in my own life or someone else's, from dreams, wishes, hopes, fears.

Some ideas take a tremendous amount of work to come together. I don't work on them continuously but rather sporadically while they percolate in the back of my mind. Some never come together.

And then there are the *thank you!* stories: ideas that come fairly complete with characters, location, and plot. A HERO TO COME HOME TO was definitely one of those.

For some time, I'd been thinking about doing a series with a military setting (my husband is retired from the Navy, and our son was in the Army), but it wasn't on my mind at all one summer day when I watched a news segment about military widows. That evening I saw another news segment about a woman who'd thought her dreams had ended when her military husband died in the war, only to find a new love.

By the time I got up the next morning, I knew the seven widows from the Tuesday Night Margarita Club, as well as Dane, the soldier who would restore Carly's dreams, and Dalton, the rancher who'd lost his wife to war as well. I knew the setting, too: my home state of Oklahoma. Of all the places we lived on active duty, Oklahoma is my favorite. I took time off from the book I was writing and wrote the first few chapters, then sent it off to my agent.

The Department of Defense really nailed it a long time ago when they came up with the slogan that "wife" was the toughest job in the service, though since there are plenty of women on active duty, "spouse" is a better choice. Trying to have a career of your own? Good luck when you move at the whim of the service. Need roots? Better learn that home really is where the heart is. Worry too much? Take a deep breath and learn to let go. Never wanted to be a single parent? Start adapting because deployments are inevitable.

But being a Navy wife was great, too. I met some wonderful people and lived in some wonderful places. I learned a degree of independence and adaptability that I never thought possible pre-Navy. Our Navy life gave me ideas and exposure to new experiences for my writing career. Though I already had a lot of respect for those who serve, I also learned to respect their spouses and children and the sacrifices they make.

One of the best parts of writing romance novels is giving all my characters a happily-ever-after ending, and no one deserves it more than the Tallgrass crew. I hope readers agree.

Oh, one final note: that morning A HERO TO COME HOME TO popped into my head? It was the Fourth of July. Fitting, huh?

Happy reading!

Marilyn Pappano

♥ ♥ ♥ ♥ ♥ ♥ ♥ ♥ ♥ ♥ ♥ ♥ ♥ ♥ ♥

From the desk of Molly Cannon

Dear Reader,

The theme of food is woven into almost every chapter of CRAZY LITTLE THING CALLED LOVE. Etta Green is a chef in the big city, but her love of cooking came from her grandmother Hazel. For Etta, the sharing of food represents love, caring, and nurturing—all those things we need and crave our entire lives.

When Etta returns to Everson, Texas, for her grand-mother's funeral she discovers her grandmother had been in the middle of turning the old family home into a bed and breakfast. The responsibility of finishing the work on the old family home falls to Etta, and after reading her grandmother's notes on the project she sees that each of the guest rooms has been named and decorated with an old-fashioned dessert as the theme—desserts that evoke comfort and fond memories of days spent with her grandmother.

I love dessert, so deciding on the room names was deli-ciously fun, and I didn't have to count a single calorie. For the first room I thought back to my school days. Buying lunch in the cafeteria of my elementary school was not high on my list of favorite childhood memories, with one exception. The cherry cobbler was scrumptious with just enough tart fruit to moisten the pie crust on top. I've had other cobblers since then, but that one remains my favorite. So of course *Cherry Cobbler* had to be one of the rooms. I decorated the room in different shades of red and taupe, cozy throw pillows scattered everywhere, and topped it off with pictures of cherries in bright white bowls. A cheerful room that could brighten any day.

Next was the *Banana Pudding* room. Banana pudding was one of my father's favorite desserts, so I always think about him whenever I make it. I still think the recipe on the vanilla wafer box is the best I've tried. And making the pudding part from scratch is simple and tastes so much better than any pudding from a box. With that as my inspiration, I decorated the room in pale yellows and fluffy meringue whites. A light and airy room that wraps the guest in down comforters and soft pillows.

But food can evoke other powerful emotions as well.

When I was a barely a teenager my older brother went to a summer camp, and when we went to visit on family day all the boys greeted us with a meal they'd prepared themselves. The star of the meal was the Ham in the Hole. They dug holes and lined them with slow-burning wood, and then buried the hams, cooking them until they were tender. It was their gift, their offering to the visitors. And it was delicious. The campers were so proud of themselves.

When my brother found out a few years ago that he had cancer, he decided on his own course of treatment and chose the path he wanted to take. As he got weaker we watched him stay strong in his resolve to live the rest of his life on his terms. One of the last things he did was to invite his family and friends over for a special gathering. He'd gone into the backyard and dug a hole. Then he lined it with slow-burning wood and buried a ham. When it was done he fed us more than a meal. It was his last gift to us all. It was a thank-you for loving him and being his family. I let Donny Joe Ledbetter borrow my brother's gift as the gesture he uses to show his home town his appreciation. It makes me happier than I can say to make the Ham in the Hole such an important part of Donny Joe and Etta's story.

I hope you enjoy it, too!

Molly Cannon

Learn more at:
MollyCannon.com
Facebook.com
Twitter @CannonMolly

♥ ♥ ♥ ♥ ♥ ♥ ♥ ♥ ♥ ♥ ♥ ♥ ♥ ♥ ♥

From the desk of Kristin Ashley

Dear Reader,

I have an obsession with names, which shouldn't surprise readers as the names I give my characters run the gamut and are often out there.

In my Dream Man series, I introduced readers to Cabe "Hawk" Delgado, Brock "Slim" Lucas, Mitch Lawson, and Kane "Tack" Allen. My Chaos series gives us Shy, Hop, Joker, and Rush, among the other members of the Club.

I've had quite a few folks express curiosity about where I come up with all these names, and I wish I could say I knew a load of good-looking men who had awesome and unusual names and I stole them but, alas, that isn't true.

In most cases, characters, especially heroes and heroines, come to me named. They just pop right into my head, much like Tatum "Tate" Jackson of *Sweet Dreams*. He just walked right in there, all the gloriousness of Tate, and introduced himself to me. And luckily, he had an amazing, strong, masculine, kick-ass name.

In other instances, who they are defines their name. I understood Hawk's tragic back story from *Mystery Man* first. I also understood that the man he was melted away; he became another man with a new name so what he called himself evolved from what he did in the military. His given name, of course, evolved from his multiethnic background.

The same with Mitch, the hero from *Law Man*. The minute he walked into Gwen's kitchen, his last name hit me like a shot. What else could a straight-arrow cop be called but Lawson?

Other names are a mystery to me. Kane "Tack" Allen came to me named but I had no clue why his Club name was Tack. Truthfully, I also found it a bit annoying seeing as how the name Kane is such a cool name, and I didn't want to waste it on a character who wouldn't use it. But Tack was Kane Allen and there was no prying that name away from him.

Why he was called Tack, though, was a mystery to me, but I swear, it must have always been in the recesses of my mind because his nickname is perfect for him. Therefore, as I was following his journey with Tyra and the mystery of Tack was revealed, I burst out laughing. I loved it. It was so perfect for him.

One of the many, *many* reasons I'm enjoying the Chaos series is that I get to be very creative with names. I mean, Shy, Hop, Rush, Bat, Speck, and Snapper? I love it. Anything goes with those boys and I have lists of names scrawled everywhere in my magic notebook where I jot ideas. Some of them are crazy and I hope to get to use them, like Moose. Some of them are crazy cool and I hope I get to use them, like Preacher. Some of them are just crazy and I'll probably never use them, like Destroyer. But all of them are fun.

All my characters names, nicknames, and the endearments they use with each other, friends, and family mean a great deal to me. Mostly because all of them and everything they do exists in a perfectly real unreality in my head. They're with me all the time. They're mine.

I created them. And just like a parent naming a child, these perfectly real unreal beings are precious to me, as are the names they chose for themselves.

I just hope they keep it exciting.

Kristin Ashley

Find out more about Forever Romance!

Visit us at
www.hachettebookgroup.com/publishing_forever.aspx

Find us on Facebook
http://www.facebook.com/ForeverRomance

Follow us on Twitter
http://twitter.com/ForeverRomance

NEW AND UPCOMING TITLES

Each month we feature our new titles
and reader favorites.

CONTESTS AND GIVEAWAYS

We give away galleys, autographed copies,
and all kinds of exclusive items.

AUTHOR INFO

You'll find bios, articles, and links to personal websites
for all your favorite authors—and so much more.

GET SOCIAL

Connect with your favorite authors, editors, and
other Forever fans, and share what's important to you.

THE BUZZ

Sign up for our monthly romance newsletter,
and be the first to read all about it.

VISIT US ONLINE AT

WWW.HACHETTEBOOKGROUP.COM

FEATURES:

OPENBOOK BROWSE AND SEARCH EXCERPTS

•

AUDIOBOOK EXCERPTS AND PODCASTS

•

AUTHOR ARTICLES AND INTERVIEWS

•

BESTSELLER AND PUBLISHING GROUP NEWS

•

SIGN UP FOR E-NEWSLETTERS

•

AUTHOR APPEARANCES AND TOUR INFORMATION

•

SOCIAL MEDIA FEEDS AND WIDGETS

•

DOWNLOAD FREE APPS

Bookmark Hachette Book Group
@ www.HachetteBookGroup.com